DARIA

We gratefully acknowledge the support of the Canada Council for the Arts and the Ontario Arts Council for our publishing program. We also acknowledge the financial support of the Government of Canada.

This is a magical realism historical novel where fact and fiction intermingle.

Cover design: Val Fullard

Library and Archives Canada Cataloguing in Publication

Title: Daria : a novel / Irene Marques.
Names: Marques, Irene, 1969- author.
Series: Inanna poetry & fiction series.
Description: Series statement: Inanna poetry & fiction series
Identifiers: Canadiana (print) 20210182105 | Canadiana (ebook) 20210182164 | ISBN 9781771338417 (softcover) | ISBN 9781771338431 (PDF) | ISBN 9781771338424 (EPUB)
Classification: LCC PS8626.A683 D37 2021 | DDC C813/.6—dc23

Printed and Bound in Canada.

Published in Canada by
Inanna Publications and Education Inc.
210 Founders College, York University
4700 Keele Street, Toronto, Ontario M3J 1P3
Telephone: (416) 736-5356 Fax (416) 736-5765
Email: inanna.publications@inanna.ca Website: www.inanna.ca

DARIA

A NOVEL

Irene Marques

inanna poetry & fiction series

INANNA PUBLICATIONS AND EDUCATION INC.
TORONTO, CANADA

To Mother and Father: A and A.

To Isabel.

"Everything in the world began with a yes. One molecule said yes to another molecule and life was born."

—Clarice Lispector

"Language is a skin: I rub my language against the other. It is as if I had words instead of fingers, or fingers at the tip of my words. My language trembles with desire."

—Roland Barthes

"If you have ever peeled an onion, then you know that the first thin, papery layer reveals another thin, papery layer, and that layer reveals another, and another, and before you know it you have hundreds of layers all over the kitchen table and thousands of tears in your eyes..."

—Lemony Snicket

I write myself in the intervals of a lifetime to see if I find my true name.

D ARIA. Your name is Daria. Daria Mendes. Mendes with an *s*, not a *z*, like the lady at the bank counter pronounced, and then wrote on your receipt, the other day, when you were sending money to your old mother who still lives on the other side of the world. You came to this side of the world when you were young and bountiful in body and mind— beautiful too, men kept telling you when you passed them on the street, whistling with wide shiny eyes, as if looking for something different from what they had ever seen, something that would remind them of the many good things there are in this universe, just waiting to be taken, eaten and loved, danced with. You left alone. You left the village on top of the mountains—that place where the stars were so close that you thought the sky was only a fingertip away and the god with a small *g* was kind, not mean like the one Padre Lévito always talked about in church when you went on Sundays. You didn't always go because the church was far away and you needed to walk ten kilometres to get there. And also because your mother, even though a fervent Catholic in many ways, did not really teach you to be a diligent worshipper. She prayed to Saint Gregory only in the middle of the night when angry thunderstorms were brought down on us by the God with a capital *G* who was treating us like peasants, peasants who had not yet suffered enough for their sins. You left the village on top of the mountains. You left and took things in your own hands. Things that you knew were there to be taken, to be tried by those brave enough to evade the rigid destinies of old stubborn Catholicism, that sturdy current imprinted even in the smallest stones of the country you left and seasoned with nearly fifty years of Salazar's fascism. Salazar's parents, truth be told, were landless peasants who lived in a village just next door to yours, but they found a way to give their son an education by sending him to the seminary and then to the University of Coimbra. He then became an acclaimed professor of economics and, shortly after, the iron fist of the country.

Despite all that he did and did not do, your father still says that what we need now is another Salazar to make things work, to take us out of the shameful debt and sinful spending that makes us look like incompetent lazy bastards who cannot govern their own households. What we need is another Salazar, not Socrates who has disgraced our house such that we are now called the PIGS of Europe. He says this despite the fact that his oldest son, Alberto, was killed fighting in Angola during the colonial wars that lasted thirteen years. Alberto was blown away in the dark, deep Mayombe and no one ever saw a piece of him again. Your mother mourns him frequently, with prolonged sighs and teary, motionless, cow-like eyes trying to spot particles of him in the air, love remnants that might have flown upward, back to its source; he was her first child, born when she was only seventeen, and he was a boy with fair, fair skin and curly black hair. The taxi drivers picking you up at the airport, when you return for a visit, tell you similar stories. They are eager to inform you about the news of the country, sensing that you come from another world, governed by other laws where good money is to be made. "What we need, *Menina*," they say with their finger in the air, "what we need is another Salazar

2

to straighten things up, to put these people in their place and teach them some proper old values. Ah, good were the days then, when we worked from sunrise to sunset to get to the belly of the earth and lift the minerals out of there, or just to find enough good soil to plant some corn and potatoes without the intrusion of the stubborn stones, our domesticated cows pushing the plough to turn the earth, guided by the sharpened metallic ending of a long stick piercing their back—because all beings need discipline. Even though we had to divide one sardine among three of us, and we felt tired to the core at day's end, we were proud citizens and owed nothing to no one." You listen and you smile, and think that nothing much has changed. But things have changed, as they always do, and perhaps you are only wishing that they did not change, that they had remained the same as when you left because that's how you remember them or think you remember them. That's how your country plays itself in your mind and body, making you feel like you do indeed have a sturdy, stable house to walk upon, even if you abandoned that house more than twenty years ago and it is no longer stable, no longer the same—as you find out when you enter it more deeply, noting the deep and mysterious shadows that inhabit the old corridors or the new colours that the walls have or the water now running in the sink. In the old days you had to carry water by the bucket or the crock from the ancient fountain, on your hands and head, balancing an intricate act, as if you were a dextrous African woman who could do many things at the same time because she knows the many needs people have and the choices are scarce. Yet it does not seem to matter much, for you find ways to make it stay the same, like a stubborn child who refuses to see her own children grow or her mother die and get old—only so that you can access the beautiful.

THE DREAM OF LAVENDER. She woke up in the middle of the night possessed by the astounding beauty that she had seen in the dream she was in. In this dream, she was dancing, or sometimes walking, in the middle of the most beautiful field of lavender somewhere in Avignon. She felt herself in a forest of open fields, moving through the ups and downs, bouncy and serene, where only lavender had been allowed to flourish and find mineral food from the belly of Mother Earth. She had never been in Avignon, but she had seen the images in postcards countless times, and so she felt that land, or the colour through which it tells itself, was somehow imprinted in her soul, remembered by the eye of the white eagle, which never forgets. She always knew that lilac, that colour that comes out perfectly only in the flowers of lavender, spoke to her from some transcendental place that she could not quite understand or grasp with the logic of her mind. But today, this morning, after having been inside the peaceful and floating sensation that those plants and their sight and scent had gifted her, she felt extraordinary, like never before. Extraordinary. It was as if the world—this world that often imposed so much on her shoulders and her lower back, making her cry and contort her body in sheer pain—had suddenly revealed itself as the perfect place in which to attain sanctity and find mercy. A mercy. Like the title of a novel by Toni Morrison that she adored, a book where finding a cure is all that matters. It was as if her body, habituated to the loads she carried, an overweight and overflowing sac pressed down by the many sad stories of the world, had suddenly discovered that flying is not only possible but that it is required. She had suddenly realized that, in fact, the ability to fly may just come when you least expect it: in the middle of your dreams at night, when darkness takes over your soul only to allow for a new dawn, that moment when flight and light will be possible and the twin sisters living in the little girls of your eyes twinkle in newly found redemption.

First, she remained seated in her bed, symmetrically positioned, so that her body would feel and remember the sensations of the dream fully and deeply. She then rolled out of bed carefully—like a gazelle in slow motion, ready to canvass the fields and graze in fresh grass—and walked out the door. The night was still high, and the darkness that enveloped her felt like a bath of wisdom or a blanket of carefully stitched pieces of fine wool, protecting her from the bad elements and the witch stories she had heard so much in her infancy. These were tales told by old ladies who knew only how to scare the soul. They knew how to suffer in this world; they had mastered it. Yes, because this world was only a passage through the painful tunnel, after which heaven would appear to you, clearly, very clearly, like an open field, finally ready to give you some happiness and much deserved rest. She walked slowly but with certainty; she was eager to feel every element under her naked feet. Seen from afar, she appeared like a nude virgin, an incandescent being, who descended to the streets of that place only to allow its inhabitants to feel and know what bliss is, how bliss is. Seen from afar, she brought tears to your eyes. She made you want more, want a lot, and deeply feel the loss that your life was. It was as if she, that woman of the night, a sudden nymph roaming the streets, was an *incumbida* entrusted with delivering a message to a dying generation, a generation who had forgotten how to be happy in this world and how to experience god right here under this starry sky. As she moved through the streets, the god with a small *g* suddenly became big, like a gigantic transparent ball of water where you and all the rest bathed in a muddy hug, finally clean of all the crimes of the world. She was finally ready to be the forever bride of all there is, all there will ever be, floating in a nothingness that kept her in the greatest company. She danced like this through the streets of the town, corner after corner, line after line, meticulously, until she found the tunnel that took her into the field of that marvelous lilac. In that field, which she entered fully in body and soul, she roamed freely and aimlessly, time after time, because she knew—and deeply felt in her bones, as if the line of her life went way beyond her—that wisdom comes to you only after you have been lost in the maze that scares you to death and makes you bleed and bleed, lost in the logics of the non-logic, where there still lives a certain sparkle of beingness. She knew that the perfect is caught only in that moment of unawareness. Unlike what the scientists at the Hospital of the Soul say and keep telling those who have disease in their being, those who are hurting to the core and speaking in tongues; they scare the masses who then run away from them on the bus and on the streetcars, pretending that they are not a related species at all. Pretending that they themselves do not speak in tongues sometimes, or wish to speak in tongues to be released from the iron bar that holds them down, preventing them from finding meaning outside the ordered webs of their everyday lives. They pretend. Pretenders they are.

Daria roamed and roamed in the lilac sheet until her body was nothing but a mound of lilac and she became indistinguishable from the landscape. She felt pure then. She felt pure and young and clean. And in that state of being she woke up. Blessed like never before and ready to be anything—the secretary or the professor or the nanny—because labels did not frazzle her, did not weaken her, did not bring her to the lower point, at least for the time being. She felt she could be anything under the sun, and in fact she wanted to be anything under the sun. She wanted to feel the entire universe upon her with the wisdoms of different people entrenched in her cells, making her immensely erudite. She wanted to be a shoemaker living in the Middle Ages producing a stunning shoe, from beginning to end, with her hands; she wanted to feel that sense of completion and wholeness that only creation, holy, holistic, without division of labour, can produce. She wanted to be a seller and maker of coal like her mother had been, pulling deep, sturdy roots out of the earth and smelling its fresh moisture; or a nun enclosed in a remote thirteenth-century monastery praying avidly to Christ with eyes shut and bosom pulsating, praying rosary after rosary until she found bliss and orgasmic divinity; or Nelson Mandela wanting and waiting for the idea to realize itself; or Wangari Muta Maathai at the moment when her ashes were spread by the trunk of a young tree and it all suddenly made sense. *Ad infinitum.* She wanted to be all stories and all people and beings and things—without any commas to intrude.

THE UNKNOWN UNDERDOG. Daria, you think you are the unknown underdog. You think you have personally been a victim of maltreatment, misunderstanding, harassment, and discrimination on several occasions. You think your people, your community, are not represented sufficiently in positions of power in Canadian society because they are not visible minorities. Even the current mayor of Toronto, you say, António Palavreiro, whom you have nicknamed *a merchant of words*, a man of Portuguese descent who has made it to the top but seems to have poor knowledge of Portuguese geography and has mixed up the Atlantic with the Mediterranean by saying, during his election campaign, that he grew up in Pombal, surrounded by beautiful mountains and the Mediterranean sea—maybe he wanted the non-Portuguese voters to think of Portugal as Greece or Italy or Spain for those are much more often advertised on TV and other mediums, and have likely more deeply entered the consciousness of Canadians and therefore are more likely to be associated with the quintessential Southern European culture—even he, you've noted, and I do know that to be true because I heard him myself, even he has stated on national television that the Portuguese are the underdogs nobody pays attention to. "We are poor and the sons and daughters of the poor. We have the highest high school drop-out rate, higher even than Black people according to some recent census. Our people clean and build the city of Toronto and parts of the rest of the country. Our older people, men and women, were born and raised in the throes of Salazar's regime and escaped here—and God knows how! Maybe by swimming through the vast and perilous Atlantic, like many others crossed the frigid and wolf-infested Pyrenees by foot to go to France and Germany. Our old people don't know how to read and write—like my own mother, in fact—and many are abused by their children who have brought them here only to get their pension cheques and make them care for their own children.

As the mayor of this great city, and a proud Luso-Canadian—another term for Portuguese-Canadian, for those who may not know—I intend to address this long-overdue wrong by creating specific affirmative action, municipal laws that will correct the problem."

You've also added that he, the mayor, won because of the ethnic Portuguese vote and not because he is in fact smart or even well-educated or particularly thoughtful. Although he only has a BA in General Arts, he indiscreetly acts as if he is the only educated person in the Portuguese community. Here you also add that you don't like the term "ethnic" because it implies that only some Canadians are ethnic, while others—namely, the so-called founding European fathers of the nation—are not. As everyone knows, we are all ethnic! We all belong to a certain group. Of course, that is changing too because, here in Canada, the so-called mother nation of a truly successful multiculturalism, groups have mixed so much that we no longer know how many people there are *in* us. The whole thing has, in fact, become quite complicated and difficult to label neatly. It's a muddy, muddy affair. And here you also noted, and I quote you directly: "I am not saying that this is a bad thing." You have further indicated that your dislike for the mayor of Toronto goes back to the time you both spent in a Portuguese literature class at the Northern University in Toronto years ago, the one taught by Professor Marcus Whiteshilgel, a German-Canadian who was very passionate about all things Portuguese, including, rumour had it, women of Portuguese descent. Whiteshilgel led a very insightful class, in fact, one of the best you've had so far. He used to joke and say that whenever he went to Portugal to a conference, his colleagues in the field attacked him, pointlessly claiming he could not teach Portuguese literature properly since he was not only a Saxon but a Canadian-Saxon and therefore quite far from possessing the necessary authenticity and aptitude.

You developed a particular distaste for Palavreiro when you were discussing a novel by Lídia Jorge, *O dia dos Prodígios*, and another one by José Saramago, *O ensaio sobre a cegueira*, because during the break he asked you what part of Lisbon you were from, and you stated sarcastically, "Oh, I am not from Lisbon, I am from a little place in the middle of nowhere, just like Vilamaninhos or Azinhaga." You are firmly convinced that the only reason he said that is because he could not fathom that someone who spoke Portuguese like you and knew how to argue like you could in fact be from a place other than Lisbon, which you claim has always been the privileged centre of the country and perceived as the only cultivated place in the nation. I have tried to point out that perhaps he has changed since then—it's been quite a long time now since this encounter you had with him in the classroom, and your assessment may be outdated because he was just a young boy then and people do change. But when I point this out, you insist that your intuition is seldom wrong, that we are all basically born with the general inclination to be good or bad, and that some things, once expressed, cannot be retracted and do indeed show the core of the person's being. You insist that this man does not, cannot fool you. You add that you don't like Palavreiro because you tend to dislike politicians and see them as either unethical sophists or very good networkers. And you also don't like him because of other specific reasons that are yet to be disclosed. Maybe that will come with time, with more trust between us.

You tend to take everything as a personal attack, and you think the world is out to get you. Those are very clear symptoms of paranoid ideation mixed with borderline personality. Daria, I have to be honest, so I am calling the chestnut by its name. As a therapist, I don't believe I should dance around the subject and use all kinds of euphemisms in order not to break the shell of an already broken egg—and this is, I believe, the reason you chose me as your therapist. You dislike, as I understand, those too Anglo-Saxon Canadians who never say what they mean and never mean what they say. You keep complaining that, because of that attitude, you can never forge rightful relationships with these people and that you feel you are always operating on a non-genuine level. That very operation, you say, prevents you—and them too—from attaining your potential as a human being. You also complain that these people, these types of Canadians, always end up by infecting the rest with their bad habits of extreme kindness and political correctness. You complain they can never handle negative emotion. For instance, if your voice shows you are upset and your words match that state of being and feeling, they say you are being unruly, too aggressive, and disrespectful. They say you must control your anger in order for any communication to take place. You say that type of behaviour is just bullshit—complete dung! In fact, it is quite the opposite, you say, because, and I quote you, "How can I be a full being if I am not allowed to express what bothers me? If I'm not allowed to show it with my own body, my own voice? How can I smile and maintain a low voice if my blood is boiling and my emotions are commanding me to express them, to release them? How can I do that? My thoughts and feelings cannot lie, should not lie to my voice!" You feel you would be lying to yourself, and you fear that the party listening to you would not understand the level and intensity of the concerns and feelings you are expressing and, as a result, wouldn't do anything about it. You have concluded that because you don't express that raw emotion—the emotion that is to be expected when something is wrong or when someone has done wrong by you—the other party will never address the wrong or really feel and understand you. She may nicely say she is very sorry that you feel that way and that she will change her behaviour to prevent the respective situation from re-occurring, but you feel that these are just words. You feel that if you don't express your feelings about the matter with emotion, body gestural language, and intense direct words, the other person involved in the altercation will not be faced with the uncomfortable feeling that arises from that expression, and thus will never change, will never understand. She'll just revert back to the same old bad habits shortly after—especially if the boss is not around and if she perceives you in a certain way because of your label as a departmental secretary. She knows that we live in a society that does not have to mean what it says; it only has to appear to be sincere and to speak with calmed nerves and tamed words. You add that because of all these fake, pretend-to-be-situations, you always suffer the consequences. You say that no meaningful, true exchange between human beings can actually take place.

You also say that the reason you invented the phrase "Communicate deeply with yourself, others, and otherness"— and placed it in the signature of your personal email account— is to teach people the value of openness and true dialectical communication. You compare it to the women you see at the Y wearing T-shirts that say *To be a feminist is to believe in the equality of the sexes.* And here I must note that I don't quite see the direct connection, Daria. But maybe I can't read between the lines, and I don't see the interconnection between everything like you do. You firmly believe that a good open fight, like dogs barking loudly at one another, is good for the soul—and that Canadians need to do that more often so that their full being can come to the surface and their soul and body can be cleansed. You express this conviction to your students at the university all the time with the hope that you will catch them young and teach them something about real communication. You feel that even at the Hospital of the Soul, where you currently work as a part-time departmental secretary, this non-confrontational way isn't helping anyone.

You call this attitude "walking around the egg" in order not to break it; this is your own saying that, in fact, deviates from the original "walking on eggshells." You notice that if anyone— staff member or patient—screams or shows negative emotion, they are immediately sent to a workshop on how to manage aggressive behaviour or put under physical or chemical restraints, respectively. This should be basic knowledge, you add: the idea that humans need to vent, scream, cry, and run wildly sometimes in order to then recover energy and start the fight of life again—a fight that is as hard as hell and breaks you over and over again. You keep complaining that at the hospital, people who viscerally dislike each other never confront one other about their unpleasant feelings, especially if the one viscerally disliking is subordinated to the one being viscerally disliked in the hierarchical ladder. The CEO is a woman (finally, thank God!) named Simone Montgomery whom many people dislike. But they will always smile and say nice things to her because she is the big boss, makes over a million dollars, and is a medical doctor who specializes in neuro-psychopathology. She doesn't have a PhD, but that does not really matter because she is a medical doctor and is therefore "clinical" and automatically awarded the category of superior. You continue, saying the staff only get rid of the patients' urine smell, which has now spread throughout the entire hospital, when the CEO comes to the site because her office is not even in the same building as the patients. Her office is in a very nice off-site corporate space that smells like roses and geraniums and has colonial furniture. While it is extravagant by most standards, it is less opulent than the dwellings of the previous CEO, which, rumour had it, had been nicknamed "The Beautiful World" by some patients who had wandered off and found it.

VASCO DA GAMA. You were abused by Vasco da Gama. Not the famous sailor who travelled to India, though both shared the name and the Indian connection. The first was the ingenious explorer and navigational entrepreneur who sailed to India in the very late 1400s, the very first European to do so. He made his journey at a time when Portugal was the proud king of Europe and was in the middle of its Golden Age. To this day, the country is still mourning and mourning the loss of this Golden Age, a fact that explains the country's constant obsession with *fado* music and *saudade*, that deep, deep-seated nostalgia for what is gone and is very dearly missed. This Vasco da Gama sailed to India in search of Christians-to-be and spices. There he implanted his seed. Much later, the second Vasco da Gama, a product of that old half-millenary seed, the son of a Goan father and a Portuguese mother, emigrated to Canada with his high-class Lisbon wife to become a Portuguese-Indo-Canadian or perhaps an Indo-Portuguese-Canadian—it would all depend on the day and the convenience of the moment. This Vasco, this Vasco da Gama, who no doubt is related to the famed explorer—if only because he also initiated the connection between two countries and two continents—was, for a bad and brief time, your boss. And you were abused by him, this Vasco da Gama. You were young, very young, in body and mind; you thought the world was there to be taken by you, with both hands, like an offering from a god with a small *g*, that kind divinity that is not greedy and believes in the equality of all beings. The world was there to be taken—like a perfectly round and perfectly clear white or brown egg with no marks on its shell. You were young, you had come to Canada not very long ago, and you were all ready for this American dream. You had heard all about it through vague stories of the beautiful Marilyn Monroe and songs of freedom by various people who, like you, felt that life ought to be lived without constraints. They spoke of shaking off the shackles attached to their toes, to their souls, to their bodies by all kinds of harsh masters, from white plantation farmers to mean priests that keep preaching about a soulless God who is jealous and sees himself at the top of the pyramid, raging down on us uncontrollably.

You became acquainted with these American dreams, first through the black-and-white images of a man landing on the moon, which kept being played after the fact, long after the year you were born, on that tiny television that your mother bought with money she made from selling everything that she could, everything under the sun, from rabbits, to coal, to goat cheese, to sardines. (Yes, sardines. They made us who we are today, even though then it was believed sardines were the food of the poor. But god is kind. God is kind, so he made those little fishes full of vital vitamins for the brain to grow healthy, for the mind to become visionary and brave.) You had finally encountered this American dream. Even though you did not, at the time, understand that this dream you had come to was different from the American dream that you had forged in your mind. But it did not matter. What mattered was that you were coming to America, not Europe, like many in your family and in your village had done. You yourself had spent some months there. But you did not like Europe. Europe was old and full of ideas that you were trying to evade, ideas about class and social status, about peasants and non-peasants that you were trying to escape. Perhaps you were ashamed of your own parents, or perhaps you thought, deep inside, that there ought to be a place, a world, where those things do not matter, where you look at someone in the eye to measure their worth rather than at the clothes they are wearing, where it does not matter whether they speak with an accent from Lisbon or one from Viseu. And so you came. But after a while, and because you came under a restricted work permit—like the many thousands of Filipina women that we still keep seeing on the street pushing the strollers with the blond babies—you thought that freedom and the American dream, your American dream, were taking too long to happen, to show their smiling faces and embracing colours. You thought that. You thought and thought, and you decided, one more time, to take things into your own hands, things that were there to be taken by those brave enough to evade rigid destinies. And so you left. You left the children in Richmond Hill and ventured into the streets of Toronto by yourself. The mother of the children—she herself a woman from the village where you came from, who had already reached her Canadian dream, or so it seemed at the time, and who had brought you over—was quite angry at you. She was angry that you had the audacity to leave; you had no shame, she said, biting the hand that fed you like that, just like Vasco da Gama told you later on. She threatened to call Immigration to tell them that you were breaking the contract, that you were ungrateful for the opportunities this great country had given you. She was very angry, but then she calmed down and said, "Because of the long history between our parents in the old country, because they worked very hard all their lives and helped each other like brothers and sisters of the same tribe, recognizing themselves as beings from the same suffering clan who ought to extend a hand to one another, I am going to let this pass. I am going to let this pass, but when the contract is up, don't think I am going to do anything else for you. You'll have to find someone else to renew it because you are no longer my responsibility. And be careful. Toronto is not that big. Don't think about going to the street corners there because we'll know what you are doing." And so it was.

You left, Daria. Alone, scared but intent on trying again, trying to grasp that dream with your hand. After a while of working here and there, in cafés and cleaning houses for the friends of the friends you managed to make, you said you needed to become more than that, and you needed to do so quickly because you were young and impatient and wanted the dream now. You had the blood of a twenty-year-old running through your veins: that red liquid that runs upwards and downwards with the velocity of thunderbolts and makes you a danger to the world, like a hotel manager once told you in Portugal when you went to him to get a job for the summer. He told that to you while staring at your chest and your legs with shining glutinous eyes that made you run away and go beg somewhere else. You wanted to break free from that kind of work, being the maid for others, because you felt that was a label that you and your entire family back home had carried for long enough. You felt the responsibility to make the dream of your entire family visible. At first, you thought it might be better to leave, to go back home or to France, where your sister, who has bipolar I disorder, was already living. She was working like a maniac day and night to prove to herself, her mother, and the world that she could be more than the label, that she could in fact amass vast wealth. And she has indeed been able to amass considerable wealth, and yet she seems to remain unsatisfied, as if she still has not found what she is looking for—just like the beautiful song by U2. The song calls for more, more please, because this life has to be better, ought to feel better. We are all after this thing; we all pursue it incessantly, like mad wild wolves who do not know where their lover is and keep howling, howling into the wind only to hear back the echo of our own loneliness. You have a dog like that, back home. His name is Pastor. He is massive like a bull, and on long winter nights he goes out into the dark and freezing cold and howls to infinity. He wakes up the entire village, and they shout at him, wanting to quiet him down, but then when that does not work, they all join him in the chorus until they fall into exhaustion and finally go back to bed, sinking into something beautiful, something otherworldly.

Yes, at first you thought you wanted to leave, that it may be better to go back home or to France where your sister was, cleaning houses from morning to night. You wanted to leave because you were lonely and scared. You were working illegally here and there instead of doing the nanny work your permit had indicated. It had clearly stated this was the only type of work you could do for two years before you could apply for an open permit and eventually get your citizenship—just like the many Filipina women who leave their own children and husbands at home to come here and make it all happen. You thought you wanted to leave, that it might be better to leave because Immigration could find you and send you back for breaking the contract. They could find you and make you feel like a real criminal, even though your only fault was wanting to leave, to work hard, so that the dream could realize itself and the label that you and your entire family had been carrying for so long would finally break down—diluted in the clear and pristine waters of the Great Lakes.

But you did not leave. You did not leave because you felt it would be a failure. You thought about what your mother had had to endure all her life, and you realized that your plight was nothing compared to hers. You wanted the American dream, this American dream, and Europe still smelled like mould: old and stubborn, full of class and dress codes and perfumes, impregnating itself in every one of your cells—like a man who does not know that no means no and thinks he can buy young women who must work as maids. That's exactly what a boss of yours once told you when you were only twelve and had breasts with nipples like red strawberries just before the spring. He said that as he put his sloppy fat hands on your chest: *criada para todos os serviços.* Just like Fernando Pessoa, the famed poet, as told by Saramago, conveyed to Lídia through his actions, for he was still blind, he was blind and in love with the other Lydia, a mere creation of another blind man, and could not see the pulsating beauty of the being that was in front of him: those hands that do so much, those breasts that keep you warm, those words that say what really matters and do not pay attention to the superficial gibberish that those who are attached to rank tend so often to display. When you see Strauss-Khan and Berlusconi on TV, your first reaction is to say PIG in big capital letters, as though you are delivering a verdict before hearing all the evidence. Your husband calls you on that, saying you are too judgmental, that you think all men are alike. But he does not know. He does not know everything, can never know everything. Because some secrets can be told only to the passing wind— that gentle breeze that cleanses and takes away dirt, leaving you feeling light, so light that you can fly, so empty of pain that the world suddenly reveals itself with astounding beauty. And you see god.

ENDLESS SENTENCE. In days like these, I want you to read me in endless sentences, without punctuation marks, nothing between you and me, or the wind or the high tide that rises and bathes your eyes and mine, the shores of your being mixing with the shores of mine like nothing ever existed between us, not even the two footprints left on the sand floor, nothing, nothing but soft untraceable encounters between two beings who have been in prolonged mourning, all-encompassing loneliness, and now accept the embrace that awaits us all when we go from here to the other side of the river, where Jesus or Buddha or Isis or Gioconda are, in pure expectance and with peaceful mysterious smiles and arms in the horizon to receive us in the single and only hug that there is for all of us. In days like these, I pray you put aside your grammatical logic and let us be in the infinity of the universe, floating between nothing, between things that do not have names and never will because they are far, far away from our language and our dictionaries and exist only in the blind between-the-lines like Clarice Lispector says, the only place where existence is in fact possible and does not cut you into pieces of a and b and c, where the letters form a rainbow that has no beginning and no end, for it is a circle, wide and vacuous like my throat when I open it up universally for you to see and stare in awe at the darkness of my insides. In days like these, all you can do is pray on your knees in the unassuming position of a lotus flower in the middle of a long white desert in a land with no name, no oil, no thirst, and no refugees, just like the free Libya, finally a beautiful woman without the shackles on her perfectly naked ankles, roaming the oasis in search of the gardens of the future. In days like these, I am barely breathing and walking, I fly above all and all is mine and yours, I am a thoroughly alive woman and I communicate with you using the infinity of my soul power, I call upon you using a mixture of tongues that are not Portuguese or English but possess the incantatory capacity to transmit the dark matter that exists in all of us—that fire that speaks without a tongue and creates *logos* on your body and mine, marking your hands' intricate designs as if you were an Indian bride in pure expectation of the beautiful day. In days like these, I can easily dwell in that small space between the toes of goats or in that fresh cow dung, which I so miss here in Canada. I miss that fresh herbal scent that comes from the wombs of cows when they descend from the mountains at the end of the day to rest in peace for the night in the home next to yours, barns and homes joined in the dwelling castle. I think of animals and people living together, and remember the pigs who lived under your kitchen and whose smell came to you, strong and rotten from their feces, until one day their smell and their bodies would disappear because they would be killed with that long sharp knife that your father kept hidden from his children. They would be killed so that their blood could be used to make blood sausage, and you ate them like a cannibal who eats her own, only because you loved them so much and wanted to forever incorporate them into your self; their blood was your blood, our lonely self was now enlarged with the infinite, just like some tribes in the Amazonia who eat their own—or parts of them—when they die so they don't die. They don't die. Yes, because love is the ultimate embrace of us all. In days like these, there are no paragraphs, no commas, no stops, only long, unstoppable, unwounded sentences that go from here to where you are, from Egypt to Lebanon and then to the North and South Poles, magic currents of meaning that do not need linguists and semantics specialists to write, to catch a beautiful language. In days like these, what your Russian student writes makes the most astounding sense, for in her obscure language, there lives the wisdoms of all the celebrated Russian writers like Dostoevsky and Tolstoy and the dark existential philosophy of pure profound life that searches for the uncanny and tries to evade the fiery tongues of fake communist leaders like Stalin. In days like these, you never dance alone, for in your steps you encounter the feathers of birds and the pollen of hydrangeas and get lost in their colours, which are so many and difficult to name using only the shades of the rainbow, extraordinary brightness(es) that one cannot but gasp to see. In days like these, you extend your forehead from Australia to Madrid so that Australia becomes a city and Madrid becomes a country down there at the end of the world, where once upon a time Aborigines were considered primitive beings who knew nothing but to hunt and eat flowers. As if that were not enough, as if that were not the whole point of living communally, as if that is not the whole point, the exact point where encounter between self, other, and otherness actually manifests itself in the most sublime sense. And then everything is roses. Roses and roses—and endless sky. In days like these, I chant poems to my grandmother and my darling friend Isabel and my father too. I pray a long rosary, Hail Mary after Hail Mary, Our Father after Our Father, and the Creed too, and then after a while everything is and is not—everything makes sense, the most sense of all, and I can sleep in peace and not be assaulted by what I could have done for them but did not do. In days like these, I see Toronto as the language capital of the world, not because there are over 150 languages spoken, languages that come from all the corners of the world, but because those languages have merged into English, making it less logical, less cold, and so much more profound—profound because it has in it the wisdoms of each language, the cadences, the hidden meanings, the open syllables, the un-ending vowels that make your mouth wide and your soul so much richer. It is then that I fully understand the awkward ways of Natalia, my Russian student. It is then that Jung's collective unconscious manifests itself in my brain, revealing the *Magna Carta* of the universe in one sole blow—like a big bang of sorts—when "yes" became a reality, like Clarice says. It is at that point that I know I have a soul, which is much more than a brain with cells and corpus matter. It is a revelation—the revelation of the IQ. In days like these, there are no DSM compendiums that classify and reclassify the intangible, there is no HR that writes job descriptions that destroy the beautiful shoe made by the shoemaker in the Middle Ages with immense and concentrated love, there are no men or women, or wolves or birds, for we all join in the crimson orange that is each of us and scream the great scream. In days like these, I am pure. And there are translucent light rays emitting from the corners of my being, so great are they that they cross thick compact walls, breaking the solitude that you feel at night, the solitude that makes you cry often because you feel that all there is are darkness and unbreakable barriers, which you have put up in fear of bareness and connection with your true self. In days like these, I write myself through breathless sentences with nothing between to stop me so that I can find my true name. In days like these, I extend my bareness from here to where you are. In days like these, I am pure, colourless like the dawn of immemorial times. And perhaps, if you truly join me, this long sentence can become our liberation and the commencement of a beautiful love affair.

YOUR FATHER DIED. My father died. He was eighty-seven years, two months, and five days old. You can't tell the number of hours because he died on the other side where time is five hours ahead, which often makes you feel that you can never catch it and are always in between something. Something that is not the present, not the past, not the future but some other time, a time where all is confused into an entanglement of possibilities. You can see this confluence clearly in your mind, but when your hands extend themselves to grasp it, they quickly realize how difficult it is to find a palpable body, stumbling upon a bare nothingness that leaves you disconsolate and uncertain, submerged in a vacuum of sorts. Sometimes you get up early with the intention of calling your mother and speaking to her when she gets up in the early morning because you want to hear her voice, a voice that goes through the day displaying different cadences of happiness, different possibilities of being. You get up early with this intention and quickly dial the phone, and then when you first hear her you get confused because you are thinking that it is the morning and that her voice should sound a certain way. At first you think that the distance between the two of you and the time away from her have made it impossible for you to recognize her. You feel that you have lost her, that you have lost that connection that comes only with presence, and you get sad, very sad. But then you suddenly remember that the time is ahead there and you become calmer, thinking you still have that connection, that you can still detect the different tones of her voice, and that this was nothing but momentary confusion. And with that insight you recompose yourself to seem cheerful to your mother on the other end of the line. She always speaks very loudly on the phone because she truly believes that if one is far away from the other, some extra work on the vocal cords is necessary if communication is to take place. You recompose yourself and promise yourself that next time you call her you will get up at three o'clock, which will be exactly seven o'clock there. Then you will be able to capture that seven-o'clock voice, her precise state of mind and feeling at that time of the day. And indeed you do precisely that, but still you fail to feel like you remember feeling when you were there and would see her in the morning speaking in a low voice, slowly awakening to life, a life that had been very hard on her. You fail to feel like that, and then you say it's likely because you yourself are speaking to her in the middle of the night, and are not, cannot, be in the same morning mood, in the same state of awareness that she is. You are desynchronized, and really there is nothing to do about that except imagine how things were and how they might now be.

My father died two days after I came back to Canada. I could have stayed longer—should have stayed longer like my initial intuition was telling me—but then I discarded the idea as if afraid of trusting the non-logical too much. I was striving to be a woman of reason, perhaps influenced by the Canadian Anglo-Saxon ethic and aesthetic. I discarded it and left him there at the hospital after the second stroke when he could no longer speak and only his eyes could murmur through that shining, merciful, and pleading intensity they emitted. I silenced that initial intuition. I thought that maybe he was a man for life, as my mother had said, a man that would still have days and days to live. She had said that after she went to see him at the hospital, two days before he died. She had not been to visit him in a while. She came home and announced to all of us, "We have a man for life there. His cheeks are rosy, and he has that overall colour that gives off health." And my mother's words always carried weight in the house. She was the boss of the castle, the one wearing the pants. But my father died two days after, and then my mother said in a suffocating lament, "Oh Lord, that is not possible, for I just saw him and he looked so handsome and healthy. Oh Lord."

She said that, and then she did not say a word for the rest of the day, my older sister told me. She went into the back of the house to look in the old trunk and take out all her black clothes because she had now become a widow for life. She was a woman who had had ten children and only one man in her life and would not conceive of ever having another one. She would not want to be called a woman of the world like her mother had been. My grandmother had been a single mother with two little girls to raise alone. It was the 1920s, when things were tough and to give away that thing that you keep tightly hidden between your legs was the ultimate sin; it made you *a condenada* for life. Condemned for life. Later on we told mother that father had waited for her visit at the hospital—he had maintained his body alive in this world because he had been waiting for her visit—and that after she came and he had had the chance to say goodbye to the mother of his ten children, he was ready to go. She smiled and said maybe that was true and so it was a good thing that she had not gone to visit him earlier because had she done so, he would have died earlier.

My father died two days after I came back to Canada. I could have stayed longer, should have stayed longer, but duty was calling me. And my mother, always afraid that I don't have enough money and thinking that Canada is very far away from Portugal, said to me before I left, "If he dies soon you should not come back because it is very expensive and you were just here so there is no point. Don't be stupid." I thought to myself, this woman is very crude, very crude, always thinking about money, always putting money above love. She also still doesn't seem to trust me, doesn't seem to think I have now grown up and can live without her constant advice. She thinks I don't know how to manage my finances. I screamed at her and said, "Listen to yourself! All you care about is money. Can't you see how your husband, my father, is worth much more than that? Can't you see that? If he dies, you call me; someone call me. Do you hear me? Do you hear me? I will never speak to you again if you bury my father without telling me." And they did call me two days after I returned to Canada. My sister left me a message on my voicemail announcing it in a low voice. My father was tall and thin and good-looking. He never went to the dentist or brushed his teeth despite the fact that I tried to explain to him, on several occasions, the benefits of having healthy clean teeth and would bring him toothbrushes and toothpaste quite often. He would always say that he drinks clean, pure Lusitanian water from the central fountain—a fountain that has been there since even before the Celts came to the Iberian Peninsula—and that's all he needs to cleanse his mouth and to live a long and healthy life. He loved to eat cod and pork sausages, and when my mother offered him sardines he would say that she did not know how to treat a man, that she thought that a man can eat like a woman and still be able to plough the earth and cut the hay from sunrise to sunset. He would say that she was lucky to have married him because if she had married other men in the village, like Mateus or Magnífico, she would have truly learned how to behave like a proper woman. My father loved the land and his cows to infinity. He would go to cow fairs frequently, and his cows would always be given the first prizes. This gave him great happiness, the greatest happiness, and earned him an equal amount of envy from the other villagers.

My father was a peasant—not a landless peasant though, like Salazar and Saramago's parents—and being a peasant was all he had ever wanted to be. I grew up hearing his and my mother's stories about the trials they had endured to be able to buy all the land they had from their siblings or other family members. But they did it. They did it with lots of sacrifice. People would always trust them, often lending them money for the purpose, which they always paid back. They would often both list the several pieces of land they owned, naming each one by its specific name—just like my father did with the cows and my mother with the goats—and explaining exactly how they'd come to buy or inherit it, to whom it had belonged, the communal water that it had, and the days that that water was theirs. Sometimes they told stories of the many fights and altercations, verbal or physical, they'd had with other villagers because of this communal water. When I visit, I am eager to hear these stories again—now told only by my mother. She tends to be the better storyteller, many say, though I think my father had his own special ways of transmitting poetry and emotion, often using fewer words but injecting them with the wisdom of the old ways. This land that they owned, lost up there in the mountains, is now divided among their nine living children, making me an owner too. It is not worth much. It's mostly subsistence farming and was always so, but for them, for my parents, this land was all they had and it meant the world. It made them proud. It gave them corn and beans and wine and all they needed to feed themselves and their children. And it was theirs, earned through a lot of work at a time when having land was a mark of being rich and powerful and important— and mostly, self-sufficient. It meant something to be a peasant with land, a *componês* of means. Some means at least, for the land was harsh and difficult to penetrate, full of rocks. It was a collection of tiny little pieces lost in the slopes of hills, mountains, and narrow valleys, and it did not easily open its womb to the wishes of the villagers. But through the will of love and need, they managed to pull from there bread for their abundant offspring—boys and girls created in the long wintry night after the rosary prayers. Today most of this land is abandoned and most of the youngsters have run away. If they stay, they buy their food mostly at the supermarkets. Only the elderly people, who are slowly disappearing and who represent a different way of life, still cultivate a piece of land or two, or as much as they can—to maintain their reason for living, to keep their dignity alive. My eighty-two-year-old mother, stubborn as a mule, still has a goat and still makes cheese to sell to the judges in town, even though she now needs a permit, which she refuses to get. She has been arrested by the police for doing what she has always done to feed her children. One day, as she was walking in town with her *tabuleira* on her head as usual, an officer asked her to show him her ID. She said spitefully, "I do not have it," and when asked where she was from, she stated, "I am from the earth and the sky." She was taken to the police station for her insolence. A few months later, when she went to see the judge to pay the fine, she told the judge, "Madame Justice, this is not the last time I will be selling cheese on the street. I have been doing this for over forty years, and you yourself have bought cheese from me on many occasions." The judge said, "I know, I know, Dona Alzira. I know, and I must admit that I really like your cheese, but things have changed, and now you must be careful."

My father was a proud peasant who loved his land. He loved getting up early, in the midst of that fresh air of the morning, to go feed his animals. The cows would moo when they heard his voice. They would moo very gently like sisters who knew their brother well or daughters who were happy to hear their father's song. My father had a third-grade education only, which was significant for a man of his age. My grandmother, his mother, became a widow at the age of twenty-seven and was left with five boys to feed and educate. Her husband died of pneumonia; in those days there was no cure, and the few hospitals in the region were far away from the mountains. My father knew the letters of the alphabet, he could read and write, and he could sign his name. He knew the letters, the numbers, and some history, which he would occasionally recite when we were sitting by the fireplace. It may very well have been these recitations that made me want to study and read, read a lot. He also knew a lot of proverbs. When I was enthusiastically telling him something that I had read about, he would say, "Books suffer what people put in them." When I told him the earth is the one revolving around the sun and not the other way around, like he believed, he shook his head and said, "Nah that can't be. Books suffer what people put in them. Tomorrow I want you to spend your day looking at the movement of the sun from dawn to dusk. I want you to do that so that you can stop talking and reading nonsense."

My father died on July 2. He was born on April 27, which made him a Taurus, a man of the earth who liked earthly pleasures. For a long time, all my boyfriends were Taurus. Some said it was my father in them that attracted me to them—that girls will always do that, go for the father-like figure. I told them they had been reading too much Freud who is a patriarch of first order and thinks that my clitoris is envious of the other clitorises. He, my father, died just after I'd published my first book in Portugal, a book dedicated to him and to Isabel: "To father Adelino, who lives dwelling between memory and the memory of non-memory, and to Isabel, who simply dwells in the movement that is proper of true memory." I don't know if this makes sense translated into English or if it even makes sense in Portuguese, but it makes sense to me and it helps me see them, my father and Isabel, as parts of me—entities that are not really gone but rather keep living somewhere in my chest or my forehead or my little toe. I could not read the dedication at the funeral. It was my brother-in-law—the one who is a Portuguese high school teacher who went to the seminary and then gave up on the idea of finding God through those means—who read this dedication while I was crying and crying. I was looking both at my father's coffin sinking down in the earth and at my friend Isabel's marble tombstone that stood at its side—making them eternal neighbours, friends in the afterlife. Isabel had died five years earlier, and I did not go to her funeral even though she and I were best friends, even though she and I had spent our childhood playing in the mountains of Caramulo while keeping the goats. Playing and inventing beauty—we would make it fresh, from scratch, with wild daffodils, wild carnations, and those little blue flowers that grow in humid hidden spaces, so discreet and profoundly gorgeous.

Isabel died very young. I had a dream about her the night before she died, which I captured in a poem that I wrote somewhere. I had a dream of her in white, with the priest, Padre Lévito, chasing after her. They were in a church that was full of people all working with the priest, and everyone was trying to grab this *noiva em branco para Deus*, this bride dressed in white for God. But she eluded them. I saw her escape through the church's wide and heavy wooden door that only a goddess could move. I saw her escape and walk into the serene plains of hay and then slowly ascend to the mountains where we played as children—like a child angel in white, flying in beauty, happily leaving this world. In this dream, I felt for a second or two as if I too were dying; I felt that affliction and that inability to breathe when they were all chasing Isabel and trying to grab her. And then I also felt the release when the large church door opened and the wide plain field revealed itself to her. It was as if she and I, Isabel and I, were both dying, dying and then really living. It was like a circle of love. When I went to Portugal last year I shared this dream with Isabel's sister, Lucinda, and she told me that the day before Isabel died, her mother went to visit her at the hospital. She had already sensed the end of her daughter's body, and the breaking of her dark, thick, lush hair. She asked her in a careful voice, hiding her own mourning, "My darling daughter, how are you feeling today?

What did you dream about last night?" When Isabel spoke, her voice was prolonged and tonal, exhibiting that singing, swaying, and lamenting quality that only those who are near the end can display, and that can be revealed only through the open, endless vowels of the Portuguese language that make time immemorial. She said, "Oh *mãe*, I dreamed I was in this place, this place where there were lots and lots of people, *muita, muita gente*, lots and lots of people, all around me, all around me, and I wanted to be free." When I heard that I said, "I was there with her. It was the last time I saw her." And then I remembered, like I do now, that the last time I actually saw her was in August, three months before she died. I had helped her put her thick black hair in a ponytail because she was already feeling weak and could not lift her arms up high. At the time she had no clear diagnosis and was at home. It turned out that she had been misdiagnosed pretty much the entire time. It was only a week before she died that they said she had Diffuse large B-cell lymphoma. They attempted chemotherapy then, but it was to no avail for her insides were all damaged and she could no longer say yes. I told the family that they ought to sue the hospital and her family doctor. Isabel had been complaining to her doctor for years and years, only to hear that she was not well in the head and was imagining the whole thing. The doctor believed that she could not know her own body because she was a single woman of thirty-six, who was still a virgin who had not yet encountered a man. The truth is that she had encountered many men, but not a real man or a real doctor. As if a woman does not know, cannot know, when her body is hurting and telling her that there is something going on, something going on...

When she could not endure the pain any longer, she finally went to a specialist who told her to go to the hospital immediately. She did go immediately, but they screwed up too and did not diagnose her properly. And so she'd died just like that at the end of her thirty-sixth year, *na flor da idade*, at the flower of the age, as my mother says. Her mother, Piedade, a fervent Catholic before her daughter's untimely death—she used to sponsor twenty-four masses a year for her dead mother, ever since she'd died twenty-five years earlier, and pay ten euros to Padre Lévito for each one—has never stepped into a church since. She rages and rages against God. When I go there, I cannot go see her or even run into her. I was her daughter's best friend and we were the same age, and when she sees me—which happened once—she breaks into an endless lamenting scream that goes on for weeks on end, causing the entire village to become immersed into an abysmal melancholia that only fades when Piedade is taken to the hospital to be medicated into a state of non-cognizance, forgetting everything and everyone. When Lucinda is around—which is not always because she married a French man and lives in Marseille—and the mother is not at home, I visit Isabel's room to see all the photos she has there, photos of us when we were young and beautiful and believed in fairy tales, when we often stayed up all night dreaming up the perfect man. The mother, like many do in these circumstances, refuses to touch her room; she is still hanging on to the idea that Isabel is alive in the dead cells that she left spread on the floor among all the other dirt that time collects. My mother, who tends to be less emotional and more pragmatic, says that Piedade is crazy and needs to stop the crying and the hysteria. She says she needs to go on with her life, for she is not the only mother in the world to lose a child. Many more have had the same fate and they don't just keep blaming God for it—they get up and go do things even if they have that constant black cloud weighing down their chest. When I hear my mother say this, I think that she is a woman of action and resolute expedience, for it is indeed true that many mothers have lost their children and, some would argue, in much more dire circumstances—like those women in Somalia who carry their children on their arms for hours and hours under the scorching sun of the horn of Africa, only to bring them to the overcrowded camps in Kenya and find out it is too late, for the limbs and the eyes of their children have stopped living among us. They have slowly slipped into the other side, where surely the body won't hurt so much and some sort of god must live, one that gives bread, equally, to the orphans of the universe.

THE SIGNS. Vasco da Gama is the executive director of the Lusitanian Social Service Centre. In his CV he says he has a soft spot for the underdogs and that's why he is running the centre, to help disadvantaged Lusitanians or other speakers of the Lusitanian language. Rumour has it, however, that he took this job only because he could not pass the bar exam in Canada even with a law degree from England, a country that also follows common law. And it would make sense to believe this rumour because, despite the fact that he openly proclaims his love for and interest in the underdog, he only employs women at the centre and often refers to the Portuguese community as a bunch of ignoramuses who cannot even read and write properly, if in fact they know how to read and write at all. When she thinks about him using the word "underdog," she laughs because when she first heard it, it came to her as an insult—like he was comparing people to dogs, or even suggesting that people were less than dogs. Even though she had always been very fond of those loving animals, her intuition, that fine intelligence that tells you to see things in its own way, was slowly but keenly informing her that he, this man, may not be what he seemed to be after all. But she dismissed her intuition, thinking that a man of his stature, his education, and his age ought to be wise and kind. She told herself that she was likely being irrational, and that she ought to follow that straight Anglo-Saxon logic now that she was in Canada. Other signs would come later that would tell her that that first intuition, that little voice stirring somewhere down there, was in fact very well founded. Also, at the time, her knowledge of the English language, though strong, was still insufficient for catching certain subtleties that only a savvy and experienced speaker could grasp. For instance, she sometimes would make the mistake of taking words and phrases literally, thinking that the parts that composed a word or a sentence created a specific, matter-of-fact meaning. Take for example, the saying "chicken soup for the soul," which she first heard on *The Oprah Winfrey Show*. She took it to literally mean that if one eats chicken soup, one cures spiritual wounds. And she actually put this into practice. On a particular day, when she was feeling profoundly desperate in body and soul, she ate nothing but chicken soup. When that did not appease her pains, she bathed herself in it, the result being that she smelled like chicken for an entire week. It was as if her cells had been transmuted into those of this now-dead bird, making people on the street move away from her and causing her to feel worse than she had at the beginning of the uncanny attempted remedy.

She had a similar experience when she went to Subway, the sandwich store, and asked for TTC tokens. She was convinced that if the place is called Subway and if it sells things, it ought to sell tokens that allow you to ride the subway and all the other affiliated transit systems. But she was wrong. She went inside and said timidly, trying to speak in an accent-less voice, as newcomers often do, "Can I have five tokens *pleaaase?*" The store clerk, a chubby well-dispositioned fellow who looked South Asian—though she was likely wrong about this because, as she later came to realize, people in this new country may look like they are from one very particular place when they are in fact from another—had a good laugh at her. This incident was very much like the case of the word "underdog," which she also naïvely translated to mean a dog being superior to a person. Though this interpretation made some sense, the matter was much more complicated than that; there is always more than meets the eye. Only experience in the language, the city, and its people would teach her that things are not always what they seem. Only experience and time would teach her. And then there was that incident that took place when she was working at a restaurant on College Street. Most of the patrons were of Italian and Portuguese descent, and several were also drug dealers. When she asked one customer what he would like for lunch, he said to her, "I would like you." She replied quickly and without any hesitation, "I am not on sale." He looked at her and smiled that Southern European smile, revealing white teeth. She noticed that he had dark, long eyelashes and a complexion to die for, and she trembled with both expectation and embarrassment. She wished she could hide herself under the ground, just like when she was in Portugal and had to pass by construction sites and men would say dirty things to her, commenting on how she had curves that could make a man dizzy and cause a dangerous road accident, how her behind was as divine as wine, and how they wished they had a good enough truck to carry such a precious asset. Then she realized, her pride a little wounded, that she should have said, "I am not for sale." Still, she thought that what she had said made complete sense. When she went back to his table to give him his change back, she directly placed the change on his hand because she thought it was more polite to do so. As she did that, he took the opportunity to tickle her palm with his savvy moving fingers. She felt her body shiver, and even though it felt like he had been inappropriate, it did not bother her because her body was touched. This incident then resulted in an intense short-lived love affair, the first she had ever had. Every time she listened to his voice, she felt she was going to die, and die happy. Despite the intensity of her emotions and the screams of her body for his complete, deep touch, she refused to go all the way with him, for she still believed in fairy tales and wanted to give it to someone who fully understood, appreciated, and knew what it meant. Not to mention she had taken to heart her mother's constant credo, repeated often as she was growing up and still quite present in her mind, even though she was now far away from the source: "I do not want any whores in my house. You keep your legs tightly shut, and if they come to you, you kick them right in between the legs with all the force that you have."

And then it turned out that he was a drug dealer, and she decided that she could no longer go on with this connection. He tried to convince her that he did not sell drugs to little kids, but she didn't think this was a sufficiently convincing argument because even if he only sold to adults, those adults could very well sell to children, and his innocence would end there. He still argued the matter from another angle by saying she did not know how hard the life of a man in this country could be, especially a son of immigrants. His parents had failed to achieve the American-Canadian dream themselves and had deposited all their frustrations on the shoulders of their eldest son, wanting him to become a doctor or a lawyer because nothing else is good enough. Everyone knows that doctors and lawyers are the ones who command the world and earn the proper respect. He claimed she did not know how it feels to work in construction at the height of the Canadian winter until your hands get raw and start bleeding. She did not know how hard the life of a man could be, and she acted like a princess who thought she was better than everyone else, a princess who had had it easy all her life. She would say, "Well at least you grew up in this country. There were jobs anywhere you turned if you really wanted to work, and you could have gone to university. You still can. I grew up in the old country and had to almost beg to get a summer job here and there, where I would have to work fifteen-hour days, seven days a week. I have done this every summer since I was twelve years old. Not to mention that I had to stay away from the sloppy hands of my bosses and their sons who thought I was part of the deal. And then I also went to France for a few summers to clean old ladies' behinds and take care of all their needs, like many Portuguese women do. In fact, if it weren't for these hardworking Portuguese women, many more people would have died during that fateful summer of last year in Paris when there was a ferocious heat wave. Thousands of French elderly people perished because their family members didn't feel they had to take care of their own old blood and vehemently defended the philosophy of individualism—claiming we are born alone and will die alone. Instead of caring for their elderly parents, they were enjoying the coolness of their *maison à la campagne* or the refreshing beaches of Greece and Portugal, the poorer Southern European counterparts, and paying very little for their pleasures. In fact, some say this is reason enough to keep Europe together, that that is what keeps the European Union going, while others say precisely the opposite. They say the EU will not work in the long run, for you have countries with very different cultural habits and economic advancement put together, countries who cannot possibly see eye to eye. At this point he would become impatient with her and would start saying that she was mixing everything up, mixing apples and roses, that she had been reading too many books on philosophy and economics and was not making much sense.

Daria did indeed think that "underdog" was a rude word for a man to use in his CV, especially a man like Vasco da Gama. It seemed like a crude, insensitive word. Later on he would tell her that she was too repressed, like a Catholic virgin, and that that is why she became damaged by every little thing. She had left the nanny work some time ago, and she lived in fear of getting caught by the immigration officials. She had been working here and there, in cafés and restaurants, and she felt like she was not going anywhere. She was still attached to blue-collar jobs, as if being a maid for all services was her only destiny. She was waiting and waiting for her open work permit, which was delayed—the immigration officials kept telling her—because they were overworked and had a great backlog. And so she was waiting. But she wanted the American dream, this American dream, to manifest itself, and so she took things into her own hands again. She was impatient and had the young blood of a girl in her twenties running through her veins, up and down, incessantly reminding her that time does not wait, that we have to grasp it firmly in our hands.

IN THE INTERVALS OF A LIFETIME. You came to me at a time when I was dying to love, dying to taste the solace that can come when two souls meet completely and the world stops for a beautiful eternity. I was dying for that unparalleled illusion that one ought not to deprive oneself from, even if one has been hurt before by the many bad characters that walk on the surface of this world. You came to me at a time when my entire being craved intimacy, that closeness that makes you forget the borders of your own body and the loneliness of your soul. It makes you feel as if the sea that you are is suddenly visible and you have found the eternal swim, where your limbs and all your pores taste the love of god through the salt that tempers the universe, making it the hospitable house that we all need to find true meaning in our lives.

I sit alone at the Frankfurt airport, always in transit as if constantly trying to find my way home, the node of my eternal soul. I see them kissing, and I imagine what I am missing with you. I sink into melancholia, deep down, into a space of non-belief. I am a well that cries endlessly, a rainy day that does not stop watering the earth. I see the couple playing lovingly with the blond little girl full of curls. The father teases her and teaches her words in a language that I cannot understand even though I attune my ear to its sounds. I write a poem while waiting for the connecting flight to Toronto, the place that I have made my home even though the coldness of the climate sometimes reaches the marrow of my bones. The cold forces me to go to eHarmony to find harmonious words that soothe all my limbs and make me believe again—believe that the dream is still there to catch and that the stunning man will come to me easily, called through magnetic cybernetic pulsing waves that do not deceive and mystically know how love is to be found.

I see the smiles of the passengers through the poem that I write. They, the smiles, the people, do not seem real; or if they are real, they do not enter my core. Instead they leave me stranded at an airport eternally, like a child with no parents and no country. The poem that I write is about my father's death. He was eighty-seven years, two months, and five days old. I cannot name the hours. He was that old when he decided to no longer resist the promise that death brings. His legs could no longer move, so thin were they. I still spoke to him when he barely emitted sounds; his mind had been slowed by blood clots formed in the heart, which then travelled to the brain, that house of memory, of memories, like the doctor told me on the phone. I showed him the book that I wrote in our language, *Habitando na metáfora do tempo* (*Dwelling in the Metaphor of Time*), and I told him that I wrote it for us. I wrote it to remember love stories that we never told one another in open words because our household, commanded by Mother, saw loving language as weakness. In our house, love and tenderness were transmitted through harsh Portuguese words that only the insiders could understand. But love does indeed come in many forms. I told him that this book was written for us, to house the stories that we knew we felt. I told him love that could be heard in the silence of our meetings, or in his facial expressions when he looked at me, or in that phrase he said to me when my sister and I had a ferocious fight: "We forget everything. Everything passes, washed away by the weight of time and the weakness of our solitude." The fight had erupted because I'd threatened to call the social services on her. She was in one of those dark moods of her illness and was beating up her six-year-old daughter, Ana, with a long wood stick. After my father spoke, my sister replied, "I don't know if this will ever pass. This will never pass. This is serious, very serious, to threaten to take my child away from me. She has no shame, no respect for blood ties. She is a dishonourable cunt walking freely through the world." And then she and I did not speak for an entire year. It was just like what had happened between mother and me when I was twenty years old. She spent an entire day calling me names because I was wearing a skirt above the knee, because I went to a party and came back in a car with a boy she did not know. It was only because I was beautiful, and men, young and old, kept wanting to smell my scent up close, even though I always said no. I too, had a dream, a dream that was different from my mother's. I did not want to be tied down, not yet, not with them, not there. I wanted to go away and find another world, other men, another type of life that I could call my own, where I could be free, where I could be clean, cleansed, and walk under a dancing abode without bad names pulling me to the dirt. But she kept calling me names, bad names, names that would spoil this diary. I do not wish to repeat them, for my intention is to talk about love: love and my father, and the other love too, the one that never came to be.

I am at the hospital trying to speak to him, my dying father, trying to love him, read him my love, a love that feels guilty for going away and leaving him anchored in his old ways on top of that mountain. It is a love that promises more than it gives, always leaving one feeling that the thing, the reason why we are here, has not yet been found; it is delayed and then delayed again, like a vengeful *ad infinitum*, a fatalistic logic of some illogical religion where God with the capital "G" is the commander-in-chief. Love, that thing that could be, is in truth the only fundamental reason for life. He, my dying father, looks at me. He is sitting in the chair where the nurses had put him, with his eyes open and shiny as if his soul had all travelled there. It is as if his eyes are announcing the approaching moment of truth, one that we will all face; no one can take your turn, nothing can buy you out—not the tie, not the millions, not the mansion, not the servants all at your service. I ask him questions to revive his mind a little and to get some assurance that he is still there in some way: "What was the name of your mother? How many brothers

do you have? Who lent you money to buy the lands from
your American uncle? Who found your wallet at the annual
cow fair of São Pedro do Sul? How many cows did you have
when you were the most affluent farmer of Almores?" I ask
him these and other simple questions, and he mumbles some
answers. His lips have been almost paralyzed by the last stroke,
when another clot travelled from his heart and installed itself
in a vein somewhere in his brain, not wanting to move—a
tired old mule the owner can no longer command. I feed him
through his mouth, spoon by spoon, giving him an unsavoury
pulpy mass. It is the same food we give babies before their
teeth grow and they learn how to grasp the flavours of life
with certainty and greediness. He eats, little by little, even
though he mumbles sounds of protest because his throat has
been affected and swallowing has become very painful. It is
an act that he does not remember how to perform. They had
put him on a tube a few days ago, but I insist that his throat
can learn again how to swallow food. I poetically protest that
a man cannot live when he is being given food like this, as if
he were a chicken in a factory being fed tasteless mashed stuff
instead of running free in the fields looking for soul food. The
nurse smiles and asks me if I am his only daughter. I say, "No,
there are four of us." She says that the reason why she asks is
because he responds very well to me. I smile, happy that I am
seen as special by a nurse who does not know the dynamics
of our large family.

A man lies beside my father, a man much younger than my
father who was caught like that in the spring of his life, and
who, like my two brothers, went to the colonial wars in Africa,
as revealed by the tattooed blue numbers on his uncovered
arm. His wife asks me if I am my father's granddaughter.
I smile, happy about the confusion, and think that it must
be the gentle Canadian sun that keeps me fresh and young-
looking. Men also still call me *Menina* when I am in this

country, though the other day one said, "Should I call you *Menina* or *Senhora*?" Likely he was wise in matters related to age and women, or perhaps he had travelled abroad and knew that women in other countries can fool your eye with cosmetic enhancements. The lady says that I look very young so my father must have had me when he was already a very mature man. "Oh, I am not that young," I say, telling her my age, adding that it must be the long Canadian winters sheltering my skin from the rays of the sun and the ease of life in that country. I don't tell her I have bad habits and deep irrational insecurities about becoming old and not being able to find a beautiful man while I still can. I don't tell her that I spend thousands of dollars to tame my body into order and smooth my wrinkles so that I don't become deformed prematurely by the natural and unkind processes of life like my mother, who carries her large arthritic and varicose vein–ridden body around like a dinosaur. I add that the Portuguese sun and the harshness of life in this country are too brutal and that the light in Canada is less blinding to our eyes, keeping us looking younger. Sometimes, however, that gentler light can cause deep-seated depression and make people take their own lives by jumping in front of fast-running trains, their bodies suddenly ceasing to be. I added this last part as if to tell her that there isn't much difference between Portugal and Canada, for everywhere people die. And pain is pain.

I am at the airport again. This time it's Gatwick, in England. It's Christmastime, and I left Toronto to be with my mother who is a widow for the first time at Christmas. I sit at the café called Costa—not Costa Rica, just Costa. I hear people mumbling words and beautiful dreams in different languages. Some are English, many are continental Europeans, and some come from India and faraway African countries. The plane that I took from Toronto, an Air Canada flight, has a service director who reminded me of you even though he was white. I kept looking at his name tag—"Barry White"—and I thought of you working this very shift. I thought about how polite you might have been with people and how perhaps you would have felt embarrassed if we had run into one another under these circumstances. Or maybe you would have come up with the jokes that you use all the time to hide yourself, or your pain, or something else that I never had time to figure out—assuming that I could ever do that, figure you out, that is, even if I had all the time with you in this world. I thought about how hard you work and have worked all your life, how you must have been so exhausted sometimes, flying by night and going to school by day to earn another degree, to learn how to take care of the bodies and bones of tired people. I imagine your hands, long and slender and black, touching those bodies, healing them to the core; and then I imagine them touching me, all over my starved being, which has not been close to another body in a very long time, a very long time, avoiding as it was the pains that always come after the beautiful unparalleled illusion that falling in love is. But your hands never did touch my starved being. We never got close enough for that. At least not in reality. If you had read the poems that I wrote about us, the imaginary us, you might have laughed; or perhaps, I kept thinking, you would not have disappeared before we could really know one another; or you would come back so that we could really start—at exactly the right point. If you had read the poems that I wrote about us, the imaginary us, perhaps you would not have left me hanging like a bride that never was, a bride only deluded by the hunger she had been experiencing for a long time, one hundred years of solitude, which had forced her to go and search for love in the magnetic cybernetic pulsing waves where your photo and your words were stunning, absolutely stunning. I kept thinking these things, these thoughts. But perhaps I have been alone for so long I no longer can distinguish curiosity from pure awe. My friends tell me I can't go fully into these things, I can't fall for a man I met only a couple of times and with whom I had not much more than a dozen conversations. My friends keep telling me that, that I must stay cool while using this electronic harmony dating thing where lonely people search for soulmates. I must be careful because sometimes people play games, games that they themselves do not understand or even know they are playing. Meanwhile, we are all so alone, so alone, and we keep waiting and waiting, waiting for the beautiful idea to manifest itself—like a Mandela of sorts, imprisoned in a lonely cell, on the island, nurturing that which is in fact fundamental for life to be called life. And I keep sitting at airports, solitary, alone, imagining how beautiful things could happen, how truly beautiful love must be possible, has to be possible in this world of so many human disencounters.

But he stopped calling, not even a word, and I am left hanging, trying to reconstruct a story that never fully was, trying to see if its denouement could have been fully realized, clarified, explained, or if destiny made it happen this way on purpose for me to learn, for him to learn. Perhaps you were not just into me, like I wanted you to be, like I needed you to be, like you thought you would be. Perhaps it is as simple as that, and so I must continue my search, the journey that I have barely just started, for I have been hiding in the cave for ten long years, hiding from the disenchanted beings, the bad characters, who have spat on my body. I have been hiding like a scared virgin who is afraid of the roughness of true lovemaking. It is cold now, and I must go. My flight to Porto is here. Soon I will see my newly widowed mother with her big swollen body and the veins on her legs on the verge of bursting. I will touch her, and in that very act perhaps I will feel the love of my own blood. Perhaps I will be reminded that I was not born to give birth to boys and girls and repeat that cycle of blood and plasma wounds.

I am returning now, going back already. The time was so short. Duty calls me again, and I leave my mother behind, like I did my father just two days before he died. I left him at that hospital bed, alone and naked, and I ran away to earn a living. Now I sit here again, eternally waiting, as we do for our whole lives. The city is London and the airport is Heathrow. The murmurs in the air bring me the scent of many people. I hear the familiar voice of Brazil, recognizing the lazy syllables of Adriana Calcanhoto—sounds that go on forever as if language were trying to really grasp meaning and avoid silence. And then comes Spain, or its old empire, in a voice that I cannot name. Is it jazz? The world is no longer like before. We are everywhere at the same time and yet feel as lonely as ever, searching for a unity of time and space that never seems to come. And so we keep going and going, like wounded animals, forever yearning.

ANOTHER TRANSCRIPTION. Today during your shift at the hospital, you had to hear another long speech from the mouth, mind, and soul of someone who wants to escape the walls of the hospital. You hear him and think, my good God, this man needs help, please deliver him from the sorrows that inhabit his nights and days, open the heavy wooden door like you did for Isabel, and let him live. Let him be among birds in the garden with sun and pathways of deliverance. Let him be part of the dance of snowflakes that the stunning Canadian winters bring, the dance that makes the world feel equal and transforms all of us into little brothers and sisters. You have to transcribe his speech word for word so that the doctors can see clearly what he needs and confirm, one more time, the diagnosis. Once again, they refuse to grant him the freedom dance that he craves and has been craving for the last twenty-five years since he got here. All this because of a misunderstanding between him and the society where he lives, a misunderstanding that robbed him of his life, his right to stretch his limbs outside under the oxygen that the sky gives to all of us equally like a father that loves all his children, whether they are in Africa or Europe or Asia. Though lately we have heard that humans have created holes in the atmosphere that are depriving some people in Russia and Africa of the pure air they need to go on. Instead these people are inhaling poison that kills their lungs. You have to transcribe word for word, gasp for gasp, trying to catch profoundly mystical metaphors, where dyslexia of mind and body join, entangled in all the truths of the world, creating aphasia, beautiful in meaning, the true language, which only the super-mind, unhabituated to simple logical words, could comprehend—a mind of an advanced future or a sublime past that we have lost somewhere, somehow. No one seems to know who is to blame. We accuse one another and go outside to protest against Wall Street and Bay Street, like guilty mobs pretending to be innocent; but deep down, we all know. We are guilty for the state of things. We know that in order to re-invent life and give bread to the children of Somalia, we have to kill ourselves and start from scratch. We have to sell our cars, our boats, and become acquainted with the nothingness of life. Perhaps in that moment of bareness and lucidity, we can find another way of life that will be the true communism that father Marx dreamed of.

But you have to transcribe him (Mackenzie) accurately and according to the limited capacities of a supposedly normal being. You need to be accurate so that your mind does not become his and vice versa. You also don't want to confuse the doctors, as this could be grounds for a lawsuit against you and the hospital. Not to mention you could be the cause of his misdiagnosis and spend the rest of your life feeling guilty because you kept this man in prison for longer than necessary, preventing him from tasting the sun and feeling the wet sand under his feet on a day when it is just good to walk outside. You attune your mind, your body, and your deeper self, preparing your being to understand his plea. Then you send his message to the doctors, who have the power to deliver him or to keep him. You wish you could lie and fabricate his story so that it would make more sense, and then they—the powerful doctors who are well versed in DSM compendiums and have read articles by other doctors from all over the world—could send him outside. He could sleep one more time under the stars of a summer night, or merely kiss his mother. She is now eighty-nine and has not seen him in ages—except that time when he was brought to visit her, but he was all in shackles. Looking at him then, she could not really see him as her son, a free boy of four dancing happily, like only children do, by the shores of Lake Ontario. She remembered that it had been a spring day—when greenery and transparency and light merge to create the incredible, the incendiary—and she had looked at him and thought, *He is fucking beautiful, fucking beautiful, and if I were to die today, if I were to close my eyes for eternity, I would not be mad at God, for my purpose on this earth would have been achieved.*

I am Martin Luther King from 3-5, here at the hospital on Slight Street, I have been here for twenty-five years, I have this doctor who is really a bad lot, hanging around with demons on the wall who dress in white, red, and green, all of them making faces and saying that I deserve to stay here, they abuse her and then she abuses me but there is no master that lets me be abused, I call corporate lawyers and they all say there is no mantra to keep me here at Slight Street, I have a case, strong lawsuit against the hospital, I have billions, millions of dollars assured by your incompetence, the judge says there is no case, there is no reason in this unreason of yours, how you keep calling the board on me, I was paying my bills and then the police stopped me and asked me my name, I did not want to give the name, the name is mine, I don't have a name but the name that you give me, on nights like this I dream of marked forests and unmarked graves and I am swinging between them, caught only by the force of gravity and the grace of Snow White, my mother holding the line of my vision before the demon came and took me away to the other side of the river, where there is no lack of pain and I see men in knives trying to drink your blood, I see them often on the walls of this hospital too, them again trying to make me a prisoner like they did then, I see them faded in others and green like the leprechauns, the police say I must take off my jacket, I don't have any money, I pay my bills, I turn around and I do what I'm supposed to do, I turn around and do things right, I am competent, I turn around and turn off the light, I put my blanket up to my face to keep the cold off and I say goodnight before I go, I have a case, there is no case you have against me, the lawyers have stated it very clearly, you have imprisoned me without charges, I have millions of billions to be made, I'll sue the hospital, I have billions of millions to be made, it is a sure case, absolutely supported by the condition of the patient, I cannot see the sun or the birds, my eyes are like closed stars that have stopped believing and emitting light, my feet have sores that signal the lack of vitamin D and my tongue is nauseated with the food that you serve me, your nurses treat me like an imbecile who does not know what the word "good" means, I know things, I am smart, I do things right like I am told to do, I don't deserve to be here, my mother is dying and I have not seen her or been with her, my mamma is dying and I am dying, God please open the doors and let me fly above the city buildings and become acquainted with the true beautiful angels like I used to do when I was a boy running around with blond curly hair, the sun, I was the sun, and mamma coming after me like a being out of this world, mamma coming after me and loving me like that, and now the leprechauns on the wall don't leave me alone and my doctor is in on it with them, I turn around and I want things fixed, I'll sue the hospital, I have an absolute solid case, strong as the iron shackles that you have put around my wrists or the injections you give me that make my tongue lazy and I can't say a word, the language that I have in my head becomes frozen in the space above me and then the demons grab it and they speak for me as if it was me but it is not me it is them trying to be me, I am me, Martin, Martin Luther King from 3-5, Unit 3-5, please call me so that we can discuss, call me at 545-555-2211, hello Madam, my name is Émile Rousseau, a French citizen of Greek origins, a doctor in philosophy, ontology, and epistemology, hello Madam, I call you to tell you what I am, have been, and still want to be, I have been an agile soccer player in the arenas of Barcelona where now the bullfighters no longer are allowed to continue and with reason for the animals are part of us and killing like that was an absolute crime, absolute, absolute crime, I turn around and want to sue the hospital, can you turn around Madam and call me please, I am in 3-5 here on Slight Street, I have an absolute solid case, the corporate lawyers from Bay Street tell me, absolute one billion million dollars to be made for wrongful convictions for twenty-five years, I turn around and I want to sue, I have been a soccer player, better than Cristiano Ronaldo, showing the prowess and agility of the best of this world and beyond playing with the ball like I own it, a toy that I toy with fooling my adversaries, I used to make millions and billions before you put me here all because of a misunderstanding between you and me, I have been Miss Canada and then Miss World and then I soared above and became Miss Universe to escape the dirty hands of old pig men who could not keep it in their pants and wanted to dirty my long beautiful body that God gave me to give only to those I chose to give it to, I became Miss Universe travelling through the ancestral lights and then coming back to this hole the police and the board and you have brought me to, I turn around and I have been a Buddhist, I turn around and I have been a Christian, I turn around and I have been a Rastafarian, I turn around and I have been Astrild the Goddess of Love, I have been the prophet Mohammed and have had the pleasure of having ten beautiful wives all for myself with their legs open widely at my disposal and I delighted entering the realm of God that can be found only in the dark moist insides of a woman, I have been the Virgin Mary and have had to explain to the world, and not without discord, why and how it is possible for a woman to give birth and at the same time maintain her virginity in body and mind, I turn around and I was going for a drink with twenty bucks in my pocket and the police start harassing me and asking me for my name, I don't have no name, I have a name that I can't give you, I tell you this but you and I do not speak the same language, I came from a long line of people who have wisdoms beyond your grasp, who run with the long snake of time close to the ground so that their seeing is all-encompassing and does not suffer from the fallacy of logics, I turn around and I see all of you and the ones who came before me and I turn around and I can read how you think of me, how you can't see the entirety of my being because you have been in the factory where division of labour is all you understand, I have a painting called *The Division of Labour* that I must show you to see if you understand, and I turn around and I am Astrild, I turn around and I am Buto the snake goddess, and I am Buddha and Mohammed and the Virgin Mary, I possess the power to navigate inter, intra and transcendentally, I am Émile Rousseau, a French citizen of Greek origins, I am Émile, a doctor in philosophy, ontology, and epistemology, I turn around and want to leave Slight Street, I have an absolute solid case, absolute solid case, the lawyers have confirmed, millions of billions, billions of millions, I turn around and I want you Madam to call me back, I am in Unit 3-5 here at Slight Street, thank you Madam, 545-555-2211, thank you Madam.

Martin Luther King did not use any commas or any full stops in his message. He told himself through a single boundless sentence until he exhausted his breath and I could no longer manage his discourse. He told himself through a single breathless sentence. I only put commas here and there so that the doctors could more easily navigate through his person, that maze with no end and no beginning, but which is in itself everything that it is possible to be: a beautiful soul trying to experience being. The *chora* that we all are. The space of the universe that is constantly expanding, leaving the inhabitants of the earth enveloped only in the luminary of the Milky Way. Blinds of wondrous holes, valleys, and hills: black, white, infinite rainbows of beingness... The fear is that I may not have fully understood the incantatory profundity of his message and that, for that very reason, I have failed him and myself. I can only sleep tonight if I tell myself that his fate is not in my hands anyway but rather in the hands of the doctors, for they hold the power. I am merely the transcriptionist in the sturdy tower that is the Hospital of the Soul.

DON'T BRING FLOWERS TO MY GRAVE. Don't bring flowers to my grave; give them to me while I am alive. I brought flowers to your grave because I did not know how to offer them to you while you were alive. And for that, I humbly ask your forgiveness. In the hospital, the nurses and the student nurses keep surrounding you and your father. You feel there is no privacy. If only they were not there, constantly coming and going, intruding on the intimacy between you and your father, you could read him the story from your book, the book dedicated to him and Isabel. You could read him the one titled "The Mountain Musician" because that is the one you feel relays your love for him most clearly, a love that you feel you ought to show more directly now that he is approaching the hour of the scorpion, now that it is almost the end of everything. After the end there will be no more chances, no more days or hours to tell the untold. You want to tell him the story, to read him your love, but the nurses and the student nurses are there. And there is also the other man with the colonial war tattoo on his arm—the one much younger than your father, with his wife by his side—and you don't feel you can tell the story to your father with the intrusion of those strangers. He ought to be at home, dying in the intimacy of his old house, smelling the cow dung and the pig dung like he did all his life. He ought to be with you and your mother and all the rest of them who would care, should care to be there and show him their love because blood is supposed to speak louder, to know better, to be thicker than the trunk of the old oak tree. But he can't go home. He is very sick; he can't feed himself. They have put the tube in him again because last night he had an episode and almost choked. Nurse Idalina says we can't take the tube out anymore because not only can he choke without it, but he has also refused to eat anything since yesterday morning. They are obliged to preserve his life, for this is not Switzerland. With the tube, they can just send something down there and feel at ease, feel they are doing their job.

He can't really speak. He had a seizure last night, and he is in this comatose state. But you feel he knows you are there, you feel he knows. You touch his naked legs and his feet, and you massage them. It is hot and humid in the room; the sticky heat of the approaching July is becoming unbearable. There is no air conditioning like in Canada. He is covered only with a white hospital bed sheet, like Christ in his last hours, thin, in agony, and distanced from this world. His sides have sores because he has not been able to move enough for quite a while now. When he came home, your mother and the rest of the family members who were there did not move him enough, did not take him on wheelchair walks. They thought there was no point, or maybe they were just burdened by the duties of their own lives. He was supposed to leave the hospital and go to a long-term care facility last week when the nice Cuban-born doctor finally agreed to sign the papers, but now he can't go because he has developed bronchopneumonia, the type usually developed in hospital settings. You blame yourself because your family was fighting for weeks. They couldn't agree about where he should go, and because there was no agreement he stayed at the hospital. You blame the doctor who refused to sign the papers that would have allowed him to go to the long-term care facility near your village where your mother could see him regularly. You felt like that Portuguese doctor was a masculine authoritarian bastard who did not like you to argue with him. You thought of your old days there. You thought of the types of men that you had encountered there. Then you thought you were in fact lucky that you no longer lived in that country, that you did not have to constantly put up with arrogant pigs like him who keep perpetuating gender and class lines as if they were living in medieval times when kings received their powers directly from God.

The other nurse, Marta, was extremely inappropriate with you on the phone when you called her from Canada and tried to ask questions about why your father had been sent home on a feeding tube that your mother could not manage, that no one in the family could manage. She said your family and yourself have no shame. She accused you of leaving your father there in hospital longer than necessary; she blamed you for his bronchopneumonia. She made you feel guiltier than you already felt. You told her she was stepping out of her bounds and that she was being unethical, and you promised you would launch a complaint against her for professional misconduct. You did launch a complaint against her after your father died. It took them a year to reply, and they stated—in cold, obscure, roundabout bureaucratic language that says nothing—that no one had ever complained about Nurse Marta and that therefore they could not find any fault in her conduct. You still tried to argue with the hospital director about the response to your complaint. You pointed out to him that they were following outdated deductive Socratic postulates in their investigation, for they were basically saying that "All actions of Nurse Marta have been exemplary, therefore Marta is exemplary and could not have conducted herself otherwise in the case of your father." But it was all to no avail. Your father was dead. Isabel was also dead, and her family did not confront the hospital about any wrongdoing. They said there was no point because she was dead after all and nothing would bring her back—nothing. Yes, perhaps it would not have mattered after all; perhaps they both would have died when they did even if things had turned out differently. But you still think the hospital needs to be accountable, that the doctors need to be held accountable. You still think they're stuck in some antiquated class system. You think they're treating villagers however they want because they don't see them as equals, just like the slave owners did to their slaves or the colonizers did to the colonized in Angola and Mozambique. The latter accepted their treatment for a long time—a very, very long time, in fact. You think that people need to rebel and protest and step out of their resignation. They need to stop saying, "That's life, that's the way things are, what can we do but accept it?" And then you remember the story that your mother tells about your grandmother. The latter had gone to see a doctor because her fingers were all twisted and she was in horrible pain. She extended her hands to the doctor so that he could see them and said to him in a supplicating voice, "Senhor Doutor, look at my hands. Look at how they are, how twisted my fingers are. Look at them, Senhor Doutor." He looked at her and merely said, "I know, I know." He did not explain to her that she had rheumatoid arthritis and that there was no cure for it. He said nothing to her. Your grandmother was a peasant woman living at a time when there was no health coverage, and she had spent one thousand *escudos* to go and see this doctor because she wanted to know how her hands could become better. She wanted to know if they could become better and would stop causing her so much pain when she was washing the clothes in the river. He said nothing, nothing. And your grandmother, who was a woman of her time and station, did not feel she could ask the doctor questions and went home just as confused as she had left, accepting life as it came to her. Isabel's parents said nothing also, did nothing to protest the actions of the hospital. They went home and cried over their fate. This bothers you immensely. You think that people ought to say things, that they ought to speak back to the beast when the beast is being a beast because that's how things change, that's how the beast becomes less of a beast. Last year when you were in Portugal, you saw a mother on TV saying, "Every last cent that I have will be used to sue the hospital for what they did and did not do to my daughter and her unborn child. Every last cent." And you thought, *This woman is doing what others ought to be doing in circumstances like that.* Her pregnant daughter had gone to the emergency four times complaining that she was in extreme pain, and every time the doctors had sent her home saying that nothing was wrong and assuring her the baby was just fine, just fine. The fifth time she was taken to the hospital, she had spent the entire night bleeding and bleeding, her blood trickling down her legs and dirtying her bedroom floor. It was too late, and both she and her unborn child died shortly afterwards.

There is no privacy in the hospital with all the nurses and the student nurses coming and going, not to mention all the sick people and their waiting families, but deep down you know you don't have much time left and that you must express your love to your father, that you must tell him now before it's too late. There isn't much time left. But you need to redeem yourself and your family and the entire hospital, for no one did enough it seems, no one did enough to take away your father's pain and make his last days bearable. And so you need to sing him a lullaby, a lullaby of goodbye, a song of last love, for the time is now. You read him the story, the story that you think will best speak to him in this place where he already is, in this unconscious valley where his memories all dwell, intermingled in unison, in a circular nothingness that carries everything. You sing him the story so that he feels less afraid, less alone, less in his own self. You sing it in your language, in his language, that perfect Portuguese with wide endless vowels. You enter the echoing *a*'s of the imperfect past, and the *o*'s and the *u*'s and *e*'s, and then the nasal ending sounds of the *n* and the *m*, forming an extended chime, a magic current that makes time transtemporal, creating a perfect past, a perfect present, a perfect future. You feel that all you are recounting is really there, forever lingering around, like the songs of Gilberto Gil in that voice that cries and sings and loves all at the same time. That voice that cries and sings and loves, forever living in the poetic nodes of his intricately long dreadlocks.

The mountain musician. Sitting on top of the highest peak of the astonishing mountain range, this musician was the treat, and also the fear, for all the inhabitants of Almores and its surroundings—the fear of that which is uncertain. Wherever they were, far or close to the magnificent event, people could not ignore the music he played and the aura that it brought. It was as if the wind—or whatever exists in it that permits the sound to travel—was a lover of the entire world and wanted everyone to listen to the deep, cavernous sounds coming from this enchanted musician, this pilgrim of the mountain.

The player was a strange man, *sui generis* to the extreme, without name that was known, without revealed origin, with long hair, so long that it covered the entire mountain peak and walked downwards ahead of him, dressing the mountain sides and making them appear inhabited by hairy, spirited goats in search of the sacred, fresh herbs that grow only in the highest regions of the world. He had come to this place seven years ago after that premature disgrace that was the death of the birds of Ti Feijó, which sung like no other, followed by the death of Bitalina Bocage's seven hens, which always rose before the cocks and before the moon was eaten by the sun to announce, in pure eagerness and beauty, the beginning of the world. This is what the people of the region would recount. But Ti Mangueiro da Poça, a man who carried the impressive weight of time and knew how to see things others couldn't, would claim, with perfect certainty, that the musician was an eternal, motionless presence. He had always been on top of that mountain of Almores, sending down beautiful and aural rain so that the inhabitants of the valley could truly discover how it is that the parties of the end of the year ought to be conducted: "Celebrating the eternity of time," he would proclaim with incendiary voice and conviction.

In days when there was little rain falling from the sky, or when a fog—sometimes dense, sometimes light—wandered across the mountain top, down its slopes, and into the valley where Almores was located, the music would descend in slow motion as if enmeshed in the intricate circles of a happy and erotic dance. And then it would install itself in the bodies of all the inhabitants; in all the plants, trees, stones, and animals living there; and even in the abundant waters that ran fast and heavy in that region, which was known for its unending springs. The water flowed eternally, as if telling us the sea was not that far away, or merely reflecting an act of great audacity engendered by great love—a love that would not permit thirst to afflict those mountaineers, living high up there, close to the skies and the stars at night. The music would envelop everything and everyone, cloaking all with acute persistence, and Almores would become immersed in a pure silence, that silence that comes when body and matter cease speaking so they can hear, in deeper cadences, the circling song that echoes in perfect repercussion, within time, inside of them, in that hollow and concave space that lives in everything that is life: human life or life of any other important nature.

On days when the rain would fall in passionate and violent aggression, something else would happen, something else even more astounding. The little boys and the little girls with less than eight years on their bodies and souls would enter a state that was impossible to put up with. They became noisy little rascals, and there was no way that their dance could be tamed. The heavy slaps of their fathers and the light caresses of their mothers ceased to have any effect. It was as if the children were possessed by a life that was vaster and fuller, vaster and fuller than the life that commanded the other inhabitants of Almores. They were little devils, these boys and girls. They were constantly fighting and with such intensity that after a while it was not possible to discern whether we were listening to the music coming from the mountain, to the heavy rain against the glass of the windows and the zinc covers of the houses, to the sounds emitted by the little girls and boys who had not yet arrived at the octave year of their life, or to everything densely intertwined in one single whirl. After this singular fighting among the children, another thing would happen. The girls and boys would start singing, but their singing did not seem to come from their own mouths, but rather from the entire extension of their bodies. Pore after pore seemed to emit sounds similar to those that came from the pianist planted on top of the mountain, up there on the highest peak, closest to the sky and the blue indigo. It was as if the little boys and girls had themselves become flutes and trumpets, drums and violins, whistles and light bird songs, powerful machines endowed with vast musical experience. It was as if they knew how to create the world's eternal chant, a song composed of the most varied instruments to create the perfect, the complete.

At this point, the fathers and mothers of the little ones could no longer understand why they had been upset at their children; they no longer knew why they had wanted to tame them with heavy slaps and light caresses. They became indifferent, as if they could not feel or think. They were only aware of the sound that was coming out of their little boys, their little girls, that dilated and feathery current of impossible music. They were now dispossessed of any individual will, becoming mere spectators of the music that had been engendered as if by a miracle of a God until then unknown—a God who was only now bringing to them, through a chance of sorts, that which they had never consciously thought could exist, that which they never thought they would need. Ti Mangueiro da Poça would remain motionless, with his eyes open, listening and feeling this scene, this music—as if he were dead, unable to transmit any sign of life. And then, when the silence returned, he would pronounce the following judgment: "Only the mountain pianist can teach us how to listen to the true music

of life. Only the mountain pianist can bring us the instruments
that we were missing. Only he, that man between the yes and
the no, the full citizen of the here and the there."

When the sun was shining and not a speck of fog, light rain,
or even thunderous, violent rain could interrupt the passage
of the pianist's sound, everything attained a magnetic and
glistening look. At times like this, the inhabitants of Almores
would position themselves at the window or at the door,
and they would carefully examine the sun's rays from the
very moment they started to appear behind the mountain's
peak until their very last goodbye. They would remain there,
immersed in the immutability of time, capturing the light
the star was bringing to them, in the multiple tonalities that
the passing of the day allows. In that deep and motionless
meditation, they were able to see, with the vivid clarity that
only musical experts have, the trans-incendiary illumination
created by the mountain musician. This illumination was
brought down to the people in each of the reflecting light
particles from the sun, as if the sun, the musician, and the
musician's music were all the same substance, the same
illuminating unity. As the people watched, this unity entered
their beings in full gradual waves, reminding them, through
its slow and peaceful message, of the Reason—the Reason
being that everything and everyone was part of the same
light, the same sun, the same piano, the same mountain, the
same pianist. And after this there was yet another junction—a
confluence of waters, of land, of rivers, of people, of animals,
of plants—that left in their consciousness the only possible
conscience: the awareness that one exists without existing,
that one exists in oneself but outside of oneself too. Or, as
Ti Mangueiro da Poça would say, in his observations always
injected with profound lucidity, "The consciousness that
the unconscious is the conscience of the pulsating earth, the
knowledge that one exists in a ring of fire, a ring of light, a

ring of the moon. Like a dancing unicorn travelling between cavernous spaces that hold the universe together."

But the preferred banquet would take place when the snow arrived—immaculate and white, almost virginal in its sensual hugging state—to visit Almores and the surrounding regions. On such occasions, people would get up from the nocturnal silence that had enveloped them during their sleep and, when laying eyes on that circling expansion that was all around them, they would become stunned, bewildered for hours on end, oblivious to the thread weaving them, stitching them together. They would enter a lukewarm, dizzying trance as they looked at the white nothingness that displayed itself in front of them in all directions like a quilt, a wide bed ready for the magnificent nuptial night of the prince and princess. They felt as though they were in a dream, a dream they had never, never, been able to glimpse, not even in their most beautiful and relaxed sleeps—those where they were clean, gliding, silvery swordfish, without a single trace of heavy scales slowing down their flight. Only long after, when the sun was coming down directly onto the snow, blinding those who could still see, would they awaken from the orgasmic reverie they had entered. They would awaken, and suddenly they would realize they were not the same people who had gone to bed eternities before, right after the crepuscular dusk. They vaguely remembered who they had been, but they had only a faint memory of themselves. It was an alienated remembrance, similar to the one we have of those people we met long ago—in another country, speakers of another language—and with whom we spent only a day or two in those vague distracted conversations that we are forced to have with strangers who, for one reason or another, come our way. After they awakened from this state, which had been induced by the appearance of the snow, they started to hear, as they had never been able to hear before, the music of the mountain pianist.

They would hear it, the music, in silvery medals whirled in rings of white gold, that brand that leaves traces discreetly, as if loving slowly, the way only true grownups know how to do. They would also hear the sound of the streams and fountains gushing in tamed slowness underneath the white snow, a snow that was sure of itself, so sure in fact that it did not need to change the aquatic state of the many things that were meant to remain in their original malleable substance— eternal birds gliding between spaces to kill the thirst of many. It knew the aquatic must remain aquatic so that we would not die of thirst and are able to see the various bodies that compose our primordial soup. The villagers heard, with unprecedented distinctiveness, the twittering of the birds as if they had only now remembered, after a prolonged muteness, how to sing. The villagers had suddenly become perplexed lovers of the Lord and the Virgin Mary, who was now spreading her body in a wide and perfect mantle in order to cover the green, the dry, and the arid, all those distinct states that the land we walk upon can sometimes attain. They could hear the sound of their own breathing—low, almost imperceptible, almost mute—announcing to them the life that was running in their being. They would grope their own breasts, their most intimate parts—the hollows under the arms, the spaces between the toes and the fingers—to make sure that they did in fact exist and that they were made of compact, dense matter. Their bodies sometimes asked for more than the villagers could give, distracted as they were by their daily poverty, which required the constant baking of bread and beans, the earning of a living for survival. They could hear the children of all ages playing in the soft, fleecy snow, losing themselves in the humid freshness that emanated from it in magnificent luminosity. To them, the snow was a magnetic, smiling lady who came from all corners of the world, bringing love and caresses to all and erasing all the inequalities that had been there before and which had often caused fights between the son of Dom Mouro and the son of Lavrador. They would hear everything like never before. They felt more alive, more conscious. They felt fuller, poorer, and richer.

On those occasions, those days of pure and complete being, Ti Mangueiro da Poça would enter a state of the highest elation, becoming a venerable professor, ready to retire. He would kneel down, prostrated on the fresh, cool, and soft snow that gave off a light salt smell, as if it had come from the seaside, and he would proclaim in a high voice, so that he could awaken those who by chance were still dormant: "Oh Lord, pianist of the mountain, man with hair longer than the darkness of time, God of the gods, music of the music, today is the day we have always been waiting for. After today, everything will be more. After today, time will become time, an uninterrupted time of the soul. Time of everything. Time of yes and no. Time of here and there. Oh Lord, pianist of the mountain, musician of the darkness of time. Transgressor of intemperate battles."

DON'T BRING FLOWERS TO MY GRAVE; give them to me while I am alive. Father, I have brought a flower to your grave because I did not know how to offer it to you while you were alive. And for that, I humbly ask your forgiveness. Don't bring flowers to my grave; give them to me while I am alive. Isabel, I have brought a flower to your grave because I did not know how to offer it to you while you were alive. And for that, I humbly ask your forgiveness.

POEMS AND OTHER LOVE WORDS. It is over. He has passed, my father. He is buried underground in the cemetery of Almores beside Isabel. He is also beside António Ayres de Gouveia, a famed figure who lived in the eighteenth century and had been the Bishop of Betsaida, the Archbishop of Calcedónia, and later, the Minister of Foreign Affairs during the stern regime of Marquês do Pombal—the powerful minister of the monarchy, who was practically running the country. The Marquês do Pombal had an iron fist like Salazar, only perhaps much more illuminated by the Age of Reason; he was able to resurrect Lisbon after that disgraceful earthquake of 1755, and he was ruthless enough to get rid of Jesuits and nobility who did not serve his needs well. It is over. He has passed, my father. He is buried underground in the cemetery of Almores, beside Isabel and António Ayres de Gouveia. His Highness, the Excelentissímo António Ayres de Gouveia, also a son of that region of Beira Alta, had been brought from the beautiful capital of Lisbon—*Lisboa, sempre menina e moça*, Lisbon, forever a girl, forever a young woman—because one must go home when all is said and done, done and said. One must go home. And at the end of everything, we all go to the same place; we are all stuffed in a narrow fleecy cabinet and put under the earth. Ministers, bishops, archbishops, peasants. Ashes and pollen. The beautiful nothingness. We are returned to the all that we are part of only to start again by feeding the worms and the small herbs that insist on having their turn, sprouting to the surface to be loved by the sun. Ashes and pollen. We all return to the same place; it doesn't matter whether you are the son of a minister or the oldest boy of a young widow—a boy who had to become a man at the age of ten, who had to grow up suddenly even though his mind and body were still playing the games of a mountain boy, up there in the Serra do Caramulo.

I am going back to Toronto. I am at the Frankfurt airport waiting for my connecting flight, thinking, feeling that my life is always running from me, running with me. I try to catch a glimpse of it between the narrow spaces of my fingers, a complicated task that leaves me feeling inadequate, vacant, wanting more, waiting for more, all the time. My heart does not yet know how to feel. It feels many things. I feel my father's body before it died at the hospital in Viseu, that body lying on the hospital bed wrapped in a white sheet, that mass in diapers, suffocated by the heat and the bronchopneumonia bacteria that had entered his lungs, preventing him from breathing, from breathing and living. Bacteria caught in the hospital, the doctor and nurses say, because he'd stayed there too long. Too long. But how could we have cared for him at home? How could mother, who is a stubborn mule, have cared for a man who was nearly ninety and could not move, when she herself pulls her body—a swollen living corpse—around like an ancient and overly tired matriarch? How could we have cared for a man who was being fed by a tube and could no longer swallow anything? We told that to the hospital staff. We told them we could not bring him home like that because we could not manage the tube and would end up choking him. We told them that, but they insisted that the matter was simple. "Very simple," they said and proceeded to show us how to manage the tube, how to insert it in the narrow dark hole that is father's throat, the one going to the stomach and not the one going to his lungs. I felt the tube descend into myself, and I mourned the taste of cherries and avocados, my favourite foods. I mourned his own taste, his love for pork sausages and codfish. I had dreams where both he and I were choking because the food went to the wrong hole. We had tried to pull the tube out several times because it was so uncomfortable and foreign to our being, but it would never come out. I woke up in the middle of the night gasping for air. I had panic attacks at Walmart when I was prowling the shelves to find the diet pills that would finally make my appetite disappear and my body become smaller, like my father's—less dependent on the flavours of this world, so that when my time came, I could be ready for the final beautiful event, when we are released from our narrow boundaries and enter the beautiful nil—the magnificent Yes.

Nurse Marta told me on the phone that we did not care, that I did not care, that he called my name all the time, "Daria, where is my Daria, my Daria is in Canada, bring her over here, she knows how to speak to me, how to tell me stories of America, America, where my uncle Casimiro went long, long time ago never to return, Daria, where is my Daria, bring her over here, she is the only one I can speak to, the only one that hears me, my wife is a mule, a mule with two legs who always insults me, telling me that I am dumb, I am slow, that I can't even go to the bank, I don't even buy a piece of bread to bring home when I go to a cow fair, she tells me I am not even a man, for a man takes charge, my wife is a mule, a mule with two legs, who spent her life making my days unbearable and the only way I could get up in the morning was because I had my cows, my cows know me by name, know me by voice, they moo and moo when they hear me, they moo and moo and stare at me when I caress their head, they stare at me with those large open eyes, so full of stories, so full of being, so full of love, Daria, Daria, where is my Daria, bring her over here, a man spends his life listening to a mule of a wife who does not even know how to cook for a man, how to feed a man, a man that spends his days unearthing the earth to find good soil to plant potatoes and corn and beans so that we can all eat and she doesn't even see that, always saying I am a good for nothing, a good for nothing, Daria, Daria, where is my Daria, bring her over here, I go to the cow fairs to look at the beautiful animals, the most beautiful animals, I go to cow fairs and my cows, God is witness, and all the Mayors of the town, all of them know, 'There are no cows in the region like those of Adelino Mendes from Almores, no cows like that, look at those feet and nails, and that splendid back, that clean polished skin, and he speaks to them, when he speaks to them it is as if we are seeing God and the Virgin Mary, God and the Virgin Mary in the most beautiful act of lovemaking, a cow and a man speaking like that, one is the other and the other is the one,' that's what they say, the mayors of the town, Daria my Daria, where is my Daria, bring her over here, and then that wife of mine, a mule with two legs goes through my pockets every time I return from these fairs, these fairs that are the only moment I have to encounter God, she goes through my pockets and counts the *escudos* that I have left and the ones that I spent and goes on a rant for days and days, I am a good-for-nothing, I never bring a piece of bread for the children, I was only good to make them, giving her a belly every sixteen months, a good-for-nothing who can't even buy a piece of bread, but she does not say that I give her all the money I make on the cows, the money I get from the cow prizes and the little calves that I sell every season, I give her all the money and then she counts the *escudos* that I spend when I go to the cow fairs and eat a dish of *dobrada* or *bacalhau* at Senhor Sampaio's tavern, which she can't even cook at home, she boils some food and expects us to be grateful and eat it as if we were pigs, the pigs who live under our kitchen, which we kill every fall to get some sustenance throughout the year, she counts the *escudos* and goes into my pockets to search and search, a wife who is a mule with two legs, Daria, Daria, where is my Daria, Nurse Marta bring her here, Nurse Marta, my Daria, my Daria, bring her over here..."

It is over, he has passed, my father. And I was not there. I had left for Canada two days before. I should have stayed like my initial intuition was telling me. My intuition used to be sure of itself when I was much younger, very sure of itself, but then I let too many voices enter my mind, my body, my soul. Those of my mother, those of Vasco da Gama and his acquaintances and many others. And now it is too late. It's finished. I missed his last moments. I am at the airport in Frankfurt returning to my life on the other side of the world. When my sister left me a voicemail message announcing that he had passed, that my father had passed, I called the hospital right away. I wanted to know how he had died. Was he alone, did he say something, did he recover from the unconsciousness that he had slipped into after the seizure, did he call my name, did he open his eyes, was there a last breath audible to the one standing by? I asked all these questions, and many others, in one single, long sentence to the nurse who answered the phone. It was not Marta. It was another one, the nicer one, the one who had asked if I was his only daughter because he responded so well to me. Her name was Ana. Ana Magda. And she had a soft voice and very sad eyes like someone who had witnessed a lot, someone who had been at the hospital too long working the geriatric care ward, inhaling all the sighs, all the screams, all the disillusions of old dying people. She said my father died peacefully, that he just gave that last breath, almost imperceptible, like an angel ready for departure, that he went to the other side meekly accepting the destiny that awaits all of us. He died peacefully, and there was nothing else that we could do, nothing else that we could do, nothing else to be done. God delivered him from sufferance. It was a *grande esmola*—it was a great act of charity—and he was now in a much better place, a much better place. You hear Ana Magda's voice on the other side. A gentle, peaceful voice. With your heart choked and the tears almost at the surface of your entire being, you think, Ana Magda is nice, very nice. She knows what I need to hear, what I need to hear to move on and not carry the guilt of my father's death on my shoulders. She is nice. A woman who has seen a lot. She knows love. She knows suffering. She knows human beings. She knows guilt. Ana Magda. What a beautiful name: short, soft, and simple. A sister of the other one, whom Jesus helped when she needed so much.

When people die at the hospital, the body is left there for four hours before it is taken down to the morgue, which is located in the basement. They want to make sure that the body is indeed dead. They did that with my father, my older brother told me. They waited four hours to see if the body would, by some miracle, come back to moving life. They did not want to kill him before his time, before God had given permission for him to leave this earth. I hear ghastly stories about the old days, when science had not yet arrived to the people of the mountains. I hear that many people, who had entered unconsciousness due to some illness, were often buried alive because those poor peasants did not possess a stethoscope to detect the pounding of the human heart. They used only their own hearts and ears to sense any sign of life in the bodies of their loved ones. I hear stories of how the son of old Maria Matos was buried alive. His mother discovered this when she went to visit his grave one day after he had been placed underground. She went to the cemetery to visit her son at his new dwellings, and she saw, in disbelief and choking pain, how the earth that had been covering him was all scattered throughout the cemetery, dressing all the other graves and hiding the beautiful marble stones and the flowers that had previously adorned the graves of the rich dead people. It was a strange, uncanny scene that made the cemetery a site of momentary equality, just like when it snows in Almores and all becomes one, all becomes the same. Ashes and pollen. All of them. All of it. Padre Lévito was livid when he saw how the cemetery of his parish had suddenly become a place like any other with no beautiful roses or stones covering the dead bodies, and he summoned his staff to immediately come and clean up the mess, that disgraceful sacrilege that had taken place during the night. Maria Matos was beside herself when she got to the cemetery and came upon this scene. She had carried, in beauty and love, a fresh bundle of red carnations to place on the grave of her beloved son. Later on, these flowers became the symbol of the beautiful revolution, when soldiers and army generals said no to the dictators and started shooting flowers instead of bullets through the barrels of their guns. The revolutionaries made Lisbon a city of love instead of blood. Finally Luanda, Lourenço Marques, and other capitals of the African colonies were going to whirl in the exhilarating feeling that liberation—that magnificent gazelle that dances stunning somersaults in the savannah, as if she were both a bird and an animal—allows for. There was finally hope that those who had been imprisoned, killed, viciously persecuted, and tortured by the PIDE,[1] Africans and Portuguese, would see their beautiful idea triumph, the same idea that Mandela had nourished, with the patience and hope of a mystic, for twenty-seven years at Robben Island.

When Maria Matos first got to the cemetery with those lovely and nice-smelling flowers and saw what had happened, the flowers flew from her arms, leaving behind their inebriating perfume, and she started crying as if it were the end of the world. "Where is my Manuel? Where is my beloved son? What have we done to you, my son? What have we done to you, my son? Oh God, forgive us all, us all, sinners who bury the living, arrogantly killing those whom only you have the right to call to you at the right time. Oh, my beloved son, what have we done? God have mercy on us." It was Sunday morning when all this happened, and so when the people came for the Sunday mass, they were horrified by the sight and even more horrified by the cries and screams of Maria Matos. She was frantically scratching the earth that was left on top of her son's coffin to see if she could still rescue him and find his heartbeat. But it was too late; it was too late.

---

[1] *Polícia Internacional de Defesa de Estado*/International and State Defence Police: the Portuguese police during the fascist regime of António de Oliveira Salazar, which came to be known for its secret activities and use of intimidation and violence against those opposing the regime.

When she finally got to him and managed to open the tightly sealed coffin, her son appeared livid, with his eyes open and his fingers securely attached to the ceiling of the coffin and separated from his hands, a sure sign that he had spent horrific hours trying to unlock the coffin with all his force. The force had been so great that most of the earth covering him had been scattered throughout the cemetery. When she saw him like this, she lifted his body and carried him around the cemetery, in a trance, or a dance of sorts, of sorrows, invoking all the prayers that she knew and others that she invented on the spot, those that come out only when we are faced with suffering of the highest degree. She was a little old woman carrying the body of a young, tall, and sturdy son like that in an enduring *romaria*, a suffering pilgrimage. The force that she summoned from her entire self must have been colossal. She then took him to the church, where people were already gathered for the Sunday mass, so that everyone could see what had been done to her son. Most of all, she wanted to show Padre Lévito what he was responsible for, because she felt that as a man of God, and as the man who had pronounced the last rites for her son, he ought to be accountable for the killing. The priest was not there yet, and so Maria went to the altar and, still carrying her son in her arms, spoke to all the saints who were there: St. Mathew Our Lady of Snows, Our Lady of Sorrows, St. Anthony, and St. Peter. Then she spoke in more detail, and with more supplication and resentment, to the Virgin Mary and her son Jesus Christ, who was there, elevated at the centre, as always, in his painful and heavy cross, eternally bleeding. To the saints, she asked, "How could you not see what took place in the night? How could you not see what was going on out there in that cemetery? How could you close yourselves inside these doors and be unmindful of my son's struggles? How could you?" And when she spoke to the Virgin Mary and to her son, her words were even less kind, more accusatory, as if she were spitting venom from her tongue: "How could you, Virgin Mary, stand there all dressed up in blue and white and only care about the suffering of your own son? Are you not a mother to us all? Do you not feel, in the entrails of your being, the suffering and agony of the one you gave birth to and the suffering and agony of all the sons of God? Are you not made of flesh and blood and bone? Do you not see how those others of flesh and blood and bone suffer, how they scream day and night, trying to escape the dark hole where they have been put before their time? What about your son? Is he not a brother to mine, the son of God, the Son of all sons? Does he not feel that prickling of the cross on his skin? Does he not know the cutting knives of the Roman soldiers on his flesh? Are you all dead? Do you even have eyes for this world that you claim you created and keep an eye on?" And on and on she went. She did not address God directly because, for her, those figures on the altar were all parts, dimensions of God. This priest and the scriptures said that "The shepherd is your Father, and you are in the Father. There is no division between Him and us. Sons and daughters of the same current. Apples of the same tree. Rivers of the same sea. The Trinity becomes the infinity of all there is in this universe." Receiving no answer from any of the divine figures on that altar, she resorted to washing her son, from head to toe, using all the holy water that she could find on the sturdy granite stone plates attached to the walls of the church, hoping that some miracle would eventually occur. She baptized him again, this time on his death, with God's waters calling him back to life. She undressed him and washed his body cell by cell, node by node, trying to get rid of all the signs of death that were quite evident all over, and putting her ears and mouth everywhere to see if she could find something, something that gave her hope.

The parishioners, who were there waiting for the mass, watched all this with open motionless eyes and did not move except to allow her to pass with the body, whenever she was going from place to place inside the church in her frantic attempt to revive her son. They were all frozen in that moment of suffering that Maria was exposing before them. It was as if her suffering had taken on another dimension, swelling up gigantically to include all their own sufferings accumulated throughout their lives—and they had suffered, they had suffered and suffered, they had suffered a lot. When the Padre arrived in his white-and-purple dress, the body of the dead Manuel was resting on the marble steps of the altar, naked, uncovered, and bearing witness to what had happened to him. His mother was crouching over him, still doing anything that she could think of to make something happen, for we must never give up in the face of disgrace; we must always see if we can find some grace in the disgrace in which we are immersed. We must never give up. The Padre immediately gave orders for the body to be dressed and taken to the cemetery again. He also ordered the parishioners to clean up the cemetery and the church, which had been ravaged by Maria's doings, so that the proper order and peace could be restored. The parishioners obeyed the priest, and they all took action to return things to their proper places. When all was clean and Manuel's body was buried again, this time surely dead, the Sunday mass took place. The same sermons were read, the same advice was pronounced, and when the people left to go home and have their Sunday meals, that event at the church, the image of Maria Matos carrying her son around, was nothing but a faint memory. For the parishioners, it was something akin to their own suffering, which they had learned to push down to that place where it lives while also letting them live. Before sitting down at the table to eat their lunch and enjoy a little bit of roasted rabbit meat and potatoes, their special meal reserved only for Sundays, they went to the closed trunk kept at the back of the house and took out some bay and olive tree leaves—and also a touch of rosemary from the bouquet blessed last Palm Sunday—and then threw all of it in the fire. While they ate, they could inhale the scent from the burning blessed plants and feel purified and ready for the battles of the coming weeks. Maria Matos, like Piedade, the mother of my darling friend Isabel, stopped going to church after that. She also stopped sponsoring masses for her dead relatives, claiming the priests and their company were all a bunch of imposters who had killed her son before his time. She claimed the Virgin Mary had just stood there, composed, in her clean nice dress of blue and white, while Manuel was trying to breathe. As if she were not a mother and did not have blood and bile running through her.

My father, being younger than Manuel and having died at the hospital, did not suffer the same fate. He was interred only when it was certain he was fully dead, fully cold, fully inert. I felt it was so when I kissed him at the little chapel of Almores, where his body was on display as per the local custom. I had just arrived from Canada, and they had been waiting for me to perform the funeral. It was July and very hot, and the body could not wait much longer: it needed to go to the ground quickly. I was tired from travelling—tired from crying or sometimes holding in the tears so that the kind flight attendants and the passengers would not ask questions that would only bring about a greater river of emotion, an entire sea of tears. I entered the village with sunglasses on, the car sliding smoothly through the streets, passing by a line of onlookers who were all there for the funeral—all there waiting for me so that the rituals could proceed. I could sense them looking, and I knew what they must be murmuring to one another, common gossipy things: "She came all the way from Canada in America for her father's funeral. She came all the way from there, and she left just a few days ago. It must be costing her an arm and a leg, all these trips. But America is rich, America is rich." I got out of the car and I entered the chapel, and there he was: my father, dead, cold, dressed up in a suit. He looked like a man of stature, even though in his life he had been a peasant and dressed as one. I think he would object to that style of clothing, for he was a simple, content man who liked coarse pants of *burel* in the winter and cotton in the summer. For him, nothing more than that was necessary to walk the earth and enjoy the moments of time that life gives us, that we often let slip by, distracted as we are with the less fundamental. But it did not matter, for he had no say now. My older siblings had chosen the clothes my father would wear for his final voyage; they had suffered deprivations most of their lives and had a deep need to dress well so that others would not put them in a certain category of peasant mountaineers: rude, dirty, classless, and destitute. It was necessary to keep face. They also had, still have, an incessant need to clean—to clean over and over again that which has already been cleaned. It is as if they are trying to invent a farmhouse that is by nature immaculate, forgetting that life on the farm is always dirty. It is dirty but beautiful— immaculate at the core, that is. But I know that when the snow covers Toronto or Almores and everything becomes dazzling luminosity, there is no need to clean. At times like these, everyone rests; gazing, unblinking, out of the window; immersed in a transcendental awe; not daring to go outside and step on the justice that is covering the ground. Because we all yearn; we all yearn ... and sometimes there is a god that listens to us.

It was necessary to keep face and hide the truly beautiful inside. My grandmother once told me of the shameful story of Albertina de Azulis, a woman who died at the age of ninety-seven. When it was time to dress her up for the final voyage, they could not, for the grace of God, find a piece of clothing to put on her dead body. She had burned all the clothes she owned before she died—the mound of ashes and the empty trunks in her backyard giving witness to that act—and all she had left were five simple white cotton sheets, the *kafan* for the female, carefully folded on top of the chair beside her bed. On top of the *kafan*, she had left a Quran in ancient Arabic with a note on the cover that read *There is no god but Allah*. And inside the Quran there was a beautiful poem written in Tamazight, the Berber North African language. The poem was encircled in two great horns and when read out loud sounded more like a song. In the sounds of that song we could detect the cadences of a vigorous warning, that we must never forget the womb that gave us life, the breast that gave us milk: "Your body came from the earth, and the earth came from Ammon. Summoning his helpers, through the sharpened edge of his great horns that hugged everything, he created the stars and the trees. And then, flowing through him, came the cows and the beautiful horses, those animals that run wild, becoming dancing butterflies in the serene endless deserts of this land, where your mind and mine become numb, only to ascend to the dazzling vacuum." When Albertina was found by the friendly neighbours who visited her frequently to check on her—since she was a single woman who always lived alone and never married—she was naked in her bed, her wrinkled old body fully exposed. Because goods were scarce in Almores and no one had any clothes to spare, they had no choice but to bury her wrapped in the white sheets she had left beside her bed. She in fact was not a true Christian or a true Catholic, but rather one of those covert Muslims, a *conversa*, a *mourisca*. Her family went back to the sixteenth century when the Inquisition got rid of the infidels of the faith in ways more horrid than it is possible to describe with the scribbles we have at our disposal when trying to name the unnamable. She had been hiding her faith, just like the Jews of Belmonte who had been able to keep their secret since the twelfth century. That was why she wanted to be buried like that, in simple white sheets, as per the Muslim custom. However, given the poem found inside the Quran, which referred to another god, it is very difficult to know Albertina de Azulis's real religious affiliation. She was, it appears, a secret inside a secret inside another secret. She was her own *ad infinitum*: the circle with no end.

Those who found Albertina de Azulis in her home like this did not say anything until after her burial. They really loved her, and they did not want the priest to refuse to perform her last rites. They thought these rites would in fact absolve her from worshipping the wrong God or god all her life, save her soul, and open the door to the right heaven. One of her best friends later said that Albertina had confided to her that she came from a long line of strong women and that she had remained single all her life because she wanted to enjoy the company of as many men as possible. According to her friend, Albertina had said that no religion had the right to put a chastity belt around her crotch. She was following in the footsteps of her ancestor, a fiercely independent Muslim woman from the sixteenth century who pretended to have converted to Catholicism during the Inquisition so that she could stay in Almores. She did not go back to Tangiers with the rest of her family, who refused to convert and had to flee to avoid being burned at the stake. She stayed because she wanted to escape the very unfair Muslim custom of polygamy, which allows one man to have several women but does not allow one woman to have many men. But she still wanted to be a Muslim and not a Catholic. She wanted to be a Muslim on her own terms, so she found a way to work with what she had. Albertina de Azulis was merely honouring the name of her ancestor, the matriarch of her family. She was merely following the call for liberation of body and soul, a call that is singing deep down inside all of us, as she used to say.

For my siblings, it was necessary to keep face, to show that one has enough money and means to dress well. My mother was quite happy to go along with their thinking; she felt it was especially important to dress decently when embarking upon our final voyage to meet God. I would sometimes argue with them and say that such ideology is contrary to God's preaching of equality, poverty, and humbleness. Don't they know, I would ask, that Jesus told his disciples they ought to abandon everything and follow him in bare shoeless feet in search for true light and salvation? Isn't that what Padre Lévito and the preachers he brings on special occasions say over and over again? Haven't they learned the meaning of a true religion, the true God they preach about? But then Padre Lévito dresses in dashing suits when he is not doing his official religious duty, and even during his official religious ceremonies, his dresses are all very elaborate: robe after robe after robe of stunning golds and whites and purples. He also drives a Mercedes-Benz directly imported from Bavaria of a magnificent shade: a never-seen emerald green. This colour, he argues in his sermons about paradise, when he gets lost in long, lyrical, and passionate diatribes about the route to salvation, is the colour of the true heaven. He argues that those who are lucky enough to enter heaven, after they leave this sorrowful place that is our planet earth, will forever dwell in it. Our Padre also charges an arm and a leg for the masses he says for the souls of the departed. And my mother tells me that lately, rather than saying a single mass for each soul like in the old days, he will say a single mass for ten souls and charge each family for one single mass, making quite a fortune in one single breath. It is, as the proverb goes, as if he is killing ten rabbits with a single stroke and then having meat for quite a while. The villagers are not happy with that. They say that one single mass told for ten souls cannot possibly have the same impact on all the souls that it is trying to save and that they should get their money's worth. But they love their dead relatives dearly and do not want them to suffer in the fires of hell for eternity or forever dance aimlessly in purgatory. Apparently one of the parishioners was bold enough to confront the priest about his new practice of mass *en masse*, and our Padre responded, "There is a great shortage of priests nowadays, and until we bring more priests from Africa, the continent where Christianity is growing at the highest rate, I can only do so much. I am only one person, and I am not that young anymore, and I therefore cannot repeat the same mass time after time." When this parishioner asked why he kept accepting requests for all these masses if he couldn't handle all of them—not to mention why he didn't tell people that they should wait until the African priests arrived so that supply and demand were in sync—the Padre informed him he had a responsibility to his community now. He said it takes time and patience to bring the African priests up to Almores because there is a certain amount of training necessary to bring them to the practice of proper Catholicism. Then he added that the people who wanted to sponsor masses for their dead loved ones now may be dead by the time the African priests finally got here and were ready to go. This, he continued, would mean that the dead souls, who are the beneficiaries of the said masses, would not receive the benefits of the masses and could therefore be forever condemned to live in purgatory, or worse yet, in hell.

My father's body was prepared at the funeral home. My family did not handle his body after he died. The staff from the funeral home, efficient and polite, picked up his body directly from the morgue at the hospital, where it was kept cold and fresh. Then they washed it thoroughly and did other things that are done to dead bodies to make them appear alive and still pretty to the eye when in fact, inside, the primal worms are already hard at work attacking the human core. Ashes and pollen. My family did not handle my father's body after he died. They passed his body onto strangers. My mother is afraid of dead bodies. She cannot go near one, and she never goes to funerals. She did not go to her mother's funeral or to my father's funeral. It is as if she has always been running away from something, running away from her first-born son who died in the Mayombe of Angola, his body spread in thousand pieces. He became pollen and ashes, floating above the heavy forests of that African country that was once part of the powerful Portuguese Empire—the Nova Lisboa, where people were sent to make fortunes and create havoc with the locals. Unlike my father, my maternal grandmother died at home, and her body was washed and cleaned at home. I played a big role in the process when I was only sixteen. With the help of my cousin Celeste, I made my darling grandmother ready for the final trip. I cleaned her and I washed her. I sang her songs. I dressed her up. Her body was put on display at our house. My grandmother was ninety-eight years old when she died, and I had taken care of her for quite a while even though I was just a young girl, young enough to be taken care of myself. She had lost her mind and would say all kinds of things that made no sense but that sometimes had an ironic twist. She said the most truthful things that can ever be said. Because the mad mind is free from everything, it knows the most fundamental things that ought to be known. She had been a single mother all her life and had lived through hardship after hardship at a time, during the fascist regime, when church and state worked hand in hand to keep the country and women in their place. And then she lost her mind. Shortly afterwards, she lost the movement of her legs and was bedridden for the rest of her days.

I am still assaulted by her suffering, by her thin body on the verge of expiration. I can still see her, a matriarch of the old times giving the last sighs at the end of a life that had been so full of suffering. I used to blame my mother, and perhaps still do, for not taking care of her properly and leaving her at my mercy, a girl of sixteen who was herself vulnerable and could not know any better. I blamed my mother for not calling the doctor more often, for not seeing that my darling grandmother was suffering, for not rescuing her from her dementia, for giving her only Nestum with milk because that was all she would eat and swallow. I blamed my mother for not seeing the need to offer more care, to give my grandmother more water, more vitamins, more love. But my mother was a peasant woman with many responsibilities on her shoulders. She was trying to carry all of them with pride and resignation as one must do because one must always carry the suffering God sends down on us. It is our fate, it is our life, this life that is nothing but a passing moment before the real one comes. I used to blame her, my mother. She would leave my grandmother alone, and sometimes she would lock her inside the house so that she would not wander off. My mother was afraid that my grandmother would get lost in the middle of the night and be eaten by the wolves of the region, which at the time were still roaming the Iberian land, claiming their right to live and howl and mate. I used to think that she, my mother, was cruel. She was more interested in going from town to town, carrying baskets of cheese and fish and legumes on her head to sell to whomever could buy them, than she was in caring for her mother. She would leave my grandmother alone or under my care. And I was only a girl of sixteen, struggling with my own struggles and trying to understand why men would stare at my full body, a body of a young woman, with astonishing waves of yeses and noes. They would stare and say dirty things, and sometimes they even touched me, trying to feel the softness of my flesh. I have recurring dreams of my grandmother where she appears to me time after time as if she is not truly dead, or as if she too blames me for the lack of care. My grandmother was born at the end of the nineteenth century. In the 1920s, she had two little girls with a man who never saw how truly beautiful she was and exchanged her for a wife of better means. In the last dream I had of grandmother there seemed to be some sort of resolution. I sensed that she was close to me, down there in the basement, somewhere, in a hidden drawer perhaps. I was upstairs but I had the haunting feeling of duty calling me downstairs. I went down there, my heart pounding with the affliction of the guilty, in order to rescue my grandmother. Then, when I opened the drawer, I saw her body before me in the form of a mummy—as if she had been living in Egypt thousands of years ago, as if she were a queen of ancient times who knew and played with Cleopatra. I saw this body, all wrinkled and brown and elongated, just like mummies are, and then I thought she was dead, that I'd killed her. I'd allowed her to die and now she was nothing, a nothing upon another nothing upon another nothing. While these feelings invaded my consciousness, or perhaps my mother's consciousness, a sense of guilt took over that I thought would never leave me. I thought, God, what have I done, God, what I have not done? In the dream, I felt as though I was trapped in a never-ending well, doomed for life. I had an acute awareness that I'd had this dream, or others like it, countless times in the twenty-five years since my grandmother left us. I felt I was doomed for life, that there was no escape from her, from my mother, from myself. But then I looked at the face of the mummy, and, in the midst of those brown and dark colours of nothingness, I saw her white teeth exploding into a large smile, a field of light irradiating from a centre. The smile travelled all over her body and then came to me like a beautiful electric current that gave me life and solace and closure. I felt at peace. I felt that my grandmother had accepted her life and her death, and that the ashes and pollen that she had become were sufficient for her to feel alive. I felt that perhaps part of her lived in me, through this light that she had sent me. I have not had another dream of grandmother since this one. Perhaps this case is resolved. Or perhaps my deeper self grew tired of the many pains that I had been sending down there and decided to take charge so that I can move on and have space for the other deaths, for the many other pains that will come after this one.

I am at Frankfurt Airport, returning to my life in Canada. I write poems to deal with him, my father, and all of us involved in his life and death. All of us who could not save him, could not make his last days better, all of us who left him alone to face them. We, fallible beings in the face of the inevitable.

Passing the Passage

Under the tip of my tongue I grasp for words, sounds, before meaning, that will say who you are, how you lived, and how you left us to go away and swim in the other current, under the node of dark nymphs, those goddesses that sing of winds below the sphere and breathe breaths under, under your skin

My mother sighs constantly, giving voice to those kisses she never gave him even in the moments she really wanted to forget the repression of the Catholic Church and the somber sermons of Padre Lévito

I want to cry for you, a real cry from the right side of my soul, I want to but it does not want to come, not now, not yet, as if avoiding the time that has passed between the moment you were born and the moment you died, I want to cry but I am not willing, not yet ready to emerge from the full summers of uncontained hydrangeas, those wild crazed flowers that do not know what thirst is, bursting into miscegenated colours never before seen

Under my tongue I compose meanings and words outside of the alphabet, things that do not yet say how I feel about your passage to the other nether, after this nether full of fulls

Very below my consciousness, I think thoughts of guilt, I hear voices that tell me I could have saved you, or at least given you more days to live, more walks in the full vines of your many lands, or that when you died I should have been there, present, easing the moment of the last blink of your heart, or that I should at least have lifted the veil of the coffin completely to stare at your entire body and touch your cold hands directly, like I did with your face scaring away the flies that could not wait to feast upon you and your sacred nothing

I could have or I should have because nothing is enough in the face of your timely death

The curious book
There is a book on the shelf that is unlike all the others

I can tell just by the spine, which is wearing out its wings, as if the book itself contains insufficient knowledge, as if it is reaching out to its neighbours to peek at their messages in an attempt to decipher the mysteries of the world, which are many, ancient, and so profound

The neighbours of this book, though, as if jealous of the God they know, like mean-spirited or insecure priests, the type you find in *The Name of the Rose*, do not voluntarily open themselves to this curious counterpart, and instead hold their pages tightly together and find a way to become closer to the rest of the books in that same shelf, those that are not eager to get at the bottomless pit that is our universe and meet all the beingness that in there dwells.

I sit on my old sofa, which is also wretched by its own condition, and I watch this spectacle in silence, savouring the manners of the curious book and the ways in which its brothers and sisters lie down in their sleep and are satisfied with their own self-contained knowledge, like premature dead children or perhaps only cynical elders who have learned that curiosity can get you killed and in fact bring you so much unhappiness

And it is in this reminiscing that I remember my father Adelino, recalling how happy he was, just knowing his cows and using their dung to seal off the oven where we used to bake fresh corn bread, bread that exhaled the sublime scent of the mountains where the cows had gone grazing just the day before

I recall his shiny eyes and how he kept saying that happiness and good living can be found in the most unlikely places and fools are those who keep going in circles and circles trying to unveil what must remain closed off from the eye of reason, like primal dogs who cannot stop trying to catch their own tails, even though they are old now and have tried such useless exercises countless times before

The days
The days may be gone, but the light still simmers through your sturdy bones, I learn how to become mute through the orifices of your nose, and I do not expect any compensation for the minutes lost in adoration meandering through each part of your body

I watch the movement of your barely moving hand, and I remember how it is to live fully and then suddenly be assaulted by the weight of days

I touch your forehead and perceive, through your breathing skin, that your life and mine (in this state) are but ephemeral moments that go away in less than the blink of a butterfly's wing

I look around your room and concentrate on details that have passed by my eyes without any second thought but which now appear as vivid and fundamental as fresh mornings when your senses are lazily awakening and life makes the most sense: your blood flowing slowly but surely to meet the challenges of a long day

I smell your body and the decay that is approaching, and I imagine the stunning beauty of your limbs when you were a child running unimpeded as beautiful as a morning mercy

I put my head close to yours, and I hear the inner thoughts your dying soul is reminiscing about, and I envisage all the dreams that you have had throughout your long life, from birth to this very moment, dreams of utter beauty and victory in life, from days filled with vigorous tasks when your body felt the most alive, the most able, the most noble, to days when mornings and nights gave you moments that nothing, nothing can recreate, moments of simple merciful beauty, like the gradual darkening of the approaching dusk or the arrival of a new awakening clarity with all its promises, after the night has passed and the dreams have left their vivid notes

Your days are all there, entangled in your wrinkled body, which I am observing with the melancholia of a daughter who is losing her father and also imagining the loss of her own body, a body still young and yet already feeling, in its universal memory, that its days too are numbered

For we are nothing but intersecting light passing through

Or the momentary beauty of the horse cavalcading through the open fields

At the end you feel so much better, so much better, and you think, *without words, without art, love could not be properly told, properly shown, and you would feel as if you were choking all the time.* Father, I have brought flowers to your grave because I did not know how to offer them to you while you were alive. Forgive me, Father. Grandmother, I have brought flowers to your grave because I did not know how to offer them to you while you were alive. Forgive me, Grandmother. And you too, darling Isabel.

THE DAY IT HAPPENED. Vasco da Gama is extremely nice to Daria. "Daria, you are a wonderful young woman," he says. "You remind me of my daughter, Santeria. And those eyes, those dark brown and wide eyes, full of mystery. If I were a man of age, and if I were to go into a place and see you sitting there with Luísa and Milena, I would choose you. You have that thing, that thing that men look for. You are a wonderful girl—a wonderful young woman. So much like my daughter, Santeria—so much like her. You know, Daria, that what men most crave is scents—pure, raw, inebriating scents. And I smell those scents in you. You know, Daria, that my homologue, Vasco da Gama went to India because he was profoundly dissatisfied with the old scents of Europe. He went all the way there in a fleet of three ships and a little caravel, facing monsters and titanic waves at sea because he could no longer stand his stale life and the air he was breathing. What he really wanted, Daria, was to feel alive again, to taste cinnamon and pepper and ginger and cardamom and saffron. He wanted to exhale and inhale so that his lungs would became alive again. He wanted the elixir of life. Do you know the first thing he did when he got there, Daria? Do you know? He got off the ship, took off all his clothes, bathed himself in the waters of Bombay—that good, splendid bay—and then he ran to the pepper mountain like a crazed man looking for the spice. He did this even though he had been warned that the mountain was infested with vicious serpents—timeless, alert, and vengeful sentinels protecting the pepper crops— and that he needed to follow the proper rituals and be invited by the locals before entering this carefully guarded site. When he finally got to the site where the sacred creeper plant was growing, whose scent he deeply craved with all his being, he vigorously rubbed himself all over with pepper seeds and ate as many as he could. He became insane for a few days with all the fire he'd ingested from the burning seeds. He then climbed to the highest peak of the mountain, all naked and red, screaming day and night. He did all this so that he could feel alive and taste the world anew. What men most desire, Daria, is scents, scents that make them feel alive again, scents that speak to their soul and bring the world to their doorsteps, scents that inebriate them from top to bottom and make them fall on the floor crying for mercy, mercy for more...."

This was what Vasco da Gama, the executive director of the Lusitanian Social Service Centre, kept telling Daria, the young and beautiful Daria, almost from the very beginning. She had just started to work as his executive assistant. It was as if he was pleading, pleading with her, pleading for something mystical, something grand, something beautiful, which she did not quite understand. She had been tired of waiting for her open work permit and fed up with working here and there after she'd left her nanny's work in Richmond Hill and had come to live in Toronto. One day when she was going up and down College Street looking for a decent job, she decided to go into the Lusitanian Social Service Centre to ask if they were looking for someone who spoke Portuguese very well, someone who could translate. The receptionist, a nice older Portuguese woman from the Azores, said that she ought to speak with Mr. Vasco da Gama about the matter. She called him and told him about Daria's query, and he asked her to send Daria up to his office. Daria was only twenty-three years old then. She was shy but full of life, full of dreams, full of energy and willingness to work, to work hard and please. She went up and entered his office. He got up from his chair, shook her hand with a tight grip, and introduced himself in a nice Portuguese that sounded continental to her. She was wearing a long flowery dress with an opening on the side that revealed part of her leg, and which made her body appear longer. The dress displayed her curvy figure splendidly, a figure accentuated by her narrow waistline and the generous hills of her breasts and hips. She had that ripe and full voluptuousness of a young woman from Southern Europe, though often people would assume she was French for some reason or other. People would frequently insist that she had that *je ne sais quoi* that only the French have. Some would swear that her accent and her manners could only be French. And when she spoke French, they had absolutely no doubt that she was *française* indeed. Some would claim that she had that look of a Mireille Mathieu or an Audrey Tautou or even a Juliette Binoche. She would feel honoured by such comparisons, and would say in a jovial, slightly mocking manner, "Oh, no, I am only Portuguese, from the continent." On her way to the centre, as she was walking on College Street, she felt the eyes of men on her, and the words too, which some did not care to hide. She often felt confused when this happened to her: she wanted to be beautiful and noticed, and yet when men gave her those messages that part of her wanted, she felt uncomfortable and ashamed. She felt as though she were naked, nothing but prey before the eyes and teeth of a ferocious and undeserving beast.

It was May, a month that she found to be of astounding beauty in Toronto, a month of exuberant greens and long rows of tall trees that went on and on from the beginning of the streets to their very end, revealing a magic, sacred world of sorts, a charming intimate abode. Perhaps they reminded her of Almores, with its oak, pine, and eucalyptus trees standing tall and strong. Vasco da Gama had that middle complexion of a man that could easily pass for Portuguese, but, as Daria later found out, he was half-Indian and half-Portuguese. He appeared to be in his early-to-mid-sixties, and his upper lip had a full sensuality that gave him a certain appeal and also perhaps told of his mixed heritage. Daria explained her reason for dropping by, listed her qualifications, and gave him her résumé. He glanced at it briefly and then glanced back at her. He looked her directly in the eye and said that, in fact, he was just trying to find someone who could speak and write Portuguese, someone who could translate from English to Portuguese. He said that he had had great difficulty finding people in the community for the job. He added that the Portuguese community in Canada had very little education, and that certainly she was a blessing that had come to him when he least expected. He agreed to let her know the next day about whether he could hire her as his executive assistant. He also asked briefly if her papers were in order and if she could work legally in Canada. She said yes with an expediency that was perhaps too obvious, too quick to assert itself, and which he later used against her. But at the time he did not seem to care; he had other needs, other intentions that would become obvious to her only as time went by. Daria left the office happy, very excited, with a sure feeling that her luck was starting to change, that she was moving toward another line of work. She was overjoyed to be leaving the blue-collar jobs, which she had been doing pretty much since the age of twelve, and entering the upper class. She would no longer be a maid for all services, she would leave her past behind, and her parents and family would be proud of her. The next day, Vasco da Gama called her to tell her that he had checked his budget, that he could indeed offer her a part-time job at the centre, and that she would be his executive assistant and the official translator for the centre. Daria felt elated, happy, happy, like never before. The new beginning had arrived. Her American dream was finally starting to manifest itself. She felt thankful, thankful for the world, thankful for that nice receptionist lady from the Azores who had sent her up to meet Vasco. Thankful for the sun and the moon and the beautiful goats she had left behind in Almores.

Daria became Vasco's protégée at the office. There were three other older women working there whom Vasco did not like very much. He kept saying they were uneducated Portuguese women who had no more than Grade 4 and had put on a little makeup just to appear educated. They did not fool him. He was a savvy man who had travelled the world and had a law degree from a prestigious university in London, England. He was married to a woman from Lisbon, the beautiful capital. He knew class when he saw it. When Daria told him that she was the daughter of peasants from Beira Alta, he said, "Yes, but you are different. You are very different, Daria. You emanate class all over." Today, when Daria thinks about this, she always remembers another conversation she overheard around the same time at the university between a Black student and a Filipina student. The Filipino student was telling the Black student that she was not really Black, and the latter kept telling the former that she must be blind and needed to open her eyes, for unless a miracle had happened on her way to school, the last time she saw herself in the mirror she was very black. Daria remembers trying to understand what Vasco and the Filipino girl meant. Even though Daria appreciated Vasco's comments and treatment because they made her feel distinguished, she was at the same time assaulted by an uncomfortable feeling: she felt that he was somehow insulting her parents, who were uneducated people from the countryside. She felt that he was automatically putting them in a low category, a category from which she had somehow escaped and should therefore be thankful. She should be thankful for him because he was able to see something in her that was special, very special. He was a savvy expert, a shrewd connoisseur who could easily separate the wheat from the chaff—or as he said in Portuguese, *o trigo do joio*. And she, Daria, she was *trigo*.

In addition to the three older women working at the centre— and Daria, Milena, and Luísa, all young girls in their early twenties—there was also another woman working there: Helena Santos. Helena Santos was in her forties, she was from

Pico—one of the Islands in the Azores—and she was visibly in love with Vasco da Gama. Or perhaps it was not love she felt, it was awe. Helena suffered immensely, like many Portuguese do, continental and otherwise, from a class complex. But her complex was also compounded by the complex of region and language, for she was from the Azores, and—as Daria discovered when she first came to Toronto—there was between continental Portuguese and Azoreans a wide rift. The rift was, in fact, laughable because, as Vasco da Gama consistently argued, most of the continental Portuguese who immigrated to Canada were just as classless and uneducated as the ones who had emigrated from the Azores. He couldn't really see what all the fuss was about. He would say, however, that the Azoreans were more religious than the continental Portuguese and that Azorean women were trashier or perhaps just more desperate. They used their "bottom power"—in other words, their physical attributes—to exploit men, often acting like shameless Madonnas or outright prostitutes. He added that he had done his military service at Air Base No. 4, in the Azorean Base of Lajes in Terceira, where he had learned how to fly a plane with American military personnel and had witnessed all kinds of sordid events—or stories, as he would put it—happening between Azorean women and the posted servicemen. He did not say whether he had been a participant in any of the events of these stories. Helena, who had a common-law partner, a very hardworking and nice man, was indeed deeply afflicted by the issue of class, region, and language. She constantly craved the attention and the compliments of Vasco, and she tried to speak in that neutral Portuguese so that people would not see her as the Azorean that she thought she was. It was painful to watch her constantly trying to impress Vasco. She was jealous when Daria came along. She felt that this pretty young thing—who had some education, could speak proper Portuguese, and was from the continent—was stealing her chance to escape her class and climb up the ladder. She was the secretary at the centre and had always been so, even though she had been working there for over four years. And now Vasco was hiring Daria as his executive assistant. It was not fair. Simply not fair.

A T CAFÉ UN-DIPLOMATICO. At first Daria was quite naïve and couldn't see all the networks at work at the centre, and especially in Vasco's head. She was naïve, and she also felt very happy with her own luck, happy to land a job like that after enduring so much and in so many places. She felt distinguished because Vasco thought she was special, smart, and classy. They became friends—close friends, she thought, but friends only—and they disclosed many things to one another. He would often start talking about his own daughter, Santeria, telling Daria how shy she was, how she had never been with a man and had never even had a boyfriend, and how she and Daria were really alike. Being naïve and eager to please her boss, but also mainly because she believed Vasco was her friend and had the best of intentions towards her, Daria eventually disclosed to Vasco that she too had never been fully intimate with a man. She had never gone all the way. She was a virgin. She told him about the intense love affair with the drug dealer whom she had met at the restaurant on College Street, just a block or two down from the centre. She told him how she still felt very attracted to him but that her morals did not allow her to be with him, to go all the way with him. She told him this and that, gradually, in the many conversations that they had when they stayed late at the office working on a grant proposal or some other important project. It got to a point where she felt very comfortable with Vasco. She felt he was indeed like a father to her, a trusting and concerned person to whom she could speak about love and sex, and from whom she could even seek advice. She could never do this with her own father, who was not only on another continent, but who was also too shy and much too religious to discuss things of this nature with his own daughter. But then the conversations started to become somewhat awkward because Daria felt that Vasco would always find a way steer the conversation toward the same topics: sex, love, and relationships. But even though she felt uncomfortable, a voice in her head kept telling her: *This man is like my father; he is old enough to be my father. I am like his daughter Santeria, as he constantly tells me. He is a man of stature, of standing in the community, intelligent and educated. He can be no harm to me, can mean no harm to me.*

One day after work, Daria and Vasco went to Café Diplomatico to have dinner. They had been working hard on a project, and he had told her that he wanted to thank her for her devotion and all her hard work. It was a spring day in May, the time of year when Toronto starts to come alive and people sit on patios eating and watching the world pass by in its new clothes. It's the time of year when people are cheerful and excited because finally the long darkness has passed and they can have a break, a break in pure daylight, their limbs emerging from their recoiling sadness to fully stretch and taste the sun. Vasco and Daria had ordered Pizza Napolitana and a bottle of red wine, Dão, a wine from Daria's region in Portugal—the Dão-Lafões winery belt. She can't remember exactly how it had started, how the conversation had shifted to that topic, but suddenly she became aware that Vasco was doing it again. He had managed to switch the topic of discussion and was asking her if she knew how a woman becomes aroused. She felt very uncomfortable this time, her face now clearly red. She thought that the people sitting at the nearby tables would hear what he was saying and would know that something inappropriate was happening between them, something sordid between an older man and a younger, naïve woman. She wanted to leave, but she was afraid to stop him or upset him. She did not want him to think she was being disrespectful or ungrateful, so she remained there, praying that he would stop saying what he was saying, asking what he was asking. She did not really say much, just a "yes" or a "no," an "I am not sure" or an "I guess." He went on and on about it saying the first thing that happens when a woman is aroused is that her nipples get erect and her thighs get wet. Daria became more and more uncomfortable and eventually worked up the courage to say she had to go home because she needed to study for her psychology class as she had a midterm test the following day. At the time she was taking continuing education courses at the university to earn a degree in social work. He said he would drive her home even though she said she could walk as she did not live far. He also insisted on paying even though she pulled out her wallet to share the cost of the meal. He drove her home in his silver BMW, and he said goodnight by touching her hand. She did not sleep well that night. It was not the first time that she had felt that things between her and Vasco were moving in an inappropriate direction, and she had spent several sleepless nights thinking about it, worrying about what it all meant. Every time, she would eventually force herself to go sleep, reminding herself that this man was like a father to her, that he was in fact the same age as her father, that he was a man of stature, an educated, intelligent man. How could she think he meant her any harm?

The three older women working at the centre would often smile when they saw Daria and Vasco leave the office in his car to go to some community meeting or another. At first, Daria did not quite know why they were smiling. She thought they were just being jovial and courteous to them, courteous to their boss. But then one day they approached Daria and told her, "Daria, my daughter, you must be careful with Mr. da Gama. You must be careful with him. There are rumours about him liking young girls too much. We mean no harm to you, Daria. We are like your mothers, and so we just want the best for you. We want the best for you, so you be careful, my daughter. Be careful." Daria thought it was odd they would say this to her, and she felt that perhaps they were just jealous of the attention Vasco was giving her, like Helena often was.

And she would be reassured when Vasco would say, as he often did, that they were all just uneducated women who were jealous of younger women like herself, Milena, and Luísa, who had other lives, other opportunities that the older women had not been given. But it came to a point when Daria felt that Vasco wanted to be seen with her. It was as if he wanted to show the world in general that he was still a virile man, a man capable of keeping up with the ladies. In her mind, she compared him to that RCMP boss who apparently did the same thing with his novice female officer, frequently going on rides with her in his car. He claimed they were investigating the case of the BC pig farmer who was murdering dozens of women, but in fact they were just going around in circles so that he could have the chance to convince her to sleep with him. No wonder she developed PTSD and has been off work for many years. Another time, when Vasco drove Daria home again after working late, he stopped the car in front of her house and took her hands in his, holding them tight for some time. By this time, her apprehensions had grown bigger and bigger, and she could no longer fall asleep that easily by simply telling herself the usual story about Vasco's good intentions. So she told him she did not feel comfortable with him holding her hands like that, and she abruptly removed her hands from his. He became quite irritated and said he was merely showing his affection towards her and that she was being irrational and childish. He said she was, in fact, acting like a frigid, scared virgin. The next day at the office he was as nice as always, and she tried to forget the incident using the usual mechanisms.

THE MOZAMBICANS. Francisco Magno Motumba is a friend of Vasco da Gama. He is a magnetic Mozambican who also has an eye on Daria, the beautiful Daria, who is currently working at the Lusitanian Social Service Centre as an executive assistant. He comes to the centre frequently to visit Vasco, or so he says, but anyone who knows him or has taken care to observe some of his behaviour can easily see that the man always has a double agenda. He cannot stay away from women, beautiful young women. He has sex to give and sell, as he proclaims. The first time he saw Daria, his eyes kept scanning her from top to bottom. It was difficult for him to concentrate on her face, even though her face was as beautiful as her body, as Vasco would often say. Magno Motumba has a very interesting story, and truth be told, when Daria saw him for the first time she was entangled by his fierce penetrating eyes and she felt water running between her legs. She did not mind that he was eyeing her from bottom to top, and it didn't matter to her whether he started at the top, at the bottom, or in the middle. He made her body boil and her mind get dizzy, and she knew it was time to give away her virginity. And then, as she discovered more and more about his past, she became slavishly enamoured, entangled in his grand life story, the story of a poet, a soldier, a man of the world. She felt sure her virginity had been kept until then only to give to Francisco Magno Motumba. Motumba held the post of general consul of Mozambique in Canada. He had been appointed to this post by the government of Joaquim Chissano, who had taken the place of Samora Machel after the first post-independence Mozambican president died in a terrible plane crash. The accident had taken place in 1986 in the Lebombo Mountains in South Africa, and the circumstances had still not been fully clarified; many claimed that the crash was the result of evil machinations by the South African Apartheid regime. Because Daria was wholeheartedly infatuated with Magno Motumba, it did not take him much time or effort to convince her of what he had in mind. As Daria found out later, Vasco and Francisco were more than just friends—they were very close friends, intimate friends, who shared many secrets and mostly a fetish for young virgin women. This meant that when Vasco found out that Daria was a virgin, he immediately told his close friend Francisco Magno Motumba. This was why he had started to visit the centre more and more, roaming around like a greyhound in search of prey. He was thinking about that precious hymen lying between Daria's round thighs, and he would not rest until he got a direct taste of it. Daria being naïve, or dreamy, or just guided by the constant pounding between her legs, a pounding that was asking her to finally and completely surrender, was easy prey for the Mozambican. He asked her out the first time he met her at the centre, and immediately started declaiming beautiful love poems to her, making her feel that she was indeed his princess and he her prince.

Motumba told Daria that he was separated from his wife, Ana Magalhães, a Mozambican white woman, who had stood side by side with him throughout the many trials of the ugly colonial war. Both had been members of FRELIMO,[2] fierce fighters for the independence of Mozambique. They had boycotted the colonial regime in every way they could, directly and indirectly. Both had been incarcerated by Salazar's regime in the Prison of Tarrafal in Cape Verde. For two long years they had stayed in that dungeon known as the Camp of Slow Death, where the guerrilla fighters—or anyone thought to be against the regime—would be punished severely. Prisoners often did not come out alive at all, or came out with their memories all twisted, as if they had been suffering from advanced and very pronounced dementia. Both Francisco and Ana suffered immensely at the hands of Salazar and his fascist counterparts. They would show up anywhere to spy

---

[2]Frente de Libertação de Moçambique/Mozambique's Liberation Front.

and eavesdrop on suspected rebels so that they could catch
them and take them to the dungeon. He told Daria how he
had been persecuted and eventually captured by the PIDE,
and how he had always had to exercise the most care in order
not to be caught. He told her, in great and amazingly lively
detail—where blood and passion and love intermingle and the
great depth of human beings is revealed—about that doomed
day when he had been caught unaware, how he was turned in
by someone whom he thought was his friend, someone whom
he thought was also fighting for the same cause. He recounted
how Fernando Nobre Montenegro became a traitor to their
memories, their childhood, their common goal of liberating
Mozambique from the shackles of the oppressor. His friend
had told the PIDE agents to pick him up, told them how and
where to find him—and his wife too. Nobre Montenegro
was a white Mozambican of Portuguese origin, and he had
been a close friend of Francisco. They had both attended the
same school in Lourenço Marques—Lourenço Marques High
School—and had been the closest of friends in that beautiful
city of acacias and jacarandas, that city full of light by the
Indian Ocean. They had been the closest of friends since they
were little boys, irrespective of race. They had shared dreams
and ideologies, and they had written passionate poems and
manifestos about an independent Mozambique. They had
written beautiful stories about hope and the resilience of the
Mozambican people, and they had spread the word among
the populace as much as they could by acting out plays in
public, reading manifestos or poems, and engaging in other
literary work—firmly believing that art must be put at the
service of the revolution, otherwise we would all die buried in
metaphors that though splendid, do not feed the hungry. They
had put on plays in which Mozambicans were represented as
the masters of their own country, the owners of their own
cotton and corn plantations, and in which Black women,
who were being constantly abused and raped by colonial

overseers, were displayed as full human beings who rebelled against their abusers and kicked them in the crotch, instead of just lying there quietly under their dirty white weight. The two friends had even travelled throughout the entire country—covering it *lés-a-lés*, from corner to corner, province to province, from Cabo Delgado to Maputo, from Zambezia to Inhambane, from Nampula to Sofala and beyond—always carefully hiding from the colonial state informants. Their goal was to bring awareness to Mozambicans and awaken them from their oppression and dormancy, a dormancy that had made them into something that could not be called human. Francisco and Fernando made them see how they had been suffering the blows of the colonial master's iron fist since the capture of Ceuta in 1415, and how it was now time to regain their dignity, their land, and their dances by the bonfires. They had read the works of Agostinho Neto and Amílcar Cabral and Che Guevara, and hope—that stubborn and beautiful flame—was burning deeply within their core.

Francisco and Fernando had thought that the fact that one of them was white and the other Black worked well because they were of the general opinion that the fierce fascists would never think that a white man and a Black man could be together, unless the Black man had accepted the white man's will. And so they tended to go unnoticed for the most part, even though they had to exercise extreme care in all their activities. They had both gone to the USSR to train in communist liberating tactics and armed combat for some time, a common practice in African colonies, and they both spoke Russian fairly well. They were avid lovers of Tolstoy and, of course, Karl Marx, and they passionately transmitted their ideologies to their oppressed brothers and sisters. They read to the people the profound lyric poems of Agostinho Neto's *Sagrada Esperança*, which called for action. They emphasized Neto's juxtaposition of pathetic images with heroic images, showing the Mozambican people what they had been, what they were now, and how they could again become what they had been—how they could regain their full humanity, their beautiful African citizenship. Fransciso and Fernando read to the people out loud in public reunions arranged with the utmost care and secrecy. They read "Western Civilization," "Saturday in the Musseques," and then "Reconquest"; they read "The Path of the Stars," "Bleeding and Germinating," "Confidence," "Green Fields," "We Will Return" and then "Haste." They read the poems in an order that was meant to generate a certain reaction, a certain action. They declaimed these beautiful verses with intense purpose and visceral emotion, sometimes screaming them out in sheer love for liberation, with tears in their eyes, and sometimes even dancing like proud African kings. In so doing, they showed those oppressed souls the power of brotherhood, the power of justice, the power of revolution. They showed them the need to revolt, to engage in armed struggle. Salazar was not going to give in easily, and no diplomatic talks would sway him to return Africa to Africans—he was a stubborn mule who was not going to yield. They, Francisco and Fernando and many of their comrades who believed in the same ideas of justice, had these powerful messages and poems translated into various Mozambican languages—Shangaan, Ronga, Sena, Swahili, Zulu, Macua, and Makonde. They knew that most Mozambicans did not speak the language of the oppressor and that this was largely why they were being oppressed. The people did not understand, could not understand the malignant seeds living inside the brains of those *tugas* who had come from a faraway land in the fifteenth century to impose their ways upon them. Francisco and Fernando also took it upon themselves to learn Mozambican languages because they too wanted to get closer to the Mozambican soul, the real Mozambican soul. They wanted to regain that thing that had been taken from them, because they too had been whitewashed; they were the real *assimilados*. In fact, some have pointed out that the *assimilados* were the ones who did not know who they were, not the mass of Mozambicans who did not doubt the gods they worshipped and the many sounds that twisted their tongues. When this beautiful idea finally came into being and Mozambique finally saw itself free from colonial rule, Machel became the man at the helm of the independent nation, and Portuguese the official language of Mozambique. The other many languages, the languages that transmit other ways of being and seeing and sensing the world, have been perishing and perishing since— the foreign one becoming more domestic and the domestic ones becoming more foreign. Every day one of them dies with the last elder of the tribe, and with it an entire vision—an entire way to access truth, beauty, and knowledge—is lost.

They, Francisco and Fernando, did all this and much more. They did it together and with the help of many other guerrilla fighters and lovers of justice. And then Fernando became a traitor. He dishonoured all their promises to fight for justice and equality for all. He told the state secret police, PIDE, about Francisco and his wife in exchange for a high-ranking post in the colonial administration. And then, at the end of colonial ruling, just before the Mozambicans took control and Samora Machel became president of the newly independent nation; after thousands and thousands had died or lost some part of their bodies and souls all over Africa; just before the Portuguese army said no to the colonial war with a peaceful *coup d'état*, feeding carnations into their guns (when Lisbon woke up to Zeca Afonso's beautiful song, "Grândola, Vila Morena" on the memorable dawn of April 25, 1974, when Daria was only five years old); just before all these memorable events, Fernando, sensing he was running out of luck, managed to escape the country. Had he stayed, he would have suffered a bloody end at the hands of those he had betrayed. As it turns out, and as Francisco had recently discovered, Fernando was in fact now living in Canada; he too had become a Torontonian. He was actually a board member of the Lusitanian Social Service Centre. And since Francisco was also a board member, they had once again come face to face, now in very different circumstances that had nothing to do with the ones they had faced together in Mozambique—for Canada is a peaceful country, at least of late, after its own abundant blooshed.

Daria was ecstatic with Francisco Magno Motumba, who was twenty-five years her senior. He described his life with such passion, love, eventfulness, intensity, and manic grandiosity that Daria could not resist. He became the man that she had been waiting for: he was educated; he had experienced suffering; and he had a poetic leftist soul, the type that is so rare to come by. And he also had that link with the colonial wars, where her brother Alberto had perished never to be seen again. He told her he was now forty-eight years old and that he had been separated from his wife Ana for two years now. She had returned to Maputo with their two twin children, Otu and Quintana, now adults in their early twenties, because she could not stand the coldness of this country, of this city, of these people. She missed Maputo, that bright bride, that blinding pearl of the Indian Ocean that sends rays of light in all directions. She missed the clarity and the sun of Africa and that warmth that people have there—always singing, always smiling. She missed their capacity to remain human even when faced with the most inhumane conditions. They had both decided that separation was best for them at this point in their lives; they had beautiful memories to hold onto, memories to make their children grateful to be who they were, proud descendants of distinguished revolutionaries. The twins sometimes came to stay with him, and sometimes he would go to Mozambique to visit them. They would take turns. Francisco planned to remain in Canada until the end of his term, which likely would be a long one because, he said half-jokingly, post-colonial African presidents frequently end up becoming presidents for life, and Chissano would probably not be an exception. He planned to return to Mozambique after his term, but for the time being he was happy to be in the Northern hemisphere where everything is so neat and organized. He had a degree in Italian Renaissance Literature from the University of Bologna, and he had had four books of poetry published by Caminho, the most prestigious publisher in Lisbon. "The next one," he added, "is going to be called *Beautiful Daria, My Finally-Found Home.*"

Motumba was Daria's love affair. Blood with blood. Blood in blood. He was the key to the mysteries that had populated both her life and the lives of her long-suffering peasant family. They had also endured the jug of Salazar's regime—one that had forced them to work from sunrise to sunset; divide a sardine among three; and send their young sons to combat, one of whom never came back, forever lost among leaves, worms, and nothingness in the Moyombe. Motumba was a man of the world, a lover of pluri-continental and multiracial nations—and not in the sense that Salazar had advocated but never really practised, despite what he claimed. As Motumba explained, the apartheid in Mozambique had also been fiercely imposed, even though it was not neatly written in a book of laws, as was the case of the neighbouring nation of South Africa. He explained to Daria how he and Ana had often had to conceal their marriage; how he had had to pretend to be her houseboy, especially when they were in public spaces and when they went to South Africa together; and how Ana had been called a dirty traitor and a disgrace to the race, a dirty vagabond who sleeps with Black men and brings beings into the world who are closer to eunuchs than humans. Daria had no doubt about how she felt: she wanted to give to him that precious thing she had been keeping tightly sealed between her legs. Blood with blood. Blood in blood. He deserved it. Daria started imagining a life with Francisco. She started seeing herself as a woman of the world with two little biracial children. Their beautiful children would tell the world that redemption and forgiveness are possible, that the thunder can become silvery and gentle, and that dreams can fly and swim in the rainwater that gives to us all. She started dreaming and dreaming about a world where nothing could impede one from becoming happy, a world where everything makes sense. A world of roses. Roses and roses. Red pulsating carnations sending inebriating perfume to the soul of all of us, that deep self that sees with the great eye. As she thought of this beautiful world coming to her, Daria remembered how her mother always said that all flowers were roses. Daria realized that, in that very act, her mother may in fact have been applying metaphor—or would it be metonymy? Or perhaps even synecdoche?—even though she never went to school and would not know the meaning of such a word. If Daria were to say it in front of her, her mother would respond, in her usual foul mood, "What are you saying? Are you stupid?" And, as Daria thought all this, she smiled to herself or perhaps to her mother, communicating across a great distance the way only a mother and daughter can.

MASKS, STATUETTES, PHOTOGRAPHS, AND OTHER IMAGES. The first time Daria and Francisco made love, they both felt it was the end of the world. Or at least she felt that. And she really felt that he felt it too. He had been as gentle with her as possible and as his desire had allowed, and he had only entered her after many inventive games of foreplay, when she could no longer endure his teasing and started to scream dirty words, words she never knew she could pronounce. Later, when reflecting upon the event, she could not understand where she had heard them. It was as if she had in her, hidden at seven keys, all these sordid ungodly words. It was as if they were just ready to come to the surface at the right moment, the moment of incendiary heat, when body and soul give into the visceral instinctual urges that lurk in the animal that lives in all of us. He had invited her to his home, a home full of comfort and decorated with a mixture of western and African things—again indicating that Francisco was indeed a man of the world, a man between worlds who seemingly felt comfortable in all of them. When she first got there, she stared at the masks he had on the wall and the many naked statuettes of Black and white women he had in the many parts of the house. She felt excited and scared at the same time, as if anticipating him in her—his full lips, his hands going up and down, *rivering* her body with his skin, his colour, his magnetic pulse. (*Rivering* was a word she herself had invented just because it sounded exactly right to describe how she felt when she thought about him like this.) There were photos of his twin children, the ones he had had with Ana, Otu and Quintana, in several parts of the house too. This pleased Daria because it showed that he was a good father, a man who had his children in his mind; it showed that he needed to stare at them every day so that he did not forget the light in their eyes. The photos displayed the children at different stages of their lives—from birth to their current age—gradually revealing their growing bodies and facial features. She would stare at them, going from photo to photo, trying to see if the twins looked more like the father or the mother. In them, she saw remnants of the children she would have with Francisco. There was a photo of Francisco and Ana embracing one another in a comfortable hug. They were young in that photo and seemed happy, their eyes full of shining hopes and their facial expressions without any trace of worry—the faces of two young people who believe in love, who believe in the beauty of the world. Daria tried to imagine them meeting for the first time and then making love for the first time. She wanted to know how it was, how it felt, if he found her more beautiful than her. She was indeed beautiful, Daria thought. She had long dark hair and a slender long body, unlike Daria's, which was full of curves and valleys; Daria had the type of figure that often makes men lose their vision and causes dangerous road accidents, as many kept reminding her. She did not quite like that comparison because it made her feel guilty for things that were out of her control.

She imagined the two young lovers dressed as guerrilla fighters and running around in the dense forests trying to deliver messages or food to their comrades or even fighting with AK-47s. She saw them on impromptu open-air podiums singing and screaming poetry and manifestos with the ferocity that the yearning for justice can bring about. She saw them surrounded by a vast acclaiming public that chanted O povo unido nunca mais será vencido. She saw their rugged, tired, and scared faces at the end of a very long day—one of those days that go on and on forever, making you feel that the idea is taking too long to manifest itself and that perhaps it will never shine through, that it will never come. She imagined the nightmares they must have had together and then alone in separate cells in Tarrafal, that dungeon of slow death, far away from their native land. She imagined them trapped, surrounded by another ocean—the cold, strange, and endless

Atlantic Ocean, which had once carried the caravels. They had set sea a long time ago, only to bring blood to the waters, only to discover what had already been discovered. She felt jealous, and she almost regretted not having met him earlier, not being older, not being born in Mozambique at the right time. She regretted only having images and sounds and stories in her head, things that came from far away, because she was too young to have lived through them directly; things that did not have a secure ground in her being and almost appeared as fainted romantic murmurs of a distant past, a time when people really took action and suffered injustices, a time when everything was more important and made your heart pound more vigorously. She recalled her mother's constant stories about her brother Alberto. She recalled seeing photos of him in a green-and-brown military uniform with tall black boots, a boy-man with a moustache. She recalled the deep vivid crimson paintings of the carnation on the walls of her primary school—side by side with the *foice e o martelo*, the hammer and the sickle—and she heard the sounds of the mailman who came mounted on a horse to deliver news to the people of the mountains. He had been blowing a horn and singing, *O povo unido nunca mais será vencido*—the happy gay song that was going from mouth to mouth everywhere, like a beautiful symphony that made you fly and see colours from above. She recalled the radio announcer speaking from Lourenço Marques or Luanda or Bissau, lands that seemed to be part of her country but where all kinds of commotions were taking place. She recalled hearing names like Humberto Delgado and António de Spínola, Marcelo Caetano and António de Oliveira Salazar, Samora Machel and Agostinho Neto and Amílcar Cabral, names of important personalities but whose significance she, as a five-year-old girl, could not really grasp. She remembered the full moon up high in the clean dark azure sky of Almores, a magnificent ball that she could reach with her hands, and then remembered it being shown on TV. She saw the Americans and the Russians, people who were doing things to one another and trying to land on other grounds above the sky. She saw them as dancing butterflies, moving, moving in slow motion, trying to achieve meditation of body and spirit, as if they were truly flying like she did sometimes in some of her best dreams.

She remembered her brother-in-law with a long beard and long hair cursing the fascists. She remembered her oldest sister marrying him on that sad, rainy, November day. They had just moved to the new cement house, a house that had two bedrooms, a living room, and a bathroom with only a toilet in it and no running water. She saw the old granite house, with the very dirty wood floors and the walls that had been blackened from the smoke because there was no chimney. Her mother still cooked in that house so many years later. It had only a kitchen and another room with two beds. She remembered sleeping there, sharing one end of the bed with her brother Marcos, who was barely older than her, while other people slept on the other end; she remembered feeling their feet close to her face. She remembered the smell of urine on the floor and how everyone either peed in a pot or went outside and did it by the cowshed just beside the house. She remembered the smell and the noise of the two pigs that lived under the kitchen. She remembered how her older siblings would scare her by pretending they were going to put her inside the pig's body hanging from the ceiling in the kitchen, after it had been killed with that long sharp knife that made it cry for what seemed hours on end. She remembered hiding in bed to keep that scream away or sometimes even running far away so that it would not reach her. She remembered moving to the new house and then having nightmares in which she was falling down from the roof in slow motion. She remembered the deep fear she felt of reaching the floor and having her body smashed by the impact. Sometimes these nightmares were mixed with her fear of wetting the bed, and if she managed to reach the floor intact, she then would pee right there on the street and she would feel a great sense of relief. She remembered all this through a mixture of internal images made up of real memory and of the distance of the memories, a distance that adds and takes away. And she also remembered it through the black-and-white photo that she stole from her sister's wedding album and that she brought to Canada with her. This is the only photo she had of herself when she was very young because at the time no one took photos up there in the mountains of Caramulo. They had enough misery to stare at every day from sunset to sunrise; they did not need to stare at it when they went home at night because they knew nights were meant for resting and dreaming. Or perhaps it was all tied to the bare and simple fact that they did not possess the means. In this photo, she and little Marcos are wearing lilac and yellow sweaters, respectively, sweaters their oldest sister—the one getting married, who is also their godmother—bought for the special occasion. The sweaters are full of waves and intricacies that Daria had never seen before, and they made her feel so happy, happy, happy. In the photo, she is a little girl with thin twisted legs, open eyes, and hair cut abruptly at the front, as if she herself had taken a pair of scissors to do the job, perhaps trying to play a game or become an adult. In this whirling of memories flowing through her, Daria felt like a little girl again, a little girl who cannot grasp that past of real suffering, of real struggle, of real importance. And in this moment of remembrance of her faint past, she wished she had been a warrior with him, Francisco, down there in that land full of light by the Indian Ocean. But then she thought she was being silly, that she was being childish, for she had him now, he had her, they had each other, and everything would be all right. She went from corner to corner of the house, deciphering and feeling the nest of this man she already loved so much.

She was in a daze of white and blue, of black and white, her body and mind pulsing with expectation about the great night ahead of her. She had imagined it since she was a little girl, often spending nights awake visualizing it, savouring it in anticipation. She and Isabel had had many conversations about this magnificent night, and they would often play silly childish games about a man and wife in preparation for the big event—which would come one day, they were certain, when they became older and truly beautiful. She saw roses and roses, gardens of endless colours covering her life, a life that was just starting and that would be, she felt sure of it, beautiful, full, bountiful. Francisco had changed from his suit into something very light, a white cotton shirt and loose khaki pants; he had no shoes, just bare feet. She stared at the soles of his feet as he walked as if fascinated by their whiteness, and then, as he was preparing a drink for himself and juice for her, she also stared at his white palms. She went to him, took his hands, and put his palms against hers to see how similar they were. She then moved to his soles, bending down on her knees and lifting his feet one by one to inspect them. She stared at that whiteness in silence, as if trying to understand the type of cells he was made of. He told her that widely known tale of how God was in a hurry when he made Black people and so He forgot to paint their soles and their palms black like the rest of their bodies. She laughed and said she had heard a version of that story, but that her version was much nicer, for it claimed that God gave Black people white palms and soles so that the white people could see themselves in them and thus consider them their brothers and sisters. He smiled and said, "My darling Daria, that is a truly beautiful version, which I confess, I have never heard before. It is indeed beautiful, and perhaps the prophecy that lives there is close to manifesting itself. Daria, you are the bearer of very good news." It was late June, and she had just turned twenty-four. She was wearing that dress she had worn when she went to the Lusitanian Social Service Centre to look for a job. She felt pretty, loved, protected, and wanted. He told her how she was the most beautiful woman he had ever met and how she possessed that courage of a warrior, a courage that he admired immensely in women, a courage that pushed her to leave Portugal by herself at the age of twenty to come and meet the world. He told her he understood how difficult it was for her—a girl of her age and station, who had been raised in a sheltered way by overly protective Catholic parents—to come just like that to the other side of the world. Listening to him, she felt loved; she felt special. She felt unique. She felt protected. She told him how she had had a hard time, how sometimes she felt misunderstood, especially among the Portuguese living in Toronto. She told him how the family of one of her Portuguese friends did not want their daughter to be friends with her because they thought that a proper young woman, a woman properly raised by proper parents, would never leave her country alone at the age of twenty to cross the Atlantic and go to a strange faraway land where all kinds of dangers and evils existed. She told him how that had upset her, how that had hurt her feelings, for she was indeed a proper young woman who just wanted to see the world and go after her dreams. There was nothing wrong with that, she said. Francisco mentioned that many of the Portuguese people living in Toronto came here many, many years ago and that they still carry that very old way of thinking. He told Daria she shouldn't take them seriously. He told her that he knew her, that he knew how pure she was, how deep, how beautiful. He told her he loved her very, very much. He said he had never, ever met a woman like her before, and he had met many, many women: Russians, Mozambicans, white and Black, South Africans, Portuguese, Italians, and Canadians, and the many Canadians that there are in Canadians. She felt loved; she felt special. She felt unique. She felt protected. Perfect the way she was. She utterly and completely believed in love.

He came behind her as she was studying one of those tribal masks that she had never seen before with intense curiosity. She was trying to discern how it was made, who made it, what ritual it was used for, if it had a particular significance and was used on special events. As if he had read her mind, he told her that that mask represented the God Ogun, a very fierce God, the most powerful God of the Yoruba pantheon. He told her the Yoruba were a people in Nigeria, the richest nation in Africa, where oil gushes out of the earth with the force of thick milk coming out of the engorged breasts of a nursing woman. As he said that, she felt shivers running though her. Sensing her shivers, he placed his long elegant hands around her full breasts, feeling them tenderly but firmly. He kept his hands there long enough to feel their readiness and their size, and then he slowly turned Daria towards him. She felt good but also very embarrassed. Her face was red like a carnation flower, as if there were a revolution going on inside her that she could no longer control, did not want to control. He told her she was stunning and that her body had the curves of a goddess, and that he was the luckiest man alive because she was kind enough to offer him that very body. She blushed some more and felt happier than ever before. He unbuttoned her dress slowly at the front so that he could reach her breasts. He stared at them for a while—they were still hidden by the white and lilac lacy brassiere she was wearing—as if wanting to prolong the moment of expectation, the moment before the ultimate revelation. She started to tremble and said that, as he well knew, she had never gone all the way with a man and was therefore scared. He calmed her down by saying he knew that very well and he would be as gentle as possible. He told her that the first time is always a little painful, just a little. "But then my darling," he continued, "it's all roses, all roses..." He then proceeded to take off her brassiere so that he could see those splendid breasts for the first time, all exposed before him. First he smelled the brassiere, holding it against his nose and mouth with his eyes semi-closed, telling Daria that it smelled like cherries, cherries in full season, ready and juicy. Then he looked directly at her breasts and gasped. He seemed momentarily dizzy, but then he regained his composure and told her they are just perfect, just ripe, ready to be taken. He told her he had never seen nipples like hers, so erect, so brownish, and so pinkish, and surrounded by such splendid wide aureoles. They were like roses inside roses, Russian dolls inside Russian dolls, abracadabra mysteries of the most sacred kind. As he said that, he put his lips on her nipples, first one and then the other, initially moving them slowly and tenderly and then becoming more impatient and aggressive, like Daria imagined babies would get when they were really hungry for the mother's milk and have been waiting too long for her to show up. At that point, she too became impatient. Suddenly, her body was no longer hers to command. He helped her undress, and she helped him take off his cotton clothes. He took off her last piece of clothing, her underwear, which she had chosen carefully that morning to match her brassiere, and he held it in his hands for a moment before bringing it to his nose, to his lips, like he did with the brassiere. Then he murmured something in Makonde which Daria could not understand.

They were both naked, standing up in front of one another in middle of the living room, in front of dozens of statuettes of naked white and Black women, and surrounded by just as many tribal masks and photos of Otu and Quintana. They moved around the entire house, as if to fully claim it as their own, entangled in one another, feeling their bodies with their hands, from head to toe, not missing a centimetre of each other's flesh. She felt his strong member in her hands without shame, and without her mother's words entering her mind. He then rivered every inch of her flesh with his tongue and his lips, leaving his saliva all over her, and Daria screamed and screamed, thinking that it was not possible to live like this one more minute. She thought she was going to die, she thought the neighbours were going to hear her and she would not be able to face anyone the next day because everyone will know what she had done, the shameless devilish games she had been involved in. She thought all this in a momentary flash, but then Francisco's games became more intense, more urgent, his tongue concentrating persistently, patiently, and vigorously in the very middle of her being, which she had been keeping so tightly closed, so tightly guarded. He went up and down in motions circular, horizontal, and perpendicular—first slowly, then more aggressively—and she really thought that this was the end, the end of her life, the end of time. She screamed some more, like she had never, never screamed before. They took turns until he could no longer wait and then he entered her slowly. She opened herself fully to receive him, happy that he was finally fully hers and that she was fully his. He thrust and thrust until he was all there, until the net she had been guarding at seven keys gave in and the blood erupted, staining his expensive brown sheets, the sheets of a well-paid diplomat. She felt pain and made a contorted grimace; he tried to console her by saying, "Oh querida, oh my baby. This will pass. This will get better."

They slept well, feeling the night through a single uninterrupted sleep, sheltered by the love and passion, and the commitment of their promises to one another, promises sealed with the blood and waters shed during that first intense night of lovemaking. They woke up happy, consoled, rested. It was Saturday and no one had to go to work. He walked around the house naked with an easygoing demeanour that embarrassed Daria. Suddenly she felt ashamed of how she'd behaved last night. Again, her mother's words came to her: "She has given it away to a stranger and she was not even married to him. He was a strange Black man from Africa, where my beloved son

Alberto died, where they killed him, those animals. Oh God, Daria, you are the disgrace and the shame of this family!" She thought this, but then she said to herself that she no longer lived with her mother, that her mother was far away on the other side of the Atlantic. Her mother was an old peasant woman who never left that village on top of the mountains, so she could not understand the world and all its beauty. She could not understand the love between a man and woman. She could not understand. Francisco asked her what she was thinking about and why she had put his shirt on, which on her looked like a long dress. Why did she feel that she had to cover her body? A body like that, he continued, which was so beautiful, full of caves, concave, the sacred abode that had made him the happiest man alive last night. She smiled and said nothing, only blushed. He noticed her shyness and went to her, giving her a kiss on the forehead. She liked that. She had always liked a kiss on the forehead given by a man. It made her feel that the man was not only after the rest of her body, that he saw her as a full human being, a being with a soul, a mind, and emotions—an endless circle that was connected to the entire universe. She also liked to be kissed on the back, slowly, while sitting between his legs, with her back to him. He sensed that, and so he placed her just like that, between his legs at the edge of the bed, and kissed her over and over again on her back. He kissed her gently, very gently, murmuring tender words like a father to a child, or a man to a woman, a woman whom he thinks he really loves and really, really wants. After this tender sensual ritual, he got aroused and tried to reach for the rest of her body again, but she said she was hurting, she was sore and needed to take a shower. Resigned, he said, "*Sim querida*, I understand."

She went into the bathroom alone, took off his shirt, and looked at herself in the mirror, carefully examining the signs of last night. She could see and sense the mark of his teeth, his lips, his breath, on her neck, her breasts, her nipples, her thighs, her belly. She felt herself between her legs and tried to find evidence of what happened last night between her and Francisco. She felt pain as her fingers reached her intimate part, where he went last night. She put her fingers in deeply, trying to find him there, mixed with herself, and she emerged with a mound of blood and plasma—a wound where surely they both now lived, their union forever sealed through an act of pure love. She then jumped into the shower and let the water slowly bathe her body, another rain of tender love coming down on her, mixing itself with all the love that Francisco had given her last night. They had not used protection even though she had protested a little. She had said that it may be too early for the babies to come because she wanted to finish her university degree first and did not want to be dependent on him. He had hushed her by saying, "Oh *querida*, there is no need to worry about that now. I am financially very well off, and I really, really want to have a baby, your baby, our baby, the most beautiful baby in the world. We'll call her Santuaria if it's a girl and Muranio if it's a boy. And if we get twins, which is quite possible because I come from a very fertile lineage, we'll call them Merania and Meranio." Daria had smiled and said she liked the names, that they sounded strange. A good strange, she added, like very old rivers that came from the beginning of the world to meet us at this precise moment in the present and bless our existence. He told her she was a very deep soul, an old soul, full of wisdom and poetry, like the ancient Mozambican Goddess Bulane. And again she had felt happy, whole, understood. She felt at home.

A PETRARCHAN SONNET. Every day that passes I am more and more in love with Francisco. He is my life, will always be my life, me in him, him in me. Last night when we made love again he went all over my body and sung to me the most beautiful Petrarchan sonnet. A man of letters, lettering me all over, his body in mine, mine in his. His tongue and his chest, his hands and legs tour me up and down in a dance that I have never thought could be danced. I enter the land of beautiful oblivion, and I see all that has been missing from me is no longer calling out.

*Daria, this is my body, poured upon yours with the cadences
    of waves that do not know black and white,*
Skins intertwined in one carousel.
*Daria, this is your body offering itself to me like a white earth
    finally feeding the baby it had abandoned and rejected.*
*Daria, we are the river and the sea, the sun and the moon, the
    night and the day.*
*Our babies will be nothing but light upon light lingering
    through tears of joy,*
*Torrents of splendid water, marbles dancing in the
    vacuum of God*
Daria, your body and mine are the world.
Daria, your body and mine make up the totality of all there is.
They are all there will be, and all there ever was.

He sings these letters to me—incendiary verbs and just adverbs, consonances, and assonances, eternal music walking me up and down—and I open myself to this enchanting chant. I am Laura. He is Petrarch. Francisco and Laura, eternal Petrarchans, weaving the sounds, weaved by the sounds. His black chest against my full breasts that are flowers inside flowers, Russian dolls inside Russian dolls.

I am in him, he is in me. Nothing is missing. Nothing will ever be missing again—from him, from me, from the world.

He tires me out, and yet I cannot have enough of him in me, enough blackness pouring light down on my pale skin, on my blushing shame—me, a prudish Renaissance Laura. I am nothing without him, nothing but a lost, fading, tiny, dying star in a night without the light that can only emerge from that pure black that shines and lives. He letters me all over, rivering me over and over again, and sometimes he sings me his Petrarchan song in all the languages that he knows, languages that he has learned while travelling the world to discover a way to liberate his people and help them regain their dignity. He sings to me in Latin, and then in Italian and Russian, the same poem spoken in all those different languages. He speaks with all the beautiful sounds that all the world's peoples have invented so that we could be rich and learn from one another, so we could see life and wisdom where we thought there was none, expanding the corners of our irises beyond belief, so that we could believe more and more. And then he switches to Makonde, to Macua, to Swahili, to Zulu, to Shangaan, to Ronga, to Sena, and I no longer know where I am, who I am, or who I want to be. I only sense the sounds and the murmurs of the world in me through the tongue and mouth of Francisco. He circles my belly with his fingers, then his mouth, putting his tongue in the rift of my belly button, and he chants a lullaby to the baby or the babies that are living there. I feel pregnant, and my breasts suddenly become engorged with milk—thick white milk, thick white milk that he sucks slowly, following an ingenious methodology, so that he can live in me and I in him. I feel full, I feel empty, I feel adored. There is nothing missing. I am happy. I am safe. I am at home. I see my brother Alberto flying happily above the heavy Mayombe of Angola. He is happy. He has invented another method of seeking and finding justice: his Truth and Reconciliation Commission. He has forgiven his Black brothers who blew away his young and naïve body and turned it into pollen, food for the many bees of that dense tropical forest surrounding the Congo river, the great Amazon of Africa. I imagine the now nourished bees flying over that deep body of water that travels throughout many countries to quench the thirst of the needy people across the continent, a continent that suffers immensely from droughts and the depletions that foreigners and locals cause. He has forgotten, forgiven Salazar who forced him to go down there and exhaust his body for nothing. He has forgotten, forgiven the helplessness of my mother who allowed him to be taken away from the safety of her skirts and the milk of her breasts. I am at home; I feel safe.

There is nothing missing. From him and me, Francisco and Daria, another Alberto will be born. The son of two former enemies, he will teach the parents how to forgive one another and how true love is to be found, fostered, discovered, rediscovered. I will bring this new son home to show to my mother, and she will open her sad mourning eyes, seeing in him her very own first-born—who had curly, curly hair and fair skin—her first-born whom she never saw again after he went down there, to that place down under. He was lost because Salazar, the son of landless peasants, was so poor that he felt he needed to conquer all the land he could find to grow potatoes and corn and beans to feed his children. He went on and on in a frenzied *ad infinitum*, excavating deeply into the bellies of the African land, much like my father did, pounding hard—hungry and angry—at the granitic entrails of the Beira Alta mountains. They had been trying to assuage their deep famine that never, never seemed to leave them. They were desperate, like a beast whose stomach reaches into the depths of its soul, making it forever doomed, forever hungry. They were eternal beggars for the material, never able to find flight in the immaterial, forever chained to the lower realms. Their penitence, his penitence—he, Salazar and his Lusitanian ancestors, who felt poor and therefore needed to expand his horizons so that they could call themselves men, fathers of a potent nation. Every day that passes I feel growing in me another world, another being, an Alberto, a Muranio, with savvy wide eyes, full of love for all the corners of the world. A future king, a future leader that possesses in him the duality necessary to make this world liveable, a new genetic code in which all the potencies and memories of many people live. He will be of a race that surpasses race only to engender the beautiful, the dream of lavender that I dreamed in the most startling of the nights when I entered the field and the sacred enveloped me in one single mantle of goodness. There will be a new flag waving at me and him and calling on to you. A new flag forged with the greatness of love and forgiveness. There will be Ghandi and Mandela and Mother Teresa and Jesus and Buddha and Allah singing happiness and justice with open smiles at the wide window of the world, sending shredded petals of camellias and hydrangeas down on us, making us eternal, walking gardeners of light, of beauty, of love. The world will be a pathway of deliverance, of magic and belief, pure belief—just like when I was little and went to the circus and saw for the very first time how donkeys could become horses and how horses could become unicorns, suddenly taking flight and swimming through the mountains, the rivers, the seas, the skies. Everything was, everything lived. It was beautiful. And I believed in everything that appeared in front of me: a vast totality of you and me, and me and you, and all of us, in one single wide step from here to the beginning of the world, making us all giants of the best and most sacred kind. A world dreamed out of love and suffering and hope.

There is nothing missing from me, from him. I am in him, he is in me. I am happy. I am at home. I kiss his back where the marks live. I travel my fingers and then my tongue through the crosses and the minuses and the multiplication signs that he has all over his back, torturous remembrances of what they did to him in Tarrafal when he refused to speak, even when they brought Ana in and made him watch. Torturous remembrances of the games men play in their darkest hours, games in which humans become mathematical codes that generate no meaning, no wealth, no bread, leaving body and soul hungry and waiting for death, that last liberating dark bride that makes it all end. While immersed in lovemaking, we play Bach's Violin Concerto No. 1 in A Minor and his arias from Cantata No. 202, *The Wedding Cantata*, his favourite, the one he had listened to time after time since he was a young boy, and the one he says kept him alive in Tarrafal, for he would train his mind to hear it over and over again, so that he would forget where he was, flying above the cement cell, and the deadly sun, and the stench of urine and feces, and the pain that they were inflicting on him constantly, using the most unimaginable methods, methods so inhuman that he was sure these people could not be people, but only agents of the lowest and darkest forces. I sing a song to him in silence as he letters me all over with his grace.

He rediscovers me through the sonnets of a Renaissance man. We are immersed in the true age of humanity, when European universalism is no longer the arrogant current of thought that steps on everything that falls outside of its lens. It now bows to give voice to other voices and chance to other destinies, to hear the suffering, to take responsibility, to accept guilt; it bows to be forgiven but it never dares to forget. It is a Truth and Reconciliation Commission. I am richer; he is richer. We are richer. My mother has not lost her son for nothing. She has gained another son, offered to her through the shades of the sublime where everything dances. Her eyes dream again. She no longer spends her days sighing and carrying that black cloud in her chest. She, who so deserves a rest after a life spent carrying the fleshy weights of all of us, we the ten children who came every sixteen months, not thinking of the heaviness of her legs and the varicose veins ready to burst into heavy bleeding.

A NA, FRANCISCO, AND ME. My love affair with Francisco matures as he discloses more and more about his life and the perils that he and Ana suffered because they both firmly believed in the beautiful idea and never ever let it slip. One day, when I was alone at Francisco's home, I came across a book he was writing called *The Idea Against Tarrafal*. He had mentioned this book to me and I was very curious to read it, but he did not offer to show it to me and I did not feel I ought to ask. I thought that perhaps he was not yet ready to show it to anyone. But that day I came across the working manuscript by accident, when I was cleaning the shelves of his library and browsing through his impressive collection of books, and I could not stop myself from reading it. I felt I wanted to know everything I could about this man, this man I loved. He had a rich and varied collection of books, which included transnational fiction, African politics, Marxist political theory, and Italian and Portuguese Renaissance poetry. The collection also included many enigmatic books pertaining to the sisterhood between mathematics and poetry, a highly perplexing topic that hinged on the oracular or the mystical, and made me vaguely think of the stars and the act of travelling through space. I saw myself as a light monarch butterfly in cadent and slow motion, perfectly circular somersaults of ups and downs, through the vacuous nothingness of the skies. But when I tried to mentally match numbers, quotients, minuses, and pluses with words and metaphors, my mind would go blank. Later on, I had a professor who also swore there is a very intimate link between these two seemingly unlikely subjects: mathematics and poetry. To my surprise, I also found on the shelves some scandalous pornography magazines, the kind that made me blush and feel very guilty. I could not stop looking at the vivid images and fabulous games so clearly depicted on the pages, sensing deep down that I wanted to engage in some of them with Francisco. Francisco had gone to an important function at the Mozambican consulate that had to do with the visit of some Mozambican ministers to Canada. The two countries were attempting to foster trade relations, something Mozambique badly needed, for even though the country was now independent, its economic and ethnic situation was far from perfect. And this was to be blamed, some argued, on the hardcore Marxist post-independence regime and the ensuing bloody civil war between RENAMO[3] and FRELIMO. The war had just ended in 1992, and it had seen the deaths of over 900,000 people, some dying by starvation and others through various other viscerally ugly means. It was a wretched conflict that gave rise to gang rapes, amputations, child soldiers, and the ravaging of the land. *The Idea Against Tarrafal* was based on Francisco and Ana's life and described, in distinct and entangling details, many of the things that had happened to them. As I read the manuscript, I became more and more in love, more and more in awe of this man who had come my way—this man I was lucky enough to meet so that my life could become more fulfilled. I knew I could tell my children that their father was a true hero, a true man of substance, the Che Guevara of the African continent. The more I read about Ana and Francisco, the more I loved them both. I even felt that I was Ana's sister in love and pain. I felt like I became her, and I offered myself to Francisco, body and soul. I was her; she was me. Daria and Ana, Ana and Daria, transmuted beings, forming one single woman who knows well Francisco's pain. Through her, I came to live the real revolution and was thus equipped to be Francisco's true soul mate. Through both, I too, defended and embodied the beautiful idea.

---

[3]Resistência Nacional Moçambicana/Mozambican National Resistance.

The Idea Against Tarrafal

DEDICATION: To those who persevere even in the face of the ugliest evil eye. To Nelson Mandela, who withstood the thickest walls.

THE SUN AT SANTIAGO ISLAND. Ana Magalhães was picked up by the PIDE when she was blissfully sleeping in her apartment in Lourenço Marques. Francisco was away in the north of Mozambique doing some important revolutionary work with other FRELIMO members. When the secret state police came in the middle of night, Ana was taken by surprise, for she was immersed in the most beautiful dream. In this dream, she was in the middle of the city of Lourenço Marques, in the central avenue of this stunning pearl of light, the famous Avenida do Ultramar, standing on top of a military convoy with Francisco and many other comrades, men and women. The Avenida was full of people, Black and white, poor and rich, young and old, mulatto, Indian, Indian Black, Chinese, Chinese Black, and many other tonalities that the world can engender. There were all kinds of people in the convoy where Ana stood and all kinds of people around it—people of all genders and sexes. The crowd filled that entire long avenue that went on for kilometres and kilometres, only to end at the bay by the Indian sea. They were all were chanting, dancing, and hugging one another. Some were even making love in open view, all naked, frantically thrusting into one another and going from one to another, as if they had forgotten the vows of monogamy that certain types of marriage can impose. It was as if they could not care less if they were doing it with a white person, a Black person, or all the others that fall in between. Perhaps they were followers of a truly democratic polygamy, a future trend that was to take over in Mozambique and other countries around the world, African and otherwise. Ana herself was not just offering herself to Francisco, as she had done up to that point. She was opening her legs and her blouse to anyone who came to her to offer love and tenderness. And Francisco was doing the same and smiling and smiling, a smile of solace and contentment, the smile of a man who has so much love to give and receive that he cannot stop giving it and receiving it.

People were also drinking and smoking *ganza*. Everyone was high, everyone was happy, and everyone was thanking the gods for this thing that had finally happened, this thing they had been nourishing for a very long time and for which they had suffered so much, for which they had lost many of their friends. This was a true *festa*, a *festa dos vivos*, a feast of the living, where everyone felt that finally the idea had manifested itself. At some point in the dream, Ana looked up. It was just at the moment when she had finished the most ferocious act of lovemaking with a man that she had never seen before, a man who made her go to heights that she did not remember ever having climbed with Francisco, even in the early days when their love was intense and fresh and their need for one another did not seem to ever appease itself. She looked up and saw the name of the street, and she realized that she was in the middle of Avenida da Liberdade and not in the middle of Avenida do Ultramar. At that moment of sudden awareness and cognition, she could not contain her happiness. She felt drunk to the core, inebriated with the sudden discovery that she no longer lived in a place that made her keep her mouth closed and forbade her from making love freely with the man of her choice. She felt sure that she had reached the place that she and Francisco, and all the others, had been trying to reach, that place where everyone could be paid equally for the fruits of their labour. They had reached a place where the light of the sun, the gentle lunar illumination, the soothing coolness of the weather, and all the other sensations that time and place allow us to have could be shared by the people of Mozambique. She felt so sure that she screamed from the top of her lungs so that everyone in that long avenue, which ended only at the bay by the Indian Ocean, everyone in that city, and everyone in that country could hear her. She screamed to everyone, shouting about her sudden discovery and pointing to the sign that now said *Avenida da Liberdade*. And as she did that, she also saw the magnificent administrative building across the avenue, and she became aware of the slogan in big letters hanging from it: *This is Mozambique.* She screamed again. She screamed louder than before, pointing at the street sign and the banner frantically, trying to inform the others of her sudden discovery. Everyone looked up, and everyone stopped what they were doing for a moment to stare at that blue neon sign. It was surrounded by a gentle dark light, as if it were dawn and the people were now waking up, waking up to stare at the beautiful dream that was no longer a dream but something very tangible they could grasp with their own hands, their own fingers, their saliva. There was a general silence, and everyone prayed with their hands held up high. Some even knelt on the floor and murmured words of gratitude to the forces that made it all happen. At that very moment of happiness, meditation, and beautiful realization, before all the people could really see the slogan hanging down from the building across the avenue and truly understand its significance, Ana was shaken violently by two rude and sturdy PIDE agents, one Black and one white. And that was the beginning of a long and arduous nightmare, one that lasted for two years, two days, five hours, and seven minutes.

She was twenty-five years old then. She was a tall fierce woman with long black hair and unending legs that seemed to be made to walk the world from corner to corner or to penetrate deeply into the jungles of Africa and compete resolutely with the tall trees, without getting lost or breaking. She loved Africa more than anything, and though she had not visited any other continent, she knew she was home and had no desire to leave that home. Her ancestors had been living in Mozambique since the early nineteenth century. They had come from a region in the northern interior of Portugal, the province of Trás-os-Montes, a land full of mountains and rocky granite stones and snow and poverty, with little houses lost in the middle of that vast chain of mountains. The territory extends to the Spanish border, and many say that the most hardworking and fierce Portuguese people can be found there. She had never felt drawn to visit this land where her ancestors had come from, like many people do—people who are always looking for that which can never be found. She had no desire to travel the world and go from place to place to find happiness, to find wholeness. She was happy and whole where she was—or so she had thought before she had met Francisco. She first met him when she was twenty-one years old in a public gathering of FRELIMO members that had taken place in a recondite corner of Niassa, away from the vigilant eyes of the PIDE secret agents. When she saw Francisco, she could not resist his magnetism, the passion that shone in his eyes and the assurance that his thick sensual voice transmitted as he declaimed manifestos and poems about the destiny of man. He spoke about the right that everyone has to wake up in a land that they can call their own; a land that feeds all and allows people to speak their minds, their emotions, their souls; a land that allows men to make love with women in open air, without shame; a land that makes people want to wake up in the morning and walk slowly through the day, so that their feet can savour the feast of the early cooling dew, or the heat of the midday sun, or the mystery of the dark night. That blessed day when she first saw him was a new beginning for her. Just like Daria, the beautiful Daria with the poetic soul, Ana also felt that Francisco was the man she had been looking for all along. He was the purpose for which she had been made a woman, the purpose of her entire existence. He was her love, her revolution, her land. He made her want, and want more. He made her feel at home. He made her want to lie under him so that he could teach her how to become a woman and how to wake her body into wholeness. There were many people at that event, people of all ages, ethnicities, and colours. There were men and women and even precocious children who already had in their souls the desire to feel freedom, even though they were children and ought to feel free all the time, ought to feel that fairy tales are not tales but pulsating truth illuminating their night.

The next thing Ana was aware of was waking up somewhere pitch dark and very cold. Though she did not know at the time, she was on Santiago Island in Cape Verde, very far from the Indian Ocean, inside that swamp of slow death that was Tarrafal. They did not take her to Machava in Mozambique where most of the political prisoners of that distant Ultramarine Province were often kept. They chose to take her far away, to the other colony, on the Atlantic Ocean, so that she would be isolated, trapped on that lonely inaccessible island, cut off from any of her relations and thus impeded in continuing her cause. When she woke up in Tarrafal, in a freezing, small room, she was naked and felt her body was bruised all over. She was hurting. She was hurting a lot. She did not recall how she got there and did not know whether it was night or day because she was imprisoned in a small dark cement cell, completely sealed, in which no ray of light was visible. She was shivering and talking to herself, words that made no sense, disconnected, disjointed words that only those who have endured a hard and long punishment can murmur: Francisco, the boat, the sun, the sea, Avenida da Liberdade, the blue neon light, cunt, Chief Oliveira, magnificent legs, what a waste, this bitch, that *preto* motherfucker who has been fucking my own women ... After a long while, Ana Magalhães felt that her body was boiling. She could not breathe, and she felt sweat all over her and even on the floor she was lying on. As she tried to feel and understand her surroundings, she crawled all over that small space that was enclosing her. She crawled and crawled like a lost helpless animal or a baby with no understanding of the world yet, and then, unable to get her bearings, she started screaming.

Her visceral scream seemed to go nowhere, for she was in a tomblike prison where nothing came in and nothing went out except for the infernal heat that was somehow able to enter that space and come down on her like a sentence from the meanest God or the most wretched human souls. She went on screaming, or howling, into that boiling darkness that she had fallen into, like a buried dog or a wolf trying to encounter another sound, but it was all to no avail because the only sound that came to her was her own cry, her own agony, her own pulsating pain—the echo of a profound abyss. She was doomed; she was dead. She was forever separated from her magnificent Francisco Magno Motumba, from the beautiful idea, from the beautiful two-year-old twins they had, Otu and Quintana. The children often stayed with her parents for safety reasons and because the couple moved a lot due to thier political activities. And so, on that fateful day, the children had been with her parents and were saved from the brutality of the state police, who likely would have had no qualms squashing their heads with their heavy boots—those thunderous feet of men who cannot walk lovingly and lightly on this earth, destroying everything in their wake.

Sometime later, she could not know how long because she had lost all sense of time, someone came into the cell where she was. The door was abruptly opened, letting in a light so intense that her eyes could not see it as light but rather as a burning blinding darkness that did not permit her to gain any knowledge of her situation, her surroundings, understand where she was and why she was there. She was dragged out of the cell by two guards and taken to a cold shower somewhere in the compound. She felt some alleviation as the water came down on her and eased the suffocating heat she had endured in that dark closed room for God knows how long, even though the force with which the water came down on her was extreme, fustigating her bruised body and making her feel a throbbing pain all over. One of the guards held the shower and pointed it at her, often hitting her intimate parts. She felt uncovered, unguarded, and she wanted to hide from the assault, from the gaze, from the humiliation. The other guard stared at her, murmuring some unintelligible things that she could not understand. She tried to hide her body by recoiling and facing the wall or by assuming a fetal position, but the force of the water did not allow her to do that for more than a second and so she quickly ended up sprawled on the floor, totally exposed, totally at the mercy of the guards. They then took her, naked and clean, to the private office of the Director of Tarrafal, the feared Chief Arsénio de Oliveira. The Chief's private office was nicknamed The Freezer or The Experimental Chamber. Oliveira ordered them to exit, and they left her there alone with him. Ana was now getting a better idea of what was happening, and she recognized Chief Oliveira because she had seen him many times on TV, along with other protectors and enforcers of the regime. She had heard him speak words of fear to those who were fighting for the cause of liberation, calling them dirty communists who had no idea of the faith awaiting them once he got his hands on them. She particularly remembered one day when she saw him making a speech that sounded more like a warning. It was June 16, 1964, exactly four years after the Mueda massacre had taken place in Cabo Delgado in the north of Mozambique. The Makonde nationalists had organized a protest demanding independence from Portugal only to be shot dead by the colonial administration. She remembered how Oliveira spoke, how he minutely described what had happened to those people who had dared to ask for independence from the great Lusitanian empire and from father Salazar, a remarkable man, who had come from nothing and was now the greatest leader in Europe. Salazar was a man of God, Oliveira said, who considered them, Africans, not distant relatives of a lower species, but in fact equals to the citizens of the metropolis. The Portuguese Empire was unlike other colonial empires, which did not promote assimilation and even forbade mixed marriages. He went on, telling the crowd that they did not know how good they had it, that they were much better off than their neighbours in the south, and that the Portuguese could not be compared to any other empire. The Portuguese were the fathers of miscegenation and did not feel that making love with a Black man or a Black woman would make them lesser. On the contrary, they felt honoured and strengthened by such a union.

Ana knew then that Oliveira was just being a demagogue. He was a son carrying the message of his father, a father who knew his days of glory were numbered. One can only swim against the currents for so long; if the currents are saying "Give independence to the Africans," then independence will come sooner or later. She knew it, and she would not be fooled by such empty rhetoric. But what she remembered most vividly were the words Oliveira kept using to describe how the protesters had been killed. He said the ones who dared to rebel would also suffer the same, or worse, fate. And indeed, he had not been joking when he said that, as she was now finding out first-hand. He ordered her to stand still in front of him while he asked her specific questions about her associations and those of her husband. He wanted to know details about FRELIMO's next moves: Who was running the operation? How many associates did it have? Who was the *comandante*? Was it her husband, or Samora Machel, or another son of the devil communist? And so on and so forth. She did not reply because she had taken an oath, an oath in the name of justice, an oath that could not be broken even if her life had to be sacrificed. She did not vacillate, even though he kept asking her the same questions over and over for four hours straight, telling her she could not move until she answered his questions truthfully. She stood there in front of him like that, naked and terrified, yet resolved to keep her oath. She stood first with her back turned to him and then, as per his orders, directly facing him, like a frozen statue asking for mercy. But no mercy was coming. When Oliveira's tactics did not achieve any results, he told her he was going to try another dance with her, a dance he was sure she would not enjoy. He told her she was a traitor, a dirty cunt fucking any *preto* that came her way. He ordered her to come near him, and he unbuttoned his pants. He then forced her to perform oral sex on him and swallow whatever came out of him, adding that he was a clean man and that she should be honoured to get so intimate with him, to get so close and personal with a man of his stature. Ana felt sick, very sick, body and soul. She had never been with anyone other than Francisco, and she could not stand the smell of this dirty man. This was a man who came from the same place that her ancestors had come from a long time ago, but with whom she had nothing in common. The mere sight of him gave her nausea, a nausea that came from the deepest in her being. After he was done with her, he shouted for the guards to come and ordered them to take her back to the sealed and dark cement cell. The door was closed behind her, and she felt like she was entering a tomb, a tomb with no light and no air, and from which there was no hope of ever escaping.

TRAVELLING BY SEA. Francisco was picked up on the road as he was driving back from Nacala, in Nampula, to Lourenço Marques. It was a Friday night, and he was travelling to rejoin his beloved Ana, his warrior princess, a woman who gave him immense pleasure in body and soul. His car was accosted by two men dressed in plain clothes and carrying pistols that they pointed at him in the middle of the road, making him abruptly break out of his thoughts and hit the brakes of his old Peugeot. At first, and because Francisco was not expecting such an intrusion into his night—a night high and dense and illuminating—he thought that a wild animal, like an elephant or a zebra, was trying to cross the road and had become disoriented by the intense lights of the car and the noise of the motor. He had been travelling peacefully and feeling a sincere contentment all over his being—the party's meetings in Nampula had gone very well and he sensed that the change, the beautiful change, was not far from occurring. This was a change that would allow him to walk with Ana and enter cafés and restaurants without being harassed; a change that would make Mozambique the beautiful country that it truly was; a change that would honour the memory of all his ancestors who had fought the Portuguese since they realized that Vasco da Gama and the rest of the visitors, who had first reached that African coast by the Indian Ocean in 1498, were not there just to see the beauty of the place but actually wanted to settle and build mansions. In Nampula, he had met many of his colleagues and close associates who were doing important political work either in Mozambique or in Tanzania; he had also met many other supporters, young and old, Black and white, men and women. They were all people he had never before seen, all eager for change, all willing to fight with all their being for the beautiful idea to finally occur—that palpable, stunning child that they had been nourishing for a long, long time. He had shaken hands with Samora Machel, his closest associate and friend, the current president of FRELIMO, an extraordinarily courageous and intelligent man, and a true visionary who could bring freedom and goodness to Mozambique. He was currently exiled in Dar es Salaam, Tanzania, but he had managed to sneak into Mozambique for this important meeting. Machel had taken the reins of the party after the assassination of Eduardo Chivambo Mondlane in 1969, who had been brutally killed by a bomb at his headquarters in Dar es Salaam, the source of which was still being investigated, some claiming it was the dirty job of the PIDE and its international allies, others insisting it was an even dirtier affair—an inside job of FRELIMO pointing to dissidence and rivalry among party members. The bomb had been secretly put inside a book addressed to Mondlane that detailed the tactics of communist successful revolutions. When Mondlane saw the title of the book—O *Comunismo Vencedor*—he hurriedly opened it but the treasure hiding proved to be fatal and he was blown into pieces. Despite all this, Francisco felt hope. He felt reenergized. He felt that his life had a real purpose and that this time FRELIMO was going to attain its goals.

The assault took place as he was reaching Beira in Sofala. When Francisco realized that his luck had come to a sudden halt, he instantly assumed the demeanour of a strong man who would not be scared by two Estado Novo secret agents. He maintained that impartial, frozen look, the look of a mask that no one can decipher because the secrets are well sealed within it. He had learned this from his selfless Russian tutors during his mandatory training in Russia before he became accepted as a high-ranking member of FRELIMO. He was told exactly the type of posture and facial expressions that he should assume whenever he faced the enemy. He was also made to train for several hours so that he could display this persona and display it well. The teachers were relentless and very methodical in their instructions, and they were satisfied only when Francisco acted exactly as they had in mind. They had specific sessions devoted to enacting scenarios of physical torture or severe mental manipulation. They were well aware of the tactics used by the PIDE and also by the South African Police (SAP)—apples of the same tree who often worked in conjunction—and they wanted Francisco to be well prepared to handle what came his way. At first, Francisco thought this training was unnecessary and that the Russians were overdoing it—and perhaps even enjoying the torture of an African in the process—but when he watched some PIDE and SAP videos that the Russians had somehow managed to obtain, he became convinced that this practice was essential if he were to be successful in liberating his country. He understood that he had to suffer in advance as preparation for the real thing. He knew this exercise was not just a game, but, in fact, absolutely required training. It was important that his body and mind could withstand the real beast when it was thrown at him. And there it was, right in front of him, in the form of two pistols pointed at his forehead by two PIDE agents. They had somehow managed to get him, even though he had exercised the most care by making it look like his travels to the north were related to his polygamous customs, that he had just gone there to visit one of his wives and the children they had. And indeed, he had stayed with Sarif Matou at her house, and they had made passionate love to one another. But the PIDE agents were wise. They would not be fooled by a pretend polygamist, for they knew that Francisco was an *assimilado* and that he was legally married to Ana Magalhães, as the records in Lourenço Marques very clearly indicated. They had done their job, and they had done it very well.

They ordered Francisco out of the car, put handcuffs on him and a blindfold. They then dragged him to their car, which was hidden in the bushes on the side of the road. As they reached the car, they put a powerful substance on Francisco's mouth and nose and he lost consciousness, his body falling down as an amorphous helpless mass. They then picked him up and placed him carelessly in the trunk of the car. They drove to the coast, and Francisco, still unconscious, was put on a ship that would take him to his destiny in Tarrafal on the other coast of Africa. He knew it took him many days, perhaps months, to reach Tarrafal, where Ana already was, but he did not have a precise sense of how long. He remembered spending days on the ship and being assaulted by fits of nausea; he remembered he was being fed little food, or food that seemed to taste rotten in his mouth. He remembered being interrogated by the agents who picked him up and accompanied him on the long voyage to Tarrafal. He remembered being hung from the ship with his head down for what seemed like a very long time. They would hang him like that, his head just slightly above the water surface, and they would tell him that at any moment he was going to be food for the sharks. They said they were reaching the South African coast of KwaZulu-Natal, and that there were plenty of these sharp-mouthed beasts there that would shave off his limbs and head in a matter of seconds, with the precision of giant and unforgiving razorblades. They would do this, and sometimes, to scare him even more, they would throw something in the water to make Francisco think that indeed the shark was coming to him to swallow his head. They would scream and point, saying, "There it is! There is the beast of the sea, the Adamastor monster, bigger than the world, bigger than the universe. There is it! Laughing its teeth at your bold Black head." They did this type of macabre exercise many times throughout this long and agonizing voyage as they moved from point to point along the African coast. And, as they moved, reaching different important ports or locations, they would name the many Portuguese sailors who had travelled that same route and taken up their posts here and there, putting up their flags to claim the territories.

They talked about dates, names, ships, legends, events, timely deaths and noble births, kings, kingdoms, rivers, monsters, mermaids, astronomical inventions, navigational instruments, vacuous and infernal labyrinths inhabited by heathens and naked savages, conquerors and conquered, and much more. The long, seemingly endless, speech went as far back as 1415, and even long before that, to the time of Viriato the Lusitanian. It was as if they were singing a song or writing another version of *The Lusiads*.

Francisco was a well-educated man, and like any Black child who entered the formal school system at the time, he had studied Portuguese history in detail. His studies had first started when he entered primary school, or perhaps even before. His father, an *assimilado* from the Tsonga group, had been a powerful overseer for the colonial administration in the sugar fields in the Province of Maputo. This gave Francisco the advantage of being able to know both sides of the equation, both sides of history, to understand both the colonial master and the one being mastered. He knew well the arrogance of the colonial empire; he had known it since he was a very little boy. He had seen it everywhere—in his father's obsequious and sad bowing, in his adulation, in his abuse of power as a man on the right side of a deeply unbalanced equation. So the proclamations of Francisco's torturers, as he was being transported to Cape Verde—following the same route as the great Lusitanian adventurers—were nothing to him but attempts to re-establish something that in his mind, and in the minds of many people like him, was already lost, doomed to fall, sooner or later. The stories his captors told were nothing but empty and tired rhetorical schemes to make him bow, to make him spill his secrets. Though he was in extreme pain— his body exhausted and depressed by heat, seasickness, lack of food and water, not to mention the drugs in his system— and all his being ached with deep *saudade* for Ana and their children—he did not give in. He had made a vow many, many years ago, when he witnessed one of the most horrific incidents of his life. He was just seven years old when he saw how his father had chained a group of men working under him, his brothers in blood and skin, and made them work for an entire day on the sugar fields under the burning sun with no break, no water, no food, no shade. He did this because he wanted them to produce higher quotas. He said they were getting lazy—lazy like their entire race. Francisco remembers pleading with his father to unchain the men, to give them at least a sip of water, to allow them to rest for a few minutes under the frangipani tree. He pleaded and pleaded but it was to no avail. And then, defying his father's authority—and feeling like the world was going to end and that God or the gods were going to kill him, his father, and his entire family for allowing such malignance to take place—little Francisco took it upon himself to bring water and bread to the working men. He tried to do it discreetly so that his father would not notice, but his father had eagle eyes, and he caught him in the act. He brought him home and he spanked him with a long belt all over his tender body, and then he chained him to the frangipani outside of their house and made him spend one night and one day there alone. He had no water, no bread, and no company except for the ancestors, who spoke to him from the ground just under the sacred tree. He knew they were there, for they could sometimes be seen and sensed everywhere above or below the earth, or in the weeping willows and ridges of the stars—one only needed to be truly awake. He would never forget how scared he felt, how alone, how powerless—how he wished he would die. His father told him that he should learn from that lesson not to disobey his father, his superior. And indeed Francisco learned; he learned how it felt to be a man with no power, no shade, no water, no father, no God. He felt what those men working under his father's iron will felt, and he promised himself that he would do something to change this world, this way, this life. He promised to bring back to life the ancestors who were now mostly silenced because no one had eyes to see them, ears to hear them, or a voice to speak to them. They were truly dead. And ever since that day, Francisco had been reading about everything and everyone, learning and thinking about how it is that men can do things to one another that are so horrible and how it is that he, as a man, can learn how to do other things that can undo such acts.

REMBRANDT AND OTHER METHODS. When Francisco finally arrived at Santiago Island, he had no idea how long he had spent at sea. He looked tired, his eyes were red, and his gums were almost diseased, for no one had given him fresh oranges. He was dazed and confused, but he still knew why they had taken him and why he was there. He was a tall man with broad shoulders and an athletic body. He had been trained through hard-line discipline at the Greco-Latino Wrestling Camp during his stay in Russia, a famous place where all the best Russian athletes trained before going on to win abundant gold medals in international sports competitions. This was also the place where African guerrilla fighters and the followers of a certain line of Marxist liberation ideals were sent to learn the ways of victory so that they could then go back home and start the revolution to free their beloved countries. Francisco had had the habit of shaving his head since he was very young. It was as if he had predicted the trend that would arrive much later on in America, when Black men, eventually followed by many white ones, started to boldly show their naked heads, like beautiful sparkling earth spheres, the big guiding eye for their bodies. But now, after the long voyage at sea, his hair was long, a real Afro that grew very evenly around his head in a perfect circle that made it look compact, intense, and sealed off, as if it were a vast unexplored map where all kinds of new lands could be devised, a vast endless field where dreams could be nourished. His hair was like a ring of stunning black fire where the knowledge and the passion for justice danced, hiding in the intricacies of an entangled and freshly made nest. His beard and moustache had also grown, and seen from afar, Francisco almost looked like a messiah coming from an unknown and faraway land to deliver the beautiful news to the waiting people. When he arrived at the compound, they took him to the barber and to the showers so that he could be cleaned up. The same two guards who had dealt with Ana took him to the showers, where they also flogged him with water, in a malicious teasing, hitting his member very hard and making him fall sprawled on the floor. He was now a naked Jesus under the hands of merciless Roman soldiers. They were following orders from a modern Pontius Pilate who had no doubt about his righteousness. They were servicemen who had forgotten their own thoughts, their own capacity to see the terror and pain in the other's eyes.

After the shower, and still naked, Francisco was taken to the chief's experimental chamber, which was located at the end of the compound in a hidden corner. When he entered the chamber, he immediately recognized Arsénio de Oliveira because, like Ana, he had also seen him many times on TV or sometimes even in person delivering speeches and trying to intimidate the people with his poisonous words. Arsénio was a small man with a belly dancing in the middle of his waist. He had small eyes and fat little hands, and his hair was sparse, only a few silver threads combed to the side so that he would appear less bald. His voice was raucous, filled with hatred for his subordinates, fear of his superiors, and sometimes raging disappointment, especially when he had tried all the methods of punishment he could think of on his prisoners and nothing had worked, when he was left without the secret he was after: the classified information he was then to take to António de Oliveira Salazar, the chief of state, also known as Sr. Presidente do Conselho de Ministros and Arsénio's own first cousin. Arsénio had gotten the position in Tarrafal because of this powerful family connection. There were rumours that Arsénio suffered from a profound jealousy of his cousin that had developed into a serious complex of inferiority or obsession. He was always trying to find ways to impress his cousin so that his aunt, Maria do Resgate Salazar, would stop comparing him to her famed son, and his father would stop making him feel he was a good-for-nothing who was not as clever or manly as his cousin. Whatever it was that was commanding Arsénio's actions, it was something very dark, very macabre, as those who ended up at his mercy inside the chamber found out.

This chamber, which some also referred to as a laboratory, was called the experimenter's chamber because Arsénio was experimenting with all kinds of techniques to arrive at his devised goal. He was well versed in the psychology of the mind and had read and tried many techniques that were popular at the time, including the various subhuman behaviour modification techniques developed by Pavlov, Skinner, Watson, and several others who were less well known. He had also invented a unique method that consisted of hanging many of Rembrandt's portraits on the walls of his chamber and then forcing his victims to decipher exactly what the portraits were communicating. He wanted the prisoners to tell him what the mysterious faces were hiding. He deeply believed that underneath Rembrandt's enigmatic expressions was a clear line where the truth shone, a transparent soul that could not hide from anyone. This method, he thought, would eventually make the cryptic and lying faces of his prisoners lose their masks and show their true selves, and, in so doing, spill out the messages that he wanted to receive. The chamber was the most insidious place Francisco had ever known. The Russian training sessions that were meant to make him withstand the most horrible tortures fell way below Arsénio's evil machinations. What really intrigued and puzzled Francisco, who was also an avid admirer of Rembrandt and an excellent art connoisseur, was how Arsénio had managed to obtain these original paintings from the seventeenth-century Dutch master, given that Salazar had decided to play it safe and had closed off the country to the world during the Second World War, without showing any open or obvious support for either the Allies or the Axis.

And more than that: *How the hell did he manage to bring those paintings all the way down to Tarrafal and then create an environment there to preserve them, considering that his nation had remained neutral during the conflict?* Francisco had no answer to this question at the time. But he was interested in knowing what really happens in the world, in knowing the truths that often stay out of history books, so he planned to solve this mystery later on, when he could, when the time was right and he had access to documents that were hidden or not yet known to exist. He knew that history only truly makes sense when looked at from a certain distance, when you can hear different voices that sing their own songs, some sad, some gay, some powerful, and some wretched. And indeed, after the ordeal of Tarrafal was behind him and he was safe in Canada, enjoying the many fruits and liberties that the country had to offer—though it hadn't always been like that, at least not for everyone and not in equal measure—he came across information about Salazar and his dealings with the Germans that would account for the presence of the famed paintings in Tarrafal.

Most of the time, Arsénio conducted his sessions alone with his prisoners, with the chamber's door closed. He always wanted them to be naked. It was as if he suffered from some perverted disease that forced him to stare at the beauty or fragility of the human body and do with it whatever he wished. He had no wife and had never been married, but he had frequent access to women. Not only would he use and abuse many of the female prisoners, but he would also have women brought in just to serve him whenever his appetite so required. Like the prisoners, they would always be brought to his chamber, not his bedroom. These women would be locals sometimes, but he had a preference for white women because he was a racist and believed in the superiority of his race. He would force Black or mixed women—or those who had been mixing with Blacks, as in Ana's case—to do the most hideous and demeaning acts, including sodomy, oral sex, eating their own feces, and many other dirty things, the kind of things that are explicitly described in Le Marquis de Sade's *La Philosophie dans le boudoir*. With the white ones he would be gentler, much more prudish, much more restrained; he would barely touch them, and most of the time he would just stare at them or walk around their standing naked bodies with a long pinkish flamingo feather. He would comb their bodies up and down with it, causing them to feel ticklish and sometimes burst into incontrollable fits of laughter, which he would then stop with a slap on the face, saying, "Are you a whore or a virgin?" Sometimes he would venture a little further and would point the feather at their nipples, circling them over and over until he felt aroused, his member erecting gradually from inside his pants and vigorously pointing towards the woman. And as the thunder and rain came, he would fall on the floor, whining like a rabbit for several minutes until he recovered his strength and called his guards to remove the woman from his chamber.

Francisco stood naked in front of Arsénio, who introduced him to his method of punishment and intimidation by using two specific Rembrandt portraits: *Head of Christ* and *Head of a Young Man or Self-Portrait*. Arsénio started his attempt at deciphering the enigmatic with *Head of a Young Man or Self-Portrait*, for he thought that Francisco was a young man and somewhat of an artiste himself, a poet in fact, an artiste of many abilities who was evading his government's regime by using all kinds of metaphors and coded language to fool him and his counterparts, and he was keen on breaking him down. He told Francisco to stand directly in front of the portrait and he started asking him all kinds of questions with the intent to eliminate any obscurity that danced in that enigmatic face fully exposed in the painting. They were meticulous questions aimed at cracking the code of the secret that hid in that fluffy head full of hair falling down unevenly everywhere, on the roundish eyes, on the slightly bent posture, the white nose, the shadow covering his upper face, the light that exposed his left cheek, the brown of his jacket, the fullness of his right ear, the meagreness of his right eyebrow and the thickness of his left one. Every time the answer came from Francisco—because the answer was wrong every time, at least according to Arsénio—he would strike him with a leather belt that one of his friends had brought to him from Brazil, a long, sturdy belt made of crocodile's skin. Francisco would control the pain most of the time and would seldom emit a cry or show a contortion on his face, resolved as he was to preserve his dignity. It was as if, like the artist, he resisted being decoded and touched by the strikes of Arsénio's violent belt, so intent was he on maintaining his persona, on protecting the sacred cryptogram. He reacted like a brave hero, a war soldier who was not afraid of dying, whose body had in fact ceased to exist. His soul, where the idea throbbed, rose to the chamber's ceiling, up high, and looked down on the meanness of the world, composing Bach's arias or just hearing them over and over again like a mantra. He was himself without himself, and he was no longer naked in front of Arsénio. He was no longer receiving blows from the merciless poisonous belt, a belt that was made of the skin of that powerful animal that once lived in the wetlands of the Brazilian Amazon, that had once roamed the canals and rivers, trying to find the sun and the water and the murky mud where the life of the rainforest could be tasted.

"What is Rembrandt hiding in the obscurity of his upper face? Is he concealing the secret of FRELIMO's next attack on the empire's troops? Does that shadowy upper face represent the darkness of evil, the darkness inhabiting the hearts of the people of this godless continent?" Arsénio would ask. And

Francisco would reply, "The upper shadow, sir, represents the sacred mysteries of the night when God visits Africans and delivers the messages of the angels, these angels being the ancestors who live on the other side of the river, on the wings of the sun, on the morning dew, or on the beautiful eyes of women who only ask for love and children as if their wombs are nothing but lands of plenty where many beings and futures are waiting, waiting to see the sun directly through their irises. Or, sir, these ancestors live on the beautiful frangipani tree in its full blooming season, when it's enveloped in those little white flowers and becomes a stunning umbrella that covers you from the rain, when it becomes the pure African bride dancing in the savannah like a translucent, transpersonal, transnational gazelle." This answer, which was overly metaphoric for Arsénio, would only exasperate him more and make his belt strike harder and more frequently, so hard and so frequently that Francisco's skin would sometimes give in, letting out a silent cry in the colour of red tears. "What is the meaning of the clarity that dances in his right cheek? Does it mean that Salazar's troops are making progress in the Mayombe of Angola? Or does it mean that Amílcar Cabral has been killed? Does it mean that civilization is spreading and securely implanting itself in this disorderly continent? And does the darkness in the left cheek mean that there is still a lot of work to do to spread the light fully, to reach those people who know nothing but the tremulous and uncertain brightness of bonfires?" And the reply: "No, sir. The left bright part of Mr. Rembrandt's visage means that he wanted to capture the ambivalence inherent in every human being, in every race, in every soul—the ambivalence within himself. It means that in painting himself, he, the artist, the man, the human, was trying to find out who he was even though, as he discovered, he was something that could never quite be unveiled. He was like a shadow moving perpetually and gradually towards the final light, even though the light could never be fully reached, never fully perceived through his own sight. He understood this after finishing the painting, when he finally looked at himself from outside of himself. There is a story, sir, about Rembrandt spending two days looking at his portrait after he finished it, as if in some meditative trance. He was trying to become acquainted with himself, to find the grounding and the peace he felt he was lacking. But then, disappointed that this feeling did not come, he went on painting face after face after face for the rest of his life. He painted the faces of everyone he found, as if everyone was a vehicle through which he would finally arrive at himself. And then, sir, when he was in his bed, ready to depart, he said to his friends and admirers, 'No man should ever think that truth and understanding can come solely from within himself. One must look at the other, note her differences, the roughness of her hands, the longing in her eyes, the many lights and shadows that dance in her face, how the sound of her voice comes out throughout the day, how it changes when it's sunny or rainy, hot or cold. That, my friends, is the way one truly finds oneself. Otherwise we are always alone and afraid, and because of that, we inflict pain onto others and ourselves.' His philosophy, sir, was truly dialectical. He believed in the otherness of selfhood or in the selfhood of otherness." "What is he hiding under his fluffy hair that seems neither black nor brown, neither blond nor reddish?" Arsénio would continue. "Again, sir, I think I already answered that question. He is, through the medium of painting, showing the art admirer that one does not, cannot, live alone on an island; that one is always made of many others; and that those others may be blond, black, brown, or something else that is not depicted in the colours of his hair, the colours he chose to paint himself with at that particular point in his life. He is using metaphor and metonymy, sir; metonymy, sir, comes from the Greek metōnymía, which means 'a change of name.' Both metaphor and metonymy have in them the word 'meta,' which means 'beyond' or 'after.' This ultimately suggests that our language is always trying to catch something beyond itself, always after some unreachable golden mean that it can never attain, making us all eternal simpletons unable to stare at the true essence of things. In some cultures, it is believed that this is a punishment from God and that the true language will only come to us when all the injustice plaguing our world has ceased. Now, I would even go so far, sir—and forgive me the many examples—as to suggest that Rembrandt is using a syllogism and that syllogism is as follows: *All humans are part of me* (this being the major premise); *I am human* (this being the minor premise); *therefore, I am part of all humans* (this being the conclusion). This could otherwise be stated as follows: *therefore, all humans are in me*, or *therefore, I am in all humans*." At this point, Arsénio would become enraged. He would land his hardest strike on Francisco, not even looking where he was hitting, and he would say, "You stupid bastard, you think you can fool me with your mumbo-jumbo imitations of western philosophy, rhetoric, and literary knowledge. You stupid bastard. The correct expression is *All humans are mortal* (this being the major premise); *I am a human* (this being the minor premise); *therefore, I am mortal* (this being the conclusion). And obviously this syllogism does not even apply to you because you are not human. But you are mortal, as I will soon show you."

The next test was conducted using the painting *Head of Christ*. Again Arsénio forced Francisco to stand naked in front of the head of the saviour and asked him a series of questions about the particular message of the portrait. This time he started with a general question to see if he could trick Francisco into divulging anything; he was hoping that if he could find out one secret, it would then somehow help pull out the other secrets he really wanted to know, secrets pertaining to the particular activities of the guerilla fighters anywhere in the several Províncias do Ultramar. "What did Rembrandt intend to say when he painted Jesus Christ this way?" Arsénio asked. Francisco replied, "I think, sir, that his posture reminds us that he, Jesus, that is, was an intelligent and kind man and looked at the world in a gentle fashion. Don't you note, sir, the gentle light in his eyes, a light that is then projected with the utmost goodwill on that which is in front of him? And what is in front of him, sir, is you and me, is the world, a world made of many peoples, many races, many men and women, all of them his children, all of whom he loves very much. Don't you see that, sir?" This answer, which came with a question, really irritated Arsénio, making him curse Francisco, calling him all kinds of very bad names, and striking him several more times with the thick belt. As he was striking and cursing Francisco, he was thinking about the last letter he had received from his cousin Salazar, a letter of unprecedented urgency.

Dear cousin, we do not have much time to save the nation from the communists, and the Americans seem to have an eye on us too. Dear cousin, we do not have much time, and the time has come to do whatever is demanded from us to save our nation and make our brave ancestors proud. Dear cousin, I am counting on you and the miracle that you can produce to stop our doom. And you know what the reward is. You know what your reward is.

"You motherfucker from the jungle, what the painting is saying, motherfucker, what it is saying and what master Rembrandt wanted it to really say is this: Christ is Portugal and Portugal is Christ. Can't you see that Christ's head is directed southwest in the direction of Portugal, the most southwestern country of Europe? Can't you see that his head is full of wavy dark hair, and that he has a dark beard and a dark moustache, which most men in Portugal have? Can't you see that even though Rembrandt was a proud Dutchman, he knew that Christ had been born in Portugal and then travelled the world to preach his faith? Can't you see that Rembrandt predicted that the Virgin Mary, God be with her, would one day come back to the place where she received the divine seed from God? He predicted she would come back, that she would appear to the three little shepherds in Fátima and give her blessing to the country, the country of God's predilection."

"But sir," Francisco would counterargue, "can't we also say that the colour of Christ's hair and its waviness is possibly indicating that he may have been born in Africa or at least that he chose to appear in a colour that is neither white nor Black, but rather one that stays in the middle, to tell us that all races and colours are good and should therefore be equally valued? Have you read, sir, that part in the Bible that says, or seems to say, that Jesus was from Ethiopia, which is in fact not so far from my country of Mozambique?" Another deluge of blasphemies and name-calling would fall on Francisco followed by heavy strikes with the crocodile's belt.

The last part of Francisco's answer had a particularly negative and infuriating effect on Arsénio: "Mozambique my country? Your country? You are delusional, my friend. Have you not seen the inscription on the municipal building in Lourenço Marques? Have you not seen it? Have you been blind? What does it say, my friend? Tell me what it says!"

"I have seen it, sir! It says, *This is Mozambique*. And the name of the city, sir, is not Lourenço Marques but rather Maputo." This answer, of course, only added insult to injury or, as the proverb goes in Portuguese, made the bad much worse, with a predictable result. The two of them wasted hours like this in front of one painting or another, hours and hours on end devoted to sad fruitless exercises where art and life were being used for evil purposes. By the end of the session, Francisco was still an enigma to Arsénio and Rembrandt an enigma to both Francisco and Arsénio. Meanwhile, boys and girls all over the falling empire were dying, their limbs exploding into a wasteful nothingness, the wealth of minerals and oil and pearls never reaching them or their poor peasant parents, who worked from sunset to sunrise.

THE TWO COUSINS. That night Arsénio went to his room in a very foul mood, still cursing Francisco, the communists, and any other bastard who was after the great nation, trying to damage his cousin's hard work. Sitting on his bed with tears coming to his eyes, Arsénio thought about his cousin and himself when they were two little boys in Vimieiro. He reminisced about his cousin with a mixture of melancholia, love, and, at points, envy. He thought about Vimieiro and their time together as little boys and then young men, beings trying to understand the world and find in it a place for themselves. He respected his cousin immensely. Salazar was a man who had come from nothing and was able to straighten up the country, pulling it out of the anarchy that had befallen it after the Republic's endless succession of governments with its unending violence, poverty, and economic doom. He had made the *escudo* gain some value and respect again. His cousin was a taciturn man with a shy sensibility, a love for flowers, and an iron fist, who still thought of himself as being poor and as the son of the poor. It was as if he could never leave behind Vimieiro and the clogs he had worn in his childhood during those harsh winters of Beira Alta. He remembered the times when the snow and the frigid, cutting wind could turn you into an inert mound of shivering or rigid nothingness, when you have to hide inside the granite houses that had no mercy for the weak. They were like dark, sad coffins that reminded you of the death to come, when we all go underground, immobilized by cold and stiffness. Arsénio had worked very hard all his life. He had sacrificed a lot, and he had worked particularly hard ever since he came to Cape Verde years and years ago when his cousin had asked this great favour of him. He had felt he could not say no even though he hated the sun of the tropics. Its sticking humidity made his body and mind slow, a dead man walking, incapable of swift action and thought. But he could not say no because he owed a lot to his cousin. He owed him everything. He owed him his life. But things were getting very hard, very hard indeed, and the only thing that kept him going was the idea that one day he would be the second man of the great nation, as his cousin had promised him, and if his cousin died before him, he would replace him. He only needed to catch the depraved red communists who did not believe there was a God commanding us all and that God was a great friend of the vast and magnanimous Lusitanian nation. He only needed to catch those reds and any other bastard who was trying to undo the beautiful nation that had been fathered by his great Lusitanian ancestors in the 1400s and then cemented by his patient, loving, and powerful cousin in the twentieth century. He only needed to catch those communists and their friends. But things were getting harder, and he had to become more and more inventive with his methods in order to extract any truth from the wretched entrails of those bastards. The first time Arsénio was able to provide his cousin with a big name on the list of the most-wanted red guerrilla fighters, his cousin had rewarded him with a great collection of European art that had kept him going and had, at least initially, revived his soul. He rediscovered his deep desire to paint, to be good, and to believe in the goodness of the world, like when he was a little boy, before his mother went away. António had sent down to him dozens and dozens of paintings that he had received as payment from the Germans in return for wolfram that he had sold to them. Many of the paintings had belonged to the Jews who had been annihilated by the millions in death camps throughout Europe. They had been burned into nothingness, the chimneys expelling dark and grey smoke for days and then months and then years, causing the sun to hide in profound sadness, even as their neighbours swore they knew nothing about it. António had also sent a savvy artsy engineer—a devotee of the postmodern before the postmodern, who dressed like a Parisian *flâneur*—to design a special room in Tarrafal, a place with just the right temperature, humidity, and light to properly preserve the paintings and ensure that their beauty and power would not fade. Salazar knew that his cousin was an avid art admirer, and he knew that these paintings had to be hidden in a place where no one could find them so that he would not be accused of aiding Hitler in the killing of Jews. He also knew that one day the paintings would be worth millions.

Ever since they were little boys, Arsénio would paint and draw beautiful things. He would often stare in ecstasy at the stained glass or the religious art at the local church in Vimieiro. It was as if he had been born an innate artist. In art, he found the solace that most human beings need to be at peace with themselves and the world around them. He would always carry with him a pencil and paper or paint and a brush, and he would paint and draw everywhere, on any surface that could take in his designs and desires: stones, walls, the kitchen floor, white or black clothes. His mother understood his calling and, though she would be annoyed when he damaged the walls and the floor and the clothes with his talent, she would seldom show him her anger. But his father would become very upset, spanking him with a long, sturdy stick and ranting about how his son was a good-for-nothing, not a real man. He insisted that real men do manly things, and he was intent on making his son into a real man; he needed no queer person in his family to bring shame and dishonour. Little Arsénio suffered a lot at the hands of his father, a man full of fury, an ugly fury that could not be tamed, understood, or neatly linked to a source. Arsénio's calling was so profound and visceral that it became an obsession, and he could not stop drawing or painting. In primary school he was always praised by the teachers for his talent. He would glow with pure pride and happiness, the pride and happiness of human beings who are allowed to do what they love and are valued because of it. The other youngsters were envious of him and would find ways to hurt him, teasing him more and more, telling him his mother was a cuckoo head who needed to go to the *manicómio*, the lunatic asylum, and that he was just like her. They would call him names and sometimes even accuse him of not being a true Christian, of having tainted blood. They would also tease him because he was always dressed with his clothes inside out and always smelled of garlic as a result of garlic cloves he was made to carry in his pockets. This was part of a plan to cure his mother's illness—a recipe given by a renowned *bruxa*, a witch doctor, also referred to as a *curandeira* (a healer) by some who saw no distinction between two professions whose end goal was the same: the healing of bodily and spiritual malaises.

Arsénio's mother, Camila das Dores, suffered from a powerful delusional disorder. She was never properly diagnosed or treated, for doctors were scarce then and cost money. This illness brought her many moments of joy but also many moments of sadness and profound suffering. Despite the suffering, if she could choose, she would not have been born any other way because the happy moments and the illumination that she gained through her illness outweighed all the suffering. The illness gave her the ability to see into the world in slow motion, as if she were flying, dancing, up in the air like a bird-woman, a being between the here and the beyond, a being that travelled through the cosmos to find meaning and meet God. It gave her the ability to freeze the beauty that exists in the world, or in a moment, and stare at it for hours on end until she became satisfied and replenished, until she was ready to face the ugly again. It gave her the courage to take off and go on many journeys, fabulous wandering trips in search of the sublime. This power would come to her at any given moment, when people least expected it: when she was in mass with the rest of the villagers or when she was working hard in the land on a sunny August day, with her back bent, tending to the corn or the bean crops, steadily moving her heavy shovel to turn the earth around the plants and take away the bad weeds, her body sweating and exhausted. She once had an episode at church, on the day they were celebrating Queen Saint Isabel, the patron saint of the Church of Vimieiro. At the exact moment of the communion, when the priest was putting the sacred wafer in peoples' mouths and saying *Corpo de Cristo* over and over again, as if it was the only prayer he had learned in the seminary, and just after Camila had taken her own wafer, she ran to the altar and started hugging all the saints. The hug she gave Queen Saint Isabel was much more prolonged and effusive than those she gave to the rest of the saints. Queen Saint Isabel was a magnificent, saintly, and holy woman who lived in late thirteenth and early fourteenth centuries and dreamed up ingenious ways to feed the poor, transforming bread into roses, roses into bread, or sometimes even roses into gold. She died from a fever at the age of sixty-five, though, as the story goes, her body remained intact for centuries after it ceased breathing. It was as if she were bearing witness to the fact that the life of the body goes on eternally when fed with the real dreams of a beautiful soul, or that the very existence of the material is part of some great master plan developed by someone with immense power and vision. Camila then proceeded to take down the cross where Jesus Christ stood, placing it flat on the altar's floor and took off her clothes. With her white undergarments smelling of fresh eucalyptus leaves, which she used as disinfectant, she wiped the blood and sweat oozing from the body of Jesus Christ. She saw him as a happy, happy man, ready to make love with her and show her that this world where we live is much more than a valley of blood, tears, and suffering, that it possesses an astounding, pounding beauty that is pure piano music for our ears and honey for our splendid bodies. She then started fondling the suffering man with her own body, a body still young and full of needs, her large breasts going up and down on the inert, cold body. As she did that, she felt the happiest she had ever felt. She repeated the words of the priest, *Corpo de Cristo*, and she felt a shower of benevolent illuminating light coming down on her, kissing her body with love—love and life. She felt complete and no longer alone, as though she possessed within her all there was to possess: the Body, the Father, the Son, and the Holy Spirit. She became one with the One and had, all over her face and body, the signs of the great possession. The people in the church, many of whom were still taking the wafer from the priest and allowing it to dissolve slowly and gently in their mouths so as not to be called cannibals of the divine, were horrified at the scene they saw at the altar between Camila das Dores and Jesus Christ. They shouted in disbelief, and some, their moment of solace and encounter with God suddenly interrupted, used their teeth to hastily finish up the wafer they had in their mouths. Or they swallowed it intact, quickly and haphazardly, with one single movement of the throat that left them without breath, their air canals momentarily agonizing in affliction. The priest, thus suddenly interrupted during his sacred task and dedicated concentration, let the wafers fall on the floor and break on the hard granite medieval stones of that very ancient church. The church had been built under orders of King Dom Dinis in the fourteenth century when he was about to die. Its completion had taken over seventy-five years, and so the king never got to see it finalized. Dom Dinis was the husband of Queen Saint Isabel, and he was a clever intellectual who composed poetry and had an unrepentant and voracious appetite for women, a man known and commended by nationalist historians for his efforts in solidifying the nation. He even planted the seed of the great empire when he ordered the plantation of Leiria's pine tree forest, which, years later, provided plenty of wood to build the sturdy and fearless ships and caravels that sailed into faraway seas, facing the darkness of the unknown. This magnificent church, which many called the sublime cathedral, was a stunning medieval building with stained glass everywhere that depicted red roses and big loaves of bread entering the mouths of hungry peasants, recreating Isabel's miracle of the roses. It had been built to honour her, to display, for all to see, her saintly virtues and inclinations; though some say that the king had it built because he felt an immense guilt for being a womanizer and not sufficiently loving his wife. He wanted to obtain some pardon from God and his saintly wife, they claim, by building this beautiful sturdy cathedral that reminded human beings of the power of charity and all the goodness that exists in this world. The less religious, and perhaps more devious, showed no qualms about the womanizing inclinations of the king and would jokingly say, laughing out loud, "What do you expect from someone who is married to a saint?"

The people observing Camila's behaviour, including the priest, stood in disbelief at what was happening inside the sublime cathedral. They became frozen for what seemed to be an eternity, staring at Camila and her depraved, shameless actions, as if they had lost the capacity to think or act. It was as if they had entered another realm, a dream zone where they did not know that they were dreaming and felt incapable of moving their own bodies. It was as if everyone was being magically manipulated by a great manipulator, tricked by the clown of clowns, who put before their very eyes the image of the impossible uncanny, the image of the stunningly beautiful, the beautifully ugly. Then, suddenly recovered from their apathy, they ran to the altar. Some covered Camila, dressed her, and then removed her from the church, and others picked up Jesus and placed him high up on the altar, in his usual pose of bleeding martyrdom. Camila's husband, being the brute and insensitive man that he was, took her home and gave her a beating, accusing her of being a wretched whore from Galilee. Arsénio was only seven years old then, but this scene has stood engraved in his mind and body ever since. Even though the way his father treated his mother has always evoked sadness, whenever he thinks about that day he also feels a great sense of joy and astonishment. He remembers it was the first time he felt very happy inside the church. He remembers how he'd felt at home when the congregation was singing "Ave Maria" and when the priest and his helpers were going around inside the church with their lanterns and baskets of burning incenses, bringing to the people the light and the smell of God. He remembers closing his eyes, inhaling the incense, and feeling the hand of the priest touching his, blessing his existence and making him a true son of God. He was in a trance of light and feeling and sensation, lulled by the music and the smell and the priest's touch. And then, as he opened his eyes, he saw the stained glass images everywhere in the church, illuminating images of that charitable woman smiling a pure smile, opening her mantle and throwing pieces of bread to the people. He saw that as the bread entered people's mouths, it became white and red roses, and he saw how the people became happy as they ate the roses, how their faces became fuller and their eyes shinier. They then began to sing and dance, and hold hands, and then, when fully satiated, they approached Queen Saint Isabel and lifted her up, raising her above their heads and chanting in a thunderous chorus: *Saint, Saint is the Madonna, Saint, Saint is the one who gives bread and roses to the people. Saint, Saint is the one who makes me see that this world smells of perfume...* Arsénio was bewildered by the beauty of the scene. He felt at home in this place, and this place felt as real as anything else he had ever seen. It was a place that reminded him of the beauty and magic of the world, of what things were and what they could become, a world where the verbs *to be* and *to become* were all that mattered, and where one would easily lead to another. It was a place where the priest's readings and words possessed a miraculous power of incantation that spoke to your mind and soul and made you see deeply, very deeply, into things, making you dwell in being so that you felt grander and smaller at the same time. It was a world beyond this world and yet very much in this world. This experience was then completed by the happiness he felt during the procession, which took place before the communion. As per the custom, the saints were put in the beautifully decorated biers and carried by the stewards around the village, everyone following them in a *romaria* that passed through every street of Vimieiro. The streets themselves went back to the Roman times and beyond, and they were full of rough and irregular stones that would make the saints fall off the pier, were it not for the diligence and care of the stewards carrying them. Arsénio vividly recalls how the piers were magnificent that day; he remembers the variety, freshness, and colours of the flowers: wild carnations, hydrangeas of all tonalities, and white and red roses, endlessly beautifying the already beautiful and adding more grace. The patron saint, Queen Saint Isabel, was the most beautifully decorated. White and red roses had been placed on her exquisite pier, which his father was helping carry that year as one of the four designated stewards, an honour to be celebrated. That made Arsénio even happier, happier and prouder and he thought that such beauty could not pass unnoticed by his father, unseen by his heart of stone. He thought it would make his father a better and softer person, someone who would kiss him at night, someone who would speak tenderly to his mother even when she became unbearably restless and took off to places unknown to them to find what she was missing. He recalls the red colours of the stewards and the colours of the piers and the colours of the quilts that the women had put in their windows to honour the procession and the saints, and he sees the showers of flowers falling down on them from the windows: love and beauty coming together in a perfect, perfect day, a saintly day.

It was all colour and perfume and bread and roses. People with people, and people with God, with nothing between them. No one can ask for more than that. But then, as they went back to the church to finish the mass on that grand day when the Queen Saint Isabel was being celebrated and remembered, and just as the most sacred act of communion between all there is was taking place, his mother had one of her episodes and the magic was broken. She was shouted at. She was accused. She was beaten by his cruel father. And the next day in school, the children mocked him again, calling him names, bad names. They accused him of being a *marrano*, someone who carried in him the seed of those who killed Jesus Christ, the true saviour of this world. They had heard some dark tale here and there—improperly told, lacking crucial details—about the past of the family, and they were now regurgitating and adding to it, as children often do.

One day, when Camila was bathing Arsénio, when he was just an infant of three months, she had a powerful out-of-body experience. As she was moving her infant around in the aluminum basin where she was bathing him, she felt the fluidity of the water awaken in her being a lightness she had never before experienced. The more she touched her baby's soft flesh and the more she felt on her hands the perfumed water where she had soaked petals of white and red roses, the more detached she felt. She saw a rose on her left hand, and then that rose gave birth to many other roses and she saw roses everywhere: on herself, on her baby's naked body, on the walls and floor of the house, and even floating in mid-air like sublime presents brought to her for her own pure enjoyment. She felt she had fallen into a garden of colour and aroma and utter beauty, and she knew that she had to fully enter it, that there was no way to turn away from it. She saw her soul leaving her body, mixing with the floating roses and rising to the ceiling of that old house, a house blackened by smoke and years of suffering, the same house where she had given birth to her baby just three months ago after an agonizing pregnancy. Just before she had started bathing her baby boy, she had been immersed in sadness, engulfed by the depths of the dark well, thinking about her life since she had married her husband. She saw before her the life she had been living with this man ever since he became her husband, how much he had beaten her, how he demanded to use her body for his own needs wherever, however, and whenever he fancied, even when she was heavily pregnant and feared for her health and that of the baby. He was a very, very rude man, a monster who made her feel like she was worth nothing. He said she should be happy that he had married her for no other man would touch her since she had already given it away to God knows how many men, during her crazed episodes when she'd become possessed by the devil. She had always been very attracted to him. He was a tall and muscular man with an angular nose, sharp features, and piercing eyes. Whenever he had looked at her, she had gazed back at him, her eyes immobile and unafraid, and imagining how it would be to make love with this man. She loved men. She loved their hands on her and the intensity of the sexual encounters when she took charge and made them scream with pleasure, but sometimes her sexual needs were so great that she became afraid of herself. Their first time together had been a fiery one, and for a few nights after the wedding, her husband had been controlled by her sexual prowess. He would treat her well because he did not want to lose what she was giving him. But shortly after things changed: he became impossible to satisfy in any aspect. He accused her of being a whore, of not knowing how to cook, how to work the land, or how to treat a man. He called her a possessed lunatic who could only go to hell for no God would ever forgive the sins she carried in her blood. Her pregnancy was full of pains: she was beaten and raped many times by her husband, and she stopped feeling anything towards him. She could not bear to be touched by him, but she had no power to refuse him and so she endured it. Often, she found ways to exit her body when he was doing those things to her. After she gave birth to Arsénio, things got even worse. He had no respect for her body and the healing it needed before he made use of it. She endured and endured, and then she became numb. Now, as she was bathing her baby boy, her first-born, alone in her house, she felt relaxed for the first time in a long time; the water and her baby's fresh body danced in her hands like soft remembrances, telling her the world was still salvageable, that tenderness and beauty did exist. In that newly rediscovered awareness, she saw herself as a free woman again, walking or flying through the world and meeting many men and women who would give her soft kisses and a hand when she was about to fall. With her hands still securely holding her baby so that he would not drown, she saw her body ascend to the ceiling. When she got there, she felt she could go much farther. She could leave the house and walk through the clear fields; she could fly to the high mountains to feel the kiss of time and space upon her starved soul. And if she persisted in her flight, she could go to other countries, other villages, in search of men who would make tender love with her, men who would respect her breasts, her thighs, and that incendiary rose she had between her legs that always screamed for much more than it could get. After this astounding experience, she did just that, returning to her life before she was married: she would take off, body and soul, whenever she could, so that she could find life and love, so she could find a reason for eating bread and drinking water every day. These episodes became more and more frequent and often would be preceded by something very nasty her husband had done to her. She would often see herself as a breeze running away somewhere or an ancient bird that could cross the vast Atlantic in one single flight, staring at the waters below and the silvery fishes, all free creatures, all things of God.

When the Gypsies, whom Camila called the Romani, insisting that was their proper name, came to Vimieiro in their colourful carriages pulled by white donkeys selling pots and pans, quilts for the winter, illustrated books for children, and other paraphernalia, like a circus of magic life, she would run off with them and disappear for weeks or months on end. She saw these men and women as ingenious mavericks, capable of the most intriguing acts of love and grace. She loved the long dresses and braids of the women, the colours and lengths of their earrings, and she was fascinated by their ability to see into her future just by staring at the intricate lines of her palm. She loved the intensity of their dances and the longing of their songs, and, most of all, she felt helpless when a pair of deep and dark Romani eyes stared at her, asking for love. She would love these Romani men like she never loved anyone else, and at the end of their time together she felt appeased for a long time, the demanding rose between her legs calmed down and satiated. She was told by several Romani women that she was of their clan and that her ancestors had been forced to adopt the sedentary and boring life of Vimieiro. They told her that now she had the chance to correct that wrong by joining them in their nomadic life, selling odds and ends here and there, waking up in a different place every day to smell the rain and the thunder or peek at the wonders of many regions. She thought that made a lot of sense, for she always felt that Vimieiro was too small for her, too confined for her grand desires. So she would take off with them and then come back with another caravan, weeks or months later. She came back mostly because she missed her son. She thought of his little body changing, his hands and his feet growing, and his face becoming that of a man day by day, month by month, year by year, and her heart started to cry for him. She could not stay away longer than a couple of months at a time because her son came out of her: he was her flesh and her blood and her bone, and she was his mother. She would come back with her heart throbbing in love and guilt, and she would take care of Arsénio with more tenderness than before, singing him new lullabies, telling him new stories that she had heard while away, offering him little toys or trinkets for him to play with. Every time the boy saw her returning, his eyes became engulfed by hope and he ran to her, calling her *a minha mãe*. It was clear from his voice that he could never forget her, that he would always know who she was, even if she were to forever disappear. She was imprinted in his cells, and the body never lies or forgets. She would hug him tightly, her eyes watery, kissing each of his chubby boyish cheeks with a noisy long kiss. Then she would lift him up, holding him high above her head, shouting out loud *o meu filho*. Arsénio would feel very happy and secure as if he had an abode covering him, an abode made of love and tenderness, which is hard to destroy even when there are heavy thunderstorms coming down from the heavens. He tried to always be close to her, and even during the night he insisted on sleeping with her, his hand closely wrapped around hers, like a sentinel that cannot let go. He savoured her voice, her closeness, her smell, her breast milk, her food, the water cup that she had scrubbed clean. He took into himself all she could give him, to the fullest, until the time she left again, without warning, abandoning him to the ill temper of his father and the jokes of the children at school. Every time she came back, her husband showered her with a deluge of insults and a heavy beating. Like her son, he would be very vigilant, watching her every movement for a while, but when the need came to her, she always found a way to escape and go search for happiness again. Deep down, all she wanted to be was a vagabond, crossing the world from corner to corner, never settling down anywhere. Sometimes, when the guilt assailed her, she would tell herself that the reason she was a drifter was so that she could get to know the world and then die informed. She imagined that she could take her knowledge to the other side, where God lives, so that He could be aware of the many miseries that still abound in the home he created, so that He could understand how important it was for him not to abandon it to the faith of men. But the truth was that she missed the faraway lands with their starry night skies; she missed sleeping outside, in open air, warmed up by a blanket, with a passionate and tender Romani man beside her. She missed cooking outside in open fires, the smoke rising and bringing earthy smells to her nose on cold crisp days, a red shawl on her shoulders, her wavy black hair falling down freely. Her soul yearned for the pleading flamenco guitars that made the people dance in a frenetic, demanding, contorted motion, as if this music and this dance were embedded in their blood from birth. Even the young boys knew it by heart and could sing it with the maturity of old men. She missed their life, their passion, and their colours. She missed everything about those feared and often persecuted people who had been walking the continent on foot, or donkey, or horse, for centuries, refusing to be tied down by the laws of any land. She missed the sounds of the Spanish language, which had first entered her eardrums as both a familiar and foreign tongue—like lullabies she once knew but had forgotten or sent back to her deepest self— when the band crossed the border in Vilar Formoso. There, they bought contraband clothes to be sold in fairs throughout the many villages of Beira Alta and beyond. And sometimes the band would cut across Spain to reach France, Germany, and beyond, knowing no borders, crossing frontiers by night without a passport, perpetual vagabonds in search of a home. She missed the novelty of the different landscapes and the physiognomy of the many peoples, the way each pronounced the words *water* or *sky* or *air*, the way they stared at the world when they were sad or happy or simply asking for answers from an unseen force. She missed the colours of their hair and the tones of their skin, their heights, their chubbiness and their thinness, and the intensity of the bluish veins in their old hands, those powerful and mysterious body parts that had moved mountains and thrown love or hate to the world depending on the current of the wind.

Camila's family had tried many cures for her condition, ranging from horrendous exorcism sessions with the priest, to sessions with mediums, during which she would be held down naked on a cold bed of salt for hours, her mouth and nose often sealed off, making her almost die of suffocation. She would be brought into the churches, and the priests or the mediums would invoke countless liturgical orations, bathing her in blessed water and burning incense, to see if they could pull the evil out of her. But it was all to no avail, for she became worse with every session and would disappear for months, taking off with the Romani. Her husband, being the brute that he was, would accuse her of running away to be with other men and would spank her without mercy every time she came back. Little Arsénio, witnessing all this, tried to understand why his mother was the way she was and why his father was so mean. Because he was an only child, he had no support from any sibling, and the only friend he had was his cousin António, who, despite what many may think, was a very sensitive man. Arsénio's mother also sought treatment from local or distant reputed witch doctors who would boast about their capacity to cure the sickest person and exorcise the darkest of evils. Astrilda de Campanal, the most renowned witch doctor in the whole nation, was once brought to Vimieiro to diagnose and cure Arsénio's mother. Her diagnosis and treatment were as follows: "My dear Camila, I can see in you the spirit of your dead aunt Adosinda Raposo, who pretended to be a true Christian woman during all her life when in fact she was a *marrana*. In order to take her sinful and wretched spirit out of you, and in order for her to be absolved by Nosso Senhor Deus Todo Poderoso, Our Lord and Almighty God, and his son Jesus Christ, the true and only saviours, you need to say two hundred Ave Marias for her soul every day, for the rest of your life. If you do that, at the time of your death, your aunt will be saved and allowed into heaven to sit by the throne of God. If you start doing that tomorrow, you will be allowed to live in peace for the rest of your life, raise your son, and care for your husband as any other good woman does. If you miss any day of the praying or are not able to go through all the two hundred Ave Marias for any reason, your condition will return and, in order to regain what you lost and not upset the outcome, you will need to increase the number of Ave Marias by ten. One more thing: you need to always dress your son with his clothes inside out and put a clove of garlic in his pockets so that evil stays away from your house." Arsénio's mother tried to follow this daily ritual of praying, but it was very hard to keep up with it because she had many other duties and two hundred Ave Marias is indeed a lot. She would try to catch up at night after all was done, but by then she was often very tired and would often fall asleep before reaching the two hundred Ave Marias. She was always behind, so her condition never really improved and there was never an opportunity to see if the witch doctor's diagnosis had been accurate or if the proposed cure would have worked.

Arsénio had wanted to go to art school somewhere in another part of Europe, where life was gentler and where great masters had been born leaving behind illuminating wonders that remind us that this world, this world is nothing, nothing compared to what it could be, what we want it to be. He had dreamed about becoming a Leonardo da Vinci or a Rembrandt or a Jacques-Louis David. But his life had not permitted him to follow his call, and so he had to do and become what was necessary in order to survive and gain some respect, because, like his cousin, he was also poor and the son of the poor. He was poor and the son of the poor, and his father, a rude man with very bad manners who constantly beat him and his mother, could not understand the urgency of Arsénio's artistic call. Instead of going to an art school somewhere in Europe, Arsénio had to do all kinds of jobs—brutish, unbecoming assignments that were very unpleasant and that forced him to become a brute, for one often becomes what one does, especially if one does not keep continuous guard over one's deep self. When Arsénio realized that he could not go to art school and devote his life to painting and drawing, he became profoundly sad and indifferent to everything and everyone around him. The religious chants and the magnificent stained glass in the sublime cathedral of Queen Saint Isabel—including the images of the saints, the suffering, ecstatic Jesus Christ, and the Nativity scenes, many of which he had participated in as an angel and thoroughly enjoyed—had lost their incantation, their lustre, their power to bring happiness to his heart, give him any reason to think that life is beautiful, can be beautiful. The verbs *to be* and *to become* had been paralyzed, frozen in mid-air at a very high distance, unreachable. He was as sad as one can be; he saw nothing worth living for. He wanted to die so that he could be liberated from suffering, from living a life that had no meaning, no value. He wanted to return to a state in which *to be* and *to become* were the only verbs that he danced for, nourished, the only actions moving, propelling his limbs into the world. One day, when he was at his lowest, he went to the highest hill of Vimieiro with the intention of ending it all by jumping to his death. He had gone to the hill at midday in the summer, when it's so hot you can barely think, after he had witnessed his poor, deranged mother being brutally beaten by his father. He was sitting on top of the hill, thinking his last thoughts, still trying to find something that would make him change his mind. But nothing was coming, and he was ready to take the mortal somersault. At that precise moment, the point of no return, he felt a soft hand touch his shoulder and he saw his cousin António right there by his side, a sacred sentinel, guarding him, keeping him from taking the wrong step, bringing him back to life. He took his cousin's giving hand, and he trembled with both fear and relief, relief that there was someone there to rescue him when he needed it most and that that someone was his beloved cousin. In that moment, he knew that blood does indeed care. Blood does indeed speak. Blood does indeed move. They talked for a while, and Arsénio told António how he was feeling and what he was thinking about doing. Through a patience that only love and wisdom can engender, António walked him out of his miserable state of mind and made him see that salvation was still possible, that not all was lost. António told his cousin that a man had options and must exercise those options to escape desperation and failure so that the kingdom where we live can be regained and celebrated. Even though he was referring to Arsénio's state of mind, his life, and those of his father and mother—that sad and sorrowful family of three—it was as if he were already uttering another vision, articulating a vision about a country, a nation that he would later save from doom and destruction with an iron will never before seen. He spoke with passion and conviction, his face thoroughly engaged in this uplifting speech, as if he were rehearsing for another cause, an even greater cause that would come later when the situation demanded. It was this power of conviction, this quiet but sturdy belief that made him the man that he became and made the nation powerful and respected again.

"My dear cousin, think of the cool sunlight of the morning, how it kisses your cheeks and soul like a blessed branch of rosemary. Think of the beauty of your goats when you take them to the mountains. Think of how happy they are playing skipping games, up there in the high altitude, how alive they are, how in awe they are that they are allowed to go up there and stare at the world from afar. They can do this because you, you, my dear cousin, you love them dearly and gave them the freedom to go there by teaching them the way. My dear cousin, think about the splendour of the stained glass at church, our sublime cathedral. Think about the chant that you sing when you are there, the zone that you enter when you allow your limbs to fly with the Ave Marias or when you stare at the doings of Queen Saint Isabel. Think of the beauty of the crying Jesus, the fervency on his contorted face. Think of his life, how he gave it away as the most profound act of love, so that we could have less evil in the world and remember not to vacillate before challenge, before suffering, before need. Think about all of that. Think about all the light that comes from there, emanating from the deepest parts of the beautiful being, which we all possess in us. You can recreate this light when you paint and draw. Even if you can't go to art school and become a Rembrandt or a da Vinci, it does not matter. It does not matter at all because the light is in you, you are the light, and that light will shine anywhere to make the world a better place. Perhaps, my dear cousin, perhaps the solution would be for you to join me in the seminary, a place where we can pray and think, be taught and advance the soul. A place close to God, close to the blue azure that makes us melt into vast waves of never-ending magnetic pulses."

António was able to rescue his cousin from death. He gave him another chance by reminding him of the good things that were there for him, things that he needed to rediscover and embrace with both of his arms so that the light could again illuminate his darkness. After that encounter, up there on top of the highest hill of Vimieiro, where the two cousins had met many times before to share intimacies that only cousins and boys can share, Arsénio came home with a renewed vision of himself. He told his mother—who was experiencing an unusual clarity, peace of mind, and a sudden burst of physical energy, despite the heavy beating she had just endured by her vile husband—that he wanted to go to the seminary and join his cousin António. If he couldn't go to art school and be a famed painter, then he would create his own world of art. He saw himself immersed in an environment that allowed him to develop his soul and stare at religious art, and he imagined how happy he would be in such a world. His mind and body recalled that beautiful day, when he was seven years old, when Vimieiro was celebrating its patron saint, Queen Saint Isabel. He recalled the awe and the magic and the communion he felt with people, with God, with the world, and with the universe. He saw again, with the same radiant brightness as he had then, the queen feeding the hungry people during the great famine. He saw the bread that became roses and the roses that became bread or even gold. He saw her give her own jewellery away in handfuls of selflessness to buy wheat—wheat that would become bread, bread that would become body. That is how one is, becomes, truly beautiful, how the verbs *to be* and *to become* can finally be joined, finally sublimated, transfused, transmuted. He smelled the incense and he heard the Ave Marias and he felt the touch of the priest on his hand, and the light, the stunning light of that cathedral illuminating all his limbs, all his cells and then reaching the soul so that he could feel complete. He saw the red capes of the stewards and the pretty quilts smelling of naphthalene coming down from the windows, and he saw the women and the children throwing flowers down on the people. Petals of red and white roses flowed down in slow motion to gently land on his face and his head and his arms, inebriating him with their aroma. That day became fully alive, and he saw himself as a man of religion, a man immersed in God and with God. He saw himself as a priest who would build the most beautiful church ever seen, a place full of light, stained glass, and images of all the saints of the world, those beautiful souls who have performed miracle after miracle to bring the reign of heaven to earth and remind us that God lives in each of us. He would develop a global network of religious art dealers who would bring to him art from everywhere, art that had never been seen, never even thought possible to exist. If he could not make art, he would make his world into one of art and beauty, art and beauty only, and nothing more. If he could not make art, he would bring art to the people and show them that through art, God is made alive. He went on and on about his new plan, painting this future life to his mother with great detail and enthusiasm. She listened to him with her eyes wide open and a smile on her calm face, a face so often inhabited by various troubling shadows. He described the beautiful, magnanimous, and grand church— the magnificent cathedral that he had in mind to build—and he told his mother about how happy the parishioners in that church would be because they would feel at home, body and soul. They would be brothers and sisters, mothers and sons, fathers and daughters, all hugging, all chanting and rising to the stars to greet God, to find solace and redemption. He was in a blissful state of mind, one of those states that people suffering from bipolar disorder often experience after they come out of the deep-seated depression that has assaulted them for days and days, making them live in a dark, endless cave, where no glimmer of light ever enters and you feel trapped in the most unkind, wretched infinity—a well, a will or no return. At the end of his magnificent story, his mother, Camila das Dores, took him in her arms and rocked him as if he were still a little baby. Then she sang to him for a long, long time until he fell asleep:

Dorme, dorme, meu menino,
Sleep, sleep my little baby boy, sleep my little angel.

You are the salvation I have been waiting for, longing for
Sleep, sleep my little baby, sleep, sleep my little angel.
You are the son who will deliver my soul and that of my aunt
  Rosinda, opening for us the grand doors to the throne of God.
Dorme, dorme, meu menino,
Sleep, sleep my little baby boy ...

But the dream of becoming a priest and a religious art dealer could not be fulfilled either. When Arsénio told his father about this newfound wish of his, his father said that no son of his would become a priest because all priests were sissies, skirt kissers, hiding behind their golden capes. His father was a brutish, vile, and raw man; he was as cruel as they come, as if he were a mistake God made because He was distracted or tired or, worse yet, the pure unmediated creation of Satan. Arsénio's father was in the animal business: he raised sheep, goats, hens, pigs, and cattle. He also owned a slaughterhouse and a butcher's shop, and he forced Arsénio to work with him in this sordid and violent business, killing and selling animals. Because Arsénio raised the animals, he became very attached to them. Just like the Nubian master of the Romani circus, whom we will meet later, Arsénio came to have a profound connection with the animals. He would talk to them about all kinds of life matters, and he was sure they understood him and answered back. He spent many beautiful moments with these creatures. He played with the little lambs, kids, piglets, and calves. In the winter, he would bring them to the fireplace to warm them up, and he would feed them when their mother developed an udder infection and could not nourish them with her own milk. In the spring and summer, he would take the herd of goats and sheep to the mountains to graze on the grass and the fine herbs that grew abundantly there. He would spend entire days with the animals, observing them and noticing their growth. Sometimes he would stop the ferocious fights that would ensue during the mating season among the rams and billy goats who seemed confused about which female to mount—the goats or the sheep. And when it was time for the females to give birth, he became the midwife, easing the little ones in their passage through the birth canal so that they could enter this world more gently. He was fascinated by the love the mothers showed their newborns right from the beginning: licking them until they were clean, smelling them, and speaking to them in their tongues of love. Though he remembered that once he had a sheep that did not want to be a mother and kept rejecting her little lamb by charging at him and not allowing him to suckle on her nipples. He had to take matters into his own hands by separating the little one from the mother and feeding it with a bottle until it became independent and could feed on grass. A similar thing had happened with a female pig he once had which, after giving birth, started eating her own offspring, much to Arsénio's horror. He tried to stop the mother's attack on her own by using a long stick to get the piglets away from her, but his efforts did not work and he had to call his father, who took care of business by taking her outside and shooting her in cold blood with a single bullet in her forehead. He then did the same with the piglets that had been spared from the mother's cannibalistic hunger because he said that they were tainted with their mother's disease. When the animals were sufficiently grown or were getting old and could no longer reproduce enough to allow for profit, Arsénio's father would take them to the *matadouro*, the slaughterhouse. He would summon Arsénio to help and force him to watch the slaughter or, worse yet, to kill the innocent creatures himself. Arsénio would beg his father to please, please spare him from such work given that he had raised the animals himself and had fostered a very special relationship with them. The father would not listen to such nonsense, striking him on the face with a heavy blow and saying, "Are you a man or a fag? For the will that God instilled in me, I will make you a man!"

Arsénio had no choice but to take the knife and sink it deeply into the neck of the lamb or the kid goat or the cow or the pig or the hen and watch them leave life and enter death, their blood coming from every vein, every corner of their bodies, running down to fall into the bucket until it was full. During these ugly moments, Arsénio's hands would sometimes shake so much that the blade of the knife missed the mortal focal point and the animal would suffer more than it ought to, making Arsénio feel a horrible guilt. He looked at his hands tainted with the blood and life of the animals, and he felt that he was a criminal for whom the punishment of jail would not be sufficient. He thought that he too should die, that he too should be killed and die from this hideous bleeding death. He thought about cutting his own throat with the very knife he was using to sacrifice the animals so that he would no longer have to spend his life performing this evil act, killing those he had become very close to.

But his father was always watching like a sentinel of evil, and he had to do what he was told. In these last moments with the animals, Arsénio would speak to them in silence as he took their lives away, looking deeply into their eyes, asking for forgiveness, telling them through telepathic soul messages that he was very, very sorry, profoundly sorry, but that he had no choice because he was just a little boy under the command of his father's iron will. The shiny eyes of the animals stared at him from beginning to end, open throughout this entire carnage, remaining open even after they gave their last sigh. Then their back legs would kick the final kick, expelling the last ounce of their life blood into the bucket, making them inert matter ready to feed a hungry and wretched world. He would reach for the eyes of the animals and try to close them so that they would not stare at him in permanent accusation, but they would always open again, as if some part of the animal was still living and wanted to send a message. Then

Arsénio had to skin the animals, take out their entrails, and cut them into pieces that would be hung on the windows of his father's butcher shop. The poor villagers from Vimieiro and its surroundings would come and stare at the pieces of meat through the wide front glass window, imagining how they would taste roasted or in a good stew with garlic and potato and fresh parsley. Then Father would come out and shout at them, "Are you looking for something that you can afford? If not, get out of my sight. This is private property." They would leave but would come back when they could to continue staring at the hanging bloody pieces on full display. Sometimes, when all the meat was not sold and was about to go bad, Arsénio would try to convince his father to give away some of it to these people, but his father would not hear of it. He would retort, "You have no sense of business, you stupid boy. There are many like you in this country, and that's why we are in this deplorable state." He would burn the unsold product in an open fire outside his shop so that everyone could smell the roasted meat and remember that in order to be able to buy it, they needed to work very hard. Arsénio would try to skin and cut the animals as quickly as possible so that he could get rid of the staring eyes, which he would bury deep down in the ground behind his father's shop in an attempt to make them go away. But sometimes the eyes would come to him at night. He would have nightmares during which all he saw were eyes around him: open, shiny, and sometimes bloody ocular objects, moving in circles as if searching for something. He would feel he would never, never be forgiven and that he would surely go to hell when he died, where he would forever be assaulted by these wandering, moving, lost eyes that had no body to land upon. Sometimes, in his hurry to get rid of the staring eyes, he would not bury them deep enough and the dogs would get to them during the night, gorging on a macabre feast. One time, he was awakened by the loud barking of dogs in the middle of the night. Instinctively he knew that the dogs had found his burial site. He ran to the site and found a pack of dogs, twelve in total, engaged in a glutinous, uncanny ritual, voraciously eating the eyes of cows, pigs, hens, sheep, and goats. He screamed at the dogs, scaring them away with heavy stones and the hard blows of a sturdy stick. He then collected the remaining eyes, some of which were half eaten, and buried them very deeply as quickly as he could. Then he went to the river and took a bath in the cold water, in an attempt to cleanse himself and regain forgiveness for his sacrilege. He developed a profound aversion to meat and became a strict vegan. Even so, his father would sometimes force him to eat chunks of meat, which he would vomit straight away because his body, perhaps commanded by his soul, refused to be an assassin and a cannibal. It refused to eat the animals he had killed, which were like his own siblings and to whom he felt deeply attached. The day before the animals were to be taken to the slaughterhouse, Arsénio would spend a lot of time with them, talking to them, caressing and kissing them, saying his last goodbye. He would feel very lonely whenever the animals he had raised were taken away, but this was his profession: to raise animals and then kill them. And he raised and killed many.

His father had another side business that involved more cruelty to animals. On Sundays he held a cockfight tournament in the village with the rest of the villagers. His cocks would fight the others viciously until their feathers and eyes had all fallen off or been eaten and they became mere walking marionettes, awkwardly moving around the ring trying to escape the final blow of the kingpin. His father owned a particularly vicious cock, a small Indian rooster. It seemed to have little strength within it, but when in battle it would destroy all its opponents in an ingenious manner. This rooster had an infallible way of attacking the other cocks, which were always bigger than him: when they least expected it, the small rooster would fly up in the air and then land on top of its enemy with the force of a monster. The bigger cock had no chance. Because Arsénio's father always had the best and strongest cocks, he would win most of the time. He made lots of money from this cockfighting business since the losing teams had to pay in cash. The people of Vimieiro were hungry for distractions from their constantly harsh lives, and so they enjoyed the spectacle a great deal. No Sunday would go by without a good cockfight—even during Lent when one ought to stay away from excessive or unreasonable pleasures. Later on, as if dissatisfied with his own cruelty and hungry for more excitement in his life, Arsénio's father got involved in the bullfighting business and became a widely celebrated matador in the Iberian Peninsula and beyond. In 1928, when a national law was introduced that prohibited bulls from being killed in the arena, he defied it and organized secret spectacles where he continued to perform his deathly ritual, just like before. He ranted against the government officials, saying they had been neutered and no longer had balls and that the Lusitanian bullfighting was now child's play suited for pussies, not real men. "Real men are not afraid of the bull's horn. Real men teach the bull who the boss is by penetrating his spine and neck with pointed arrows inflicting the fatal blow," he would vociferate, his eyes wide open and his arm making the motion of death. There were always people who came to see him in action, just as they did before, not afraid of the consequences of disobeying the law—eager for the excitement that comes with cruelty when one's heart pounds uncontrollably with heavy fear in anticipation of the hour.

When Arsénio was about to turn seventeen—that benchmark age when he would become a man and emerge as his own human being, separate from his family—his mother stopped coming back. Two months had passed, the usual time that it would take for her to return, and she did not show up. And then the third month came and then the fourth and the fifth. Finally, on July 27, the day he turned seventeen, the news about Camila das Dores came, brought by the Romani who arrived in one of the largest caravans ever seen in Vimieiro. They were on their way to the south of Portugal to sell their products. Their business had expanded significantly, and they were now running a circus with all kinds of exotic animals to do the tricks that can make people laugh and marvel. There were lions of all sizes, birds of equatorial colours, elephants, panthers, cheetahs, snakes, and seven ballerinas. And there was a tall giraffe, with her otherworldly neck, that made Arsénio very uncomfortable. When she looked at him from such a great height, he saw himself as small and invisible, like an ant that could be smashed in a second. There was also a spectacular parrot that spoke fluent Punjab and Zulu. When it was angry, for whatever reason—and the reason could not always be understood—it would break into incomprehensible tongues that caused everyone, including the animals, to experience heavy migraines for days. The ballerinas would lose their balance, suddenly unable to execute their complex acrobatics; the master would lose his power over the animals; and the animals themselves would just lie on the floor. Not even the heavy kicks of the caretakers made them move— they would simply roll their eyes from side to side as if affected by some internal invisible disease that disturbed the functioning of their bodies and souls. Needless to say, this would cause the circus to underperform, and so it was no surprise that everyone tried to treat the temperamental parrot with the utmost respect and sensitivity. They always attended to his desires, even the most outlandish ones, like his frequent demand to sleep with one of the ballerinas, the beautiful Sophia Zarakoska. The master managing all the animals and birds was a tall Nubian the Romani had found in Spain. He had been left bleeding and nearly dead after a group of

Spanish fascists had attacked him viciously because they did not think he was in the right continent and ought to go back to where he came from. He had the capacity to make the animals execute the most unusual tricks, and he even taught them songs, which would alternate between beautiful classical music, heart-wrenching flamenco melodies, and even certain types of heavy rock melodies that seemed to have come before their time. He was the conductor of a never seen orchestra, a man capable of speaking to the animals in such a manner, that they would always respond to his commands and with a promptness and precision that made the notes come out perfectly in pitch and tempo—a hallowed, marvelling sound, entering the ears of a stunned and beatified audience.

None of the ballerinas looked like the Romani girls; they had blond hair, translucent white skin that made their veins visible to the eye, and green or blue irises—shades no one in the area had ever seen before. They looked like fragile, magic porcelain dolls—perfect for children to play with. The circus was an enchanting treat for the starved eyes of the villagers of Vimieiro, and they came to see the spectacles as often as their meagre *escudos* allowed. They marvelled at the magic displayed right there in front of their eyes, and for a moment they felt as if Jesus Christ through the will of His father had descended on earth again, dressed in another dress, singing another song, offering another kind of miracle. The children stood frozen in a daze when the ballerinas climbed on top of the giraffe, standing on one foot as the animal moved, noble and erect, like a dazzling princess of the universe or a powerful goddess uniting earth and sky. Some of them would scream, "I want the doll. Give me the doll. I want the doll. Give me the doll!," their eyes leaving their faces to follow the walking miracle.

On the third night of its stay in the village, the circus revealed something that no one had ever known existed—or at least, they had never been explained or shown its existence in that fashion before. The substance the Nubian master was about to expose had been always associated with the devil, his sins and dirty paws, his Hell or Purgatory, his inscrutable and dangerous night. The Nubian master, standing alone in the middle of the presenting platform—dressed in white, as he always was—brought out a black box from under his vest. He told the audience, in an accent of a man who speaks many languages, that the trick he was about to show them was in actuality not a trick but a very profound scientific fact that could explain the mysteries of the human brain and the space between bodies. He said it could satisfy the gurus of astronomy who had been trying to decipher the matter for a very long time without any success. "This box," he said, "contains black matter, the substance that is all around and in us, filling the vast space between stars and planets and commanding the cells and veins of our brains. No one has yet been able to see it and capture it—no one but me." He said he had discovered this universal axiomatic truth when he was travelling from Sudan to Andalusia on foot for twenty-four straight months, crossing deserts and mountains by night and sleeping by day so that he would not awaken the coast and border guards. The first time he was able to capture this evasive substance, which he had dreamed about countless times, he was in the desert, at the Egyptian and Libyan border. He had walked for a long time and had had a lot of difficulty distracting the guards on both sides of the border, who had been given very specific orders by their respective leaders that no intruders or disturbers of any order, much less Africans, should be allowed in or out of each nation. The borders had been closed so that the culture and tradition of each nation could be properly preserved. These leaders and many of their followers did not see themselves as African but rather Mediterranean or Arab when they looked into the narrow mirrors they had placed behind their front doors. After waiting for five days and five nights to leave Egypt and enter Libya, he finally managed to cross when the guards, tired of doing nothing and bored to the bone, decided to ignore their leaders and started playing a game of stones. The game consisted of throwing stones as far as possible into the desert, running to them, and bringing them back. This was not an easy exercise because the terrain was all sand, and, when thrown, the stone would sink deep into the sand. Not to mention there were other similar stones around, and knowing which one had been thrown was no task for the stupid. The team that managed to recover all or most of the thrown stones was the winning team. The prize was a bottle of a non-alcoholic and very refreshing beverage made of palm leaves. When the winning team was in a good mood, they would share the drink with the losing team and everyone would become equal. Sitting down by the palm tree, which was half on the Libyan side and half on the Egyptian side—because plants know no boundaries and need to access many soils to find water and minerals—the guards drunk together and forgot that they were from different countries. It turns out that on the sixth day, the guards of the winning team were in a good amicable mood and did just that: they shared the drink with the losing team under the palm tree. Everyone took off their uniforms and put down their arms, which were hard to carry under that blazing desert sun. They were fully naked and relaxed under the tree, and they seemed to have forgotten where they were and why they were there. The Nubian master, who had been spying on them for quite some time, noticed their tranquil mood and the sense of brotherhood between them. He observed them in their relaxed state and saw them naked and beautiful. They appeared as innocent children who had just been born and knew nothing about the names that different people go by, about which colours are considered good or bad, or about the many laws written in books—senseless, stubborn axioms that tell the world how to turn and forbid you from shaking hands with everyone. They were pure. They were in bliss. They were enchanting to watch. They were enchanted. In that moment of utter beauty, he saw floating between the whiteness and yellowness of their bodies and the endless Sahara, known as the Greatest Desert, bubbles of pure black matter, which then turned into lines and moved up and down, entering and leaving the bodies of the guards, the thousands of sand grains, the green leaves of the palm trees, the sleeping barracks, the demarcated line between Libya and Egypt, and even his own Black body. From his body, he also saw emerge Ramses the Great and other ancient pharaohs who had run away from Egyptian museums where they had been forced to wear golden masks. The pharaohs left him and walked freely through the desert, like dancing living mummies, finally liberated from their deadly condition and appearing in a vast array of shades from lighter to darker. Then, without any trace of fear— for he felt the world was all love—he walked openly to the guards, took off all his clothes, and sat among them. They welcomed him, gave him a glass of the cool palm tree drink, and asked, "Where have you been, brother? We have missed you immensely, so lost we have been in ourselves, blindly immersed in the paleness of our moonlight colour, suffocating in this endless yellow desert. Where have you been, brother? We have missed you." They all sat there and after some time all they could see around them, and flowing out of them, was the beautiful black bubbles and lines floating and dancing up and down, somersaulting like freed children playing games invented by God—the stunning games of heaven just so that the people of the world could marvel at the extraordinary. The white and beige colours that had dominated previously began to vanish, disappearing into thin air, and all they could see was the black matter executing its life, demonstrating its fundamental, everlasting, and ever-present existence. Then, before the end of this game or shamanistic trance, and just before the Nubian master sensed that the black matter was receding into the invisible realm, he got up and walked steadily into the Libyan desert. Then he moved through Tunisia and Algeria, reaching the Atlas Mountains in Morocco, where the valiant Berber warriors live. He sensed then that he would have to be careful with these people when crossing their lands; he knew they had little trust in invaders and that they have had to defend their territory from countless destructive assailants and settlers: Phoenicians, Greeks, Romans, Christians, Muslims, and many other vandals and barbarians. He wandered for seven days and seven nights in the frigid mountains. He encountered familiar animals in versions he had never quite seen before, as if the force that created the world wanted you to see yourself in others and at the same time remind you of your own difference: leopards, stags, elephants, macaques, lions, gazelles, aurochs, vipers, bald ibises, and dippers. At first, he felt afraid of them, but then he recognized that they were not very different from the many other animals he knew and had an intimate connection with. He had been born with the power to relate, on a very deep level, with animals. He did not know why he had been given such power, but he could always understand the thoughts and feelings of animals. They would come to him voluntarily, even when not called, as if they wanted to smell him or look into his eyes, and they would follow his command blindly whenever he gave one. There was no fear or distrust between him and the animals. So close was their link that the outside observer would think there was but one species in the world and that all its members got along with one another very well. The animals that he encountered in the Atlas Mountains guided his passage through the region, protecting him from the village warriors. When he was at the highest peak of the mountains, in Toubkal, an auroch—the very ancient animal that can seldom be seen by anyone or anywhere these days—came to him. The animal told him that if he closed his eyes and then opened them again, he would be able to see the amazing substance that floats through the universe and that is responsible for the equilibrium of all things. This material tones down colours that are too brilliant in order for us to be able to see the multiplicity that there is in the world.

"Without that colour," said the auroch, "we would be all blind and nothing would be differentiated. We would live in an amorphous world with no cedars and no wolves, without water, without spring. And the grey of our brain could not find its tone." Following the auroch's advice, the Nubian closed his eyes to the whiteness that was in front of him, for it was winter and the Atlas Mountains were covered with snow. He stayed like that for some time, and then, at the command of the auroch, he opened his eyes again. There it was in front of him. For the second time, he could see the stunning black matter dancing in circles, bubbles, and lines. It was going up and down, intermingling with the whiteness of the snow in a spectacle to die for. He could also see inside himself. He noted the intricate workings of his own brain: the atoms and molecules, the veins and the sub-veins, the circulating blood, and the black bubbles of the precious matter—all the fundamental elements that make us think and love and be wise.

After telling this story to the villagers of Vimieiro, the Nubian master then proceeded to distribute glasses to everyone and instructed the audience to put them on. This was the only way, he said, they would be able to see the black matter that was going to come out of his box once he opened it. He had invented these high-definition glasses himself, though he had received advice from many of the animals he had come across since the auroch had shown him how to see black matter on the top of the Atlas Mountains in Morocco. The glasses were made of uranium and mercury and had a thin layer of gold, the substance that permits the travelling of light. The villagers did as they were told, and when they all had the glasses on, the master gave a commanding whistle to signal that the moment was coming. Then he opened the box. At first, the audience saw in front of them a milky white vacuum that obscured their vision, but then they saw, slowly ascending from the magic box, spirals of black flowers. These were followed by or intermingled with black bubbles, inside of which were many black things unravelling slowly and steadily: corncobs and Pinto beans, rainbows, horses, Adam and Eve, the big apple, an oak tree, a kangaroo with a baby in its sac, a white frangipani, a rat and an ant, sardines and codfish, a cow and a mule, Galileo and Jesus Christ, Nabia and Apollo, a serpent and a comb, the sun and the moon, a hen and her egg, and many other things that they could not name or understand—perhaps because they belonged to faraway places and had never been seen in Vimieiro.

The last night the Romani stayed in Vimieiro, the circus put on another spectacle that was out of this world in beauty, in meaning, and in transcendence. The Nubian master came out dressed in his usual white silk vest. He looked stunning: tall, dark, with the unmistakable elegance of a real king. In his hand, he carried a long silver stick and a large circle, inside of which were many little circles. He stood still and silent in the middle of the podium, staring at nothing. Then suddenly he moved the smallest circle from inside the many others, taking it out of the intricate entanglement. This movement sounded like a faintly tolling bell. It sounded like it was coming to the audience from a faraway monastery or church somewhere, announcing the commencement of mass or simply reminding the villagers that it was time to stop working and devote themselves to prayer. But, in fact, this sound was calling the first animal to the podium. Out came the smallest lion, a white cub, agile and tiny. Moving with confidence, it jumped up and went through the small circle held perfectly still by the master. The circle did not move, nor did the master; the only movement was the one produced by the little lion's body as it entered the circle with a velocity of an arrow. When it came out on the other side, it landed on the ground steadily and with a calm kind of grace. After this first exercise, the other cubs, which gradually grew in size, came out to perform the same ritual as the master moved to the bigger circles to accommodate the size of each animal. As the circle became larger and larger, the sound produced by its movement also became louder and louder, as if the call to mass or prayer was no longer a distant one but rather something very present and urgent, directly addressing the audience. The last lion to come out was the mother lioness—a massive creature that roared like thunder, making the onlookers' entrails swell in fear. The Nubian master then played the same game with the cheetahs, the elephants, the giraffe, the panthers, the snakes, and the birds, all of which took turns jumping in and out of the circle. On a second round of tricks, the order of animals was changed: snakes, birds, elephants, giraffe, cheetahs, and panthers entered the circle in succession and amazing rapidity without creating any chaos. The master stood as immobile as before, efficiently switching the circles. Then he held his silver stick straight up, pointing to the sky, and the animals jumped onto its tip, each one remaining there for several minutes. The master still did not move; his face displayed no sign of distress, and his eyes were as serene as ever, even when he was holding the larger animals like the mother lioness or the elephant or the giraffe. The audience sighed in awe and screamed when they saw the giraffe standing very still on the tip of the silver stick, up high, high in the sky with her long neck stretching far into the horizon. It was breathtaking. It was nighttime, and the sky's azure expanse was scintillating with thousands of stars. It was extraordinary. It was dizzying. Then, as if this were not enough, all the animals jumped on top of the giraffe's head, one by one, building a spiral staircase that did not seem to end and went on and on *ad infinitum* to touch the wings of the stars. The seven ballerinas were the last ones to jump onto this heavenly ladder, and they were so high up that the audience could barely see them. Then, just as the ballerinas were rising farther up into the skies—carrying magic wands like true fairies of a true world—everything and everyone was brought down. One by one, the snakes, elephants, birds, cheetahs, lions, panthers, the giraffe, and ballerinas descended, falling down gracefully like trophies from the other world being offered to the peasants of Vimieiro. The villagers eagerly opened their arms to receive them so that they would not fall on the dry, hard earth and break their limbs. The result was that there were people and children hugging snakes, elephants, cheetahs, panthers, lions, the giraffe, and birds, and no one could tell where the animal began and the person ended. It was love and communion. It was lovely. It was delightful. It was beautiful. Then, in a final shower of beauty, butterflies began to descend, coming down from everywhere, mixing with the animals and the master and the people. The rain of wings was kissing everything and everyone, and everyone and everything felt like flying was all there was to do. There was, among all, the feeling that they were no longer citizens of the earth and had entered another zone—a realm of dancing and swimming where the weight of the body is no longer felt and the hunger of the soul no longer hurts. After the magic had passed, and everyone felt they were citizens of this world again, a fat, stocky man with a red face came to the centre of the podium and started laughing stridently, awakening in each person a visceral need to eat, drink, and copulate. His laughter reminding them of how alive their bodies were and the power they exerted over their lives. They started dancing and screaming, acting like true sons and daughters of Dionysius—eternal, content drunkards. Many pointed to the man and shouted from the depths of their lungs, "Zé Povinho, Zé Povinho!" When everyone was about to jump onto one another to satisfy the needs of their bodies, needs that had suddenly been awakened, the mood changed again. The fat, laughing man disappeared, and for a moment everything became dark, even the stars above seemed to have left the Milky Way to illuminate other galaxies. There was nothing now. Nothing. Only pitch and perfect darkness, a suspending blindness hanging over everything and everyone. Then, gradually, little candles start to appear, drops of light falling into the stark darkness and bringing with them the birth of the world. And then, before the audience knew it, there were circles and circles of candles, small circles inside bigger circles, so many of them, like round gardens of white flowers flickering through the night. As a final wondrous touch, the animals appeared again. Instinctively knowing its place, each animal entered its respective circle in an orderly fashion, one at a time, until all were there. Inside the big circle, the circle of circles, stood the master. He was immobile as he commanded this whole operation of blinding beauty. And then it was all over. Everyone clapped. Everyone cried and laughed out of pure emotion and love for the world. The chief of the band and the new circus—a tall, dark, and handsome man, with a long moustache and a severe look on his face—stood backstage and fondled the ends of his moustache, thinking about the magnificent beauty of his enterprise. He thought about how much it gave to people and how much it gave him both spiritually and materially. This business was good, the best he had ever invested in. The next day was a sad day. The caravan left, taking with it all the magic. The villagers returned to the reality of their harsh lives, some with tears still in their eyes, others with a longing on their faces that would not go away until the next season when the Romani would return, bringing with them the sacred creative seed that still pulsates in the world's womb.

This Romani band was the same that had taken Camila last time they had passed by. When they first arrived in Vimieiro,

Arsénio had run to them, eagerness and hope in his eyes, to see if he could spot his mother. But she was nowhere to be seen among the noisy convoy where people and animals, colours and instruments, and all kinds of other magic paraphernalia mixed up, creating a sense of disorder and chaos. The chief of the band told him and all the other villagers that Camila das Dores had been killed by a group of bad, greedy Romani she had run off with. They had been selling her to everyone willing to pay in Portugal, Spain, and well beyond. And indeed many would be willing to pay because the woman had an astounding capacity to make love with a man; she could make him feel the nectar of the bees and the feathers of God's birds all over his body. She had been buried high up the Pyrenees mountains and covered with layers and layers of snow in the hopes that her body would forever remain intact and that the whiteness and freshness of the snow would cleanse it from any dirt it may possess. When Arsénio heard this, he felt like his world had come to an end: no longer would he be able to hug his mother, to look into her eyes or to drink from her clean cup, the only cup that could make water taste like water. He went mad for several days, insisting that the Romani were liars and that his mother was still alive. He accused them of keeping her prisoner somewhere and exploiting her, and, as evidence, he pointed to the size of their convoy, the extra horses, the carts of merchandise, and the circus they were now running. He got into a physical fight with a group of boys in the band until the chief put an end to it and told him he had to find a way to become a man without his mother. Then Arsénio said he was going to the Pyrenees and that he would not rest until he could find his mother's body. He promised to bring her back and give her a proper burial in the cemetery of Vimieiro. Everyone tried to calm him down. They told him that going to the Pyrenees was an impossible task that would get him killed; they said the mountains were very high, the snow would engulf him in one single movement, and he would die a white, horrific, cold death before he could find his mother's body. He did not want to listen and took off on foot, determined to reach the faraway mountains that separate France from Spain. When he was in Salamanca, he was picked up by the Spanish police. Since he had no papers and was a minor, he was brought to Vilar Formoso, and the border authorities then drove him back to Vimieiro. When he came back his eyes were crazed and he was as thin as a eucalyptus tree. His cheeks had sunk into a defunctness that scared anyone who saw him, as if what they saw was no longer of this world. His father beat him and tied him up at home for several days to make him see reason, make him forget his dead mother. His father said she was just a whore anyway, always bringing shame and sorrow to the family. Just as Arsénio seemed to be getting more accustomed to the idea that his mother was gone forever, other news came that disturbed his fragile sense of peace, making him more distressed than ever. Malaquias Alcatraz, a Portuguese soldier who had fought at the Battle of La Lys in Flanders, came back to Vimieiro in 1918, just after the armistice was signed. He claimed that Camila das Dores was the most well-known prostitute at the camp of La Lys and had died of a venereal disease. She had been interred at a cemetery on the French side in Richebourg, amongst the many soldiers who had died in battle. Her grave was surrounded by white and blue tulips, and it had a stone with an engraving that read, *Here lies an unknown soldier—the one who fought the hardest battle.* Arsénio became angry again and attempted to fight Malaquias for spreading false rumours about his mother. He did not know if he should believe the Romani or Malaquias. He had recurring dreams about his mother. Sometimes in these dreams he would see himself climbing the Pyrenees for a long time, a circular time that seemed to have no end. And then he would see himself at the highest point of the mountain range, where he was sure his mother was buried. He would scratch the snow ferociously with his hands, like an angry dog looking for a buried meal, trying to uncover her body. Then he would fall into the hole he had managed to open and, breathless and gasping for air, he would watch the endless whiteness closing in on him until he stopped breathing and his heart stopped pounding. He would wake up exhausted, scared, confused, and feeling like he had died in his sleep and would never again be able to be a living being. Other times in these dreams, he would see himself running through Spain and then France, trying to reach Richebourg. Sometimes he would be stopped by the police in Spain or France and sent back to Portugal since he could not prove that he was a citizen of either country and all he could say when addressed was *Yo soy portugués* or *Je suis portugais*. But sometimes he managed to evade the sentinel of the police and reach his destination: the cemetery in Richebourg. He would go around and around trying to find his mother's grave, but it was an impossible task for all the graves appeared the same. They were all encircled with white and blue tulips, and the engraving on all the upright tombstone was exactly the same: *Here lies an unknown soldier—the one who fought the hardest battle*. It was as if the person who designed the cemetery was an architect of equality who wanted to emphasize the greatness of each soldier and, at the same time, annihilate selfishness and egoism. He would run around the cemetery in endless circles, feeling like he was in a labyrinth with no end and no beginning, trapped in a maze of flowers and engravings and tombstones that said nothing about his mother, that placed her in eternal anonymity and made him enter a state of profound melancholia. Still other times, he would dream that he was standing on top of the Pyrenees, and then, after meditating for a long time, he would see his beloved mother leave the belly of the mountains and ascend to heaven in slow motion, beautiful like never before, enveloped in a white cotton robe, whiter than any white he had ever seen. At that moment, he would extend his arm to reach her body so that he could say goodbye to her before she forever left to inhabit the skies, but as his finger gently touched her, her body would disintegrate and she would break into large fleecy snowflakes as if it had suddenly started to snow. As a last attempt to receive her, he would stand erect, his eyes closed, his face upwards, his arms fully extended, feeling her disintegrated body fall upon him like a mantle of soft wool, offering him a last warm moment to remember in eternity or winter's cold. For a brief moment, he would feel her gentleness on his face and all over his body—a sort of feathery embrace that reminded him of the goodnight kisses and hugs she gave him when he was a little boy just before he fell asleep, right after she finished telling him enchanting stories of faraway lands where the world is perfect and people are always happy. But then it was all over, and when he opened his eyes, all of her had already fallen on the mountain's mesa to become a nothingness that was indistinguishable from the rest of the whiteness covering the endless chain. He would feel cold to the core, falling on his knees, crying and sweeping the frigid floor with his entire body, trying to find trace of his mother: an arm, a single strand of hair, a cheek that he could put against his to feel her flesh one more time. But there was nothing; there was only a bare endless whiteness that annihilated every form or shape, killing every individual in existence and making the world dead. Sometimes he would also dream that he was watching the beautiful show put on by the Romani circus. In the dream, he would see his mother, real and intact, coming out of one giant black bubble. He would scream with joy and run to catch the bubble, but when he grabbed it everything disappeared. He would feel blind again, falling into a white milky nothingness, frantically trying to search for the magnifying glasses that had fallen out of his eyes. These dreams assaulted him for a long time, making him very tired and afraid to go sleep. He became more and more withdrawn and morose, his melancholia reaching unbearable heights. He was often alone and had that look of those who have lost something very dear to them, something that cannot be replaced with anything else. All these misadventures had made Arsénio into a very, very dark man, one who was capable of doing to others what life had done to him. It was as if he refused to live alone in his excruciating pain and needed some company to help him bear the heavy load.

There was also the affair of the priest, what he did to Arsénio for years and years. Slowly and gradually, the priest started touching his hand more and more, telling him during the secret and sacred moments of confession that he was the true son of God, a very special boy, and that was why he was so fond of him. He had been told by God that Arsénio ought to be treated in a very special way and needed a lot of guidance because of his bad father and gravely disturbed mother. God told him to become Arsénio's closest friend. And indeed Arsénio needed a very close friend, even more so when his cousin was away at the seminary, and so he believed the priest. They had long sessions alone, and the things that the priest asked Arsénio to do were many and very strange. He was just a boy, and he was lonely, and he believed in God, so he obeyed. Only when he became older, did he understand that what the priest had asked of him was not saintly, was not good, was not pure. He kept the sordid secret within himself and did not even divulge it to his cousin, his best friend who knew almost everything about him. When his cousin became the head of state, Arsénio was sent to Tarrafal to be the chief of the prison. The communist dissidents from the metropolis were kept there, as well as, later on, the guerrilla fighters of the colonies like Francisco Magno Motumba. In Tarrafal, Arsénio regained some self-respect. He felt like he was a man of power, and he made sure that no one would ever step on him again: not his father, not the priest, not the boys in school who called him names. But today he felt a sense of profound helplessness come upon him, rising from the depths of his being, making him feel alone, scared, incapable. He felt that nothing he had devoted his life to was really worthwhile, for all he had ever wanted was to be a painter, a fine artist who could capture the beauty of life. He wanted to capture the subtleties that live under the visible spheres, which only especially wise human beings can see. Because Arsénio could not be an artist, he had had to find a way to keep some sanity in the midst of the horrible work his father forced him to do or when he himself was doing something horrible. Whenever he could, he would try to paint one thing or another. As an attempt to capture the soul and body of his mother, he frequently painted portraits of her. This exercise gave him some solace, and when he was immersed in this endeavour, he would feel very close to his mother, as if they were together again, just like when she carried him in her womb or when she returned from her stays with the Romani to take care of him and love him, very, very much. As he grew older, the portraits of his mother became insufficient for his all-consuming hunger and the profound yearning he had for her inside him. He started to make life-sized dolls of her with rubber and plastic. His room in Tarrafal was full of these portraits and dolls, all trying to capture his mother's essence and bring her back so that he could go on with his life. And when things were bad and he could not get the secrets out of the prisoners with the portraits of Rembrandt, he would close himself in his room for an intimate tête-à-tête with his mother, as if there was a connection between the mystery of her disappearance and the activities of the guerrilla fighters who were working hard to destroy the great empire. He would stare with intensity and melancholia at his mother's lookalikes, trying to solve the mysteries that had affected and were affecting his life. He spoke to her in tender and supplicatory tones, trying to awaken her from dormancy. He touched the different versions of her face on all the portraits, looking into her eyes, asking for answers, asking for love, asking for something that he could not quite name but that he desperately needed to save both himself and the great nation. He spent hours alone with the likenesses of his mother, talking, observing, caressing, and supplicating. But it was all to no avail because the effigies did not reveal any secrets. They stood mute on the walls, or sitting on the chairs, like beautiful but blind mercies that could not be awakened by the needs of anyone, those cavernous endless empty spaces that lie deep within each of us. Today, after his disappointing sessions with Francisco, Arsénio followed all these rituals, observing, supplicating, and asking for guidance from the effigies. As usual, nothing of substance came and all he could see were shadows: shadows on their hair, shadows on their dark eyes, shadows on their limbs, shadows on their wombs. They were mere lifeless dolls, mirages of something that once was. Then, sipping on a glass bottle of Coca-Cola, his favourite drink, second only to the sour green wine from Vimieiro, Arsénio reread the letter he had recently received from his cousin urging him to act. He tried to summon some hope and regain strength for the hard-core punishment that he needed to inflict upon Francisco the next day. He summoned hope that Francisco's secret would be divulged and the empire would be saved from the communists, or whomever was after it with greedy eyes and dog's teeth, just like what had happened many, many years ago when he had to use one of his most efficient methods on Miguel Cunhal, the cocky communist leader who thought he could escape his hands. And to reassure himself that he could deal with Motumba the next day as he'd dealt with Cunhal many years ago, he reread that letter that his cousin had sent him then, also urging him, begging him to act, to save the empire.

My Dearest Cousin Arsénio,
It is with love and tenderness that I write you this letter. And

it is also with a great urgency that I come to tell of the things that are happening here in the metropolis, things that make me fear that our great nation has reached the brink of doom. There are many people who want to destroy us, and I am even afraid of those who claim to be our friends, like the Americans and the British. It seems to me that everyone is looking after their own interests. They want the base in the Azores to attack the Axis. They also want to stop our trade with the Germans, a trade that we need very much for fuel. We sell the Germans wolfram, and they give us coal; as much as I want to stay neutral in this ugly war and avoid the massacre of my brothers and sisters, I still have to run my country and save my empire. I never forget that I have to work very hard because I am poor and the son of the poor. I am being pulled from everywhere and by many—and with strings of many kinds. I even fear the Allies' connection with the communists, those red devils who are infiltrating our provinces in Africa, bringing arms and irrational ideas to our darker brothers and sisters. I feel pulled in too many directions, all at once. I am never certain of the nature of the wind pulling me, but I do know that we do not have much time to save the nation from all of those who have an eye on it, on us. The Americans even want to bring Coca-Cola into our nation to spoil our serenity and make us drunkards of modernity. Can you believe that? I want to preserve the bittersweet taste of our Vimieiro wine. I want to keep my garden with its beautiful wild flowers and the naked granite rocks that served as our seat in our childhood, when we conversed like true brothers and made plans for the future. The other day I received a letter from an American impresario asking permission to introduce the drink into our nation. He sent me a sample in a nice glass bottle that had the shape of a woman's body and wrote, This drink, sir, is the drink of the future of all nations: cool, brown, and with a zesty taste. This drink, sir, is the best invention since the invention of electricity, and it will make many countries rich. *I tasted it, and I could not stand its sweet, biting, gassy feel on my gustative glands. I spit it out right away on the floor of my office. This is how I replied to the ignorant and audacious impresario:* Dear Mr. Anderson, you do not understand my nation, nor do you understand my own temperament. You should know that, above all, I detest modernism and its avant-garde daughter, Damsel Efficiency, with whom you Americans are so in love. I tremble with fear and raging disgust at the idea that your large, loud, clumsy, and unattractive trucks would invade, at high velocity, our old cities, changing, as they pass, the sacred rhythm of our secular habits. We have a long history, sir, a very long history—a history of commanders-in-chief and discoverers. As long as I live, sir, I will not allow your second-rate mass-produced junk into my nation—as a long as I live, sir. *But the other day, I had a gentle visitor from America. A certain rabbi, by the name of Solomon Lapin, dropped by to thank me and my people for the help that we have provided to the Jews by making Lisbon a city that welcomes them, a place where they can safely live or just pass through en route to the Americas. He took my hand and thanked me profusely, calling me his brother. At that point I could not help myself. I pulled up my sleeve and said, "Rabbi Solomon Lapin, see these veins? Here runs real Jewish blood from my great-great-great-grandmother Catarina de Coimbra!" We looked at each other with tears in our eyes, and we hugged in a tight embrace, staying intertwined for a long while, mourning the ashes of the brothers and sisters annihilated by that damned Hitler. And then, dear cousin, that night I had the most frightening dream. I dreamed that I was in Hitler and that Hitler was in me—and I felt like I was killing myself over and over again. In the dream, I saw mountains of gold in front of a concentration camp. When I looked more carefully, I saw, mixed with the glittering gold, thousands and thousands of Jewish (and other undesirables like the Romani) bodies, men and women, little boys and girls, with their thin twisted legs, skeletal bodies, dwindling away into a desecrated nothingness. And then I saw myself rummaging through the piles of people and gold, stealing the gold away, filling my pockets and all the bags I had with me. There were sacks and sacks full of that glittering substance all around me, all mine, intoxicating me with an ugly blindness. As I removed the gold, the mountains of skeletal people became ashes: ashes upon ashes upon ashes. I was in a barren land. I had never seen anything like it before—it was burned to the core and could never again produce crops to feed anyone. When I looked again at the mountain of ashes, I saw in the middle of it, trying to stay adrift amidst that hideous nothingness of grey, my great-great-great-grandmother, Catarina de Coimbra, screaming at me, pointing her finger and saying, "You savage soul, you, body of my body, blood of my blood, you are nothing but greed, nothing but greed—rapacious of the rapacious. Let it go. Let the gold go. Let the nations become. Let the Jews find their true place. Let it be. Let all of them be. Do not send boys down to Africa to steal the gold and the yams from the people. Do not sell wolfram to Germania—the Germans are depraved to the core. Do not kill the blood of your blood. Do not eat the carcass of your own soul. Be who you are. You are poor and the son of the poor." As she screamed these insults in a passionate and raging outburst, she pointed to a burning cross on the side, and I saw myself inflamed and disappearing into a vacuum of ashes. As you know, I am a fairly rational man, but that dream has stayed with me. I have not had a single good night sleep since then, and just yesterday I called Joachim Bienbach, the German impresario, and told him that no more Portuguese wolfram will be sold to Germania. I told him that the mines are running out of the mineral, and furthermore that I have family members who work in those mines in Loumão and Carvalhal do Estanho, just around the corner of Vimieiro, in conditions that are deplorable, and I don't want them to die of intoxication and cancer or be buried alive under the earth, like many others have. He did not receive the news well and tried to persuade me to continue the exploration and export of the mineral. He even promised to improve the working conditions of the miners and double the buying price. I replied that I had made up my mind and that certain things cannot be bought with money or gold. He argued more and more, presenting rhetorical stratagems that I could not buy into. Finally, I had to put a firm end to the conversation by saying I am still the leader of my nation, and that, as such, I have the right to decline certain business endeavours that I see as damaging to my welfare and that of my people. And furthermore, I said my nation is neutral regarding this war and that therefore I have the absolute responsibility to do what is expected. He hung up the phone and said rudely, "Jude, der Hurensohn!"*

The very next day I received a very warm letter from Franklin Roosevelt: Dear friend, I write to tell you that I am very happy with your recent decision to rescind your commercial contracts with Germania in respect to the wolfram affair. I want to assure you, once more, that in the opinion of the government of the United States, the continued exercise of unimpaired and sovereign jurisdiction by the government of Portugal over the territory of continental Portugal, the Azores, and all its African colonies, offers complete assurance of security to the Western Hemisphere, and that we stand firmly with you. It is, consequently, the desire of the United States that there be no infringement on the Portuguese sovereign control over those aforementioned territories. We are ready to offer our multifaceted support in that regard, should the need arise. *And then I got a letter from Winston Churchill echoing the same sentiments. It was as if they had had a chat about the matter the night before to discuss how the letter should be worded. Still, my dear cousin, I have a lot of doubts and fears. I fear that the Allies are getting too close to the communists—these are the real devils creating havoc in our great overseas empire, as you well know. I fear, dear cousin, that times are changing and I do not know whom to trust any longer. I urge you, dear cousin—for we do not have much time and the hour has come—to do whatever it takes to save our nation and make our brave ancestors proud. I am counting on you, dear cousin, and the miracle that you can produce to stop our doom. And you know what the reward is. You know what your reward is.*

On another note, I want to tell you that I am a man in love. I am falling in love with Marianinha, but Godmother noticed it and reminded me: "António, do not forget your crocks." See, dear cousin, ours is a very sad country where people always remind you where you came from. It is as if we are doomed to determinism, falling straight into Darwin's fatalisms. That is why, dear cousin, we must work very hard to prove them wrong, we must work very hard to keep the empire. We will show them, all of them, who has the power and who does not and how power is attained and kept. We are the sons of the poor, but we do not have to be poor like Godmother says. I am telling you, dear cousin, that we do not have much time. The time has come to do whatever it takes to save our nation and make our brave ancestors proud. I urge you, cousin. I still go to Vimieiro frequently even though it's far from the capital and the roads to get there are bad. I go to our garden there, and I sit on the granite stones, where we sat together so many times. I can never forget that land, those people, my mother, my father, how hard they worked to make me into what I am today (even though Godmother always says that if it weren't for her, I would always be a Zé Povinho, a simpleton from Beira Alta). I must go now, dear cousin, for duty is calling me, but I am telling you, we do not have much time and the time has come to do whatever it takes to save our nation and make our brave ancestors proud. I urge you to do this, and I know you will not disappoint. I have all my faith in you.

With love and tenderness,
Your cousin, António

TRUTH OR DARE. As time passed inside Tarrafal, and as each day did not bring to Arsénio what he was looking for, his methods became graver, more inhumane—his punishments revealing the wickedness of the human spirit, the suffering that it must have had to endure to come to such extreme of evil execution. The compound doctor visited the chief's chamber frequently, often only to use his stethoscope to see if he could detect a heartbeat in the victim, who was invariably lying immobile on the floor after enduring Arsénio's physical punishment or severe psychological coercion. Or he would come to stop a bleeding vein, to attempt to save an eye, or to give a dose of Haldol to someone who could no longer withstand the mind games and had finally fallen into a dark well, howling unstoppably to the moon or to the scalding sun or ravaging his own body like a truly mad person. The doctor was a nice man from Lisbon from a wealthy upper-class family, a man used to the nice advantages that status can bring. He later became an acclaimed writer, unveiling in his sombre, existential, and psychotic pages some of the most atrocious miseries of the human soul, his books acting as mirrors of what we can become when possessed by the unmeasured corruption that power brings, or when abused by that power. They revealed that no matter what side one is on, one is always a victim, a victim to the fallibility and shortcomings of human nature. These were powerful books, treatises, which can hopefully teach some of us to see what we could become, to not repeat history. In his book, *The Asses of Men*, which has received high acclaim recently in Israel, he recounted tales of the horrors that he witnessed in Tarrafal. He described monstrosities that were comparable to those inflicted upon the Jews in Germany or Poland, and later on many others in Rwanda, or Syria, or Libya, or Afghanistan—that land of rugged mountains and very old customs where women still cannot learn the alphabet, cannot learn a truly beautiful lullaby to sing to their daughters just before they fall asleep. The Israeli literary judges described his writing as *That magic sorrowful voice that touches us in the deepest part of ourselves and makes us want to become better. It is a universal voice that makes humans from all walks of life stop and consider their doings, whether these doings are doing something or simply undoing the human race. This man is brilliant. Deep. A voice to be cherished. A bible for our times.* The doctor had reddish hair and freckles. In Tarrafal, he had to be both a surgeon and a psychiatrist, though he was trained as a psychiatrist and was therefore more familiar with the pains of the mind than the bloody lacerations of the body. He was not there because he wanted to be there, and he was not there because he was a friend of the regime. He was there because he was sent as a military doctor, like many others were sent as soldiers to fight and kill. He had no choice. He had a long name—Carlos Cabral Abreu Abrantes Antunes Montealva—a very long name that indicated the endless line of influential people from whom he'd descended. But he disliked being called all of those names. He even disliked being called doctor and insisted that people, all people, whether chiefs or prisoners, peasants or urbanites, call him Carlos. Despite the fact that he came from a wealthy family with royal-like dwellings and grew up in a beautiful vast mansion that looked like a medieval castle in the green region of Sintra, on the outskirts of Lisbon, being attended to by maids from Beira Alta or Trás-os-Montes, he had always felt a deep sympathy towards the oppressed, the underdog, the one who does not have luck on her side. He had always been very respectful towards the young maids he grew up with, treating them with dignity and never groping their behinds, or worse, forcing them into a corner of the house to ask for something very dear to them, which they wanted to give only to those they loved, at the right time, like their mothers had taught them to do. This was something that his father had done quite frequently and it had made Carlos deeply despise him, ever since he'd become aware of it at the tender age of four. Since then, whenever he thought of his father he saw an ugly, fat, well-cared-for pig, dressed in an expensive black silk suit with a white red-dotted bowtie around his short flabby neck. This image always came accompanied by a scary mocking voice that said, very loudly, like a bell that did not wish to go unnoticed, "Throwing pearls to the pigs." The image and the voice came to him often, even in his dreams. Whenever that happened, his body experienced a deep-seated nausea, and he had to run to the bathroom to vomit whatever was inside him. He made all efforts to keep the image and the voice buried inside him, but his mind kept calling it to the surface and putting it right in front of him—like a revolving, revolting mirror, its reflections ugly and unstoppable. He became obsessed with the image and the mocking voice, and as a way to try to tame them, he had decided at a very young age to become a psychiatrist. He wanted to understand. He now understood that the image and the voice were his consciousness telling him he could not be like his father, that he had to aim to become a better man. At the early stages though, when the image and the voice started to come to him, his family had thought he suffered from schizophrenia like a great-great grandfather on the mother's side. They had taken him to a psychiatrist. But the psychiatrist did not believe in genetic fatalisms and had basically said the boy was too lonely and that, as a result, he was imagining things that did not exist to have some company. Carlos's mother had asked, "But doctor, if that's the case, wouldn't he imagine little boys and girls of his age—nice, friendly creatures that he could play and be happy with—rather than an ugly pig with a bowtie and a scary mocking voice?" The doctor replied that the mind of a child is not yet sophisticated enough to discern between benign images and malignant ones and that it just picks random things from here and there. Still, Carlos's mother could not quite understand where he had picked up such things—she did not remember ever having read him a story of a pig in a bowtie. The psychiatrist advised the parents to have a few more children to keep the boy company, and so they did. They had four more boys and two more girls in the hopes that Carlos's visions would go away. But the arrival of siblings did not help, and after a while his parents gave up. Carlos also disliked his mother profoundly, for she knew that her husband was abusing the maids and did not do anything to stop it. She did not even confront him about it. She just acted like a nice upper-class lady who knew her station very well and was quite aware that maids were what they were: maids for all services. He tried to be all that his parents were not, and he had treated all the maids with the utmost respect and distinction. He had insisted they call him by his first name, Carlos—just that, simple, direct, human, and right—instead of Menino Carlos, as was customary in the deferential context of maid and master. This was quite ironic if one really thinks about it, for being called Menino forever could be taken as a sign that one has never managed to reach full adulthood, forever stuck in a stage of arrested development. Carlos often leaves the chief's chamber in a dark mood, murmuring the same words over and over again: "I am not here to cure the sick. I am here only to sign death certificates. Those who come here come to die. I am not here to cure the sick. I am here only to sign death certificates."

"My dear friend Francisco Magno Motumba, you have been playing mind games with me, and you have not yet revealed anything of substance that you ought to reveal about yourself or about the activities of your comrades. Now the game will be taken to the next level. You ain't seen nothing yet, ain't seen nothing yet, my friend. Now it is really going to be truth or dare, truth or dare." This was Arsénio's prelude to the next round of punishments. This round was going to be based on what Arsénio understood about behaviour modification from reading Pavlov, Skinner, Watson, and others. He had taken Watson's position and beliefs to the letter, and he was firmly convinced that he could, in his chamber, make anyone become what he wanted them to become. He kept Watson's famous quotation posted in big red letters on the chamber's wall so that he would not forget what he was there to do, and so that the prisoners would also become intimidated. He wanted them to see that statement constantly staring at them, reminding them that their beautiful idea, the one they had nourished since their birth and the one they likely were born with, was nothing when compared to the reality of the idea that had brought them to that place. But Francisco was a sophisticated, patient, and learned man, and when Arsénio used his methods on him in an attempt to modify his behaviour—to make him forget his beautiful idea, to brainwash him into accepting his ideologies, and to divulge his secret—he would not give in. Francisco was sure of himself. His resistance was unbending and his will unyielding. He had trained his mind to read Watson's quotation, which stared at him in big red capital letters on the wall, as follows: *Give me a world that is healthy, where men and women, Blacks and whites, yellows and browns can become lawyers, doctors, artists, merchant-chiefs, and yes, even presidents. Yes, we can.* Instead of what it actually said: *Give me a dozen healthy infants, well-formed, and my own specified world to bring them up in and I'll guarantee to take any one at random and train him to become any type of specialist I might select— doctor, lawyer, artist, merchant-chief, and yes, even beggar-man and thief, regardless of his talents, penchants, tendencies, abilities, vocations, and race of his ancestors.* When using the freezing method, Arsénio tried positive reinforcement: Francisco, who had been standing in the same position for three hours, was allowed to sit for ten minutes whenever he gave a response that seemed truthful to Arsénio, or at least the prelude to something big—the white whale Arsénio was after. Of course Francisco was just buying time and finding a way to rest his body for a few minutes. He was a man of letters, and he knew how to speak words that seemed to say something when in fact they said nothing, had no palpable substance. As the session resumed, Arsénio would quickly find out that he had been tricked, for Francisco's previous promise or the hint of a promise would not materialize into anything. At this point, his techniques would intensify, becoming at times seemingly sloppy or dispossessed of much logic, and he would apply negative or positive punishment alternatively or indiscriminately. He would inflict on Francisco's body electric shock after electric shock, deprive him of sleep for three days in a row, not allow him to eat for four days, and so on and so forth. During these sessions, Francisco would enter a state of semi-consciousness but would still maintain alive his idea, often mumbling it in a songlike fashion like someone who was dreaming or sleepwalking: "Give me a world that is healthy, where men and women, Blacks and whites, yellows and browns can become lawyers, doctors, artists, merchant-chiefs, and yes, even presidents. Yes, we can." He would mumble it in Shangaan and sometimes in Maconde, so that Arsénio and his assistants would not know what he was saying. They would just think he was delirious or that he was invoking some black magic that would not be of any help when compared to their scientific methods, which were founded on reason and logic. But they were wrong, for this invocation that Francisco repeated over and over again in his worst moments was what gave him strength, strength to continue. It was a mantra that allowed him to meditate and enter transcendence, to leave his body and dwell in the magnificent zone of love, where one is all and all is one, where the eye that sees is vast, spreading like sun rays on a stunning spring day. He could see the frangipani tree in its glorious blooming state, advancing in assurance and unparalleled beauty through the wide African savannahs, giving shelter to the living and to the dead.

In yet another attempt to make Francisco lose the idea that he carried deep within himself, to make him give up his secret, Arsénio forced Francisco to take potent magic mushrooms, which he had obtained through the same friend from Brazil who'd given him the crocodile belt. In that country, these fungi grew naturally and were often used by Indigenous people in ritualistic religious ceremonies to communicate with the vast cosmos and experience love in all forms. Arsénio believed that psilocybin, the magic ingredient in these mushrooms, would force Francisco to become less of himself and enter the vast nothingness, and that at this point Arsénio would be able to extract what he wanted, or better yet, to train Francisco to become someone else, something else. Arsénio thought that after having experienced the greatness of selfhood, Francisco would surely not want to return to the smallness of his African self.

Of course Arsénio had little knowledge of what it meant to be African, and he was not aware that Francisco had participated in many religious ceremonies in Mozambique at which he had taken similar drugs. Those trips had allowed him to meet his ancestors and all there was in this universe, and he had always come back safe and sound, integral in his person, because he had been trained well by the elders, who knew how to encounter greatness and still be able to remain in themselves and with themselves. Moreover, Francisco had experienced the distended ego in many other ways: when making love with Ana, or Sarif, or that Russian splendid woman whose eyes were as green as the rich moist fields of May in the northern hemisphere; or when listening to Bach's Cantata No. 202; or when writing a poem in which words became things that he could eat and smell and touch; or simply when walking outside under the dark night when he and the stars joined together in a feast of oneness and his heart beat in unison with the skies. So when Arsénio gave him the potent fungi, Francisco started to experience what he had already experienced many times. His mind knew what was happening, having already travelled to that land—and through much better routes. There was that deep voice down there that was well aware of what was sacred to him, and that voice was stronger than the venom with which Arsénio was trying to poison him. That voice was more than the voice of reason—it was the voice of the soul. It kept telling him that this moment—this moment he was in after having ingested the mushrooms given to him by Arsénio—was not a real one, not the real one. It was not the genuine *sunyata* of the great we, of the nothingness, of the handsome void. This moment was not a moment to experience real merging with the cosmos, like he had when he had participated in the rituals with his people. This was not the moment to speak with the ancestors who lived below the frangipani tree, that bride of the beautiful country by the Indian sea. This moment was not the moment to get lost in the emerald eyes of the Russian woman and become the grass of May. This moment was just an illusion; it was not a real translucent pearl. As he expected, first he felt happy, euphoric, and light. Then he saw the colours of Watson's quotation on the wall more intensely than he had before: they became bleeding diamonds or sometimes rising or setting suns. Then Bach's music, which he always kept in a corner of his mind, became louder and louder, and he no longer heard or saw anything else. He could not hear the questions Arsénio was asking him, even though his jailor was trying to pose them in different ways to see if Francisco would get distracted and let himself go. But Francisco was immersed in the protective mantle of his soul, that magnanimous sheet that served as the filter to keep out all the intrusions, all the weapons of a dirty war.

If anything, this trip made him feel more, sense more, think more. It made him see how his brain was wired and what nerves were responsible for the protection of the idea. It was as if he could see, right in front of him, his own brain, his own grey matter fully exposed right there on top of the table. Looking at it, he was able to understand the complexity of his own mental processes, like a transcendental scientist performing a thorough autopsy on himself. He stared at the left and right sides of his brain, analyzing that magnificent grey mass full of intricate neurons and little veins that connect to the rest of his being and make him walk. He started to see vividly, like never before, how he came to nourish his idea so dearly and how he came to accept that he may have to suffer a lot before he could see that very idea dance in front of him—the verbs *to be* and *to become* joined, happy to be brothers, happy to be sisters, siblings carrying the same genetic code, able to generate new life and never, never let the world die. He recalled, with the arresting sharpness and presence of today and now, that day when his father had abused the men working in the sugar fields, chaining them together and not giving them bread or water for hours on end. The bread and water that—in the old days, before the gluttony of empire took over—they had been able to gather from their fields, where they had cultivated the variety of crops they needed to feed themselves and their families. He saw and felt and tasted the painful movements of their bodies and the lack of light in their eyes. He tasted and swallowed the fear that he had felt when his father left him outside, attached to the frangipani, when he had spent the whole night alone. He smelled the lions and the hyenas as they roamed around, very close to his tiny body, trying to take a bite out of him. And he saw, with his hands and feet and eyes, how the elders had come from under the frangipani to scare the predators away and spare his life. He felt the iron slap on the face he had received when he had entered a bar in Maputo with Ana—years ago, when they were first dating—and he tasted the blood that he had had on his hands after he gave the abuser a good beating. A blood that was sour, a lifeless liquid smelling like old, moldy. He saw and tasted all the other things that he had experienced and eaten throughout all his life, in an unprecedented fashion and with a great degree of intensity. All this encouraged him to fight harder and harder for his idea, to keep it down there, guarded and sealed from the mean world at seven keys, until the world came to a point where he could let it out to walk freely in the fields of the African savannah, the fields of the entire world, like a circle of fire or a dancing wild horse. He saw with distinctiveness the nerves that are responsible for his emotions and the ones that made him compose and write beautiful classical poetry. He saw and touched the rational part of his brain that controlled the tears and the dishevelling of the self. He felt its coldness; he saw how he could use that part to compartmentalize—like many Europeans like to believe they can do, thinking they are superior because of that very capability—and he acknowledged that that part is necessary sometimes, like in that precise moment when he was trying to protect his secret and his idea. He also saw that that very part is often misused and abused, that it produces technology and ways of seeing and being and feeling that only serve to kill the innocent and annihilate the fullness of life. And then, right after, he saw Picasso's sombre painting like he had never seen it before or would ever be able to see it again, even when he stood right in front of the original at the Museo Reina Sofía in Madrid years later. He saw its magnitude taking over the entire chamber, taking over himself. He put himself right inside the dark canvas. He saw the brutality of the painting like never before—everything was in disarray, everything broken down, men and women, bulls and horses mingling, disoriented, inside a closed claustrophobic room. They were trying to reach for the candle—that old gentle light that brings so much warmth to the heart and the tired limbs and helps us to have a magic sleep. And then, above the claustrophobic room, he saw, suspended and smiling, Franco, Hitler, and Salazar, arm in arm, like comrades of the same creed. As he looked at the other part of the brain, *Guernica*'s scene became inverted: now he could see the threesome of Franco, Hitler, and Salazar inside the claustrophobic room, cowering in terror and covering their heads with their hands to shield themselves from the meteor shower that kept on falling. They looked small, scared, and very human. And the others, men and beasts, women and children—the ones who had been kept inside the claustrophobic room in the other part of the brain—were now flying around the room, roaming the sky. They were frantically trying to stop the meteor shower from falling on their fellow beings who were still stuck in their own rooms, their own houses all over Spain. After this extraordinary trip inside and outside Picasso's painting, Francisco looked at Rembrandt's *Head of Christ* and saw himself as Jesus Christ inside the painting, as if he had gone on another trip. It was as if he had become God or allowed God to enter himself, like he had learned to do in the ceremonies with his people. He felt Jesus Christ in him, and through Jesus he felt his father, and through his father he felt the entire world weighing upon his being. He felt the cows and the zebras, the elephants and the snakes. He felt the large empty savannahs of Africa and the mountain chains of the Northern Hemisphere. He entered those very different spaces in slow, rhythmic movements like a man who can fly or like a bird who is also a man. He tasted the spring berries and the figs of August and the cassava and the mangos and the refreshing watermelon and the chicken soup for the soul. He shivered in the cold Russian winter, and his body expanded in the heat of Mozambique. He sensed the peace of the night and the tiredness of a long workday. He danced again with the many women he had met throughout his life, reliving the very first moments he had spent with each of them. He returned to the moments when their romance was new, vibrant, and sacred, and made him feel like a mystic engaged in a perpetual discovery—a discovery of the beautiful other and the self in that other. And then he felt the opposite: the tired, old lingering of that which one already knows too well, or thinks one knows, and the rising need to go out again and hunt for the beautiful. And he felt too the hypocrisy of the game and the tiredness, the fear, and the hurt that it can bring. He became a carpenter, and he travelled throughout Galilee delivering the word of his father to the people. With an incantatory word, he made Lazarus rise from the dead and walk through life, stunningly erected and healed, ready to withstand suffering again. And he made wine and bread multiply, feeding the many hungry, needy people that he had encountered in his many voyages. He became his own mother, the Virgin Mary, and he felt deep within his womb the entering, in himself, of God's seed—experiencing a cosmic orgasm of the soul, one so grand and so vast and so absorbing that he would never forget it. And though, at that very moment, he experienced the vanishing of his self, perhaps like never before, he still kept sealed within himself the sacred idea. Arsénio was trying to force it out of him with all his barbarous and unscrupulous methods, like a robber who did not care and insisted on breaking down and stealing from the jeweller his most precious jewel—the brilliant bride that would illuminate the world, when the world was ready to receive its stunning and redeeming light. And then, after all this, when Francisco looked at himself from outside of himself, he saw again, in memorable detail, Rembrandt's portrait: the head of Christ full of black, thick, and curly hair, just like he himself had had when he arrived in Tarrafal. He saw his own Black face in the painting, and he saw the blood trickling down from the crown of thorns that the Roman soldiers, commanded by their bosses, had put on him. Like an endless canvas of the world's history, or like a line that never ends, Rembrandt's painting then transmuted into a portrait of Karl Marx; that man of vision and insight stared fiercely at him and reaffirmed with steadfast conviction his creed: "Break down the empire. Create a revolution. Take arms to kill your enemy if need be, for the rich man is not going to give away his mansion easily. Learn, deconstruct the constructed, denaturalize the naturalized, shatter mansions and creeds—become a rational man. Do not allow religion or any other opium to pollute your mind. Divide the field of your country equally, and equally distribute bread, water, and salt among your people. The idea, my friend, has not yet manifested like I saw it, like I envisaged it during my long nights of meditation, when I was writing the manifesto. The idea has not yet manifested, but the idea is beautiful and the idea is possible. It is possible and beautiful, my friend, and one must never stop trying to make it manifest, to make it as palpable as the sores on the bodies of your fellow men or the alienation in their eyes at the end of the day. Let's go, comrade. March ahead. No fear. No regrets." At that moment, the trip became less intense, and he gradually returned to himself. He felt the surest he had ever felt—about his idea, his convictions, the task at hand. He felt clean and rejuvenated. He felt ready for the new battle. Ready for whatever Arsénio wanted to throw at him. He had travelled deeply into his soul, and in that process he had encountered the soul of the world, the voice of voices, which had given him more strength and clarity of mind. This trip, which he had been forced to undertake, had allowed him to see everything anew—at an angle, in a light that he had never before experienced. It had allowed him to see the world as it was, how it was, how it had become that way, and what and how it could be and become. He was reminded once again of the intertwined, beautiful dance between the verbs *to be* and *to become*. These were the most important verbs to conjugate and conjugate again until one found the golden medium that each carried, until we could finally stop to admire the great house that we built, until we could finally exhale. Exhaling and inhaling, a perfect balancing act: clean air going in and coming out. We could be the citizens of a perfect world—a world that we ourselves built with our bare hands, our naked and raw dreams finally realized. He was now able to see himself clearly and understand precisely why and how he was the way he was. Francisco was, more than ever, very conscious of himself and of the outside world, and he knew that this world was not yet ready to receive his jewel. But he was patient and he would endure, and unless Arsénio decided, as a last resort or in a fit of high rage, to cut his head off, suspending the circuits that connected body and soul, Francisco knew that he would withstand.

Disillusioned with the application of this latest method on Francisco, Arsénio tried his last weapon. He brought Ana to the chamber in her naked and sorrowful condition. When Francisco first saw her, he was horrified and very surprised because he had no idea that she too had been brought to Tarrafal. He had thought a lot about her since he'd been caught by the PIDE agents on that dramatic night. He had imagined how worried and sad and scared she would be, not knowing where he was and what he was going through. But he had never imagined that the secret police would have also sequestered her and taken her to that deadly land on the West African coast, where the sun is so mortal that it takes away any drop of moisture that your skin, in its plea to survive and keep your body protected, manages to nourish. He became very unsettled, and for a moment he felt he could no longer go on with this, could not allow Ana to suffer at the hands of those dirty animals with no souls, beings whose eyes were no deeper than the snake's, lowlife dirty rats, creatures always roaming the low lands, unable to fly above and unite the universe—stare at the perfect marriage between land and sky. As Francisco looked at Ana and her bruised body, his facial muscles tensed up and he almost lost that mask that he had learned to carry to preserve his secret inside him. When Arsénio saw that glimpse of reality on Francisco's face, he smiled and thought, This is my chance. This is the day when my beloved cousin António will finally reward me and understand my true greatness. This is the day when the country and its empire will be saved, and we powerful Lusitanian citizens will live forever in honour and greatness. So excited was he with the prospect of revelation dancing in Francisco's face that he decided to go all the way with this method, to enact a particular punishment that he had only ever considered before. Something had always stopped him—perhaps the thought of his mother being exploited by soulless Romani pimps or being passed endlessly from soldier to soldier while he watched immobile and did nothing. He called two of his guards into the chamber and asked them to tie Francisco against an iron pole that had been placed in the middle of the chamber, standing tall and strong, erected like a pistol or a cross where many victims were to be crucified. He then ordered them to grab Ana and bring her to him. Then he forced her to do what he had forced on her before. He unzipped his pants, excited and frantic, and pulled her head down; she had no choice but to take his member fully in her mouth. He pulled her head by the hair, up and down, and to the sides, so that she could give him the pleasure he wanted. He grunted like a satisfied bull, looking directly into Francisco's eyes. Francisco started to scream violently, trying to untie himself from the pole. To calm him down, Ana kept telling him, as much as she could, that she was alright, that her insides were as clean and sturdy and resolved as the great Limpopo River, that magnificent mass of water that runs from southern central Africa like a crescent moon, in a weaving purposeful dance that wants to feel the many curves of the land to taste its soil, first going to the north, then to the northeast, then to the east and to the southeast—finally arriving at its destination on the Indian Ocean, where its dirt is dissolved into that immense body of water making the world clean again. Francisco would calm down momentarily, but then when the affair became uglier and Arsénio ordered the two guards to do with Ana what men who are depraved or dead or simply afraid do to women, Francisco started howling like a very sick animal, the kind that knows that life is not worth living. He howled and howled for hours on end and tried to hurt himself, like many other prisoners had done before in that dark chamber of slow death so that they could be liberated from the ugly conditions that this world had imposed on them. He was in this sorrowful state long after the whole thing finished and he had been put back into isolation inside his dark cement cell that burned his body by day and froze it by night. Because he would not quiet down, and the entire prison could hear him, feel the piercing agony of his sorrow and the plea of his soul, the chief ordered the compound doctor to pay him a visit. A dose of Haldol would make it all go away.

Carlos Montealva, being predisposed, as he had been since he was a child, to have deep intuitions that often turned into ugly and unsightly visions, sensed that the next day would be a big day—a good day, a day to remember—and that Francisco needed a good night's sleep to be ready for the new dawn. He entered Francisco's dark cement cell, let in by the two guards, to administer the calming drug on the suffering man. He opened his briefcase, took out the Haldol injection, then gently cleansed Francisco's right thigh and injected the miraculous liquid that was supposed to make the mind quiet down. He also applied some remedies to Francisco's many injuries. In so doing, he managed to slip a piece of paper into Francisco's hands without the guards noticing. He closed

Francisco's hand tightly around the paper, hiding it from the eyes of those who cannot know beautiful secrets. Francisco fell into a heavy, sweet melancholia and stopped howling and hurting himself. Then he was left behind in that dark room. Carlos left the cell with a smile on his face, which was unusual for him, a man of sombre demeanour who often left these situations with the usual fatalistic murmurs: "I am not here to cure the sick. I am here only to sign death certificates." But the cure was coming, and it was coming soon; the announcement had come from far away in the metropolis of the empire and had been transmitted through radio waves, or merely through the common dreams of the people killing and being killed. Carlos was then led into Ana's cell by the same guards, and though Ana seemed to be mentally in good health—as good as it can be expected under such conditions—her body needed care. Carlos asked the guards to take her to the showers and leave her alone there for some time. She needed to wash herself and regain some dignity. The guards would have hesitated if it had been someone else asking, but Carlos was a doctor—he was Carlos Cabral Abreu Abrantes Antunes Montealva, a man of stature and soft ways—and they felt they ought to obey him. They were young boys who came from poverty and submission, and they had only learned how to say yes: yes to their abusive fathers, yes to the priest, yes to their commander-in-chief Arsénio. When Ana was brought back enveloped in a light white robe, her long dark hair falling down her back and shoulders, Carlos treated her body as gently as he could, as gently as he had treated Francisco, and asked if she needed a mild sedative. She nodded her head, and he gave her a low dose of Valium. He respected the young couple immensely. He almost felt jealous of their adventures, of their passion for life, for justice, for a sound healthy world where race and class and gender were secondary to love and life. And he hated Arsénio as much as he hated his own father. As he had with Francisco, before he left Ana's cell, he discreetly gave her a piece of paper and closed her hand tightly around it. He felt as if he were sealing a miracle that was about to burst into life, guarding it inside the fortress. He did not want it to be destroyed or contaminated by the impure air of the cell, that stifling current that made Ana's lungs work very hard to keep her body breathing.

HORSES, SEA, AND FLOWERS. This was the night of nights, the queen of queens, for both Ana and Francisco. The cards on the table were finally showing the aces; the game was becoming one to win, not one to lose. Whether it was because of the drugs that the doctor had given them or because of something else—something that had been brewing quietly and silently sometimes or fiercely and loudly at other times—the young couple, each in their individual cells, entered the most redeeming and hopeful dream. It was a dream that was hard to wake up from, unless one sensed while in it that the real world, the one that pulsated in front of us, was somehow going to hold on to that dream, that the world of the inside and the outside would no longer live as separate oblivious entities but rather as two sides of the same rich coin: two arms of the same wise person, communicating deeply and continuously to make manifest the idea. In this dream, Francisco saw himself in an open hay field, wide and serene. At first, he sensed no life in this field at all. There was only silence, gentle light, and a weightlessness dancing around him and making his body wave up and down, up and down like a feather or flower pollen dancing gently in the air. He could barely perceive his own breathing and his own life. His being, his body felt complete even though he could not grasp what was happening to him and where he was. Then he perceived other life roaming around in the vast field. He looked straight ahead and noticed that there were several horses grazing in the field—or perhaps they were tahki, the ancestors of the horse, that splendid wild animal that has some zebra-like qualities like the ones depicted in the prehistoric Lascaux caves in southern France. The species is nearly extinct today, with only a few hundred still running wild in the desert of Mongolia because some wise humans thought it a good idea to preserve it. At first, Francisco just stared at these animals as if he were trying to see if he could trust them and sense if they trust him. The animals seemed oblivious to his presence, just grazing here and there, or sometimes running together on that wide open endless plain that seemed to have no end and no beginning. Some were short like ponies, others were stocky, and still others were tall and elegant, with very elongated bodies. They seemed capable of walking or flying great distances. There were white and black and grey and brown animals, many colours and shapes in that field that had space for everything and everyone. Francisco opened his arms wide and stretched his body to feel the vastness and the emptiness of the space, as if he were trying to measure it and detect whether there were obstacles. But everything seemed unimpeded and open, ready for him to enter it, to take flight, to taste its freedom. He stretched his body inch by inch, elongating it as much as he could, feeling its totality and its life. He then lay down on the ground with his back to the earth to smell the grass and hear the wisdom of the ground. He looked at the sky: it was clear, azure, vacuous. He felt its immensity and was almost engulfed by it, experiencing, yet again, that splendid distention of the ego which some Buddhists may call *sunyata* or *nirvana* but which many other people know and experience and may call something else. He knew that time was on his side. He knew that life, and the being or beings commanding it, were screaming at him, telling him that he must take charge again. He must run to the other side of the world, to meet Ana, to encounter the idea, to really be and become. He must run away from a place where he had been staying for quite a long time now, a place that wanted to pollute his mind and hinder his body, a place that wanted his force, his pearl, to smash it mercilessly with thunderous military boots. He was certain now that he was no longer inside the cement cell in Tarrafal. He was free. He could fly or he could sing and howl to that nothingness and no one would bother him, no one would close his mouth or assault his body. He sensed though that there was something missing in him, something missing from him. He pondered, but it was difficult to come to an awareness of that thing that he was missing, that thing that he was lacking. Then he watched the animals, hoping that they could remind him of what he was lacking. He stared at two of them, one brown and the other grey, both magnificent in their beauty and agility, and then he felt a painful knot in his chest. This knot then accelerated and travelled up and down his body. He touched himself all over to see if he could get rid of that knot, if he could find in his own body the source of his pain. He was desperate to understand what it was that he was missing, what it was that was causing him such pain. He touched his chest, his legs, his arms, his head, his feet, his hands, feeling each part of himself, and then, as he was about to stop and just when he was searching in his crotch for the secret that was paining him, he remembered what it was that he was missing, what it was that he was lacking: it was Ana, in body and soul. It was not just her body and her sex that he was missing; he was missing her entirety, and her entirety included her body and the pleasure that it gave him, but it also included her mind, her soul, her pristine spirit, and the beautiful idea that she carried in the entirety of her being. He recalled when he first met her at that event between comrades. He recalled how much he had liked her, how much he was struck by her: he liked her smile and shiny black eyes, her long dark hair, her slim body, her chest where two brief breasts stood, erected with the resolution of a volcano, which he would later tease and tease. He recalled how much bigger they became when she was pregnant with the twins, Otu and Quintana. He recalled tasting her milk when the babies were born, and how that too gave him so much pleasure in body and mind, in body and soul. He recalled her long arms and legs, the way she pronounced his name and then followed it by that sweet Portuguese expression that he liked so much: *o meu amor és tu*—you are my love. After this realization, he knew why he was there and what he must do. He approached the animals, trying to coax them into allowing him to mount them. They were not very open to that—not yet. He knew he had to search deep within himself to try to find the language that they would understand, that would make them trust him. He searched and searched, and he tried different dances and games with them. He spoke to them in their language, which he managed to rescue from some part within himself, and then, after a while, after having conversed extensively with them, one of them finally allowed him to mount it. The acquiescing animal was majestic, imposing, covered with a shining grey mantle, possessing the manner and the rich dress of a king of a past grand age. He was a being carrying all the wisdom of time and space within himself, a creature who had become the friend of man. He saw in Francisco an ally who would protect him, or perhaps he sensed that Francisco was the one who needed protection and help to travel great distances. Francisco was now on top of the superb animal, and he was not quite sure what his next move must be. They both stood still in the middle of the magnificent plain in silence, and Francisco could feel the breathing of the stallion underneath his own body. He could feel the animal's warmth and the strength of his muscles, the silkiness of his grey skin. He could feel the animal's assuredness and readiness and yet also some faint trembling, possibly a sign that there was danger to come or merely an indication of excitement, an intimation that the time was right and ready—as right and ready as it could ever be. Mounted on the horse, Francisco could see the expanse of the field much more clearly. He could see that there was a great distance to travel, which made him somewhat apprehensive, but he could also see, far away, the top of the hill. In seeing it, he felt drawn to it. It was as if he knew the hill was the place he must reach. He knew that, from the hill, he would be able to see much more clearly where he was and where he must go. He felt he must ride ahead, but he had no saddle. He considered how he could manage to ride such a long distance at a high velocity without saddle. As if reading Francisco's mind, the horse raised his front legs, causing Francisco to instinctively grasp the neck of the animal in order not to fall off. And then, sensing that Francisco was securely attached to him, the horse started to cavalcade through the plains with the velocity and assertiveness of a bird. Francisco had no time to think much or to feel afraid. He only knew that he must keep his hands firm on the horse's neck and that he wanted the horse to take him to the hilltop or perhaps even farther, way beyond the world that the hill allowed him to see. They galloped like that for a long time as if running for their lives. The other horses of the plain let them pass, staring at the moving man and horse in awe as if they were curious to know where they were going—or how it was that they had become friends and were now part of one single entity. At some point, the horse neighed that neigh that could either signify contentment or affliction, and Francisco was not sure what was happening, where he was going, or what the final outcome might be. When they reached the hilltop, the horse stopped for a moment as if to catch his breath and Francisco noticed that down there, below the hill, there was the vast sea extending in never-ending dimension. His eyes could see nothing but water upon water upon water, a world of silvery and bluish colours where many secrets may lie. The horse then quickly took off, his pace increasing to an unprecedented speed. When he reached the water, he did not stop and his galloping became even more impressive. He flew through the sea water, above the waves, avoiding being engulfed by it. Francisco felt a mortal fear invade his being, but he also knew he did not want the horse to stop; he wanted it to continue through that immense and dangerous body of water until they reached land again. And the horse did not disappoint; he kept flying through the waves like an incandescent being, a mythic figure that was both material and immaterial, both human and divine. At one point in the voyage, Francisco noticed that the water was covered by deep velvety red roses and the sea no longer looked silvery, like it usually did, but had rather become an extension of redness. Sometimes it seemed that the roses were no longer roses but rather liquid blood or floating bodies, and sometimes the roses became carnations and their sweet scent invaded both his nostrils and the nostrils of the horse, making both of them feel drunk. Yet it was a drunkenness that did not make them irrational but rather awakened them to another reality, giving them clarity—a much more complete, much more beautiful clarity. And in that reality, in that clarity, in that beauty and ugliness, they witnessed another transformation: the lifeless and bloody bodies floating on the ocean—which they had seen before amidst the flowers, and which had come from the dark belly of this vast mass of water—all took the shape of roses or carnations. They stood erect and walked through the waves, fearless, unimpeded, freed butterflies rising to the glitters of the moon. They walked as if the water were the solid floor of the house they had left behind or the house they sensed they had waiting for them on the other side of the ocean.

There were many of them, thousands of them, young and old, men and women, all Black, their shining skin against the light of the universe competing to be seen. It was a beautiful procession of people united in their suffering, evading the enemy, walking towards their destination. Francisco and the horse trotted in front of them, guiding them and giving them strength to continue. It was an uncanny image: people guided by one man and one horse, all suddenly so sure that the end was approaching and that the shore was not far away now. They knew, they sensed, that they could finally rest on secure land and build a home. After a long while, they reached the shore and fell exhausted on the ground, thanking God or the gods in many African languages, many of which were familiar to Francisco's ear. At the shore, there were thousands of people awaiting them as if they had known the newcomers were arriving at that precise moment. They offered the newcomers blankets and chicken soup—for their souls and bodies. They offered them the flags of many new countries. In the middle of this awaiting crowd, Francisco spotted Ana. She seemed strong and happy, young and unspoiled by Arsénio—just like when he had met her that first time at the meeting of the comrades. He dismounted from the horse and ran to her. They embraced frantically, touching one another all over to make sure they were not a mirage caused by a weakened mind and a tired body. Then, when they were certain that they were real beings in flesh and bone and blood, they rolled on the floor and cried out loud, like newborns announcing their lives to the world. Everyone looked at them and exclaimed, "Look how beautiful they are, how happy they are. Look. Look." At that precise moment, Francisco woke up, opened his clenched hand, and read the note the compound doctor had given him: *In the middle of the night there will be a song coming to you by radio waves. It is the end, my dear brother. I will shake your hand, and we'll sing "Grândola Vila Morena" together. You will be able to hug your wife.*

THE RIVER, THE MOUNTAINS, AND THE PRISTINE CHURCH. Like Francisco, Ana fell into a dream, a grand and awe-inspiring dream, full of uncanny revelations. She travelled to places she had never travelled to and countries she never wanted to visit, as if her mind and her body were telling her the world is a very big place and must be discovered. Or as if her ancestors from Trás-os-Montes were calling her to her roots, wanting to introduce themselves to her, wanting her to know she had many people within her and many lands she could call her home. In the dream, she first felt that her body was weak, like a castle that was old, a castle with walls that, despite being massive and thick, had in them the weight of time. They had been damaged by intemperate seasons and by the countless armies that had come to ransack the castle and take possession of its wealth, mines and mines of precious minerals that had been safely kept inside the beautiful fortress for a long time. She touched herself all over, trying to determine where the hurt and tiredness were. She thought that if she could identify the wounds, she could then attempt to cure them with all the remedies she had at her disposal. She felt her long legs and her long slender arms and noticed that they had dark spots in them, like nodules of cancerous cells—cells that had gone into disarray, losing their DNA IQ, becoming mad and not knowing where to stop, multiplying endlessly and producing tumours that would eventually take over her entire body and annihilate her being. She then touched her belly, her small breasts, her navel, and the gentle part between her legs. She wanted to make sure she was still a woman of reproductive capacity and integrity who could have many more babies with the man that she knew she loved. She could not remember his name or anything specific about him, but she was certain that he existed, that she had met him, and that she had already made love with him. She knew this because her body, or perhaps her soul, carried the memory of him. She also felt within her the cries of her absent twins: Oto and Quintana. She could not remember exactly who she was, where she had been, or where she was going, but she knew she was someone who had been to many places and had many more to visit. She knew she was still young, and—despite the hurt she felt all over her body, especially in the gentle part between her legs—she was sure that life would spring out of her in the times ahead. She knew those times were coming, and she sensed they would be better, would allow her to breathe a clean air, dance in the open field of her childhood, and make love with the man of her choice. She heard the murmurs of water not far from where she was, and she followed the sound until she found the river running upwards. She looked at herself in the reflection of the water to see if she could recognize her own her face, and she was happy to see that indeed she knew who she was. She then took off her white robe and slowly entered the river waters. At first, she felt very cold; shivers ran up and down all over her, making her want to retract and regain again the certainty and warmth of the land. But she knew this initial reaction was normal and that her body was just adapting to the new world it was entering, a world that was clean and refreshing, a world that would give her body the energy it needed to continue. She washed herself thoroughly with that clean fresh river water. It was going upwards, which she found odd, for she had always thought that water ran downwards, from north to south, and not the other way around. When she was thoroughly cleansed and her body felt reenergized, she dried herself with some leaves she found on the riverbank. The leaves looked odd to her too—they were excessively long and thin, and they had a texture she had never encountered before. Still, they felt good on her skin, emitting a cool scent she could not quite recognize but which seemed to be from a tree she had read or heard about, the eucalyptus, which was known for its healing properties. She then put on her robe and walked along the river, upwards, for a long, long time.

The river was moving upwards as if it were going to the North Pole, and it was calling her to go there too. She was enjoying this walk very much and did not feel tired though she knew she had walked a lot already and that she still had a great distance to conquer. She would sometimes stop to take a sip of water or just to refresh her body again. And sometimes she would be taken by the beauty of the vegetation she encountered on the shore of that great river. She was in awe of the plants and flowers she found, and especially of those little blue flowers with a yellow faint centre, so beautiful and so tiny. She would reach for them, wanting to cut them off from their source and take them with her, but then the yellow centre would smile at her and tell her not to do so. It said that if she did, the flowers would cease to exist, and without them the world would be poorer, with fewer species. She listened to the flower, and she respected its wishes and its tenacity to live. She also saw and heard birds that she had never seen or heard before. They were tinier than the ones she had seen in the world she had lived in before, but they were nonetheless magnificent. Their songs kept calling to her, sounding like faint murmurs of lyrics she knew she had in her memory but could not quite push to consciousness. When she finally reached the end of the river, she noticed that she was in a place of high mountains, green fields, and tiny, tiny houses made of sturdy stone. She looked at her surroundings and observed the smoke that was coming out of the chimneys of the small houses. There were many mountains and hills; there were many little houses like this with the same little chimneys, lost in the valleys, on the sides of the slopes, or sometimes even standing on top of hills or mountains, standing proud and defiant, built to withstand the harsh climate of the region. Her eyes could see nothing but that: mountains and hills and houses and chimneys and smoke coming out of the chimneys. It was dawn, and there was a faint fog dancing in the region and hiding some of the houses in the valley. Everything had a misty quality, and Ana felt at peace. She felt at home even though she was sure she had never set foot on that land. As the day awakened and walked towards its destiny, she saw people passing by with their sheep and goats and cows. They were taking them to pasture. The animals had bells on their necks, and as she heard the music that came from the bells and the language spoken between the animals and their caretakers, she knew the language was familiar. She knew the language she was hearing was Portuguese, the same language spoken in the land she had come from and had always lived in—though not by most of its people. But the tone of that language was different from the one she had grown up with. And the people, though familiar, were also strange: the way they walked and talked to their animals, and the bells those animals had. It all seemed very uncanny to Ana, and she felt somehow disoriented and out of place. At the same time, she was quite sure she liked this place, and that she wanted to be introduced to its people, to eat their food, to sleep in their beds, to hear their stories and the lullabies they sang to their children when they went to sleep. She stayed there, observing her surroundings in minute detail for a long time, and then, as the night gradually approached, she noticed the lights that were now appearing to illuminate the place. And she saw the chimneys giving away smoke and the fog coming again like it had in the morning. She saw the animals and their caretakers returning from their pastures with their bellies full. She sensed how happy they all were, animals and caretakers, coming home from the mountains to sleep and rejoin their families, to rejoice in the company of those most dear to them. She noticed how the animals lived just beside the humans, and she felt the fresh smell of cow dung invading her nostrils. She saw children playing outside, happy, happy. She saw how some of them came running when they saw the animals that their parents or older siblings were bringing home and how they hugged those animals, calling them by their names. They called them Alemania and Tulipa and Madureira and many other names. A little boy approached a goat and then touched her round belly while she stood still with her ears pricked and her eyes alive, a princess in waiting. He asked his father, "When is Bem Feita going to give birth, Dad? When, when? Look at that belly, round like the moon!" And he kissed her face. Then, when all was quiet and dark, and all the families had gone inside the house to eat dinner, Ana saw a church down by the foot of a hill. Her eyes were drawn to it because it was now the only thing emitting light. It stood there, erected, at the foot of the hill, calling you like a giant messiah. It had the pristine, unspoiled, and wondrous quality of a magic circus or an ancient primal dwelling, a home calling you back, offering protection. The land was very still and very dark, except for that extraordinary church down by the foot of the hill, and she felt she was almost blind. She made her way there by resorting mostly to her other senses, like a truly blind person does. She walked carefully and slowly, feeling the stones of the path with her feet; sensing the branches on the sides with her long arms; opening her ears to the faint melodies coming from the magic, illuminated place resting by the hill; and following the light that came from that centre of life. As she came closer to the church, she could hear distinct songs, beautiful songs, words and vibrations that sounded religious or perhaps just agreeable to the soul. Ave Marias and arias so enchanting that she thought she was an angel approaching heaven and being invited to come in by the kindness of God or the gods. And indeed, as she approached the church, which was closed for the ceremony, someone came to the door to open it and allow her in. As she stepped on the granite stone of the church stairs, and as she extended her hand to the massive wooden doorknob, she saw in front of her a little boy dressed in white. He smiled and said, "Come in, my lady. Come in. This is your home too." She went in, putting her feet on the cool granite floor. Dressed in her white robe and with her hair falling down, she looked like a virginal vision to the people inside the church who were there precisely to celebrate the birth of Jesus. There was an elaborate Nativity scene on the side of the altar where the little baby rested on Mary's arms. Mother and baby were encircled by Joseph, the Magi, the sheep, and the cows, a sturdy barrier protecting them from the wrath of Herod, that beastly cannibal who could be satiated only by the blood of innocent babies. This scene was truly beautiful even though all the figures were lifeless and made of ceramic. They stood there like statues to be adored and revered but did not seem to give much back, as if blind and mute to the cold of the winter and to the real pains of people. When they saw Ana, the celebrating parishioners came to her and chanted, "Ave Maria, Ave Maria cheia de Graça, Ave Maria, Ave Maria full of Grace." They chanted and chanted and clapped and clapped, all of them—young and old, men and women, fat and thin. The priest came to her and put around her head a wreath of white and red roses, and then he performed a ritual that involved the elaborate recital of a text in Latin and then in Ancient Greek. Finally, in a language that everyone understood, he pronounced her the virgin of the night, the true mother of Jesus, the magnanimous woman who gave birth to the saviour. They sung some more songs that seemed to be in different European languages, and then they switched to African songs, some of which Ana knew. They would alternate between languages, between songs, and they would play various instruments, some serene and low like the flute or the piano in a low key, others thunderous and potent like drums or horns. She became immersed in this feast of the body and soul, and she danced with everyone, men and women, young and old, thin and fat. Then they formed a circle and moved, hand in hand, inside the church, dancing, chanting in a collective act of profound solidarity. They did this for a long time, but no one was tired. It was as if everyone in that church, including Ana, knew the ritual had to be performed for a long time, the songs sung many times, the dances danced many rounds until the last drop of hope that they were waiting for came, announcing, strong and unmistakable, the end of suffering and the beginning of love. And indeed, that last drop of hope finally came. As Ana watched, the door of the church suddenly opened by itself and she saw healthy, strong, and upright, her beloved Francisco Magno Motumba. He was in a white robe too. She stopped dancing and chanting, took a big breath, and then ran to him: a princess running to her prince with whom she had momentarily cut ties and not because of her own accord. He took her in his arms, and, just as he had seen it in his own dreams, they felt each other fully, up and down, to make sure that they were real beings in flesh and bone and blood and not figments of a wishful and very tired mind and body. When they were fully certain that they were real and alive, the parishioners came to them and guided them to the side of the altar where the Nativity scene was. They took out all the ceramic figures and carelessly dropped them on the floor, breaking some of them, and then they took Ana and Francisco by the hand and seated them inside the scene. Their naked feet rested on the fluffy softness of moss that had been gathered from the rich floors of pine tree forests, which are abundant in that land. The people went outside, brought in their real sheep and cows, and placed them there as well. They brought in the goat Bem Feita, who was contorting herself with pain—her hour had come. They helped her bring the little one out. It was a she-goat, and they named her *a Encantada,* the Enchanted. Finally, they brought in a baby who was clearly of mixed race, even though the mother had claimed she had only made love with her husband. He had not believed her and had since divorced her, leaving her alone with an unwanted baby to raise by herself. They brought in this unwanted baby boy and placed him in Ana's arms. She received him with eagerness and love, and showed him to Francisco. They both undressed him and touched him all over his tiny body to make sure that he was healthy and to stare at that beautiful skin of his. The scene was now perfect. Everyone in that church was happy and standing still, looking at the Nativity scene, smiling, in awe of what they were witnessing. Ana and Francisco and the little one felt at home. They felt wanted, loved, dignified. Someone in the audience took a photo of this scene and then showed it to everyone. They decided to call the photo and the scene the *Mystic Nativity*, and indeed, if one were to carefully look at the photo and the scene it depicted, one would clearly see elements of Sandro Botticelli's masterpiece. There were the colours; the decorative detail; the levels of vision with three centres of power; the grand scene in the middle with the virgin and the baby; the golden, open heavens; the kind and simple magi in adoring awe; and the virgins and the angels immersed in devotion and love, and flying in sensual ecstasy. There were also the dark demons lurking here and there, reminding us of the exquisite mastery and insight of the early Renaissance painter. They also reminded us of the teachings of the Dominican friar Girolamo Savonarola, that man from Ferrara known for burning books and immoral art, who believed art should reflect the best of human nature, like a superior vision calling humans to their higher realization. The photo, as a mirror of the thing it reproduced, seemed to have a more powerful effect than the thing being depicted. It was as if the camera that had taken the photo possessed a soul, perhaps the soul of the person who took it, which would equate to the soul of the artist. That soul was a clear mirror of our lives and told us, in vivid detail, what our lives could be, ought to be, if we could get rid of all the devils roaming around, often in the most secretive places, which we often failed to even notice. Then, after adoring, in speechless wonder, the colours and magnificence of the photo and of the thing the photo reproduced, the people heard a sound: a rooster's crow announcing the Christmas Eve midnight mass. The sound then transformed into another melody, becoming a chant with very distinct and unmistakable lyrics:

Grândola, Vila Morena, Grândola, Swarthy Town
Land of fraternity
It is the people who lead
Inside of you, oh city
Inside of you, oh city.

Immediately afterwards, the church was invaded by military men and women, all singing this song and carrying red and white flowers in their berets and in the barrels of their boots. The church dwellers all joined in to chant "Grândola, Vila Morena" for a long time, and then, after a while, they all left the church. They walked first through the streets of that land and then far beyond the confines of that land. They followed the same river that Ana had followed, going back the way she had come. They reached the island of Santiago and then went even farther to Luanda, Maputo, and many other places. It was a beautiful scene. It was as if the people were going on a pilgrimage—the most fantastic, the most audacious *romaria*—to honour the promise they had made long time ago to God or the gods. When this pilgrimage reached Galinhas's island in Guinea Bissau and liberated all the political prisoners held there, Ana woke up. She opened her hand and read the doctor's note: *Tomorrow at precisely midnight you will wake up to the beautiful song "Grândola, Vila Morena." It is a message, my sister. It is the message.* Then she heard the song and a lot of commotion in the compound. The lyrics penetrated her slowly, and she felt the poetry, wisdom, and emotion that they carried. Her body was suddenly cured from the perils it had endured, and her mind saw clearly the love of the world and the will of the people.

She regained herself, fully aware that the hour of the star had arrived, and her body received its light through the thousands of rays illuminating her cell. The song and its words became benevolent rain, a bath that washes away loneliness and the dirt she had been carrying:

In the shadow of a holmoak
which no longer knew its age
I swore as my companion,
Grândola, your will

Grândola, your will
I swore as my companion
In the shadow of a holmoak
Which no longer knew its age

The compact door of her cement cell opened, and Ana saw in front of her the two guards who had raped her the day before. They entered the cell, and she noted that they too had red and white roses on them. They extended their hands to help her get up from the cold floor, offered her two roses, and asked her for forgiveness, kneeling down before her.

Francisco's novel in progress ended there and having read it,
Daria felt more in love with him than she had had ever felt.

IVAN LINS AND THE STITCHED QUILT. When Vasco da Gama found out that Daria and Francisco were dating, he became mad. He would not show that madness or discontent directly to Daria, but she noticed that he was unhappy with the turn of events. He felt he had lost his chance to sleep with Daria and break away the hymen she had been keeping between her tightly closed legs. When the Lusitanian Centre was accepted as a member of the United Way, he felt very accomplished and proud. The acceptance meant that the centre would be receiving more funding, and it was also a sign that Canada was really interested in looking after its newcomer citizens from the many Portuguese-speaking countries worldwide. Vasco invited everyone to go out and celebrate. They all went to The Boat, a splendid restaurant that served outstanding and mouthwatering Portuguese fish dishes, and then they went dancing at Copacabana, a well-known Brazilian samba and bossa nova place. The club was playing melodious vibrations for the soul and body, and the sounds of the Portuguese language became a singing, penetrating, and docile chant that made the crowd break down. When they were playing Ivan Lins and Adriana Calcanhoto, Daria became very emotional and started crying uncontrollably. Francisco, who had been dancing with the other women working at the centre and seemed at home on the dance floor, came back to the table and saw Daria in this convulsive state. He did not know quite what to think, and he was worried that perhaps she was upset about him dancing with other women. He had left her alone at the table because she was not such a good dancer and always felt sort of embarrassed when dancing. She was especially uncomfortable with the samba, which sometimes turned into frantic sexualized rapper's movements—the crotches of men and women coming dangerously close together, shamelessly entangled in one another—making her feel very inappropriate, very ashamed. When she told him the real reason for her crying, he said, "*Meu amor*, you are very sensitive. That is beautiful," and he kissed her forehead. They sat together having an intimate conversation, that tête-à-tête that only very close lovers can have, and she told him exactly the lines from Ivan Lins that had made her cry. She had never heard Ivan Lins before, and though she was used to the mournful and deeply melancholic sounds of *fado* music that often made her cry, she had never ever felt as touched by the sound of music as she did with Lins. She repeated the lyrics of the song she had heard:

The colour of the sunset

Is this Fellini or is this our lives?
In what film did our love happen?
In what port did we say goodbye?
Cagliari?
Gênova?

What is it that illuminates our film?
From what sunset comes that colour?
What pasts does passion inhabit?
Évora?
Córdoba?
From theatre to theatre,

We will love each other throughout life.
One more hour
One more scene... I don't know

Happiness is a series of nuances.
From what dawn is romance born?
Is the time I will have you, everything?
Mônaco?
Málaga?

She dwelt incessantly on the first lines of the song, as if she could not stop asking questions that did not really have an answer but for which she expected one: *Is this Fellini or it this our lives? In what film did our love happen?* He heard her repeating the song and then crying and crying some more, and he felt more in love with this woman than ever. He wanted to calm her down; he wanted to ease her pain. He wanted to possess her body and soul right there in front of everyone so that they would know that she was his and that she wanted to be his. And so he did. They made love right there, and everyone was in awe at the lovers' movements. They went at each other like never before, seemingly unable to attain satiation, commanded by the thirst that ran deep in their veins. And as they made love, the audience of Copacabana sang Ivan Lins's beautiful song in chorus: *"Is the time I will have you, everything? From what dawn is romance born?"* Everyone was feeling the love that Daria and Francisco felt; everyone was entangled in the words of Lins and in the actions of the lovers. It was as if everything and everyone had become one and the same thing, one and the same feeling, one and the same person, except for Vasco. Vasco da Gama did not feel the love or the entanglement or the happiness that everyone else felt. He was visibly upset, visibly livid. At the end of the night, when no one could take any more love, people started to leave. As they dispersed, they each became their own person and returned to their usual loneliness. Vasco drove Daria and Francisco home, leaving them at their respective places because the next day was a work day and there was no more time for play. He dropped Francisco off first and then Daria, even though Daria lived closer to Copacabana. Before Francisco got out of the car, he gave Daria a wet kiss, vigorously taking in her tongue and the freshness of her mouth, evidently incapable of satisfying his desire for her. They arranged to meet the next day after work at the Communal Mule. The next day, June 25, was a big day for Mozambique, for it was the anniversary of the country's independence from Portugal, and the Mozambican consulate was marking the date with several events. First, there would be a recital of Mozambican poetry at the Communal Mule by expatriates—Daria did not like this word, and she often told Francisco that he should call them Mozambican-Canadians—and then there would be an elaborate dinner at the Communist's Daughter restaurant with traditional Mozambican food and music. When they got to Daria's street, Vasco stopped the car completely and asked if he could use her bathroom. She hesitated. Her basement apartment was not very nice, and she was worried that Vasco might think less of her if he saw her present living conditions. She also felt uncomfortable because a part of her was concerned that he wanted something from her, but again she rationalized her worries away. She told herself she was being foolish since Vasco was old enough to be her father, he was a man of standing in the community, and he therefore ought to be a man of sense. Because of all that, and also because she did not want to disappoint him or prevent him from exercising his basic need of using a bathroom, a universal and warranted right for everyone, she brought him inside the apartment and showed him to the bathroom. When he came out, he walked slowly towards Daria and said her place was very nice, very intimate and romantic, and that it truly reflected Daria's way of being, her tender and genuine sensibility. He praised her incorruptible naïveté, which he attributed to the fact that she had been raised high up in the mountains of Caramulo—with goats, harsh winters, and splendid springs of yellow genistas and wild lavender—witnessing the harshness of the lives of those rude peasants who had to work very hard to make ends meet. She smiled but felt uncomfortable with his labelling, with the fact that he called her people rude peasants. She thought of her grandmother's great sensibility. She was a woman who spent her free time putting together beautiful quilts, each one telling a story of her ancestors or those still living. She stitched intricate, deeply penetrating patterns performed in colourful metaphor. For fabric, she used old clothes that she found here and there in her own house or by going around the village and asking the inhabitants of Almores for their relatives' tattered, unusable pieces. Daria thought of how happy her grandmother had been when engaged in this task, how she would smile to herself, or to whomever happened to pass by and see her in concentrated awe. Daria thought of how her grandmother would slip into a prolonged storytelling mode when stitching these quilts and would start reciting the stories of the lives of many of the people she knew or had heard about and whose clothes she now had in her possession. When she got a piece of tattered clothing from a certain person, and as she stitched it into a quilt, she would describe the life of the respective person in great detail, qualifying that person as good, on the way to becoming good, wretched, on the way to becoming wretched, or perfect. "Five types of people, that's all there is in this world," she would say. And she added that she was stitching clothes of people with different degrees of goodness and badness together so that they would all be joined. In that communion, she said, the perfect ones would transmit their qualities to the other ones and the end result would be a beautiful, enchanted, and colourful quilt that she would then offer to the villagers of

Almores. She hoped that, in looking at the quilt, they could see in it the mirror of their souls and realize how those souls had the potential to attain greatness when under the right company. Some of the villagers mocked her attempt to make the world better and rejected her offer. They argued that her method would fail because many of those people she was stitching together were already dead or were in fact mortal enemies, and some had even killed one another. To this, she would say that her work was of great magnitude and the quilts of great length, its effects going well beyond the here and now, to resolve the most unthinkable hatred. She would then open one of the quilts and point to the lines and colours that had the power to travel at the speed of light and reach those who were now beyond the visible horizons in heaven, hell, or purgatory. She believed the pattern had the power to bring them and God together in a fully honest and merciful conversation, giving the bad ones another chance to be allowed into heaven and to live forever in green fields, among birds, sheep, goats, and the Lord. When Daria was little, she would look forward to these sessions with her grandmother, and she would listen to her stories in expectant wonder. She thought her grandmother was the wisest person alive; she was a true philosopher, the kind that is rare today in this age of simplified psychics and capitalism; this age of toy mountains and smiling restless children with their hands always extended, eager to receive; this age that forges in us a vacuous desire for the material. This age has created an unhappiness, a void that was not there before when the world was barer and we did not eat lobster every day, when one molecule simply said yes to another and the world was born, like Clarice Lispector, one of her favourite writers, has said. Deeply entangled in all these thoughts, she attempted to explain to Vasco that the people she grew up with in the mountains of Almores were in fact full of poetry and sensibilities, and she told him about her grandmother. He smiled, listening and taking in the beauty of the story Daria was recounting, perhaps recognizing that, indeed, these people had a magnificent poetic soul. If they could engender a creature like Daria—so beautiful, so superior, and so capable of awakening one's desires when one thought they had all been spent over the years—then these people must have been special, very special indeed. Then he came very close to Daria and kissed her on the mouth. She was very surprised and immediately pushed him back, asking him what the hell was he doing. He said he was just trying to show the deep affection he felt towards her, which she thought was strange. She said that he did not need to kiss her on the mouth like that to show his affection. Maybe not in Almores, he replied, but Canada was a new country with many new habits, and this was one of those habits. She became more and more upset, furious in fact, like someone who had been betrayed in a very deep way, for she thought this man was mocking her, treating her like a simpleton. She felt especially hurt because he did what he did and said what he said right after she had told him the beautiful story of her grandmother. It was a story one tells out of pure love, out of pure wisdom, out of a pure need to show how we are all special beings, in our own ways. The story tells us that the barriers that we erect between us are just symbols of our fear—that fear of those who are different from us, yet also fundamentally beautiful, fundamentally human. They argued for some time, and then he said, "How could you kiss Francisco? How could you do shameful things with him? How could you? And with a man as black as my pants?" She said she was an adult and she could kiss and make love with whomever she pleased and that whomever happened to be Francisco.

"Francisco, not you!" she repeated loudly. She felt violated to the core in body and soul, but Vasco did not stop there. He grabbed her with more intensity, seemingly surprised that Daria could actually take such a strong stand, that she could have such a strong and sure will. He also felt upset that he seemed to have made a mistake assessing her personality, for he always told himself that he could know people well, know them better than they knew themselves. His disappointment turned into a rage, and he pushed her down onto the floor and did to her what depraved or lost men do to women. She struggled and screamed and she asked him to stop, but it was all to no avail for Mr. Vasco da Gama was in a frenzy and seemed to be in another world, travelling waters that he had never travelled but which his tired and old soul had been craving for eternities. He was a navigator sailing the waters of an unknown beautiful sea, just like the other Vasco da Gama, his forefather, did five hundred years ago to meet his promised bride—that splendid India ful of colour and flavour. He smelled all her colours and ate all her spicy delicious food, in that other vast and rich continent, far away, by the Indian Ocean. When Vasco finally left, Daria was not herself and entered a state of deep-seated melancholia. She felt dirty in body and soul. She felt guilty, but mostly she felt painfully disappointed with life, with the forces commanding the world. She was invaded by a profound disenchantment. She was an idealist and wanted to live in a beautiful world; a world she had imagined as a little girl, playing games with Isabel; a world she could grasp because it was as near as the sky of Almores. And now this thing, this ugly thing had happened to her. And it had happened at a moment in her life when everything was perfect, when she had found Francisco and he had found her. How could she get up in the morning to face the world? How could she tell Francisco and denounce Vasco? She did not know if she would be able to do that, and all she wanted was to stay in that dark place with no windows and no light. She started singing Ivan Lins's song again. The words and the melody came out jumbled, as if she could not find any meaning in it anymore. She murmured it like a sad lullaby, mourning the day that had passed: "Cagliari? Fellini or it is our lives? In what film did our love happen? One more hour. One more scene ... I don't know. Happiness is a series of nuances." She cried and cried again, like she had at Copacabana, but this time she knew that her crying had a real identifiable source. In the club, she had felt sad but happy, happy but sad; her tears hadn't been for anything in particular, but rather for many entangled memories of people and places and feelings not quite her own—like *fado* music.

TELLING HIM. The next day, in the early morning, Daria found the courage to go to the hospital to be examined. She felt weak, devastated, and broken, but she possessed in her that strength of a young girl who wants justice to prevail and who believes the ugliest acts can be forgiven, perhaps even forgotten. The nurse at the hospital was very kind. She told Daria that she ought to tell the police right away and that, given the gravity of the assault, Daria would be entitled to a lofty sum as compensation. Daria felt strange, confused, and uncomfortable when the nurse mentioned monetary compensation. She thought of how her mother had always told her never to accept money from any man, advice that Daria had always followed. She thought that if she were to accept money from Vasco, she would feel like a prostitute; she would feel dirty, and her mother would surely think the same even in these circumstances. A *puta*, her mother would say in her crude and direct way. She felt money does not, cannot pay for these things. Money just makes you feel dirtier and guiltier. She told the nurse that all she wanted was an apology from the person who did this to her, an admittance that he had done something very wrong, something he ought to try and retract somehow. The nurse smiled and said that though that was a very kind gesture on Daria's part, from her experience, and she had seen a lot, these types of men are not very willing to admit their guilt and much less apologize for what they did, unless they are forced to. Still, Daria felt she ought to give Vasco a chance to explain, to tell her face to face, eye to eye why he would do something like that to her when he had said all along that she was just like his daughter. Just like his daughter. Just like Santeria. Daria took all the medical precautions, including the morning after pill. The nurse also referred her to a counsellor in the Portuguese community, thinking she would be more at ease with someone from her own cultural background, but Daria protested right away and said she would rather go to someone else. She did not want to share her sad story with a person who spoke the same language, a language where there are some words that have certain connotations, a language that would bring her too close to her emotions, not to mention those of her mother who had entered her in many ways, good and bad. She told the nurse how, back in Portugal, she had almost been raped by a man who had offered her a job as a model. She had been a fool and had gotten into the car of this unknown man. He had approached her in Rossio, downtown Lisbon, and told her he needed to take her to his studio, but instead he drove off to the outskirts of Lisbon and tried to assault her. She had begged the man to let her go, and then, in a moment of courage and salvation, she had managed to get out of the car when he stopped, running to the side of the road and climbing a cliff at the end of which she found a home—a light that would rescue her. She knocked on the door of this home, feeling very relieved she had been spared, but when she relayed her story to the lady who appeared behind the door, the first thing she said was: "Menina, if you have a boyfriend he will be very upset and he may leave you." At the time, Daria had felt very confused about what the woman said, for she believed she had not done anything wrong and didn't understand why her boyfriend, had she had one, would be upset at her. But she did not say anything to this woman and thanked her for helping her get to the train station safe and sound. The nurse said she understood her reasons for not wanting to see a counsellor in her own community and gave her another name, an anonymous name that sounded like nothing she had ever heard, nothing she could place anywhere. She liked that anonymity. The anonymity of that name and that possible relationship with the therapist created a distance between her and the incident, a distance between her and her mother, between her and her father, between her and Francisco, between her and Vasco. And she thought that perhaps, in that distance, she would be able to find the truth as to why this had happened to her, the reason why a man takes a woman as his even when that woman does not offer herself and never gave any indication that she wanted to be taken, even when that woman is like that man's own daughter, is the same age as that man's own daughter. She then went home and did not go to work that day, calling in and telling the secretary that she was not feeling well. She called Francisco and told him he needed to come see her as soon as he could, for something very bad—and she repeated *very bad* four times—had happened. Francisco asked what it was about, but she said the matter was grave and could not be disclosed over the telephone, through those strange and defective waves that are able to transport sound but cannot fully carry the truth of what is being told and felt by both the teller and the listener. He told her she was frightening him with her philosophical proclamations about telephone waves, which sounded like very bad omens. He told her he was extremely busy but would come as soon as he could. He did come a few hours later when the sun was about to set, entering the house with a very worried face, not knowing what to expect. Given that he was a man used to very grave and ugly events and circumstances, a man used to expecting the worst, his worried demeanour seemed to reveal that he really cared about Daria. He often hid his true feelings behind a blank mask—the mask that he had learned to put on to hide his secret, his beautiful idea—so the present nakedness of his face told Daria that she occupied a central place in his life, that she was indeed his finally found home. His expression confirmed what he had told her before through the title of the poetry book he said he would write about her and for her, or about her and him: *Beautiful Daria, My Finally Found Home.* It was a title full of softness, kindness, and dreams, with open endless vowels and alliteration, which Daria found appealing and appeasing to the ear, to the body, to the soul.

Telling him was hard. She was worried that he would be disappointed, that he would think less of her, that he would blame her. She felt guilty for giving him news that would bring him sadness, that would further burden him. He was a man who had suffered enough; he had paid his dues and did not need any more ugliness in his life. She also worried that he would love her less, even though, deep down, she knew she was not the one who should be blamed or punished. She knew she did not ask for it, like Vasco's defence lawyer would try to imply later in court. And then she also thought that she should have trusted her intuition, trusted that voice that was telling her earlier that Vasco da Gama might not quite be who he says he is, might not quite act as he says he acts, might not be worthy of the name and the title that he carries—and she would get confused again and blame herself some more. She had had a dream the night after the ugly event. The dream was mostly negative, but there had also been a moment of clarity and insight that had told her, without a shadow of a doubt, that she was clean, that she had not done anything wrong, just like Ana Magalhães had not done anything wrong when she suffered at the hands of Arsénio and his aids. In this dream, or rather, at this moment in the dream, she saw herself being born, she saw herself coming out of her mother's thunderous thighs. At first she thought she was ugly and dirty and born out of sin, but then she saw herself clean and naked and beautiful, her mother speaking to her in tender tongues and repeating, "She will be my last child because my womb is already tired. She will be named Daria. She is clean and beautiful, clean and beautiful, will always be clean and beautiful. Those are her possessions, and no one can take them away from her." That moment of the dream gave her confidence and assurance, the clear certainty that she was not to blame for the ugly dirt that had come her way, a dirt that was trying to bring shame to the shameless, to that which is clean *a priori*. Still, now that she had Francisco in front of her, telling him was hard. She felt that perhaps he would no longer want to marry her and have babies with her, and that she would never experience a perfect love, a perfect marriage, a perfect life. She had wanted to be his woman, only his, and now this had happened and she felt that the damage may be irreparable. She had already imagined her wedding day, her wedding dress, and she had discussed that glorious day many times with Francisco. They had decided that the day would come in a very near future, as soon as Francisco managed to secure an important trade contract between Canada and Mozambique and his divorce papers were finalized. The latter were being delayed, he had said, because of the inefficiencies of the Mozambican bureaucracy. The clerks of the civil registry office in Maputo had not yet been able to locate Ana and Francisco's marriage certificate. It had been lost in the massive annals where all the marriages—all the love stories between men and women that said yes to one another in that city of light by the Indian Ocean, yes, till death do us part—were dully annotated, like immortal witnesses to love. Francisco had also added that the Portuguese colonial government had never been interested in developing the infrastructure of Mozambique or in teaching Black people how to run an independent country since only a handful of them had become *assimilados* and had had access to the colonial education system. He said this was to blame for the current inefficiency in record keeping. The colonialists, he had gone on to say, trying to give Daria a history lesson, were only interested in taking out the country's wealth and bringing it to their own nation to enrich and develop it. Daria smiled and said that, yes, many of his points about colonial history were well taken, but she did not quite agree with this last statement because no infrastructure was ever really developed in Almores either, since the village still had no central sewage system or running water in most of the homes. She argued that Portugal continued to be at the bottom of the

European ladder, a member of the group that had recently been given the insulting label of PIGS. They both laughed and jokingly blamed it all on Salazar's peasant background, his habits of washing and peeing in the river, and his lack of knowledge about the direct relationship between good hygiene and health. But then Daria added that, as he well knew, the situation was much more complex and should really be blamed on the politics of transport, otherwise known as triangular mercantilism, practised during much of the Portuguese colonial era. These practices consisted of bringing the raw materials from the colonies and then selling them to the wise, pragmatic, and rationalist English, who pretty much controlled the entire scene. The English would then sell back finished products to Portugal or the colonies at exorbitant prices. Francisco counter-argued by noting that the situation had not been as clear-cut as she was implying and that the blame was to be found everywhere since the Portuguese also practised the politics of transport and in fact benefitted a great deal from it—and an ugly transport it was. They were, after all, the fathers of the transatlantic slave trade. But indeed, they may not have been as wise as the Englishmen and may have indulged in too many wasteful behaviours, making chairs and cartwheels out of, or even padding the ceilings of their houses with, pure gold. The salty sweat of Black people could still have been tasted in that precious metal, or on the walls, ceilings, and marble floors of imponent cathedrals, convents, and abbeys, had the colonizers not carefully cleaned it off, plunging thousands and thousands of Africans into oblivion, dumping them into an unconscious blind denial. The conversation had gone in many directions at the time, and many angles of the matter were explored, including the fact that African chiefs had also sold their own people to the European slave traders and had been slave traders themselves. They may not have been fully aware, however, of what was awaiting the slaves on the other side of the Atlantic under the whip of the master and the unforgiving sun of the coffee plantation. The slaves would become beings without a nation, deracinated, and dehumanized to the core. In the end, both Francisco and Daria agreed that power and too much material wealth always corrupt and that Karl Marx was indeed right when he said that a revolution is the only way to take away the wealth from those who have stolen it but think they legitimately got it—those who think they were born with it like a gift from a God, when in fact we were all born naked. Naked and beautiful.

Telling him was hard. She kept imagining her wedding day and her wedding dress, and she felt that that day and that dress may very well never come. She saw herself in an imaginary land, a land full of mountains and valleys all covered in yellow genistas, and then she saw herself inside that land, dressed as a bride, her dress also yellow. It was yellow inside yellow, a never-ending circle that confounded you, but in that confounding whirl you could find the most agreeable solace, the most agreeable realization. She saw the image of that land and herself inside that land in front of her. It was a vision inside a vision, as clear and beautiful and perfect as they could ever be. But the vision, the visions, the perfect whirl, which she had seen and felt clearly before, was now graspable for a moment only. As she tried to hold on to it, it would slowly walk away from her, leaving her destitute. She now saw herself in doubles: in the valley and at the top of the mountain, and in both places she was dressed in her stunning yellow bride dress. As she tried to ascend the mountain by climbing a ladder that had been placed there, she sensed that the ladder was infinite and that she would never get to the top. She saw herself climb and climb and then climb again, desperately trying to attain the highest point of herself, the happy bride at the peak of the mountain, but the journey was hard, impossible to conclude. It was as if it had been interrupted by the voices and deeds of the people who remained at the bottom of the mountain, or by her own self, that double of her that had stood motionless in the depression of the valley. The valleys and mountains were no longer dressed in yellow genistas; they had become desolate lands. The only thing that was now yellow and beautiful in that land was her in her dress. And she did not seem to be able to reconcile her two stranded selves, one at the bottom in the depressed valley and the other calling to it from the top of the mountain. She felt lost, without a secure ground to walk upon; she had been doubled, fragmented, broken into pieces by the many voices inside her head, inside her body, all confusing and tormenting the clean beautiful naked self she had been born with—that most precious possession. She was herself in herself, but she was also outside of herself trying to see the future. She wanted to know whether that future would hold after she disclosed to Francisco what had happened between her and Vasco. He took her hand in his, locking her in his magnetic pulse, and he looked her in the eye. He stared at her, immobilized in a prolonged and silenced stillness. She felt he already knew about the ugly incident. But he did not know.

My darling Francisco, what I am about to tell you may break your heart, but I hope it does not do so. I hope that it only makes you love me more and want me more. I hope that reminding you of this ugliness may also make you more forgiving, more loving towards me, towards love, love that calls itself love. I feel strange and uncomfortable telling you this, but deep down, in the clean part of myself, I do know that I am not guilty, that I did not do anything wrong. I did not ask for anything, did not provoke anything. And so I feel like a beggar who should not be begging, but I cannot stop myself from begging. It's as if I am commanded by an invisible force, a force that has shaped me and that I cannot shake off.

Last night, when Vasco dropped me off at my place, after he left you at yours, he did something to me, something that is very difficult to describe to you. He did to me what Arsénio and the guards did to Ana in that dungeon of slow death.

She tried to say more, but her mouth could not speak those words. She went into a poetic ramble, where psychosis and metaphor become beautiful haunting images of the wounds of the human soul, those created by us and those we allow others to create for us. She became hysterical, a child wanting to recount the lullaby or the fairy tale she had heard to her prince, to convince him that happiness is still possible and that all one has to do is to believe. Belief is the mother of all, the sister of the spring, the cousin of the summer. She told him a beautiful story. She had composed it in her head a while ago under other circumstances, but it applied to this circumstance just as well as it had applied to the other; the story had helped Daria when she was searching for meaning, meaning behind the pulsating world, the water that runs and bathes and cures. The story was called "The Revelation of Camilla," otherwise known as "Rescuing the Divine." She recited it word by word, syllable by syllable, like she had the other time, trying to find meaning, convey meaning, find love in sorrow, life in death, clarity in confusion:

She was a fool, or at least that was what some thought. But God, how wrong they were. The first time I met her I was only a girl of eleven. A mere little girl, so much closer to infancy than adolescence. Unlike many of my age, I wanted so much to delay my womanhood. I wanted to impede my body from growing so that the young boys, or worse yet, the older men would not look at me with lust and unkind wonder in their eyes. I wanted to delay my age so that my legs would stay thin, my behind in the shadow of the invisible, and my breasts just little roses in a state of perpetual buds.

I wanted to remain here, between all the seasons, perhaps with a hint of spring. I wanted to imagine, always from afar, what I could be and what I may be. I never wanted to be one thing only, caught between the dreams of many people, the seasons of many centuries. I wanted to stay young so that my eyes would forever stare with wonder and wander about, taking in everything around and about me. I wanted to stay young, young, and so, like God's gift, this secret wish of the most intimate part of myself, materialized when I saw her. Lady Camilla was her name. She became my friend forever, my invisible friend who would appear to me when I most needed her. She would give me dreams and make me walk in astounding beauty in those large, unending lavender fields. She would sing me songs. She would call me to the many things that there are in this world and the world beyond this. I was not alone. I was not poor. I was.

He did not seem moved. He did not understand. His poetic vein had been suddenly frozen by the venom that the world had injected into him, once again. And this time the snake had really won.

ICANNOT. She has been wasted. I want to love her. I know she is beautiful and clean, but I cannot touch her. I see in her Ana being raped by Arsénio and his aids. I see her beautiful young body being taken by another man, and in that vision I cannot find forgiveness, I cannot regain pure love, pure yearning. I see my baby being soiled by the sperm of another man who has always been a friend to me. I see my idea being destroyed. Daria. I cannot believe he would do this to me, to her, to us. He is my friend, a man who has also suffered the shackles of colonization. I cannot forgive Ana or Arsénio or the guards or myself. Daria. I had to let Ana go, for I could no longer touch her. Every time I lay down on the same bed with her and tried to put my hands on her belly, they became frozen. She stayed for a while, immobile under my frozen fingers, thinking my wounds would be cured with time, that they would be cleansed by the beautiful metaphors that I invented to cover the ugly in *The Idea Against Tarrafal*—through an alchemy of love and the ultimate visionary alphabet. She hoped that words could in fact do that, but wounds are wounds, and sometimes they are so great that they cannot be washed away, will never be washed away. No catharsis is possible. She waited in vain: her belly never became warm to my desire. Since then, I have been covering them up, the wounds, behind this mask that I always wear. I have acted like a man in full control of himself, a rational, pragmatic being who does not allow himself to be shaken by emotion. But the truth is that I am not made of iron. Daria. My mask is a mere lie; underneath it are the ugly events that have shaped my life. And there are many of those ugly events, too many to recount fully in a lifetime, and they are too difficult to recount using this language that we humans use. We think we know what we are saying and that we can say what we feel, how we feel, but we don't. I cannot touch her. She has been wasted. She was my salvation, and now I am at point zero again. I became a sex addict after my release from Tarrafal, going from woman to woman, always virgins. I was trying to rescue Ana, to repossess her before she was wasted. I thought if I could do this, I would perhaps find a way to save her from that doomed future and that I would forever have her. I thought I could return to the time before those ugly days at the prison, that I could stare at her frank and clean smile, her hope and mine together working toward the beautiful. And now this. Daria, beautiful Daria. She was my salvation, and she has also been spoiled. I am at square one, and I am afraid that I will never be able to become a normal human being who sees women as women, not as bodies to be taken and used and possessed and dispossessed. I am lost, a man without redemption, without future. Where is my escape? I have abandoned her, leaving her alone in her pain, soiled by the dirt of another man and without my understanding. I am broken; I am gone. I no longer know whom to believe. Vasco da Gama claims she is lying. He says she is a liar who cannot even work legally at the centre because she came to Canada as a nanny and was restricted to that profession for at least two years. He says she is a woman who uses her physical beauty to trap men of power and then makes a public scandal out of her debauchery. She is shameless. Just a peasant—like her parents. She has admitted to me that she did come to Canada as a nanny and that she did not disclose her immigration status to Vasco, but that he also did not ask for any papers, any proof until after the incident. She said that, in fact, she should have had her open work permit by the time she started working at the centre but that she has not received it due to the backlog at Immigration; she says she is a victim of bureaucracy. I believe her. I want to believe her. She is a woman full of depth and poetry in her body and her soul. But Vasco is my friend, and he is a man of standing in the community. I am a man of standing in the community. I cannot look at her in the eye and tell her all this, but this is all that I feel. I must find a way to let her know our romance cannot go on now. How can I find a dignified way to tell her that? I really thought she and I were it. I really thought she was the one who would cure my illness, this vicious need to possess women who have never been possessed. I really thought she was my Daria.

My therapist tells me that I suffer from PTSD and that all I really need to do is face the pain that I endured in the past and let my mask go. All I need to do is open my soul and my heart to the wounds that Salazar and his counterparts, and all his ancestors since Vasco da Gama, have inflicted on me. All I need to do is deal with this trauma, which he calls colonial trauma. He tells me that he himself suffers from slavery trauma, which he has been trying to overcome by taking many different steps. It started slowly, but today he feels like he is a real man, someone who believes in himself. Now, when a white man looks him in the eye, he does not look down or move; he stares right back. But in South Africa, he continues, Black men still have difficulty staring at white men in the face. In South Africa, even after all that Mandela endured, and despite his beautiful speeches that pierce the soul and really make you believe, despite the end of institutional apartheid, people still live side by side but not together. The rainbow nation is just an illusion—a beautiful Daria, a flying dream running in the savannahs of Africa waiting to find a bed. We keep waiting to see this idea be made manifest, and we are becoming tired, tired and disillusioned with the distance that still remains between the verbs *to be* and *to become*. He tells me all this as if he were my own double; he tells me that I must face the dark side of my self, like he has done, that place where the pain throbs fully, waiting to be heard, felt, caressed. He tells me that is the only way for me to stop hurting others and myself. He tells me that a real man shows his emotions and lets the mask down; a real man allows the tears to roll and the lips to tremble uncertain and convulsed. But I do not think that I am ready yet. I do not think that I can let it go, that I can let this crutch go. This crutch gives me power and allows me to relive my love affair with Ana. Ana. The beautiful and fierce Ana, who begged me to father her more children after we left Tarrafal because I had stopped touching her belly and rolled to the other side of the bed every time she came to me to feel my veins. My therapist is a man of knowledge who tells me that I must read Fanon's *Peau noire, masques blancs* to understand the depth of my bondage. He tells me I have been reading too many books by European and Western thinkers, including Karl Marx. He says those books have corrupted my soul and they are preventing me from seeing who I really am. He tells me I must travel deep down there, to the place of the ancestors, in order to regain my true self and that this symbolical voyage has been taken by many in my condition and has given them great solace, great self-assurance, making them feel at home. He tells me to read Derek Walcott, the Saint Lucian poet who proclaims he has no nation but his imagination.

My therapist is a man of knowledge, and suffering too. He came from St. Lucia and has felt to the bone the damage that slavery can cause. He has felt the damage that has been inflicted upon him and his long line of ancestors, bodies and bodies crossing the sea to come to another world that was not theirs. They are the same people whom I tried to liberate in the dream that I had, that dream where I was a knight mounted on the most beautiful stallion, saving my people and bringing them from the bottom of the sea to a secure shore, where warmth and open arms were there to receive them. My therapist is a man of knowledge and I respect him, but I think his ideas are a little too utopian. I think he wants to regain his pre-colonial Africa, pristine and perfect, but that Africa has never really existed. I have seen how my brothers killed and sold one another. I am an *assimilado*, I know that, but I am a man who has lived on the soil of Africa and on the white soil too. I have lived in exile in and out of Africa. I think I can master both systems, and I am not completely convinced that constantly chasing after virgins and white women is an attempt to regain the power that the white men took away from me, like my therapist says, like Fanon says when he writes that the dream of the colonized is to sleep with the white woman and eat at the colonizer's table. To be honest, I like all kinds of women: Black, Chinese, Indian, white … I like to travel through their colours and sense with my fingers the different complexions, the different patterns of their noses, mouths, eyes, and hips. It's a "Mambo No. 5" song: *a little bit of Sandra, a little bit Jessica…*

It feels like the world is in my hands when I am with a woman. It feels like I am boundless, that I can travel the wide earth and taste its fruits, here and there, here and there, like an explorer. I like possessing women, and, let's face it, Africa is ridden with patriarchy, from left to right, from bottom to top. I understood, from very early on, that women were there for men's pleasure. I learned this from my mother, my father, my sisters, my brothers. My sisters and my mother ate the leftover food, after all the men had eaten. My father had seven wives and divided his sperm between all of them, one day here and another there. I have many brothers and sisters that I do not even know. We do not quite see eye-to-eye here, my therapist and I. And when he says that the main reason African-Canadian women suffer from depression is that they are not following Afrocentric values, I get a little confused. I ask him to define Afrocentric values, telling him that his position makes it seem as if African men and African culture are not against women, are not patriarchal. He says that is precisely what he thinks and that he has done extensive research on the subject. He says he knows that pre-colonial Africa was truly communal, a place where women were respected and had equal access to power. I note that one can find all kinds of evidence to prove an idea that one wants to prove, and I argue that his position is extreme and biased—that he is being purely reactionary, that perhaps he ought to read Wole Soyinka and Buchi Emecheta and Paulina Chiziane to find out some other truths, more balanced stories. I tell him that perhaps he has been reading too many purists, the likes of Ngũgĩ wa Thiong'o and Léopold Sédar Senghor who, though profound and righteous and beautiful, are not always as objective as they ought to be and can sometimes come across as racist or ethnocentric in a manner similar to the European colonial masters, not to mention misogynistic. "Perhaps," I add, thinking of Ngũgĩ wa Thiong'o's passionate Africanism, particularly his novel *The River Between*, "what men need is to decolonize their minds, decolonize it from patriarchy, that is." I also say that he ought to read Fanon more carefully, for one of Fanon's central points is that those who are oppressed often go on to oppress others, whom they perceive as having less power, in order to regain some power—something that Fanon in fact mourns deeply, wishing, praying that we could find another way, a better way, a more beautiful way. Perhaps that is why Black women are the ones who suffer the most, for they are dealing with what Kimberlé Crenshaw has called intersectionality. They are the victims of multiple guns trying to destroy their wholeness, their fundamental right to be. Black men are oppressed by white men, and then they oppress Black women even more as a way to regain some power. If only we could find a way to regain true power and step out of this disgraceful dynamic. If only we could find a beautiful way, the beautiful way. This is also the fatalistic dynamic guiding Arsénio de Oliveira, as I try to show in *The Idea Against Tarrafal*: he is an abused and deeply traumatized man, who feels poor and undervalued inside and out, and then goes on to abuse others in unthinkable ways.

But my therapist maintains his positions firmly, unshaken by my doubts, my attempts to contradict, complicate, and debunk them. He further adds that I am grossly misreading Ngũgĩ wa Thiong'o's intentions in *The River Between*, for his main objective in that novel is not to necessarily defend female genital mutilation—he insists on calling it "cutting"—but rather to decolonize the minds of Kenyans (and Africans in general) by making them question the Christian and European ideologies they have slavishly and uncritically internalized. The novel, he argues, is to be understood as an allegory, a type of sublimation in reverse, if you will, which could be interpreted as the author's direct attempt to dismiss some of Sigmund Freud's psychoanalytical theories, an erotic manifestation of rejection of colonial cultural baggage, a phenomenology of love, as superbly argued by the Cameroonian-American scholar Elias Bongmba in his article "On Love: Literary Images of a Phenomenology of Love in Ngũgĩ wa Thiong'o's *The River Between*." He, my therapist, recently became a chief in Ghana, and despite the fact that he lives in Canada and works as a therapist full time, while also doing his PhD in Anthropological African Studies, he manages to travel there frequently to perform his duties. This honour and title were given to him because he has done a lot of good work with different communities in that country. The other day, when he was interviewed on the national radio, the interviewer asked him how a chief must act. He replied that there are very specific protocols to follow. For example, one cannot go out on the street alone without one's aids, one cannot walk barefoot, and one must not get drunk or abuse others. As I heard his answers, I smiled, for I know that in certain parts of Africa the community chief also has the right to sleep with a young virgin woman if he so chooses. In speaking about the community that he represented, I noted how he avoided mentioning anything that would imply that the men had more power than women. He also kept talking about the Queen Mothers and their paramount role. He did not mention that even they are still mostly under men's power and that the areas that they control are considered to be less important. He did not address female circumcision. He did not address polygamy and how it often creates jealousy between the women. He did not address the many initiation rites that women undergo, rites that teach them that their main role is to please their men sexually, that their happiness is secondary to the men's, that suffering is their lot in life. He spoke like a good politician, a man who has a specific agenda. There was also an article in a Canadian newspaper, *The Canadian Times*, that described him as follows: *This man possesses the high distinction and wisdom of a true African chief. From the way he walks to the way he talks. He exudes nothing but rectitude, nothing but knowledge, and so being given the title of chief is only fitting.* Upon reading this article, I chuckled because my father too was a traditional chief in Mozambique, and he benefitted from all the perks that being a powerful and respected colonial overseer warranted him. He was all that, and yet he did all that he did to his people and to me. He had a great demeanour too, and he spoke with distinction. He had seven wives and never doubted that he had the right to have them, that they had been made to bow before him and lie under this weight whenever he needed the warmth of their thighs. When I tried to discuss the interview and the article with the newly appointed Ghanaian chief, he became very professional and said we were there to discuss my neurosis, my PTSD, not his diverse career. I did not say anything because I needed him to help me. I am a sick man trying to find a way out of my painful and confusing darkness, but I am not fully convinced of his methods, his views relating to my condition and his own condition, for I think the matter is really much more complicated than meets the eye.

The trial between Daria and Vasco is set to happen very soon. I still do not know how I should act, what I should say. His lawyer has summoned me to provide a character witness about Daria. I am Vasco's friend, but I used to be in love with the beautiful Daria. I have not seen her in several weeks. I have avoided her, and, sensing that, she did not beg. Sometimes I dream about her, how stunning she was that first time we made love, how her breasts were roses inside roses, Russian dolls inside Russian dolls. I dream about her gentle and poetic manner, and that way she has of seeing deeply into things. I dream about her like this, over and over again, trying to regain, restore that moment, that moment before the fall. If I were a perfect man, if I had really learned from the evil that was inflicted on me, I would still love Daria as much as I loved her then. But I am a mere mortal, I am an African and a European, I am a universal man, and I possess all the faults of those men. If I had become illuminated, if I had truly escaped my ego, if I had become acquainted with the big self in those magnificent voyages that I undertook inside the chamber and on other occasions—when the soul becomes bigger than the body, than the man, as I describe in *The Idea Against Tarrafal*—I would not do to women what I have been doing to them. I would not do to Daria what I have been doing to her, what I am about to do to her. I would not, because I would have truly entered her being, felt her pain. Do as you would be done by: that is the golden law.

THE DIVERSITY DIRECTOR. Daria, you used to know a very *sui generis* director of diversity while working at the Hospital of the Soul. He was hired when the idea of diversity in the workplace was really starting to take hold in Canadian society, or at least in Toronto. His name was Abassi Izuora Mbembe, but he was also known as Michael von der Post, the last name alluding to his dark history, that atrocious passage through the Atlantic that left so many marks, visible and invisible. It could not be otherwise, for the human soul and body can only allow so much disgrace to penetrate their clean, breathing core before sickness takes hold. Some still called him Michael, but he would quickly correct them, saying in a calm timbered voice—where, if we paid attention, we could detect a slight accent, but one that was impossible to locate, to attach to any existing tribe in Africa, America, or Europe—"My name is Abassi, Abassi Izuora Mbembe." He, Abassi, was massively tall and always walked as though he was very sure of himself, erect like a beautiful monument that no one could ever bring down. In his position of diversity director, he had ordered a book for newcomers to Canada to be translated into a particular African language, Akhunnia, and then printed in high numbers. To everyone's surprise, the book was never requested by any newcomers and the copies just sat there in the closet collecting dust and mould, waiting for the mysterious people from Africa to arrive. He got into a little trouble with the executive team for ordering a booklet that benefited no one. They pointed to the fact that, in this age of economic depression, we all had to be careful about how the money was spent. When they asked him why he had ordered the booklet to be published in Akhunnia, a language that no one was able to locate in any part of Africa—a fact that was confirmed by the independent consultant hired for the purpose—he became irritated and simply said, "I am the diversity director, and as the holder of this title, I know the languages spoken throughout the world. I know the languages of my motherland." Shortly after that incident, news came that Abassi was voluntarily leaving the Hospital of the Soul to pursue his other interests, which included finishing his PhD in Anthropological African Studies. He studied a new branch of Anthropology, which followed an Afrocentric epistemological approach, and his research topic was the collectivity systems in pre-colonial Africa. Later on, Daria found out through a private source that the CEO of the hospital had received a call from a very angry Caribbean woman who accused Abassi of defending and perpetuating patriarchy in his therapy sessions by insisting that Black women follow Afrocentric family values. This woman was doubly upset because she did not even consider herself African. Apparently, she threatened to sue the hospital if they did not get rid of Abassi.

After leaving the hospital, Abassi took off to the African continent for several years, completely cutting off communication with Canada and the Caribbean, where he was originally from. None of his relatives heard from him during that time. He immersed himself fully into the collectivity systems that he was studying so that he could write his dissertation (he called it a treatise) and share it with the rest of the world. His goal was to prove that evidence of true egalitarian systems could still be found in Africa, and that these systems had been ruined by the unkind interferences of arrogant white foreigners and Islamic sheiks. He spent years excavating an area where the remains of that perfectly egalitarian community had once existed. He found all kinds of utensils—like forks, spoons, and broken pots—as well as human skeletons, and he was also able to discern the precise dimensions of the houses where entire families had lived in perfect and joyous communion. To these discoveries, he applied the most modern and non-universal anthropological methodology, explaining in great and highly precise detail how the forks, the spoons, the broken pots, the size of both men and women's bodies, and the house dimensions reflected the true egalitarian system of pre-colonial African societies. At the end of page 776 of his dissertation, his conclusion read: *These ruins are the mirror of what the Europeans and the Muslims did to the great civilization of my ancestors. One ought to rebuild these ruins and bring them to full life so that the world can regain its full sense and learn how to live from ancient Africa, which, after all, is the mother to all of us, a fact to which the latest discoveries related to the origin of the humans species attest.* He had to defend his dissertation in front of a committee of twelve professors at the Northern University in Canada, one of the most prestigious in the country. Although all twelve of them specialized in specific aspects of African civilizations, they also had their own stubborn, individual views on the matter Abassi was writing about. Not to mention the fact that they all had fallen victim to what is generally known as inherent bias in the discipline. As a result, Abassi had great difficulty in successfully defending his dissertation. He presented it to the committee many times, and he failed it as many times as he presented it. He rewrote it many times to accommodate some of the committee member's viewpoints and ideological trenchant, but he also left room to explain and be faithful to his ideas. He did not want to feel like a traitor to himself, but there was always someone who would have a problem with some aspect of his reasoning, argumentation or evidence. After each failure, frustrated but resolved to continue the battle, he would go to the site again and rethink the objects he had found, re-measure the house dimensions one more time and carefully and rigorously apply the methodology of the discipline to the findings. He would end up reworking a few arguments here and there to see if the professors would all be happy this time so that the trial could end once and for all and he could move on with his agenda and work in the real world. But because his conclusion would always remain the same, when he came back to the defence table and sat in front of those who had the power to decide whether he should become a doctor of philosophy or not, and thus be in a legitimate position to teach the world, no consensus could be found and he was again impeded from obtaining his doctorate. He often would have anxiety dreams, his angst replaying over and over again and his unconscious, in conversation with his conscious, would try to find a solution to the problem he was having. One particular night, he had an illuminating dream that involved a big pot of soup. He saw himself in his kitchen in front of a big black pot of soup. His dissertation director was there with him, and he was trying out the soup, which was still cooking on the stove, with a long wooden spoon. The professor tried a spoonful and then another and another, taking a sample from a different part of the pot each time, and each time he shook his head negatively, stating that the soup was not quite ready to serve yet, that Abassi needed to add a pinch of salt, a little more Italian zucchini, a little more of the Indian yellow spice known as curry, a little more yam to thicken the texture, a cup of coconut juice to balance the taste, and so on and so forth. Abassi agreed that a little more yam and coconut juice would be good ingredients to add because they were original products of Africa, but he did not see the point in bringing in more quantities of the Italian and Indian elements because the soup was already full of non-African elements, including its very base, which consisted of Knorr chicken broth, an imported artificial product from Germany. They argued with one another for what seemed to be a very long time, and the supervising professor said that Abassi was in fact wrong for thinking the coconut was indigenous to Africa and that, had he thoroughly investigated the matter as a careful scholar ought to do, he would have found out that that fruit is actually indigenous to Austronesian-speaking nations and has, through commercial transactions and throughout millennia, been brought to and cultivated in various parts of the world. Eventually Abassi lost his temper and threw the soup on the kitchen floor, stepping on it over and over again—though what he had really wanted to do was throw it directly at the professor so that he would stop arguing with him and trying to make him push his epistemology forward. He woke up sweating and afflicted from the drama that had taken place in his kitchen. He lay awake in his bed for some time reflecting on it, and then suddenly he understood exactly what he had to do. He decided to fire his entire committee and find one that would be solely composed of professors who had been born in Africa and educated in African universities. It occurred to him that the reason he was failing his dissertation over and over again was that his committee members were all Western professors using mostly Western-based ingredients to analyze his work, just like the soup that he had been making in the dream. They could never see what he was trying to prove and would always apply their Eurocentric universal method to African cultures, just like their ancestors had done since at least the fifteenth century. They carried, still deep within themselves, Rudyard Kipling's civilizational burden and complex. When he explained his plan to an African friend of his from Nigeria, his friend told him he had to be careful because a lot of those African professors could very well be more Westernized than the Westerners. And he gave specific examples to support his argument: the way Nigerian judges and lawyers kept wearing that ridiculous blond wig regardless of the local climate, and the way upper-class Nigerian women kept referring to any girl who showed her cleavage as immoral and were even trying to impose a regulated dress code for university girls. Of course, if we go back to pre-1800s Nigeria, his friend continued, we see women selling fruit at the market naked from the waist up, fully displaying their breasts. Abassi replied that Nigeria, despite being the most populated African nation, does not constitute the whole of Africa. In fact, he continued, it is also the most corrupted one, and should therefore, not be used as a standard good example.

Abassi had a shaved head, which sharply contrasted with his long beard that almost reached his chest. The beard had abundant silvery tones that contributed to his air of distinction, making him irresistible. He was stunning, just stunning, illustrious, with skin dark as the night—not just any night, but rather the night of epiphany, the night of revelation. He had teeth like you'd never seen before: white, straight, almost otherworldly. He reminded you of the proud African kings that you would have seen in films here and there, during colonial times and then after colonialism had fallen and the African continent was trying to find its way out of the ugly mess that the Europeans had engendered during the many centuries of exploitation. He looked like a resurrected African king who wanted to show the world that Africa did indeed exist fully before the Europeans went there, that it had its own culture and its own sophisticated political systems, and that it had been happy and fulfilled and civilized without the white man. When you first met him, you could not stand to look at him directly; he made you feel afraid and ashamed and guilty, as if you yourself were responsible for what your ancestors did while in his continent, or rather his ancestors' continent. He made you want to cry—cry out of love, out of pain, out of mercy. Cry because of something that you could not quite understand or call by its true name. At the time, not long after your love affair with Francisco had ended and turned very ugly, you were starting to feel irrationally attracted to Black men and had just started studying African literatures. You went on and on about Abassi, about his goals and his beautiful ideas. You told your friends that Africa was a stunning, perfect place before the colonizers got there, a place with collective systems of social organizations that we in the West could not possibly understand, and that we were becoming poor as a result of that incapacity. Your friends would point out that you were sexualizing Black men. You didn't entirely agree with that; in fact, you thought that they, the Black men—or at least the ones you came in contact with—were sexualizing you too. And some of those same friends—the ones who had lived longer, had travelled abroad much more than you, and had read several books and treatises written by the gurus of many civilizations—appointed themselves as truly multicultural critics and said there ought to be limits to cultural relativism and that female genital mutilation really ought to go. They would say that you were very fond of utopias and that you always tried to find them. And when you couldn't find them, you would invent them, like a Marx of sorts. You were young then and impressionable, and there was that thing stirring between your legs that often made you fall on your knees and tremble in pure expectation. And Abassi did that for you. Abassi Izuora Mbembe. He was like another version of Francisco, one who was a little farther away from home, who did not speak the Lusitanian language. Perhaps because of that you were even more attracted to him. His otherness made you feel more yourself. You thought about and would invoke the deeply philosophical, mystical, and poetic writings of Emmanuel Lévinas and Luce Irigaray to prove to them (and to yourself) that indeed the other is the way to the self—as long as the self does not incorporate that other into itself, eating up his individuality, his difference, like a starved cannibal always in need of the meat and soul of someone, of something. You felt safer with him because you spoke in English with him, that neutral language that did not evoke in you all kinds of emotions, and in which words did not seem as crude as they did when pronounced in Portuguese. Even bad, dirty words, said in the heat of the moment when you were making love with him, seemed less intense, less promiscuous, less visceral. After the whole affair with Francisco and Vasco,

you wanted nothing to do with the Portuguese community—
or rather with the Portuguese-speaking community, since
Francisco and Vasco were not Portuguese themselves, a fact
they brought up in court to argue their innocence and their
victimhood. It was their defence.

Abassi Izuora Mbembe. You would pronounce his name
over and over again like you had pronounced Francisco's.
You would see him in your dreams, his beautiful body
against yours teaching you the ways of heaven and the true
spirituality of being, teaching you how to lose your virginity
and regain it again through magical African wisdoms that
only those from there, with ebony skin and shining eyes could
teach you. It was as if he, stunning Abassi, also represented
your father and his ways of being. In your mind, he, like your
father, represented the old way of being, which is also the
most modern, the most present, the most futuristic, the most
eternal. It was a true and pure attachment to the land, to
the cows, to the plants, to the skies—a perfect communion
with everything and everyone in the universe. Both spoke
that language that says without saying, that teaches slowly
and unobtrusively and allows you to truly see, feel, and be.
It was as if you were trying to recreate the beauty of your
old village back in Portugal, to make it exist just like you
left it or like you thought it was then, like you remember
it being then. You could see it: animals and people living
and breathing together, houses without running water, and
women carrying buckets of it on their heads from the central
fountain to clean and cook and bathe and drink. It was as if
you were transferring all your yearnings—all your *saudade*
for that which had been lost, for the past, for what you did
not have and perhaps never would—to Abassi. In so doing,
you proved Freud's theories of how twisted the human mind
can be—how tricky, how confused, how delusional, how
unreliable, how subjective, and also how relentless in its
search for perfection and fulfillment.

And then there were your two brothers who went to the colonial wars in Angola and Guinea Bissau, forced by Salazar and his entourage. There was the one who never came back, who was blown away by the mines hidden in the middle of the dark and luscious forest, the Mayombe full of secrets. It was as if he, Abassi, was your link to them, especially to Alberto, your mother's first-born. He had had fair, fair skin and black curly, curly hair—facts that your mother kept repeating as though she were haunted by a past that cannot correct itself, as though she occupied a space that was equally beautiful and equally ugly. You never saw Alberto because you were the last to arrive—sometime after Marcos—the last to exit your mother's tired womb, while he was the first to inhabit her new house, the house of a young woman—a clean, clean house still completely ready to shelter love and life. And then there were the other dark things, the unnameable things that your people had done since the fifteenth century, the things they had done to the beautiful continent. All of this was playing in you, playing against and with you, and you wanted to live and learn and love and remedy the errors of history to make things better, to make the pain go away, both your own and that of others. And Abassi was stunning, just stunning. And there was that vast, pounding, liquid thing stirring between your legs, calling you, calling you by its own name, like a voice coming from the remote corners of yourself, the world's self, viscerally potent, viscerally incantatory. The mere sound of his name made you see the beautiful place somewhere in Africa before the Europeans got there, a place like no other where everything made sense. It was a place where animals and people and trees, the sea and the sky and the earth were truly interconnected, creating a universal language and making humans feel complete, complete, wholes of wholes. You were much younger than him and you were white, so you tried to find a way for him to see you, to love you, to communicate with you. You wanted him to call you by your name, your name. He had a reputation of being a lady's man at the hospital, and you had heard rumours about his improper conduct with the ladies: Black, white, Chinese, you name it. He was truly multicultural. He wanted them all like a hungry man who cannot say no to any offer that openly and generously offers itself. And indeed there were many offers. They would come to him from every corner of the world, eager to give, to feed him, to lie beneath his body and feel his heavy thrust inside their virgin vaginas, vulvas utterly hungry to be penetrated to the core. They wanted to truly find their name, their purpose, their destiny. He had a reputation and you hated PIGS, so you tried to convince yourself—in your mind, in your body, in your deep self—that this man could not be what they said he was. He could not be because you needed him and you needed him to need you. You became deaf to the rumours; you became obsessed by his own voice, beard, skin; and you kept reading Africanists like Ngũgĩ wa Thiong'o, Agostinho Neto, Léopold Sédar Senghor, and Aimé Césaire. These writers talked about mother Africa incessantly, yearning and calling for a return to pre-colonial African values, to a place where justice, equality, and mystical consciousness existed—all those things that made human beings feel truly alive. You kept reading and reading beautiful poems that create, in stunning language, that Africa of the past—so how could you not want Abassi? How could you be blind to his beauty or deaf to his wisdom and his profound insights? You read about elders in the Kalahari Desert of Namibia who were still shepherds and cow herders and were trying to keep their language alive, that undulating language with lows and highs and clicks, a language like no other, a language that told millenary lives through oral stories. Long, endless lives, displayed just like that from memory, with no pen or paper, as if the human mind were indeed the greatest monument, keeping alive all the records of history, encoding them in its cells, these sturdy recording tapes that do not, cannot forget.

Stories and stories pouring out, like marvels of another world, a world that is trying to be kept alive, to preserve the beauty of the magnificent old ways. Just like your father, a peasant with land and cows, who loved his way of life so much that he needed, he wanted his sons and daughters to carry on his tradition, to cultivate the land and raise the cattle, so that what he loved and knew the most—and he himself—would not vanish. In fact, he had ten children so that they could help him work the land, keeping it alive through veins and veins of memories, vines of wine produced every spring that made you drunk to the core and satiated your most profound thirst. But then came the new ways: the tractors and the corn and the potatoes and the wine and the beans arrived in truckloads from other parts of Europe, from the whole wide world. His crops and his way of life lost value, leaving him melancholic and mourning the days of Salazar, when he worked from sunrise to sunset and life made sense. Yes, the new ways came and took away most of his daughters and sons, who eagerly entered the new modus operandi, finding ways to cross the borders. They went to France, Germany, and even beyond, trying to reach the American dream that, though farther away, was believed to be the most fulfilling one. The new ways came, and he was left almost alone, anchored to that powerful rocky village on top of a mountain. He was left there to admire the sun, still fascinated by the magnanimous way it illuminates the world and all the other small stars that visit at night. He still believed that the sun moved around the earth, like the eye tells you, and not the other way around, like the scientists insist on claiming. He was still fascinated by the way his cows mooed when he spoke to them, calling them by their own names, as if there was no fundamental difference between them and himself; they were all beings of the same god, children of the same universe. He was like a mercy of the eternal refusing to move and break the beauty of time. He wanted time to be a sphere, not a straight line that blinds us to the meaning of the world.

Your father and Abassi. Intertwined in your mind as seekers of the same truths, guards of the same fortress, and you, alone in this new world of the Americas. Alone, young, and beautiful, eager to open your soul and your legs to whatever came your way so that you could feel pregnant with fulfilment, know all there is to know, and attain perfection and completion. You still believed that total happiness could be attained and that one only needs to take the right steps—one only needs to grasp it and grow up to be able to attain it. As a child, you believed that things were not yet perfect because you were a child and were not yet formed, but that they would become perfect as you grew older, because you yourself would become perfect. He, Abassi, was another Francisco. Or he was what Francisco could not be for you. You felt you ought to try again and recreate the beautiful. It was as if you felt guilty about something, and you wanted to make up for it. You believed Vasco da Gama's claims, and then you believed the profoundly disappointed voice of Francisco when the judge asked him to tell the truth and nothing but the truth. Tell the truth and nothing but the truth, for that is love. Love bigger than the earth, love bigger than the sea, love bigger than the sky, the kind, the king you truly need, we truly need, if only we were not blind. And so you loved Abassi totally only to discover that he too could not give you what you had to find for yourself, in yourself. No one could give you something that you could not get yourself, especially when that something is love, love and forgiveness for yourself. Only when you have those, love and forgiveness for yourself, can you move ahead and look at the stars and cry with gratitude, with your full body, your full being. You were a fool, Daria. You were always looking for the beautiful, the perfect, the total, the big, the wide, that which contains all and everything. That splendid, brilliant vacuum, opening itself in front of you to take you into its immensity. Just like Abassi. And that's why you loved him, wanted to love him, wanted to believe his thesis of true collectivity. But as Hegel reminds us, and as Marx also believed, there is always an antithesis to a thesis to allow for the formation of another thesis. And the entire process is so dynamic that the past cannot really ever be recovered, at least not in palpable terms. Perhaps it is made alive only through beautiful words, through beautiful paintings, or in the stunning stories of Adam and Eve before the fatal fall. And so you yearn, constantly.

ANOTHER SESSION. Today I called Ms. Gloria Bollatti, my therapist, to ask her if she could see me pronto, for I was having a particularly bad week. My emotions were being triggered by everything and anything under the sun, and I felt like I needed to see her straight away if I was going to survive another day. I was wearing my emotions on my sleeve, as they say in English. My mother tells me a similar thing in Portuguese: "Your emotions are always at the flower of the skin, and we can't tell you anything because everything brings you to convulsive crying." And yes, everything was coming to me, like a torrent of salty, very dirty, and heavy water. My body had been carrying this water like an immense sea, but it could no longer hold its weight and I bent down to the floor, my legs suddenly seized by its force.

She sits there patiently listening to me. Today I need her to listen, only listen and not give any opinion about what she listens to. I need to get clean, to ejaculate the filth. I speak to her in sentences that make sense, and then I move to the senseless, as if I am a patient at the Hospital of the Soul and I am transcribing myself. I am both the transcriber and the transcribed, and perhaps, given my experience, there will be little discrepancy between the message and the messenger. My case is unlike that of Mackenzie, who was a being outside of myself, whom I had to capture as faithfully as I could in my report, which I then passed on to the doctor for the proper diagnosis. I was only an intermediary in an interaction that was already mediated by the cadences of his convoluted speech, words trying to find the true meaning that only exists beyond words.

I speak to her in tongues, sometimes my own, sometimes another's. I speak to her in short diary entries that I had written inside of me but had never put down on paper as if afraid to see what I had been carrying. Sometimes my entries are longer and go on and on about this or that, as if I am distracted or afraid to get straight into the matter and need to find preambles or metaphors to make it less crude and more beautiful than it is. Or perhaps, just like the medieval shoemaker, I see that everything is linked and that in order to really see the nature of the shoe, I need to talk about the shoelaces, the soles, the sides of the shoe, and the cow that made possible the existence of the entire shoe. I am me, but I am also the many others that are in me, that have entered me and made me very heavy. I vacillate under the pressure of every corner that I try to cross, in my brave attempt to see another street, another curve that might be gentler to my limbs.

At the Police Station. I summoned the courage to go the police station eventually, after Vasco fired me and said I was a liar who was working illegally in Canada. He said I was spreading rumours about him, dragging him through my own mud, that cow dung that I grew up with in the mountains of Caramulo. I went to the station with my Portuguese friend, who had also come to Canada as a nanny, like me and the many thousands of Filipina women whose own children grow up without a mother. I told the story to a young policeman who spoke immaculate English. He listened attentively to what I had to say. At the end of it all, he said nicely, "Miss, I am very sorry that you had to go through all of this. I would be very upset if someone had done it to my sister. I am very sorry, miss, but I cannot do anything about this. We cannot do anything about this, miss."

The Police Chief. I went to the police station again, his time with a paralegal, who, I later found out, also had his own agenda and almost coerced me into launching a civil lawsuit by telling me that it was the best way to make money. He charged me for his work when I refused to give in to his coercion, despite the fact that he had initially told me to apply for legal aid and said that that money would cover all the costs. He was not a doctor even by Portuguese standards since he only had a college diploma, but I remember that when I was in his office, waiting to see him, the people who came to consult with him—mostly Brazilian and Portuguese immigrants without status, who worked from dawn to dusk building and cleaning houses in Toronto—called him *Doutor*. He did not correct them, though I thought he ought to correct them. In Portugal, everyone who has a university degree is called a doctor. This practice might be changing though: my sister told me that the current Portuguese minister of economy, who has a PhD from Simon Fraser University and lived in Canada for some time, tells everyone to call him Álvaro, simply Álvaro, and not Dr. Álvaro Santos Pereira, even if in this case he could rightfully be called a doctor. Perhaps then there is a chance that he will be able to straighten up the economy so that there will be no P in the PIGS, and we'll end up with just IGS, and there will be no need to bring back Salazar—no need for the world to put the country's credit in the junk bin.

Both the paralegal and I are escorted to office of the chief of police by a young and friendly officer. The chief is a tall, middle-aged, handsome man. His name, Lawrence MacIluren, seemingly denoting he's of Anglo-Saxon origin. I tell him the story with some help from the paralegal—he who has mastered the acceptable legal jargon, which gives more weight to the truth of my story. At the end, the chief says, "It is evident that you are a very attractive young woman and it is evident that he, Mr. da Gama, wanted to get into your panties." I remember becoming very red in the face because I did not like that expression. The choice of words sounded inappropriate, dirty, and sordid, and made me feel invaded again. Not to mention I never liked the word *panties*. I much prefer the word *underwear*—a word that is less personal, less intimate, and less dirty (even though it shares some linguistic traits with *underdog*, or at least it has the same prefix). I should also mention that my mother never used the words *panties* or *underwear*; she always referred to them as *pants* despite the fact that I tried to correct her many times.

The Human Rights Commission. I called the human rights commission from a public phone to tell them my story. I don't recall why I used a public telephone; it may have been because I had just seen someone about the matter and it had not gone well and I was desperate to do something, to get an answer from someone that seemed right, that felt right. I spoke to a male agent, relaying, with an insecure and afflicted voice, the events that had taken place as accurately as I could recall them, and he listened in silence on the other end of the line. At the end he told me, "Ms. Mendes, I have a lot of experience in these types of cases, and I must tell you that you won't be getting a lot of money from this." I said, "What? Money?! Can I tell you the story again? Or perhaps I should have an interpreter with me because I think you have misunderstood what I was trying to say." He said that would not be necessary for my English was quite good, or good enough, in any case. I hung up, went home, and cried until my eyes were swollen and hurt from my constant wiping.

The Portuguese-Canadian Human Rights Commissioner. After attempts to get through the Human Rights Commission by myself failed—perhaps because I did not communicate in the same language as the agents had been trained to communicate in, or because rumours had spread in the Portuguese community about me and my case—I was contacted by a nice Portuguese-Canadian woman, named Carmina Fraga, who had worked for the Human Rights Commission and knew how the organization worked. She told me that she could help me prepare my case to present to the Commission. She was very kind and supportive. I met her many times, and we did prepare the report. She told me I must ask for monetary compensation in order to repair the damages inflicted. I said that I did not want that, that I only wanted Vasco to apologize, to admit that he had made a grave error in his life, in his judgment. He ought to admit to it, for only then could he heal as a human being and only then could I find a way to forgive him and move on with my life. Carmina Fraga became livid when I said that. She said that in that case she could not, would not help me. I did not quite understand her reaction, and I felt confused again, like I had felt when the nurse had told me that I should denounce Vasco to the police and that, given the gravity of the crime, I would get a lot of money; or when the first agent had told me the opposite of that, that I wouldn't get very much out of this. But Camila Fraga was changeable like a chameleon, and a few days later, after reflecting on the matter, she called me back and told me she would still help me despite my refusal to ask for monetary compensation. I felt understood and thought, *Here is a woman who can understand my ways, a woman who went back to her previous life in the other country, when she was younger and more beautiful, and was able to still rescue the philosophy she grew up with. A woman who does not think that money can solve matters, or at least not all the matters.* Five years later, after repeating my story to several agents of the tribunal, the case was finally resolved, or I should say, put to rest. Vasco was asked to make a donation of five thousand dollars to a woman's shelter where I had worked for some time. He never apologized openly and never admitted that he had done what he did. It was my word against his, and God, as always, was mute and did not appear in court to testify, straighten things up, or scream at the criminal. And since I'd decided to pursue the matter only after Vasco had fired me and refused to apologize, and because the nurse who treated me at the hospital had lost my file, I had no physical evidence to prove that he indeed had done what he did to me in my basement apartment that day, that evening, that summer, after I'd listened to Ivan Lins's beautiful song. My lawyer, a stylish young Black woman who had been appointed by the Commission, told me I was a very brave young lady and that my mother should be very proud for having raised such a decent human being. I did feel proud when she said that, proud of my mother, proud of myself, proud of Almores and its ways. But I did not tell my mother about any of this. She would not have understood and likely would have reacted the same way as the other woman on the outskirts of Lisbon had, when she opened the door to find me on her doorstep, scared, after I had run away from the other cannibal who had tried to hunt me down.

The Immigration Agents. I had not told Vasco that I had a restricted work permit when he offered me the job—but he also never asked, blinded as he was by what he thought he saw. And the truth was that I just couldn't have worked as a nanny for two or three years up there in Richmond Hill. I had been young and restless. I wanted to do things, many things, and those two kids, Albert and Justin, had been in my way, waking me up every day at five o'clock and jumping on my bed demanding breakfast, demanding my life, my youth, demanding that I sacrifice my dreams and remain a maid, a maid all my life, like my sisters, my mother, and my grandmothers, women who never had a minute for themselves, who were always running after other people's desires. I did not tell Vasco, but he also did not ask. He asked only after the incident, after he knew that I was very upset about what he had done to me, after I'd demanded an apology and he'd said in wretched mockery, a mockery of my self, my reason, my sanity, my right to choose, "I don't know what you are talking about. I made a mistake assessing your personality." He asked only after I'd talked to him about what happened, after he suspected that he might not get away with this one so easily like he had gotten away with what he did and likely was still doing with Helena, the Azorean woman who suffered from a profound complex of class and region. After sensing that something had taken place between me and Vasco, and because she had already sensed Vasco's interest in me and was jealous, Helena told me that he had kissed her on the mouth too. She told me that when she said she wanted something more than a simple affair, he had replied that anything more would never work because they belonged to different social classes. I was livid when she told me that. I thought I had to tell her what he had done to me so that she would gain courage and slap him hard in the face or kick him right between the legs—advice my mother always gave me— next time he tried anything with her. Sadly though, when the matter went to criminal court and then to the Human Rights Commission, Helena Santos denied everything, including having told me what Vasco did and said to her. I was furious with her. I cursed her and all the women like her, women who, instead of standing up for themselves and their kind, lay down under the men and open their legs to them freely. And they, the men, don't even have the decency to thank them for the good time.

When I was fired from the Lusitanian Social Service Centre, I went from immigration office to immigration office, trying to locate my file and get an answer as to when I should have my open work permit, when I could be free—free to work wherever I wanted without the constant fear of being caught by the immigration officials, whom I had heard could come in the middle of the night, arrest you like a true criminal, and deport you back to your country of origin. I was supposed to have had my open work permit a year before, but because of the backlog at Immigration, they kept telling me, my file was taking a long time to be dealt with. They could not even locate it. I would go from office to office and beg the receptionist to allow me to speak with an agent, and I would explain my plight, often in tears, but I received no sympathy. After many attempts, I went to the office in Scarborough where my file was finally located, and I told the receptionist, a Filipina woman, that I was not leaving until she allowed me to speak to an immigration official. She understood my plight and gave in, perhaps thinking of when she herself was restricted to nanny's work and could not take care of her own needy children, those beautiful boys and girls she had left behind in the Philippines. I went upstairs to see the nice Canadian agent with an English last name. She opened one of her drawers and, misunderstanding my last name, pulled out a file of someone called Dania Mendez. I corrected her and said that my name was Daria, Daria Mendes—Mendes with an *s* not a *z*. I told her that the *z* generally indicated that the name was Hispanic, and that that would include not only names from Spain but also names from the many countries that Spain had colonized, including the Philippines. She looked at me with surprise, smiled, and apologized in a seemingly embarrassed way, and then she pulled out another Mendes, this time the right one: me. She looked at the file for a few minutes and then said, "I am very sorry, Ms. Mendes, that you had to wait so long to get your open work permit. I really am very sorry. Because of your long wait, I am going to issue your landed immigrant papers right away. We'll forgo the open work permit step. I apologize again, but you seem very young, Ms. Mendes, and this country is open to all your dreams. I wish you the very best." I hugged this nice woman and told her how much her actions meant to me. She hugged me back, a little hesitantly at first, but then fully accepting the embrace of this stranger who had come her way. I came out elated with that paper in my hands, feeling a freedom that I had never felt before; feeling like the police or the immigration officials, or Vasco and his lawyers, were not going to call me an alien anymore; feeling like I was not a liar or a criminal as they had insinuated in court over and over again, trying to discredit my case. They wanted to apply the Socratic generalizing rule—*She has lied one time, therefore she always lies*—and it seemed to me that their method was similar to that of Strauss-Khan's lawyer when he and the judicial team tried to discredit his accuser. But the truth is that even though we may sometimes lie or not reveal the entire truth, we are not always liars. Remember Jesus Christ's saying? *He who is without sin may cast the first stone.*

But before I met the nice immigration agent who gave me what was owed to me, I met another one who was also trying to get into my underwear. When I was desperately trying to locate my file, I met a very handsome agent at one of the immigration offices. I told him my plight, crying hysterically like a little girl, and I begged him to try and locate my file, that piece of paper lost somewhere in the thick annals of the Canadian immigration backlog. I told him I was without a job now and that I needed to get my open permit to be free, free to earn a living and pay my tuition fees. He listened to me attentively, his face serious and concerned, and he tried to console me, promising he would locate my file. He asked me if he could call me at home, and I said, "Sure, you can. Please do." I left feeling hopeful that I would indeed get my open permit and that freedom would soon appear before me. Two days later he called me at home. He asked me how I was doing, and I said I was fine. I didn't say much more; I was speaking in short sentences, in yeses or noes, waiting between silences for him to tell me he had found my file. But he did not do that; instead he asked if I wanted to go for a coffee with him. Smelling another rat, I froze when I heard that and immediately said, "I don't see why I should go for a coffee with you." He changed his approach and said, "Okay, okay, but you know I have not been able to locate your file." I said thank-you and hung up the phone. I was trembling. I felt very alone, very far from my dream. I thought it would never come. My dream. I felt like most of us feel when the heavy and stark darkness falls upon us—before a ray of gentle moonlight starts peeking through and announcing, little by little, atom by atom, that love still exists in the world we walk upon, that people truly care about one another.

António Salgado. It so happened that Francisco Motumba and Fernando Montenegro were board members of the Lusitanian Social Service Centre, though they were now mortal enemies and hated each other quite viscerally. But this centre had been created to accommodate all those who spoke the language of Camões, and so they had to pretend that the past was behind them, at least during the monthly meetings. It was as if, being brought back together in Canada, Francisco and Fernando had been given a second chance to make Salazar's proclamations about a truly multiracial Lusitanian nation into a reality, to establish a place where everyone would really have the same rights no matter their creed, colour, sex, or religion—like Pierre Elliott Trudeau had passionately championed, and with the best of intentions, it seems.

It also so happened that Mr. Palavreiro, the current mayor of Toronto and that fellow I'd met a while ago in a Portuguese literature class at the Northern University, was also a board member. I was right when I told you I did not like him and that he was not a properly educated man. You tried to dissuade me from that narrow and stubborn view, insisting that he could very well be a different man today, now that he had more years on his belt and, perhaps, more wisdom. When I went to the board with my plight and told them that Mr. da Gama was a man of evil and amoral inclinations, Palavreiro was not receptive at all. He had grown up in Canada, but he still had the conservative outlook of a mama's boy. A child of peasants—just like me, but a boy—he could note only certain injustices in the world, the ones that affected him or those like him directly, those people who carry a stick between their legs and think that, because of that mere fact, they are superior by natural right. He reminded me of Abassi and of Francisco. They were all men who were deeply affected by and sensitive to the issues of race and class, deeply affected by the scars and labels with which the ignorant world had burdened them, but who were ignorant of the woes of women, ignorant of the very fact that their everyday, unquestionable behaviour towards the other sex was a sad mimicry of everything that had been done to them, of what they so vehemently rejected. I have written poems and manifestos about this elsewhere, asking humans of all casts and origins to think, and think deeply, about what has made them suffer and who has made them suffer. I have asked them to learn from that suffering. I have said this using many different words, some deep and bleeding, others philosophical and mystical, others tender and refulgent—all of them inspired by the same urgent personal call to action. I have asked these men—in direct and dynamic verbs, direct and piercing adjectives—to transcend the narrow walls of their individual egos so that they could grow wiser, so that they could develop a heavy, matured soul. I encouraged them to find a kind of forgiveness that can see in the suffering other their own self, and that can, in that seeing, put an end to their own cruelty. I encouraged them to stop the atrocious movement that they had been following as if they were automatons pulled only by the weight and wills of evil mechanisms—a bloody fatalistic fallacy. When I was younger and more beautiful, I used to think oppressed peoples were the only ones who were pure. I used to think they had the key, the key to humanity's salvation. I used to believe, like a Marxist of sorts (before I even read Marx), that the oppressed were the ones who could, who would, make the world perfect, perfectly communal. I believed in a world in which my mother and father and those of their sort could stop carrying other people's weights. I used to think that. The first time I doubted that belief was when my brother-in-law—who used to be a Marxist and hippie in the '60s and continuously sang *"o povo unido nunca mais será vencido"*—started saying that all Romani and Black people were nothing but scum and that he was working like a dog so that the government could give them free houses. He, my brother-in-law, became very rich, and every time I went to Portugal and heard him, I was reminded of what I used to believe about poor oppressed people being the key to human salvation, the key to the true, beautiful revolution and revelation. It was as if he, my brother-in-law, suffered from a never-ending thirst that drove him to accumulate wealth and show off that wealth to the world, a world that mocked him before, a world that had placed him at the bottom of the scale like a scoundrel, when in fact it was the world that was committing the crime.

And so António Palavreiro, whose real name is António Salgado, preached about bringing the Portuguese community out of the shadows and making us full participants in the Canadian dream, but he was not a good man. He only saw with one eye, and he had forgotten the womb where he came from. Mr. Palavreiro did not believe me when I came to the board and told them what the executive director had done to me. He then testified in court and at the Human Rights Commission, saying I was just one of those women without a proper foundation who had run away by herself to another country. I was *uma qualquer*. When I heard and read his comments, I could not help but think this man was being vindictive. He wanted to get back at me because I was the best student in that Portuguese literature class we had taken together, and the professor, who may have also wanted to get into my pants, would often say that out loud in class. Mr. Palavreiro could not stand the idea that a woman, and especially a woman of his tribe, could surpass his intellect. He was one of those men who would like to have fun with what he called the Canadian women, but who when it came to settle down wanted a proper Portuguese woman, a virgin still, one that he could enjoy fully, one who hadn't been spoiled (he seemed to have that in common with Francisco)— one that knew her place well. When I worked at a café mostly frequented by Southern Europeans, I heard comments like that all the time from those guys who still carried the heavy marks of the old country. Some of them, seeing me working there until the small hours of the morning, made very hurting remarks and took actions that the café's owner, who also carried his own cross and that of his very religious mother, did not care to stop. They would grab my behind without my permission, and sometimes they would stare at me with those eyes of depraved soulless dogs and mumble viciously that I was "excellent for a good fuck." I stopped serving them. I guess they saw me as a loose woman too, closer to the Canadian women and not so Portuguese anymore. They were like the parents of that friend I had, who did not want me to be their daughter's friend, for they looked at me through their narrow lens, a stagnated and dirty lens reflecting a world that no longer existed—that place they had left forty years ago, escaping the tentacles of Salazar and his close associates, the cardinals, still stuck in their memory, unwilling to let go. I felt like I was living in a world that no longer existed, and even though my mother was a fierce traditional woman, who always warned me of the evil that men can cause and the sorrows that can come from opening your legs freely without a proper contract and the blessing of a priest—like her own mother did in the 1920s when she got pregnant twice, only to be despised by my great-grandmother and everyone in the village and surroundings—she seemed more modern than these people I was meeting in this new country, people stranded between two shores, incapable of fully setting their feet on either one.

The reporter. A man identifying himself as a community reporter working for the newspaper *The Voice/A Voz* called me after he had heard on the mainstream news that I had been assaulted. I don't know how he got my name and my number because the news only noted that a Portuguese woman working illegally in Canada had been assaulted by the executive director of the Lusitanian Social Service Centre. He asked me if I could give him details about what had happened. He was writing a detailed article on the subject, he said, as a way to encourage other women in the Portuguese community to come forward when things like that happened to them, for, apparently and unfortunately, they happened quite frequently. Like the paralegal instructed me, I told him I could not share any details with him as the case was now before the courts and that any information about the matter should be obtained from my legal representative. Later on, the paralegal, my legal representative—the doctor who was not a doctor—said the journalist did contact him and told him I was "very savvy in the matter and knew exactly what to say." He said this was "a sure sign" that I had "made a career out of this." At the time, I cursed the reporter and equated him with all the other pigs that I had met in my life. Later I realized that the reporter may not have said this at all, that the paralegal may have just invented the whole story to fuel my rage and manipulate me into pursuing the matter in the civil courts, where real money was to be made, as he had put it. When I refused to launch a civil lawsuit, this paralegal also told me that with my newly acquired reputation, I would have a lot of difficulty finding a job. I was infuriated by his comment and replied that as long as I was healthy, I could find a job as this was not Portugal but Canada where jobs were there to be had, even in the '90s when the country was facing a recession. Shortly after, he gave me a bill for his services, saying that the legal aid money only covered the lawyer's fees and not his since he was not a lawyer. I paid him fully.

On the matter of race. "Why do you, Mr. da Gama, think that Ms. Mendes has launched this dirty campaign against you, a man of standing in the community, a man of law, and a man of letters?" asked Mr. Ketsukiapolous, his defence lawyer, a renowned legal expert who graduated from Harvard *summa cum laude* and often appeared on national TV to give his legal opinion about the worst of Canadian crimes, including the ones committed by Paul Bernardo and Karla Homolka. "There is no other explanation but to say that Ms. Mendes holds deep in her being a racist belief, like her ancestors who went to my mother country over four hundred years ago, raping it like savages with their dirty phalluses. She is a racist who does not want to see a man of colour running the Lusitanian Social Service Centre. That is my firm belief."

Mr. Horatio Cunningham, my attorney, argued with Mr. Ketsukiapolous and Mr. da Gama, trying to discredit the serious implications of the remarks, and asked the following question to Mr. da Gama: "Are you, sir, not a man of mixed race, a man with an Indian mother and a Portuguese father? And do you not, sir, often identify yourself as being Portuguese rather than Indian? By looking at you, sir, I could not tell the difference. In fact, I could not tell the difference between you and me, as we both have dark hair and that nice tanned skin tone, like thousands of citizens in this world of ours, and especially in this magnificent city of ours, Toronto."

Da Gama replied, "No, I am a coloured Indian man first and foremost—my Portugueseness is secondary to my Indianness." They argued and argued over this issue, and then my lawyer presented evidence that indeed da Gama often presented himself as Portuguese, omitting his Indian ancestry. He brought to the table, as evidence, a document that showed just that: it was the application that da Gama had sent to the board of the Lusitanian Social Service Centre when he applied for the job of executive director. In his cover letter, da Gama stated: *Being a Portuguese man myself, I am very familiar with the barriers faced by our community, and it is my intention, as the executive director of the Lusitanian Social Service Centre, to break down these barriers so that my fellow countrymen can all access the Canadian pie and taste its sweetness. I have a deep passion for the Portuguese underdog.* Da Gama's lawyer tried to argue that my lawyer was just playing the rhetorical game that lawyers are often forced to play. He said that comment was being taken out of context, and that if we read the entire cover letter, we would find more evidence that would show that Mr. da Gama fully accepted and claimed his Indian or mixed heritage. My lawyer then read the entire cover letter to the court, and there was no clear indication that da Gama was a man of Indian or Portuguese descent, or that he belonged to one more than the other. There was no concrete evidence of da Gama advocating for his Indian heritage, even if we were to spend time analyzing the many ambivalent passages in the letter, such as: *Having seen the world from both angles, the angle of the dog and the underdog, I am in a perfect position to run this great institution that is the Lusitanian Social Service Centre* or *I have felt in my skin the wounds of prejudice.* Both lawyers tried to argue their case to the best of their abilities, and I sat there observing this event as if I were observing an unconvincing play. It was like a dramatic scene in which the players had no intention of putting their real selves on display and were poorly hiding behind the roles assigned to them by the director, who, for his part, had failed to fully understand the characters of the actors and had assigned them random roles that had nothing to do with their true personhood, their true passion. My mind travelled to the mourning sounds of Ivan Lins's song and, rather than hearing what was happening in the courtroom, which directly concerned my life and reputation, I heard in my head, over and over again, Lins's beautifully haunting lines: *Is this Fellini or is this our lives? In what film did our love happen?*

My dress. Mr. Ketsukiapolous was sweating in the court room, breathing hard, mind and body trying to stay alert, asking me pointless questions that had nothing to do with the matter at hand: "What were you wearing, Ms. Mendes? Can you describe for us, in detail, your outfit? Can you also tell us, Ms. Mendes, why you made the decision to sit in the front seat with Mr. da Gama even though you were dating Mr. Motumba and it would have made more sense to sit in the back with him so that you could stay closer to one another?" I said I was wearing a long dress, almost to my ankle, and that this dress was my favourite because it made me feel taller and thinner, and it reminded me of the beautiful dresses my aunt Maria dos Anjos used to make for me back in Portugal. These dresses were always made out of patterned fabrics bought at the open market fairs from the Romani women, who were always singing as if they were always happy. This, despite the fact that they often became victims of the market police who conducted regular surprise raids to catch the outlaws trying to sell their products without the proper licences, just like they had caught my mother when she was selling cheese from town to town. The Romani women would chant, "Hey darling, come look at this stunning *tecido* I have here! Come, my beautiful one, come. I guarantee you can't find quality and prices like these anywhere else." These flowery flowing dresses were made to hug my own body and nobody else's; they were dresses that gave me the sensation that I could fly and that it was always spring, always beautiful, always sunny. The judge, Mr. Smitherman, a nice Jewish man with an inclination toward the lyric, seemed taken by my intricate description of my dress.

Even though he wanted to prevent me from answering—the question "What were you wearing?" was already beginning to be considered problematic in those days—he did not stop me in time and so, when I finished, he addressed the jury: "Dear members of the jury, I order you to disregard the answer given by Ms. Mendes to the question just posed by the defence counsel about her manner of dress on the day of the alleged incident. The question has nothing to do with the matter at hand, and Mr. Ketsukiapolous ought to be ashamed of himself for asking such a question. We all should know that women's bodies, including their hair, are essentially good and do not cause the fall of men. If I did not know you better, Mr. Ketsukiapolous, I would say you have some affiliations with radical Islamists or that you have been reading outdated religious books and misinterpreting its metaphoric language. Yes, if I did not know you better, I would say just that..." The judge allowed me to answer the second question, though I could not quite give a convincing answer, at least not according to Mr. Ketsukiapolous, who kept asking me the question over and over again, in slightly different words. It was as if he thought my English was not good enough and that he ought to repeat it several times, each time louder than before, and change the wording a little like we do with youngsters who are learning the language we want them to learn.

He would sometimes call me Ms. Mendez, and I would correct him straight away and say, "Please sir, I ask you to call me by my rightful name. It is Ms. Mendes." I would pronounce the word *Mendes* several times, very slowly, asking the lawyer to repeat after me until he got it right, but he would often forget or get confused and go back to committing the same crime. When I tried to think about why I had sat in the front and not in the back with Francisco, I could not come up with anything specific, except that perhaps I had done so out of respect for Vasco so that he would not appear to be the chauffeur. Or perhaps, I thought, he had asked me to sit there. Or perhaps I just took the seat without giving any conscious thought to the matter, because really there was nothing to the matter. I kept saying this or that and repeating the word *or* to go from one possibility to the other, and Mr. Ketsukiapolous was clearly frustrated with me and kept trying to make me stick to one possibility. He accused me of wanting to confuse the courtroom and all the officials of justice present, including the jury members who had had to take the day off work to be present and allow me to have a fair trial. I got nervous and started to cry, at which point the judge stopped Mr. Ketsukiapolous from asking the same question, accusing him of being either a parrot or hard of hearing, for it was quite evident that I had already provided an answer. We could hear laughter in the courtroom when the judge said that, and then Mr. Ketsukiapolous had to find another line of argumentation and defence. He was sweating more and more. He was a stocky man with a heavy moustache. I had been told that he was one of the highest paid lawyers in the field of criminal law.

She is an alien. "Your Honour, esteemed members of the jury, there is no doubt that Ms. Mendes is an opportunist, a woman who tries to entice wealthy, powerful men, decent men, men of letters such as Mr. da Gama and Mr. Motumba. She uses her physical attributes to get their attention and then she cries victim and accuses them of abusing her. The entire thing was premeditated, from beginning to end. I ask you, your Honour and esteemed members of the jury, to think very carefully about how Ms. Mendes came to this country, how she lied to be able to work wherever she wanted without any regard and respect for our sacred Canadian laws. I ask you to consider how she played both Mr. da Gama and Mr. Motumba. I ask you to consider, as our evidence—including the deeply moving accounts by both Mr. da Gama and Mr. Motumba, the true victims in this whole affair—has amply demonstrated, how Ms. Mendes holds deep within herself the idea that that these men are not on the same level as she is, simply because they are not white. These, my dear friends and esteemed colleagues, are crimes of high gravity, which require a punishment of the same order. She is a racist, my dear friends. And an opportunist. I have done my job, and now I leave it all up to your consciences." He sat down, and my lawyer took centre stage. He argued that I was a young woman of morals, a very hardworking young woman who came to this country by herself at the tender and innocent age of twenty, who was not afraid to work, as her many jobs here and there demonstrate. "She is good Portuguese stock, like many other people of this ethnicity, whom we've all met in this wonderful city of ours, cleaning and building our skyline and homes. This woman has guts. This woman has courage, for even though she had some immigration issues that may have given her a bad image and play against her, something that would scare other women and force them to remain silent in the face of the abuse, she took action. [Pause.] She took her life into her own hands and denounced Mr. da Gama's heinous crime. [Pause.] She denounced his unacceptable abuse of power. [Longer Pause.] I ask you all, your Honour and respectful members of the jury, to carefully think about all the evidence that has been presented here today. If you do that, you cannot, you *cannot*, in good conscience, consider this young woman guilty and let the dishonourable Mr. da Gama go. You simply cannot. If the Canadian judicial system cannot protect the needy and helpless, who can it protect? If it cannot protect those victims, who need the most protection, what, I ask you, is its point, its reason for being? This woman, my dear friends and dear colleagues, is a victim. Nothing more, nothing less. [Very long pause.] To suggest that Ms. Mendes is a racist just because the accused is not white is a short-sighted, ludicrous argument. On that note, I shall conclude my defense with a very insightful passage from an excellent novel, *My Father's Wives*, by Angolan writer José Eduardo Agualusa, which I just finished reading last night: "To accept that one cannot criticize someone just because that someone is Black is an act of paternalism. Paternalism is the elegant racism of the cowards." He then sat down and unbuttoned his navy-blue suit jacket. He was a handsome man with a shaven, clear face, and clever, clean eyes.

I am not. I am not a victim. I am not guilty or innocent. I may be both. I am much more than what they say here, and much more than what they have said all along. I am me and the many others that I carry within me. My reasons cannot be summed up in legal jargon, a language that compartmentalizes me and breaks my being into disjointed pieces, as if the shoe were not a shoe but rather a series of separate parts that have nothing to do with the cow who gave its life for the shoe to fully exist. I wanted to scream at them and tell them they are playing this all wrong. I wanted to say that a true tribunal has to be able to see the beautiful truth beyond any shadows of doubt; they must see the intact person that we all have deep down inside, beyond the line that protects our body from cold. Any true tribunal has to be like God, or a good novel—it has to show, beyond any doubt, the true mirror of our conscience. It has to be a true play. I wanted to say all this, scream all this, but my legs were frozen and my throat was dry. I felt like I was in a dream where a thief is after me and I know I have to run but my legs cannot move and I will soon be under the predator's paws. Despite all the hardships, the difficulties in being heard, I felt proud to be up there telling my story. I felt proud that I was facing Vasco and Francisco. I felt like I had had to withhold my voice too many times before and that this time the bag was full so I had to take everything out, I had to scream the scream that would allow me to continue living in this world without feeling that I was to blame, that I had asked for it—like I often had felt when I passed by a group of men who said dirty things, or like I felt when that woman in Portugal opened the door to me only to condemn me with her old words, stale verbs pulled from a priest's pockets.

His words hurt the most. I had not spoken to Francisco in weeks. After I told him what Vasco did, his eyes rolled to his sad side and he ceased to see me as I was, as I wanted to be seen, as I thought he had seen me before. *Beautiful Daria, my finally found home. Beautiful Francisco, my finally found home.* There was no home anymore. (Perhaps there had never been.) Not in his body and not in my body. Not in his soul and not in my soul. We became separated from our home, anchored in a nothingness that made us sink deep into an ocean that had no bottom and no algae. Our eyes were blind to the marine beauties, the corals and the scintillating fish that emit a light that takes you to the end of the world, allowing you to see the sunset and the sunrise at the same time. We could not experience those underwater dances where speech is paramount and mute and where the whales tell you there is another world above this one and then another world above that one, and then another one and another one, *ad infinitum.* Their calls are like a cadence of music or silver spirals that are both songs and visible, true things that can be touched, seen, tasted, heard, smelled. Francisco testified in court about me and Vasco—about the ugly affair, the alleged incident of rape, as he called it, as the defence lawyer Mr. Ketsukiapolous called it. He took a stand. He made a choice. Tried to make a choice. I looked at him and tried to meet his eyes to tell him that what he was doing was only hurting his soul, that his patterns—those that were dancing in his brain's intricate design, those that would lead him to his true soul—were deadly dangerous and that he was going against his beautiful idea. He was allowing Tarrafal to win. *What will become of the world, of me and you, if we allow Tarrafal to take over? What do you want from life? What do you truly want? Do you remember our love? Do you remember the dances we danced and the sound of the whales calling us from afar?* I asked him these questions with my eyes, sending these words to him through his irises, where

I thought the shining darkness might still reside. But Vasco's lawyer and mine were distracting him and pulling him into other waves, other seas, and so he could not see his full self, my full self, the world's full self—his potent black matter was seemingly absent, momentarily deceased or blindfolded. They broke him like Arsénio wanted to break him in Tarrafal. They asked him childish questions that prevented him from giving mature answers, and he got lost in the game. It seemed as though he was tired of life, of its tricks and trends. He did not possess the same strength he had when Arsénio's heavy paws tried to step all over him to kill his spirit. He could not see the whales in those waves within the sea where we swam together. He could not hear their song, their deep language calling us to the world beyond this. He was going to be lost; he was going to drown amidst dead bodies like his ancestors had, those men and women who had been sold and bought by my people and some of his, and then forced to endure the voyage. "Mr. Motumba, did Ms. Mendes have an affair with you?"

"Yes, she did."

"Did she want to marry you?"

"Yes, she did."

"Did you consider marrying her?"

"Down the line perhaps, but at the time we were just enjoying each other's company. And we were enjoying it very much, I must add. I am still a young man and I have needs. She is a young woman. And look at her."

"Please, Mr. Motumba, just say yes or no to my questions—do not add anything else. Just yes or no."

"Yes."

"Did she ever show an interest in your finances? Did she ever show any signs of being racist? Did she ever tell you she was an alien in this country working in places she ought not to?"

"Yes and no, since you are asking too many questions at the same time—and complicated questions, I might add. She did say she was happy that I was a successful man, especially because I had endured too much in my life fighting Salazar, often going on bread and water only for days on end in the forests of Mozambique and Tanzania, inside the dark cement cells of Tarrafal, fighting for the beautiful cause. She did say that she had some unresolved immigration matters, but she added that these matters would be resolved at any moment and that Immigration Canada was a very slow institution that made people wait and wait to become true Canadians. I asked at the time if she needed any help from me, as I had some friends in high places, but she said that it would not be necessary."

"Please sir, limit your answer to yes or no, or at least try to avoid unnecessary explanations. We are after the truth here and nothing but the truth."

"Yes. In relation to your last question, she did stare at the palms of my hands and the soles of my feet when we first started our encounters. She said she had heard a story about why the palms and soles of Black people were white. The story claimed that Black people's hands were white so that when white people looked at us, Black people, they would see themselves in us and would therefore not be abusive towards us. This story could easily mean that indeed Daria, Ms. Mendes, that is, suffered from what I often call the exotification of the Other. It could also mean, as we would all easily agree, that she is in fact a kind woman who was trying to get away from stereotypes, especially since the version I told her I knew claimed the reason we have white palms and soles is because God was in a hurry when he made us. This version is less kind, of course, because it implies that God had less interest in us than in the rest of humanity. It implies that we were just an afterthought, that God did not feel we were a priority and that he could just rush our creation. All this also implies, and this is a very important point, that this God is a Western God, a God who presupposes that white people are the norm and Black people are the exception, the bad copy of the model, the secondary design—the Other of the Self, in the often overly complicated jargon of some postcolonial critics that confuses more than it enlightens. This is similar to that sign they used in South Africa and also in my own country: *Non-whites not allowed*. Note the use of the double negative here."

"Mr. Motumba, I have to remind you again not to speculate about the reasons behind Ms. Mendes's actions, extrapolate about any other conclusions, or go into unnecessary digressions. So please just say yes or no."

"Yes."

The matter went on and on, and at the end of it all, no clear conclusion could be reached. I was not guilty. I was not not guilty. Vasco was not guilty. He was not not guilty. Francisco confused everyone in the courtroom, including myself. He should have known me because I showed myself to him as I was, or at least, as I understood I was. Why was he giving answers that were full of doubt? I was not a chameleon. I did not vacillate between a plague and a salvation. I was mostly good. I wanted to be mostly good. I was mostly one person and mostly good. He was mostly good. I wanted him to be mostly good. Vasco was mostly good. I wanted him to be mostly good. I wanted him to apologize, to say he was sorry for what he'd done. I didn't want this circus that we all put on in the name of law and justice and honour.

When I read Francisco's answers to the Human Rights Commission I was truly hurt:

Yes, I could see that Ms. Mendes, a woman of a certain condition, was taken with my status. Being the general consul of Mozambique in Canada and a man of letters seemed to have made quite an impression on her, and she was very drawn to me. We did have a brief and intense affair, but the truth is that I am a married man, and I love my wife dearly. I also have no reason to think that Mr. da Gama would do to Daria what she claims he did. He is a man of high standing. And a man of letters, like me. I also cannot quite grasp, rationally or otherwise, why Daria, Ms. Mendes, would invent such a story, but then again we never really know people, even the ones we think we know quite well. We never really even get to fully know ourselves, and that is why Mr. Rembrandt, the famous painter we all ought to appreciate for his superb aesthetic and deep concern for ontology, kept creating caricatures of his own self and caricatures of others, whether he was on commission or not. It was as if he suffered from an incessant, deep-seated obsession with the person he carried in himself and all the persons humans carry in themselves. These persons are always trying to fully emerge at the window, to have real conversations with the street passersby, but they are only able to peek through sporadically, when we, the observers, are the most distracted. And so Rembrandt never found what he was after, the real portrait; he always ended up with a caricature.

His sentences were long and difficult to follow, as if he himself were emulating Rembrandt's art, as if both, in their attempts to find truth and meaning, were only able to remind us that there is nothing but mystery and doubt. Mystery and doubt. And very long sentences, attempts to crack the code. He was being mimetic, parallel to the other soul, the soul of the artist. He wanted everything—the sun and what is beyond the sun—because life on this earth can be so lonely. He was a cad. Men are cads. They want the prodigious rivers between women's legs, where the world is born. They are eternal eaters of the sacred.

Abassi and Francisco. Ms. Bollatti, can you believe that Abassi knew Francisco quite well? Can you believe that

Abassi was in fact Francisco's therapist, the one who was working on *The Collectivity Systems in Pre-colonial Africa,* the one who eventually came to the realization that he had to fire his entire dissertation committee because they were not getting his point? Can you believe that when I met Abassi, he already knew who I was but did not tell me? Can you believe that? And I gave myself to him fully, still trying to recover Francisco, to make up for whatever harm I may have caused him. And for what? Another vain love affair that did not amount to anything. I am still alone. I am still searching for my full self, still trying to find my home. *Beautiful Daria, my finally found home. Beautiful Francisco, my finally found home. Beautiful Abassi, my finally found home.* Daria, Abassi, Francisco. Francisco, Daria, Abassi.

THE NANNIES AND ME. I am going to the park with Albert and Justin, the children. I am wearing shorts and a T-shirt, and I am fully aware of my thighs. In Portugal, my mother would call me names every time I wore shorts like these—and every time I wore a sleeveless shirt. The same would happen if I bent down and she could see my back because the shirt was too short, even though it was far from being a midriff. I would look at my mother and her big swelling body, the protruding varicose veins ready to burst into blood and inundate the world with more pain and suffering, and I would say to myself: My body will never become my mother's body. Never. I am going to tame it into order. I am going to prevent it from becoming out of control, occupying more space than it ought to occupy, making itself fully visible to the passersby, too visible, as if there is nothing else in the world to stare at other than a woman's body. I would look at my mother and the long line of children that she had, and I would repeat to myself: My body will be mine first, first and foremost, and then I will give it to others, to men, to children, to the world. Only after I am satisfied with it and have spent enough time alone with it to get tired of myself will I share it, will I open it to men, to children, to the world. I would listen to her and her mother, my darling grandmother, I would listen to them telling their stories and those of others like them, and I would pray in my head to solidify my conviction: My body is my own, first and foremost. I listened to them, I listened, and I saw them, their bodies, their wrinkled hands and their twisted arthritic fingers and toes, and when I had listened and seen enough, I ran away. I took a plane to the other side of the world, crossing the Atlantic on that February day, afraid but exhilarated. The cold of the winter made my body recoil, taming it into an order that I had devised, dreamed up out of need or sickness, a sickness that comes not from the body itself but from a truly polluted place. For isn't the body born naked and beautiful? I got out of the plane, and I felt the

biting Canadian frost on my starved body, a body that had
been expelling food voraciously for a few years now, as if
I were trying to get rid of my mother's own body and her
mother's body, lines and lines of swollen women. I knew I
carried their bodies in my own, dragging them with me like
weights that I could not leave behind, implacable currents
preventing me from walking the free walk, from running to
the sun or to the peak of the hill. The weight of their bodies
stops me from doing somersaults like I do in my dreams,
when the thieves are not after me and I sense that the world
is all mine, that it is all there to hug me and allow me a dance
in midair, akin to my soul, akin to my full self, reaching for
the gods with a small *g*.

I am twenty years old. It is a sunny spring day in Richmond
Hill, and I am fascinated by the intensity with which the
spring arrives in this country. I am in awe and think that
just the other day it was white with the winter snow and
today it is all sun, April, and green. I see this intense green
everywhere, bursting out of this earth that has been gelid
for months, refusing to give birth, shrinking its body into a
discreet nothingness. The earth has been gelid and dormant
and dark, sleeping the long sleep, but is now suddenly ready
to ejaculate life into the planet on this side of the Northern
Hemisphere, where the Indians who are not Indians have
lived since time immemorial, these shamans of other times
dancing in smoke. (Or at least, those are the Indians many
of us have in mind, which may not correspond to the real
ones who pass us on the street, whom we do not recognize.)
On the other side of the world, things were much slower. It
started in February, little by little, a bud here, a flower there,
a leaf here, a sprout there. But here the intensity astounds
me. It is as if the earth is too fertile and the sun too potent,
penetrating her, its sperm impatient to create instant life
everywhere. A tropical north, luscious and unbounded. I

observe the shrubs, the leaves, and the flowers around me and touch them too to determine whether they are like the ones I am familiar with on the other side of the ocean. I look for something that I know as the kids—Albert and Justin, three and four respectively—ride their tricycles in front of me, screaming in bursts of happiness, like children ought to do. I am twenty years old. They speak to me and show me the trees on the side of the road and the lush purple flowers that I have never seen before. I can't name them, even though I think they are somehow close to me and must surely have a Latin name, like all plants seem to. It is as if, when it comes to plants, humans all speak the same language; whether we are Inuit or Greek, Syrian or Sudanese, our tongues and souls understand the same sounds. It is as if we are all akin to one another, daughters of the same current, sons of the same molecule: the yes that said yes to another yes. But I am only twenty years old. I may not yet know the full story. I may not yet know the true full story of this continent, where Amerigo Vespucci arrived centuries ago. He named it after his own name, his own garden, for he brought with him his own dictionary, full of arrogant adjectives and verbs and nouns. He had been ready to teach his religion, like his ancestors had when they went to Iberia and built beautiful arched bridges and aqueducts, when they had killed the pagan Lusitanian gods—or at least sent them into hiding.

They, Albert and Justin, speak in their beautiful, childish way, helping me improve my English. We become three children learning how to pronounce the syllables of the English language, feeling its pauses, its running or lazy vowels and consonants. We learn to speak so that the world around us will understand us and respond to the needs of our souls and bodies, so that it will allow us to mature and become older fulfilled beings, with no regrets, because we were loved and cared for. Beings who, at the hour of the scorpion, will truly feel that they've made friends and that life has been good. At home, we sing and dance to "Yellow Submarine" around the living room. I try to become excited, joining them in this dance, jumping up and down in freedom, for even though I am not a good dancer, I feel no judgment from them. I suddenly allow my body, my thighs, to move like freed, happy butterflies. I dance with them in frantic excitement after our communal meal, and after I eject mine into the toilet bowl, sending it down the drain to feed the worms and Pluto, the greedy god of the underworld, who is tormenting my soul and eating me alive. Sometimes Albert, the little one, follows me into the bathroom and catches me in the act. He asks me if I am sick, his worried, slanted eyes afflicted by my gasps—a child attempting to take care of another child. Like a hypocritical criminal stealing food from the Ethiopian children, whose eyes are larger than the moon and whose bellies are rounder than the globe, I tell him that, yes, I am sick, my stomach is not happy with the food I ate. He asks me if I need *mickie and cokes*, milk and cookies, to feed my body and soul, to feel better so that we can go to the park and play on the swings again, flying our legs in midair, feeling the sunlight shine on our bones, staring at the incandescent marvel that is the spring—the spring with its incendiary green of tropical lushness.

They ride in front of me, and I look at my thighs now and then. We pass house after house, all like one another. Large, green, tidy lawns. Everything is contained. And the sidewalks are new and wide as if they were just built yesterday, as if this land has space to give and sell and everyone has access to it. The suburbs are dead on this spring day, and I see only a couple of people here and there, mowing the lawn or doing something else they could not have done in the heights of the winter when the cold cuts across your bones. I am twenty years old. I look at my thighs, obsessed as I am with those of my mother and her own mother. Even though they are on the other side of the Atlantic, one still standing and the other rotting inside the coffin in the cemetery of Almores, they walk with me here on this side. They are here with me on this spring day, when I ought to dance with the sun freely and lift my body in lightness, gay with drunkenness, like a stunning butterfly that can carry its wings to the stratosphere and beyond to intermingle with stardust and lost broken comets.

When we reach the park, the children push me to the swing, eager as they are to experience the somersault they have been trying to keep in since they got up this morning at six o'clock and jumped onto my bed screaming, "Daya, my cereal, Daya, I'm hungie." I am twenty years old and I want to sleep in. I was never a morning person. I ignore them as they jump up and down on my bed, but eventually I cannot be oblivious to my duty. Carolina, their mother, who is a nurse, came to this country when she was sixteen years old. She worked hard, very hard. She did what she had to do to make it. She first worked as a cleaning lady and then moved up. She worked very hard to be able to leave behind the old granite house without running water back in Portugal, to start anew here in this spacious house built for her and her family, built out of the newest and most modern material, with a sink and running sparkling water. And a bathroom to cleanse the tired body at day's end. A ticket of a lifetime, she thought, like I thought too, when we had both left those villages on top of the mountains, those villages that seemed stopped in time, stuck in the Middle Ages, frozen by the ambitious adventures of Salazar. She then married a Russian engineer. They made a good life together: a big house in the suburbs, two kids, and a nanny brought directly from Portugal just to take care of them. Back in Portugal, she had gone to school with my older sisters, as I did with her younger siblings. Both of us came from large, poor families, and our parents had helped one another many times, borrowing cows from each other to carry loads of this or that when it was time to harvest hay or corn or grapes. I remember a line of cow carts directed by many men that went on for many kilometres. I remember this long line of carts pulled by cows and the cows being guided by the men. I remember how my father would spend days in his *forja* preparing the wheels before events like these, a blacksmith sweating with pride, pounding heavily on burning red metal. I would watch, fascinated with his abilities, stunned by the hard metal that could turn into dripping red honey in my father's hands, malleable like water, adjusting to the dreams of humans. I remember the musical symphony that the carts made. It was a collective singing, the souls of men and cows merging together to create an amicable embrace—food for the bones. A reminder that life was indeed worth living because God was always singing in the background, even if He was often mute, immersed in prolonged silences, just watching how His children made a life for themselves. These cow freight events were a show for all of us. We would watch the carts come nearer and nearer, entering the village in an order that they knew by heart. We would try to discern which cart made the unpleasant screeching noise because it was not properly cared for, properly oiled, and then we would gossip about that person who had no pride in his job. My father would boast about the clear singing of his cart and the beauty of his cows. We were in awe watching these shows, watching carts being pulled by cows and cows being pulled by men. And then we would make fresh wine, jumping into the *lagar* ourselves and smashing the grapes with our own feet. And in the winter, when the snow covered Almores and its surroundings—leaving us inside a white, lonely, and recondite sanctuary—we fed the cows and the sheep and the goats with that fresh hay that had been carried by the cows in these carts, the carts pulled by cows, cows led by men. And then we witnessed the births of little calves and sheep and goats: the prodigious and the sublime right before our astonished eyes.

At the park, I see all the Filipina nannies with their blondish white children. When I first started going to the park, I did not quite know that these women were the nannies and that the children were not their own. I was in a new country where all kinds of people lived together, made babies together, and so it did not cross my mind that these women and these children did not share the same bloodline. Later on, I came to understand the matter much better. I came to see that these women, like me, had come from far away to reach their own dreams and get away from their own stories, that many of them had left their own children in their home country and would not see them until much later, when they were eventually able to bring them over here for a full piece of the Canadian dream. I was shy around them. They seemed to be so sure about themselves and so nice to the children: patient, always smiling. Tender. They seemed to be fashionable and thin. I would look at them and then at my thighs and feel like I was not pretty. They were friendly with me, but they remained distant for reasons that I could not quite understand. One day, one of them, Raquel, came to me and introduced herself. We became friends and went out a few times. She then told me that when she first saw me, she asked herself "Who is that beautiful European woman who comes here every day?" When she told me that I was surprised, surprised that she would think I was beautiful, surprised that she would think of me as European because mostly I thought of myself as Portuguese. She was surprised herself to discover that I was not the mother or the blood relative of the children but rather the nanny. The nanny. Just like her. Sometime later, she told me she had called at the house where I worked and asked for me only to be told by the house mistress that I was not there and not to call again.

I was surprised that Carolina—the woman I worked for who went to school with my older sisters, whose siblings I went to school with, and who had come from the same mountains I did—would do something like that. Raquel said she likely had done so because she knew that the Filipina nannies had formed an organization to fight for the rights of all foreign live-in nannies, and she did not want me to be part of it because then I would demand to be treated with respect, I would know I had rights. I was not sure whom and what to believe, and I found the situation very odd, especially because when I told Carolina the story, she said this Filipina woman was an impostor and probably a lesbian who liked me and was trying to start a feud of some sort in the hopes of getting into my underpants. I left my nanny work after five months and never saw Raquel or Carolina again, so I could never find out who was telling the truth and who was lying. And then many other things happened to me.

O F PSYCHICS, SEASONS, AND OTHER DOCTORS. The other day I watched a show on TV that addressed the strange, obsessive habit that many women have of going to female psychics to ask for counsel instead of going to real therapists, professionally trained people who are well versed in the science of the human mind and behaviour. They usually end up being robbed of thousands of dollars and not cured of their illness. Unable to stop their actions and the need to consult these charlatans, the women seeking help become addicted to their advice, falling victim to their scams and developing yet another type of obsessive compulsive disorder. One of the women being interviewed—who went to a psychic several times a week, or sometimes every day—claimed that the reason she felt more comfortable with the psychic was because the psychic told her what to do and what would happen if she did what she told her to do, similar to that witch doctor Arsénio's mother went to. The therapist, on the other hand, was always too detached and just sat there listening, never telling her exactly what to do. She saw no point in these encounters. The psychic acted like her friend and the therapist acted like a rigid professional who seemed to have no feelings, no thoughts, no humanity, and no desire to help her client. She seemed to be sitting erect behind her professional code. I couldn't help but think that what this woman was saying was true, or at least partially true, for I remembered going to therapists who did not seem to be there, who withheld their views so much that I couldn't have a conversation with them and felt no alleviation after the session. That was why I finally picked Ms. Bollatti. She had a different approach, a more direct one; she spoke her mind when she thought it necessary, since I was there for direction. I also thought, though, that the psychics of today are not like the shamans of bygone days, or the idea that I have about many of them. It occurred to me that they too, have fallen victim to the evils of capitalism. They tell you the story you want to hear because they want to profit. The message then is that we ought to be more careful about both the psychics and the therapists of today. And the message is also that if we had more friends, real men and women friends, we may not need to go to psychics and therapists as much as we do. And if we accepted sadness and suffering as part of being human, as part of finding one's full humanity and true illumination, then we may be better off. We might not run to a helper each time, expecting her to fix it all for us, to take it all away, because we suffer from this delusion that life ought to be only roses and sun. Only roses and sun. And yet we all know that each season brings us new feelings, allowing us to savour the entirety of the year. We have pears in the summer and apples in the fall and persimmons in the winter—at least in some countries. Without these seasons, there would be no fruit.

THE RUSSIAN STUDENT. *He who lacks completeness and purity does not deserve to be called beautiful.* My Russian student writes like this, in big grand metaphors that try to awaken your dormant self, that vein that has been tamed by rational knowledge and the silver factory toys that numb our children. I want to listen to her as much as I can when marking her assignments. I feel like she speaks from a part that is bigger than the world we live in, bigger than what it allows for. There is a battle between my professional duty, which tells me that I ought to teach her how to write clear, direct, and unflowery sentences, lines of thought that will call an apple an apple and will get her a real job in the real world, and my deeper calling, which murmurs to me, in stubborn persistence, that the true masters of the universe are those who can go beyond the silvery visible lines to reach the start of the sun and dance in the volcanic lava—the vulva of the vulva, where the word *yes* resides. The latter wins. The course coordinator or the dean may fire me for this. They may determine that my marking style does not adhere to the very rigid rubric they have prescribed to all of us teaching this first-year course in Rhetoric and Composition, which expects very specific outcomes in relation to the following four points: Ideas and Insights, Research, Evidence and Structure, and Style and Mechanics. We'll keep it a secret, she and I—Daria Mendes and the Russian student. While I read her paper, I mumble to myself—*she who lacks completeness and purity cannot be called beautiful*—so that I do not forget.

OF WORDS AND MEANING. Sometimes I have fights with my husband. His parents are Nigerian and strict Anglicans, but he himself grew up in London and then in the U.S. We have fights about the meaning of the word *sad*. When something happens to me that irritates me, contradicts my ideals, or makes me believe less in the world, myself, or others, I invariably say that I am sad. When something happens to him under what I consider to be very similar circumstances, he always says he is disappointed and then tells me in detail the reasons for his disappointment. When he is done, I say to him, "Don't be too sad about it." He states he is not sad but only disappointed, and then we get into a senseless long debate and heated argument about the meaning of this small word: *sad*. At the end of this long debate, our thoughts and explanations have gone in so many directions that I no longer know why we are fighting and feel this heavy sense of unease. I feel that he and I share different values, that we have fundamentally different beliefs about words and what they exist for. And sometimes the feeling is so unsettling that I think divorce is the only option, for how can two souls truly meet if they use language in such different ways?

LAST NIGHT. Last night was painful. Unlike the beautiful dream of lavender that I have already told you about, the dream of last night brought me to a state of confusion, guilt, and never-ending images of my dead father and grandmother. Of Isabel too. *Could I have saved them? I should have saved them.* Their lingering souls danced around me in circles of light or darkness, making me aware that there is more than what I see when I am awake and blinded by the sun. I don't know if they were happy or mournful, happy or sad—or just disappointed. I don't know if they love me—or if they can forgive me.

A T **PEARSON.** I am waiting for my flight to Porto. I am going for a visit, but I know I will return because this country is good. This country is good, and the other's credit is in the junk bin. Just yesterday they sold EDP, the national hydro company, to the Chinese. I also hear that the Angolans are gaining ground, that the president and his daughter are buying old beautiful palaces in Viseu. This is the same ancient city where Viriato the Lusitanian, a shepherd and a fierce warrior, fought against the Romans, only to be killed because one of his own was playing for both sides, a man wearing a mask. As for Socrates, he was thrown out and is currently studying philosophy at the Sorbonne in Paris. How times change. I write poems on the plane, praying for our salvation—because I love this country too.

I am Daria, looking for Daria. If you help me, I may succeed.

ACKNOWLEDGMENTS

Ontario Arts Council for a small grant provided.

Quotations used at the beginning by the following authors: Clarice Lispector, Roland Barthes, and Lemony Snicket.

A version of the story "The Mountain Musician" was published in Portuguese in Irene Marques's story collection *Habitando na Metáfora do Tempo* (Edium Editores, 2009), translated by the author.

Versions of the poems "Passing the Passing," "The Curious Book," and "The Days" have been published in Irene Marques's poetry collection *The Perfect Unravelling of the Spirit* (Tsar Publications, 2012).

Ensaio Sobre a Cegueira, novel by José Saramago, published in 1995.

O Dia dos Prodígios, novel by Lídia Jorge, published in 1979.

The Lusiads (Os Lusíadas) by Luís de Camões, published in 1572.

Sagrada Esperança, poetry collection by Agostinho Neto, published in 1974.

A Mercy, novel by Toni Morrison, published in 2008.

Peau noire, masques blancs, book by Frantz Fanon, published in 1952.

The River Between, novel by Ngũgĩ wa Thiong'o, published in 1965.

Head of a Young Man of Self Portrait (1629), painting by Rembrandt Harmenszoon van Rijn.

Head of Christ (1648), painting by Rembrandt Harmenszoon van Rijn.

Guernica (1937), painting by Pablo Picasso.

Mystic Nativity (1500-1), painting by Sandro Botticelli.

"Grândola, Vila Morena," song by Zeca Afonso, released in 1971, translator unknown.

"The Colour of the Sunset" is Irene Marques's translation of Ivan Lins's song "A cor do pôr do sol," released in 2000.

"On Love: Literary Images of a Phenomenology of Love in Ngũgĩ wa Thiong'o's *The River Between*," academic article by Elias Bongmba, published in 2001.

Quotation from *My Father's Wives* (*As Mulheres do Meu Pai*), a novel by José Eduardo Agualusa, published in 2007, translation by Irene Marques.

The story related to Queen Saint Isabel and King Dom Dinis is partly based on historical figures and facts.

The line "he has no nation but his imagination" is based on a line from Derek Walcott's poem "The Schooner Flight" in *Collected Poems 1948-1984*.

The statement, "I am not here to cure the sick. I am here only to sign death certificates" by Dr. Carlos Montealva (Tarrafal's Doctor), is based on real statements made by the Portuguese writer António Lobo Antunes, who served as a medical doctor in the colonial war in Angola. The persona of the doctor in this novel is partially based on Lobo Antunes.

The articles "Neutrality by Agreement: Portugal and the British Alliance in World War II" (1998) by economics historian Joaquim da Costa Leite and "Portugal and the Nazi Gold: The 'Lisbon Connection' in the Sales of Looted Gold by the Third Reich" (1999) by historian and journalist António Louçã and Ansgar Schäfer, and the book *Hitler e Salazar: Comércio em Tempos de Guerra,1940-1944* (2000) also by António Louçã were used as background sources to understand the complex relations between Portugal, the Allies, and the Axis, and the commercial transactions between Portugal and Germany during World War II.

Some parts of the letter written by Salazar to his cousin Arsénio in this novel and the letters by Roosevelt and Churchill to Salazar referenced in that letter, are based on some statements made in an actual letter sent by Roosevelt to Salazar in 1941 and a telegram sent by British Diplomat to Portugal, Sir Ronald Campbell, in 1943, to the American government—as they appear in the above noted article by Joaquim da Costa Leite. However, the letter is mostly fictional.

Photo: *Dan Abramovici Photography*

Irene Marques is a bilingual writer (English and Portuguese) and Lecturer at Ryerson University in the English Department, where she teaches literature and creative writing. She holds a PhD in Comparative Literature, a Masters in French Literature and Comparative Literature and a BA (Hon.) in French Language and Literature all from the University of Toronto—and a Bachelor of Social Work from Ryerson University. Her literary publications include the poetry collections *Wearing Glasses of Water* (2007), *The Perfect Unravelling of the Spirit* (2012), and *The Circular Incantation: An Exercise in Loss and Findings* (2013); the Portuguese language short-story collection *Habitando na Metáfora do Tempo: Crónicas Desejadas* (2009) and the novel *My House is a Mansion* (2015). Her academic publications include, among others, the manuscript *Transnational Discourses on Class, Gender and Cultural Identity* (Purdue University Press, 2011) and numerous articles in international journals or scholarly collectives, including *African Identities: Journal of Economics, Culture and Society*; *Research in African Literatures*; *A Companion to Mia Couto*; *Letras & Letras*; *InterDISCIPLINARY: Journal of Portuguese Diaspora Studies*; *African Studies*; and *Portuguese Studies Review*. Her Portuguese-language novel, *Uma Casa no Mundo*, won the 2019 Imprensa Nacional/Ferreira de Castro Prize and is now published by Imprensa Nacional Casa da Moeda. She lives in Toronto. www.irenemarques.net